ON THE EDGE OF DARKNESS

Book One in the Orca Series

By Anthony Molloy

Create Space Edition
Copyright © 2013 by Anthony Molloy
All Rights Reserved.

Characters

    Vice Admiral Sir Walter Mackenzie Chief Special Operations Group
    Lt Commander Alexander Barr CO HMS Nishga
    Lieutenant Robert Grant CO Eddy
    Lieutenant Grey Gunnery Officer
    Lieutenant Benjamin Crosswall-Brown
    Petty Officer Stone
    Leading Hand 'Hasty' Hastings
    Leading Seaman Patrick Benjamin 'Nervous' O'Neill
    Able Seaman William 'Tug' Wilson,
    Able Seaman 'Earpy' Wyatt
    Ordinary Seaman Peter 'Blur' Goddard

ROYAL MARINES

    Bushel
    Blake
    Stilson

CIVILIANS

    Charlotte Crosswall-Brown
    Olaf Kristiansand
    Jennifer Mott
    Maude Wilson

GERMANS
    Leutnant Sieg
    Oberjager Hoffmann

Prologue

Following an heroic part in the Second Battle of Narvik, Captain Barr puts the marines, his ship and certain captured enemy vessels to such good use that their exploits come to the notice of the First Lord of the Admiralty. Churchill sees how the 'Nishga's' exploits dovetail so well into his own fledgling tactic of 'Butcher and bolt'. He orders the new unit to carry out clandestine missions behind enemy lines. Already Churchill has seen that commando raids will be one of the few means by which a beleaguered Britain will be able to take the fight to the enemy. Soon Orca becomes an elite fighting unit, codenamed 'Orca' with a far reaching remit to harass the enemy held coast of Norway.

Chapter 1

First Blood

The Norwegian Sea, 0100 hours, Wednesday, 10th April 1940.

It was getting too rough for mine laying. With the long regular rhythm of the swell, the minelayer sank below each crest, allowing the sea to surge in ankle deep across the cold metal of the quarterdeck. As each wave passed under the ship, she rose up cascading water back into the sea from every scupper.

Silently and without a word of command a group of oilskin-clad figures worked in the dark, the wet, the bitter wind. Their glistening black oilskins clung like second skins flapping about their legs giving them the appearance of scavengers bent over a bloated kill. They strained, pulling and pushing at the mines moving them slowly along the greased tram-rails. For'ard, concealed in the gloom, other mines waited snug in their wheeled carriages, waited as their fellows dropped from the stern into the heaving waters of the Norwegian Sea.

5

Across the swell, the 'Nishga' and the 'Glowworm', the escorting destroyers, were darker shadows in the moonless waste, rolling their way relentlessly south.

The men at the guns huddled in their foul-weather clothing, watching the skies and the sea for signs of the enemy. Below, their shipmates listened for the submarines that were known to be in the area.

The next mine in a long line, serial number Manx. 309 /40, moved slowly towards the stern and the waiting sea, the carriage screeching its senseless protest along salt wet rails. To the men, it was just another weight to be moved, its fate as unknown and as uninteresting as the hundreds of others they had sown into these treacherous northern waters. It went over the side just the same as all the rest, opening the surface of the sea in a great foam-framed 'O' before being swallowed up by a hungry sea. It sank towards the seabed, three hundred feet below the surface. Its carriage was released, plunging on, trailing fathom upon fathom of oily chain behind it, an umbilical cord linked to the horned and lethal belly of the mine itself. Unseen it hit the seabed, and the mine, trailing its chain, rose slowly towards the surface.

* * *

HMS Nishga was steaming close inshore. To port, the Norwegian coastline slipped by unseen. The destroyer, sleek and graceful, cut through the water like a hot knife through dark chocolate sending creamy waves rippling out astern.

She was making her way south from the mine laying duties, abandoned as the weather worsened. Her clandestine mission to extract a party of Royal Marines put ashore earlier in the week by submarine. The landing party's task had been to find one Olaf Kristiansand, a

Norwegian mountain guide who knew the fjords and mountains like the back of his hand. Using the man's extensive local knowledge Army Command hoped to find out the extent of German penetration into this sector of the mountains.

Just two days before, the Navy had fought a fierce battle at the port of Narvik, along the coast to the north; five British destroyers had engaged ten German destroyers. Despite a great victory in which the British had sunk two of the enemy's destroyers as well as nine other ships, they had been too late to stop the invasion. Now it was vital to know how far the enemy had infiltrated inland.

The conifer-covered and snow capped mountains loomed darkly to port, breaking waves underlining them in white foam like an old man's moustache. The warship seemed dangerously close to the lee shore for the weather conditions, but she was protected from the worst of the storm by the Skerries, a mass of islands to seaward.

A little after two bells in the middle watch, she heaved to, head to wind, bobbing her acknowledgement to the choppy sea as her crew prepared her sea boat for lowering.

Whispered commands brought the boat level with the iron deck and ten heavily armed seamen clambered over the guard rails.

Now, fully loaded, the boat continued its jerky progress to the water line where she was silently slipped, dropping the last few feet into the water in a welter of spray.

The boat's crew leant back throwing their combined weight behind the long ash oars and the heavy boat turned in a slow laboured arc towards the shore.

As they drew away from the noise generated by the destroyer's engines, the men in the boat could hear the occasional burst of small arms fire and the rapid staccato Brrr of a Bren.

The muffled oars lifted clear of the water as she nosed in towards a battered wooden jetty. The basket fenders along the structure screeched in protest as they slid alongside and then they were up, out of the boat and running, crouched double over their Lee Enfields.

Lieutenant Grey slid in behind a stand of empty drums at the edge of a cluster of log buildings.

"Spread out and take cover! Signalman!"

"Sir!"

"Make the call sign."

The signalman's hand held Aldis chattered out, the beam illuminating the trees to their front making their long shadows jump in alarm.

No reply was received. In fact nothing moved except the shadows, no sign of the reconnaissance party they had come ashore to extract; only the ominous rattle of gunfire.

Able Seaman Wilson pulled his helmet round straight and looked to see who his neighbours were. Wyatt lay spread-eagled to his right and Stubbs to his left.

"Fuck this for a game of soldiers!" whispered Wyatt.

Wilson grinned and pointed at him "Ha! Game of soldiers…Good one!"

"It wasn't supposed to be a joke… What's up with you?"

"Quiet you men!" hissed Grey. "Keep your eyes to your front and stay alert. No firing unless I fire first."

As if on cue, two figures broke cover to their front running in short bursts towards the waiting seamen.

"Hold your fire!" called Grey.

Wyatt looked to the heavens before squinting down the sights of the Bren.

"Can't you tell them that's born to command"

The two marines, weaving from side to side as they withdrew turned and kneeled on the frozen ground. A third and then a fourth figure emerged from the trees and sprinted, heads down, past their companions.

The marine with the Bren ran past another fifty yards and spinning round, lay prone in the snow covering the withdrawal of the others.

Suddenly all hell broke loose, bursts of fire erupted from the tree line, flickering and flashing along its length, tracer arcing in towards the running marines, spurts of snow shot into the air around running feet, they spun round, dropped to the ground and returned the fire.

"Signalman make to the ship, 'Request support fire, engage the tree line'…You men! Keep the enemy's heads down… Fire into the trees… Fire at will!"

"Who's this bloke Will anyway?" asked Wilson of no one in particular. "No one seems to like him."

Branches and leaves flew into the air as the ten man landing party commenced their covering fire

A whistling noise overhead heralded the arrival of the barrage. The tree line erupted into orange flames as the enemy's positions took accurate fire. A ragged cheer went up from the seamen as the conifer plantation burst into flames and great fireballs rose lazily into the night sky.

Under cover of the bombardment the marines joined the shore party and they withdrew, scrambling along the icy jetty and down into the waiting boat. Oars hurriedly shipped they pushed off. But the enemy was not finished with them. Bullets whipped about them as slowly, sluggishly the overloaded boat made its way back out to sea.

Gradually, the firing died away and the 'Nishga' shifted her fire to the jetty. The exploding shells sent great beams of rotting timber high into the air. The small fishing boats, secured to the jetty, became blazing beacons glowing through dense, acrid smoke.

The boat reached the safety of the destroyer moving round into the lee she had provided. Alongside, under the falls, the crew wrestled the heavy blocks of the hoisting gear into place and the boat rose clear of the water.

The 'Nishga's' twin propellers started to turn and the sea astern churned into a grey froth, she began to move slowly ahead. Swinging sharply under full rudder she turned her stern to the smoking destruction ashore and headed out into a tranquil darkness.

The sea boat jerked to a stop, level with the 'iron deck'. Men ran from the rope falls to hold her glistening side in snug against the ship's side. One by one the landing party stepped back onboard grinning in reply to a cheer from their shipmates. They handed in their arms to the waiting gunner's mate and clattered down the metal ladders to the welcome warmth of the mess deck.

* * *

Leading Seaman Patrick Benjamin O'Neill, known to all as 'Nervous' nursed the rum fanny down the steep mess ladder with practiced ease and placed it on the long table.

"Did you hear about the 'Glowworm'?" The men around the table looked back at him with blank expressions.

"What you mean that bloke, the one she lost overboard in the roughers?" asked Wyatt.

"No, that's old hat," said O'Neill dismissively, "No she gone... sunk!" Now he had their attention. "When she was looking for that bloke she ran into two Jerry destroyers. She showed 'em a clean pair of screws and they eventually turned back. Her skipper wonders why Jerry's suddenly lost interest, follows them and they lead him straight onto the guns of the bloody 'Hipper'. For them that don't know she's a bloody great Jerry cruiser, eight eight-inch guns!"

"Bloody hell!" said Goddard.

"Bloody hell's right The 'Worm' she goes in and attacks the lot of 'em, the 'Hipper' and her escorts!"

Wyatt shook his head, "Officers eh? ... The lot of 'em's mad as 'atters". The mess nodded its agreement.

O'Neill shrugged, "Sure you're right there, you wait until you hear the rest. The 'Worm' zig zags in, sticking up some smoke, fires her torpedoes, they miss so she goes in again through her own smoke and rams the 'Hipper'!"

"Blimey...said Wilson, " 'Ow big's one of their cruisers, sixteen, seventeen thousand tons, she must've bounced off the bastard. I reckon 'er skipper's lost 'is rag....Was there anyone left alive?

"No one seems to know, she sunk that's all they know, no word of casualties yet" O'Neill splashed the rum into a mug and handed it to Wyatt for 'sippers'.

'Earpy' Wyatt took the offered glass, as 'ticker-offer' it was his job to tick off each man's name as they drew their ration. A sip of every man's tot was his payment for the arduous task. He was a short thickset bull- necked man with red hair and a beard. There was a long-running dispute as to the origins of his nickname. Some said it was because his surname recalled a famous Sheriff of Tombstone, others, less charitable, perhaps, held that it was because he had caught a disease, of the same name, whilst serving on his first ship.

"We'll 'ave no bloody ships left at this rate," he said, "I 'eard the 'Gurka' gone with all 'ands".

There was silence around the table, the 'Glowworm' was one thing but the 'Gurka' she was sister ship to their own 'Nishga'. A Tribal just like them it brought it all uncomfortably close to home.

"I had a couple of oppoes on board 'er," said Wilson.

"All hands you say?" asked Stubbs.

Wyatt nodded, "Sunk by Jerry off Bergen. So the 'Bunting Tosser' told me. It was only a couple of months ago she got that U Boat off the Faeroes... you remember?"

* * *

As night fell and concealed the 'Nishga' from inquisitive eyes, she turned north- east and increased to her maximum speed.

The cloud cover was total, the ship darkened, no lights showing above decks, below only the red warm glow of the night lights guided the men to their stations as the watches changed. The loudspeaker clicked in a fog of static.

"Do you hear there, this is the Captain speaking."

Men all over the ship, closed up at their Steaming Stations, stopped to listen.

"I am taking this opportunity to update you on events unfolding in Norway. You'll all be glad to hear that, since I last spoke, we've bagged two more Jerry destroyers bringing the tally to four. Ashore things are not looking so good. The Germans have landed paratroopers at all the main airfields and are, as I speak, attacking many of the large cities.

For our part, we are proceeding, under new orders to Vest Fjord, as you may or may not know that's quite close to Narvik. There we will join up with the battleship 'Warspite' and her escorting destroyers.

We will remain at Steaming Stations for the time being, I advise you all to get as much rest as possible. That is all"

The watches changed again at midnight, port watch swinging up, fully clothed, into the still warm hammocks recently vacated by their opposite numbers.

Up top Hogg, the ship's only midshipman, paced the bridge, lost in thoughts of the glories of a possible battle to come, he passed by the array of voice pipes; the bridge end of the ship's internal communication system.

He noticed one of the lids was hanging by its chain. How long had that been off? He glanced quickly at the Captain in his bridge chair.

As the second officer of the watch he was supposed to keep an eye on such things. Just as well the 'Old Man' was asleep. He put his hand out to replace it and heard someone humming a tune. It came from the wheelhouse... he instantly recognised it, 'The Girl I left behind me'... One of his dad's favourite songs, he could remember the words. His dad used to sing it as he worked in their potting shed. It seemed a long time ago now. The quartermaster on the wheel was whistling, melodiously and... illegally! He suddenly remembered with a frown...No whistling allowed aboard one of His Majesty's Ships. He was about to call down the tube when the whistling stopped and the rating burst into song.

"Ooh! I don't give a fuck for the Officer of the Watch,
Or the 'Killick' of the fo'c's'le party
'Cause I'm off ashore at 'alf past four,
I'm Jack me fucking hearty!

The midshipman's mouth gaped open and blushing brightly in the dark he quickly and quietly replaced the lid.

Lieutenant Commander Alexander Barr, slumped in his bridge chair, smiled from under the peak of his battered cap. He was a man of indeterminable age, his face deeply lined and deeply wind-tanned. His long frame ill formed for a uniform of any kind, he managed to look more like a badly dressed art teacher than a commissioned officer in His Majesty's Navy. He was, however, living proof that you should never judge a book by its jacket which unfortunately the Navy invariably did. The result was there for all to see, two and a half rings on his sleeve where at his age and with his unquestionable abilities there should have been a lot more.

* * *

Ofotfjord

"Interrogative, sir!"
"Very good, make the reply, Yeo."
The Yeoman of Signals nodded to the visual signalman and the Aldis chattered out their call sign.
Saturday had dawned furtively behind an early morning mist that hung about the 'Nishga' eerily like a wet

shroud. The visibility in Ofotfjord was down to a few hundred yards. The guard ship, posted close to the entrance had done well to spot them at all.

"Guard ship's pennant number is ... Foxtrot seven five, sir; she's the 'Eskimo.'"

Barr raised his binoculars to study her; she was a fellow Tribal.

He looked for damage; the majority of 'Warspite's' escorting destroyers had been engaged in the fight at Narvik three days earlier. He could see no visible damage. He noticed her cable was shortened in readiness to weigh anchor and proceed, it seemed they had arrived in the nick of time.

The 'Eskimo's' Aldis began to flash once more this time it was directed away from them into the swirling mist astern of her. An answer flashed briefly and then the same light transferred its attentions to them.

He heard the sound of their signal lamp chattering in reply.

'Flag ship signalling, sir.'

Barr lowered his glasses and watched as the towering structure of the 'Warspite emerged gradually like a grey ghost from the folds of the mist. She was unmistakable, with her huge gunnery director, bigger than 'Nishga's' bridge, poised seemingly precariously atop her foremast.

She was old, nearly thirty years old, if his memory served him right, he had heard how she'd taken fifteen direct hits at the Battle of Jutland but she was still with them. Rightly so, she was magnificent, her designers had her just right, a perfect combination of firepower, speed and armour.

"'Captain report to Flag', sir"

"Very good, officer of the watch, make the arrangements, if you please. I'll be below."

* * *

14

Vice Admiral William 'Jock' Whitworth CB, DSO, sat at the end of the wardroom table his snowy head leaning forward as he read a signal. He was approaching his fifty-sixth birthday and already had some considerable claim to fame after seeing off the Gneisenau and the Scharnhorst whilst flying his Flag in the 'Renown' earlier that spring. Around him sat the Captains of the other nine destroyers. Barr recognised Sherbrooke of the 'Cossack' and nodded greetings.

The Admiral signed for the signal and, handing it to the Chief Yeoman at his side, waved Barr to the one remaining chair at the highly polished mahogany table.

"Good to see you, there's coffee on the side table behind you"

"I'm fine, thank you, sir."

"No? Right then I'll bring you up to date, if I may. As you probably know we lost the 'Hunter'' and the 'Hardy' three days ago, besides that we had two other ships badly damaged during the action at Narvik; so your presence will go some way to making up our numbers and will be most welcome.

Now, according to aerial recognisance Jerry has eight destroyers and two U Boats as well as several merchantmen, all survivors from Wednesday, in Narvik. Our intelligence chaps ashore assure us they are too low on fuel to come out, probably as a result of Wednesday's action.

I intend, as they seem somewhat reluctant to come out to play, to take the game to them" He turned and beckoned to a Flag Lieutenant waiting at the back of the compartment who quickly carried forward a wooden easel with a chart of Ofotfjord pinned to it.

"The old hands with their prior knowledge of the anchorage will take the lead; 'Cossack' in the van. I will follow in the 'Warspite'. Barr your 'Nishga' will be our rearguard. I am hoping to take Jerry by surprise but it's a thirty-mile trip up fjord so it should take us about an hour, if all goes well.

The 'Warspite' will engage Jerry's shore installations which were, apparently, captured more or less intact from our Norwegian friends. This means they have eight-inch guns and shore-based torpedoes at their disposal. So be ready to receive a warm welcome.

We have aircraft from the 'Victorious' available as air cover so make sure your Gunnery Officers are up to par on aircraft recognition. I don't want any home goals!

My Flag Lieutenant will give you your written orders. Address any queries to him. Well, gentleman, we will shortly be having a seat in the front row of history. Good luck and good hunting."

* * *

Barr lowered his glasses; on the beam the Flagship was turning into the wind in order to fly off her Fairy Swordfish. Beyond the destroyer screen was nearing the headland that hid the enemy held harbour from view. His job was to stay close to the flagship as anti-submarine protection and to provide a rearguard.

"Clear away all guns!"

"All guns clear!"

At full speed and in line ahead the van of the destroyers was already sweeping round into the harbour, their Battle Ensigns rippling and snapping at their mastheads. It looked as if the enemy ships had been taken completely by surprise.

The 'Cossack' in the lead engaged a large German destroyer moored to the jetty, the target, at very close range, was hit by her first salvo and oily black smoke began to pour from her shattered fo'c's'le.

"All guns closed up and cleared away, communications tested, sir"

16

Astern of the 'Nishga' a rolling crash with the power of a thousand thunderstorms echoed around the fjord as the 'Warspite' opened fire; the broadside, from her fifteen-inch guns, howled overhead and on into the enemy's positions ashore.

The 'Nishga's' gunnery control could now see the target.

"Target enemy destroyers, Green eight seven, range one thousand two hundred yards."

Through his glasses Barr could see that the four point sevens of the lead destroyers were doing terrible damage. It looked as though none of the enemy guns were yet in action, although it was difficult to be sure through the thick smoke already drifting out across the town.

Barr stood at the for'ard screen he could hear the preparations being made for his 'Nishga' to join the bombardment.

"All guns with H.E. Load! Load! Load! Follow TVI." That was 'Guns' ordering all his four point sevens to load with high explosive shells and to follow the director rather than engage the target separately over open sights.

"Open shutters."

He could hear the men in 'B' Turret, close up and below the bridge, repeating the orders, clearly and calmly as if they were on exercise rather than about to enter what must be their first major action.

"Trainer on! Layer on!"

"Left gun ready! Right gun ready!"

"Shutters open. 'B' Turret ready!"

Guns' voice echoed down from the director above his head. "Permission to open fire"

Barr leant over the voice pipe, "Permission granted."

The words were barely out of his mouth before the blast from the for'ard guns hit the bridge, a flash of light and noise, a whiff of acrid cordite, the whistle of the shells roaring away like express trains and then the yell of the gun captain below. "Reload!"

Barr had his binoculars raised once more; this time they were focused on the 'Cossack' she was taking hit after hit. The size of some of the explosions indicated she was taking punishment from both the shore battery and the smaller guns on the enemy destroyers. Barr could only imagin the damage they must be doing below decks as each eight-inch shell, weighing more two hundredweight tore into her thin unarmoured sides.

The Navigating Officer called from the compass platform, his binoculars still raised to his eyes, "There's the battery of eight-inch we were warned about, sir."

"Where away?"

"Green eight oh, compass bearing one oh five."

"'Guns' shift target. New target the shore battery bearing one oh five magnetic."

"All guns Check! Check! Check! Shift target left…"

There was a flutter of red and white from the 'Cossacks' foremast. "Yeoman can you make out what the 'Cossacks' flying."

The Yeoman at his side yelled above the roar of another broadside, "That's Foxtrot, sir. She's disabled."

They must have hit her boiler or engine room or perhaps her steering gear. As they watched she veered sharply out of the line and began to lose way drifting downwind towards the north shore, all her guns still blazing.

Both sides were now doing terrific damage; several of the enemy had cut their moorings and were now under way. The harbour was full of smoke and the din of battle with destroyers weaving and turning, firing their guns and torpedoes over open sights.

Right ahead a Tribal suddenly appeared from the smoke of the battle. She was drifting helplessly downwind, smoke billowing from her superstructure in an oil-black cloud. Very few of her guns were returning fire.

"It's the 'Punjabi', sir," yelled the Yeoman somehow reading his thoughts. "She's a sitting duck."

Suddenly they heard a huge explosion, Barr swung round just in time to see the 'Eskimo' lifted bodily from the water. Oily bellows of smoke quickly hid her from view. When it cleared downwind he could see a huge gaping hole. Her bow had been completely blown off probably by one of the massive shore-based torpedoes.

Somehow, incredibly, she was managing to stay afloat. He could see men rushing forward across the debris-strewn deck dragging fires hoses to fight the raging fire.

Across the fjord the 'Cossack' was in even worse trouble, hard aground and under fire from the shore.

The 'Kimberley' roared across Barr's line of sight all her guns blazing away, her Aldis flashing urgently.

"She's signalling the Flag," Barr looked astern as the 'Warspite' lamp winked a smoke hazed reply.

Barr heard the clatter of their own Aldis.

"From the Flag to us, sir, 'Give covering fire to the 'Kimberley' she is about to take LO3,'... that's the 'Cossack', sir, 'in tow'."

"Full ahead both engines, hard aport... Pilot! Take us close in to where the 'Cossacks' aground."

"That's Hankins Point, sir."

"Very good. Then take us to Hankins's Point, with all speed, if you please."

"Aye, aye, sir."

The 'Nishga's' bow swung dizzily across the skyline, first the speeding 'Kimberly' appearing in the eyes of the ship and then the beleaguered 'Cossack'.

First, the 'Kimberley' and then the 'Nishga' sped in closer to the shore. They began to draw fire from shore-based mortars, machine guns and even rifles. The bridge crew took hasty shelter behind the screens as rounds winged across the bridge and smacked into the metalwork.

Barr crouched over the voice pipe array, "Bridge, Director."

"Director."

"'Guns', see what you can do to keep those snipers

heads down."

* * *

Wyatt at his station on 'A' gun had a clear view of the action in and around the crippled 'Cossack'. His turret began to turn; all guns had been following the Gunnery Director's pointer. Now the order came down to fire over open sights and return the fire from the machine guns and snipers arranged before them. He shook his head one hell of a large hammer to crack those nuts ashore.

Mind you they weren't the only nuts around, the skipper of the 'Kimberly' was right up there with them, going in after the 'Cossack' like that! Officers! He never could figure them. 'A' gun bucked and shook under him as they fired point blank into the shoreline at one of the tiny targets.

* * *

Barr heard the roar from the for'ard turret, tasted the bitter smoke as it flew past the bridge. Raising his head above the parapet he saw the fall of shot only yards from one of the shore-side mortar emplacements. The soldiers manning it scattered, leaving two of their number spread-eagled and still in the blackened snow.

The 'Kimberly' had noticeably slowed; drifting almost lazily into the smoke cloud that, momentarily, hid the 'Cossack' from view.

A lone, helmeted figure up in her bow threw a heaving line into the smoke. A sudden puff of icy wind cleared Barr's view, blowing the cloud in towards the shore. He caught a glimpse of hurrying figures as the 'Kimberly's' seamen ran the messenger line inboard, working like men possessed.

The 'hammer blows' from the four point sevens were having the desired effect; the sniper fire had died away to the occasional hastily aimed shot. When this did happen, it was answered with a fusillade of machine gun fire from both ships. From what Barr could see the 'Kimberley's' attempts to tow the 'Cossack' clear of the rocks wasn't having the same sort of success. Through his binoculars he could see the hastily rigged towing hawser was bar taut, stretching and then vibrating under the immense strain. The 'Cossack' seemed to be stuck fast.

* * *

Wyatt wiped his cordite blackened eyes on the rough sleeve of his duffle. He must be seeing things. Two figures were descending the mountain towards the stranded 'Cossack' on skis!

They reached the shoreline, quickly removing their skis they scrabbled across the rocks and up onto her quarterdeck. Through the powerful gun sights Wyatt could see what appeared to be a rolled up German flag. There really were a lot of nutters around today.

* * *

Barr removed his battle bowler, wiped at his blackened face with a handkerchief and looked around.

All the German ships and most of the shore batteries had been silenced and he could see German soldiers ashore retreating under fire from the squadron. It appeared to be over, there was time to take stock of the situation, sunk and damaged ships littered the harbour. He counted eight German destroyers either sunk or ablaze. Amazingly they hadn't lost any ships sunk, although three, the 'Cossack', 'Eskimo' and the 'Punjabi' were real 'dockyard jobs'. There could be no rest until those three were under tow or scuttled. It looked as if they would be here for quite some time.

"Pilot when's the next high tide."

"Around six, sir."

"It looks increasingly as if they won't be able to get the 'Cossack' off till then. Stand the men down."

"Aye, aye, sir... Defence Stations?"

"Yes, that will do nicely and give the galley a buzz, will you? Get something hot into the men." It was funny but he had only just noticed how cold it was.

As if by magic his steward materialised at his side. "Your coffee, sir." Incongruously, given the circumstances, Leading Steward Jenkins was balancing a silver pot of coffee and a delicate china cup and saucer on an immaculately polished tray. He could smell the fresh coffee beans and the generous measure of Jerez sherry that laced it. The man was God sent.

As night fell it brought with it that convenient high tide. They were soon employed in further attempts to re-float 'Cossack' clear of rocks. During the first watch she, at last, floated free but, because of shell damage to her fore end, she was only able to go astern.

With other destroyers fussing around her like protective mother hens, she weaved in and out of the still blazing wrecks of German destroyers and half submerged merchantmen.

Clear of the fjord, the three crippled ships, under heavy escort, headed west for the shelter of the Lofoten Islands.

Chapter 2

A Roving

The next day the 'Nishga' entered Skelfjord; where the damaged ships were already undergoing temporary repairs. Most of those that were present at the battle the night before were there, not one had escaped damage of one sort or the other.

The 'Nishga' herself had no structural damage, but splinter and bullet holes peppered her sides, her upper deck bulkheads and both funnels. With so many damaged ships the harbour had been dubbed 'Cripple Creek' by the sailors.

Shortly after they had dropped anchor, the Bosun's Mate noticed a motor launch approaching from the direction of the flagship, it was hailed, came alongside and an officer ran up the gangway carrying a buff envelope.

Within a half-hour of his arrival he had left and Harbour Stations were piped. Even before they had cleared the mouth of the fjord the rumour had circulated throughout the ship that they were under orders for another lone assignment further along the coast.

Up on the bridge Barr was more than happy with his new assignment. The action at Narvik had been his first fleet action, his first time operating as part of a squadron under the command of an Admiral on a flagship. He was thrilled to have taken part but he preferred detached assignments. Independent action was something skippers would give his eye-teeth for. Free from the restraints that the presence of senior ships imposed and able to make your own decisions. There was even a chance at some prize money.

* * *

Once the skipper had officially announced that they would be cruising the west coast of Norway looking for likely targets, the topic of prize money was the only conversation around the tot tables.

All of the men in the seamen's mess, indeed in the ship, were professionals; at this stage in the war 'Hostility Only' ratings were mostly confined to the smaller ships. So between the eight men sitting around the mess table there was something like fifty years of seagoing experience, even so not one of them had ever been awarded prize money.

Now if there was something under discussion of which they knew very little, or even nothing at all, it was usually Wyatt who assumed the status of expert and who led any debate.

"Come on then, you lot, someone must know what share of prize money goes to the ship's company?"

He looked around the table; everyone was sitting mouths tight closed looking up at the deck head or down into their tot glasses; except Goddard.

"Blur?"

"Erh.. Me? Well, I don't know" he thought for a moment, "I heard in Nelson's day they used to get a quarter..." he ventured.

Wyatt nodded sagely. "And you all know what, say, a freighter's worth nowadays?" Wyatt looked around the table; Goddard had now taken up a similar posture to the rest but Wilson… "You must know that, Tug?"

"Well… thousands of pounds, I suppose."

Wyatt nodded shrewdly. "That's right… there you go…so we all stand to get erh … a lot of money." A murmur of admiration for Wyatt's profound knowledge of the subject ran through the assembled seaman.

There was a clatter on the metal ladder as Stubbs arrived from the galley with a fanny of 'pot-mess'.

The stew pot on its rubber mat in the centre of the table gradually emptied and they wiped their plates clean with the last of the fresh bread, brought across from the flagship's bakery.

O'Neill, 'Duff Bosun' for the day went for the afters and placed it in the centre of the table with a flourish. It was, as usual, something under a thick layer of custard. Goddard dished a good helping out to each man and, with the notable exception of Able Seaman Wyatt, they all set to with some gusto.

"What's this supposed to be?" asked Wyatt of O'Neill a pained expression on his face after one tentative mouthful.

"Duff."

"I can see that, can't I! What sort of duff?"

O'Neill looked up from his plate, "Take a good bite and bloody well find out. Am I a fucking menu?"

Wyatt spat his mouth-full back onto his plate, "Well you ain't a fucking cook that's for sure!" He wiped the back of his hand across his mouth and added, "Disgusting, bloody disgusting that is."

"You mean discustarding," quirked Wilson, reaching for Wyatt's plate.

'Tug' Wilson, was a barrel of a man, short in statue, broad in the chest with laughing eyes. Heavily tattooed, he sported a beard that he was justly proud of. He could always see the funny side of any situation. A fact that endeared him to most but which infuriated others beyond belief, especially Wyatt. His favourite line of 'If you can't

25

take a joke you shouldn't have joined' would guarantee that Wyatt would 'lose his rag' to the point where he was often speechless with rage, but it could stop a moan dead in its tracks. It was Wilson's honest held and much aired opinion that people with no sense of humour had no place in the Navy.

O'Neill was not one to take anything lying down, "There's nothing wrong with that duff, I'll have you know I were renowned for my duffs on me last ship."

"Yeah, but renowned for what, not for their bloody taste that's for sure...renowned for giving everyone a dose of 'Malta Dog' more like."

"I wish I was in Malta now, anywhere to get away from your bloody moaning." O'Neill turned back to his duff; pushed it to one side, admitting to himself that it wasn't one of his best.

Wilson, thinking it was time for a change of subject, stepped manfully into the breach, "Where are we making for? Anyone heard? I heard we're taking that Norwegian bloke, the 'Royals' brought with 'em...

* * *

At that very moment, in the cramped and cold Asdic hut, Lieutenant- Commander Barr, was about to brief three men on just that subject.

In front of him lay the Admiralty chart for the Norwegian coast. He leaned over it, as a draught from the open door rippled it like silk.

"Get the door will you please, Number One."

Beside the tall thin figure of his second in command stood the stocky marine corporal, Bushel, and to his left the stark blond hair of Olaf Kristiansand reflected the dim light from the range finder. The incessant and hypnotic ping of the Asdic transmissions punctuated Barr's words as he spoke.

26

"My orders are nothing if not imaginative, gentlemen. I am to find a secure base, anywhere north of Trondheim from which we are to harass the enemy's supply lines. We will be getting most of our supplies from Scapa Flow so it will need to be within a fast night's passage of there. That means our base must be somewhere within this radius" He indicated a pencilled semicircle with one gloved finger.

As you can see there are hundreds of small deep water coves which look suitable for our purposes, at least on paper.

Jerry has, at the last estimate, over a thousand planes committed to this campaign. Wherever we chose as a hideout must enable us to stay out of sight of aircraft during daylight hours. Secondly, this coast is plagued by storms, as you know; we will need somewhere that will shelter us from the prevailing westerlies. So we are looking for a small bay, with perhaps an island, or islands to the west and preferably, with something that will give us some cover from the air, a cave, an overhang of rock, at the very least something to secure a camouflage netting to.

As I say, on paper there are plenty of likely spots. Our problem is which one. Luckily we have Mr Kristiansand to advise us. Bushel you and your 'Royals' will provide the escort and help in the selection of the site from a military standpoint?"

Barr stood for a moment, scratching the stubble on his chin and studying the chart.

"We'll stay on our present course, heading away from the land. If we are spotted by the enemy they won't know our true intentions. As soon as it's dark we'll double back and drop off the landing party. How long will it take to survey this section of the coast on skis, Mr Kristiansand?"

"No more than a day I have some likely sites in mind, so there will be no need to look into every Inlet on your chart"

"Very well. I'll give you twenty-four hours. Then we'll rendezvous here, at the southernmost end of the section, pick you up by boat. Any questions… No?…Right then! Thank you, gentlemen. You may return to your duties."

The three men filed out of the cabin and Barr absentmindedly whistling a tune from an obscure Gilbert and Sullivan opera, turned back to his consideration of the chart.

* * *

The port lookout, Ordinary Seaman Goddard slowly swept his one hundred and twenty degree sector of the sky for what he thought would be the last time before his relief arrived.

Nothing, as usual…or was that something…a speck on the lens of the binoculars, he checked the glass, nothing, he raised them to his eyes frantically searching the east again…Christ! He swung round yelling at the top of his voice, "Aircraft! Aircraft! Aircraft! Red one seven oh …Angle of sight four five!"

As he yelled the first word of the warning, the bridge crew froze; by the second the alarm klaxon began its jarring belch, before he'd managed to release the safety from the Hotchkin gun the whole watch below were moving fast towards their action stations. Metal ladders rang to the frantic and continuous stream of men emptying from the mess decks, plates left, food forgotten, their hastily acquired foul weather gear flapping about them, as they donned lifejackets and anti-flash gear on the move.

Even before Goddard had finished his report the guns were swinging around and onto the port quarter. Before the first men from starboard watch reached their action stations the guns opened fire.

The Messerschmitt 109 came in low, barely clearing the wave tops. The tracer from its wing mounted cannon drifting almost lazily towards the 'Nishga'; closer in they seemed to increase speed, ripping through the sea, crashing up the ship's side, punching their way across the bridge. The fighter flashed over the ship drowning the noise of her guns with the manic scream of her engines, speeding away fast, climbing higher, twisting and turning in a maelstrom of tracer and exploding shells.

The 'Nishga's' eight machine guns gave a last spurt of white-hot tracer and fell silent. But the greater range of the Pom Poms enabled them to continue the bombardment, the sky to starboard blossomed with exploding black mushrooms.

Impossibly the 109 emerged on the far side of the smoke, high in the clouds now, unscathed and turning gracefully, almost majestically in a slothful curve. Then back down it came, roaring for more.

This time the gun's crews were ready, this time there was no hurry, they tracked the enemy with practised precision. Calm as an opening batsman who had survived the trauma of the first over. Practised professionals make the worst of foes. This was the lesson the Messerschmitts young headstrong pilot was about to learn.

In range of the awesome aerial firepower of the destroyer his plane lasted only seconds. It began to disintegrate under him, ripped apart by a swarm of half-inch bullets from the heavy machine guns. Finally, as he wrestled with his smashed controls, a two-pound Pom Pom shell hit the cockpit and he became, in an instant, part of one of the black mushrooms he had been flying through.

* * *

The 'Nishga' stole in towards the darken shore, her sea boat slowly craned out from its davits and was lowered towards the wave crests until they were slipping by just beneath her keel. Ashore a lonely light flashed in the inky darkness.

A voice whispered "Out pins" In the sea boat, three

arms were raised in silent reply. "Slip" whispered the same voice.

The sea boat fell three feet into the waiting sea in a crash of iridescent spray and veered wildly out from the destroyer's side under its lashed tiller. O'Neill sliced through the lashing with his rigging knife and lifted his other hand palm up to his shoulder. In the gloom for'ard Wilson saw the expected signal and yanked on the towing bollard, the bow rope slipped silently into the cold sea. Free of the mother-ships umbilical cord, alone in a coal-black sea, the six-man crew pulled for the shore.

O'Neill's face glowed momentarily as he bent to the faint light of the boat's compass. He eased the tiller a little and the boat settled on a more easterly course, lifting and yawing to a stern sea.

Chapter 3

Olaf's Inlet

Norwegian Coast, Monday 2200 hours 15th April 1940

Olaf Kristiansand and the three marines knelt together in a tight defensive circle, Kristiansand and the NCO looking out to sea to where a darker shadow marked the slow but steady progress of the 'Nishga's' sea boat.

They had carried out the reconnaissance without contact with the enemy and found two inlets that they agreed were suitable for Barr's purposes.

All four men were glad to be returning onboard. It had been a cold twenty-four hours during which they had covered thirty miles of the rugged coastline, mostly at night and in truly bitter conditions.

The NCO tapped both his marines on their shoulders, gaining their attention he pointed to his own chest and that of Kristiansand's, and then pointed towards the boat. The two marines nodded and resumed their silent watch.

During their period ashore together Kristiansand had grown accustomed to the silent marines, they hardly spoke and when they did it was in a whispered clipped fashion as if they paid for every word in gold.

The ship's boat gradually materialised out of the night-gloom; the coxswain waved an arm and his crew lifted their oars clear of the water and stood them on their ends in the' toss oars' position while the boat drifted silently in towards the shore. Did these Englishmen ever talk? Kristiansand longed for the sound of a human voice uttering properly completed sentences. He had learnt his English in the United States; now there was a nation who knew how to hold a conversation no matter what the circumstances.

He clambered aboard the boat and watched as the NCO jumped the gunwale behind him. Turning, Bushel pointed to the two remaining men ashore and tapped the top of his Balaclavaed head with an open palm. The Norwegian shook his head slowly. There they go again.

* * *

'Nishga'

The group of officers and marines were gathered round Kristiansand and the chart, which he held open in front of him. The Asdic hut had barely enough room to hold them all but at least it was out of the bitter cold wind now blowing in from the north-west.

The Norwegian removed his thick gloves and rubbed his frozen hands together, "We've found two suitable Inlets, both deep enough for your purposes and both sheltered from the west. They are about ten miles apart," he stabbed at the chart. "The first is here and the second, farther to the south... here."

Barr scratched at the day's growth that shadowed his lantern jaw. "In your opinion which of the two will serve our purposes best?"

"The one to the south has the better overhang, almost a

cave."

"Right...We'll use that and keep the other in our pocket, should the first becomes compromised in any way... Pilot."

"Sir?" the respectful reply came from an ascetic looking two-ringer on the far side of the Asdic hut.

"Set me a course for this Inlet of Olaf's... Has it a name?" he asked the Norwegian.

"Not that I know of."

"Well, it has now..." He turned back to Lieutenant Usbourne. "Calculate a course for 'Olaf's Inlet, Pilot. I want to be close inshore by first light and I mean first light...Number One I want... who's got the Middle Watch?"

"Starboard, sir," replied Lieutenant Grant promptly.

"Right, I want men from the starboard watch of seamen and a good signalman in the boat, in this Inlet, at dawn... you're in charge. I want thorough soundings made... I want marker buoys... I want the sea boat to lead us in there... I don't want to take any chances inshore. I intend to warp the ship into her new berth as soon as we have sufficient light. See to it so that the Chief Bosun's Mate has the gear laid out in time. Port watch remains at steaming action stations until we are safely in."

The First Lieutenant, who had been writing on a dogged eared note pad, looked up. "We'll need to be pretty quick hiding the ship away, sir. Jerry planes will be up with the dawn. Shall I arrange for camouflage netting to be brought up on deck before I leave?"

"Yes...I've a few ideas, myself concerning camouflaging the old girl, I want 'Chippy' and his mate ashore as soon as is practical to cut wood, have him meet me in my cabin after this briefing."

"Yes, sir."

"And last but not least... the marines." the Captain looked up at the corporal, "Corporal Bushel, you and your team will go in first before first light. Make sure Jerry's not waiting for us. Signal us to that effect as soon as is practicable."

The big corporal nodded.

"I want you to draw up plans for shore defences. I want them hidden from the land, from the sea and from the air.

If an enemy patrol does turn up I don't want them to know we are here. No footprints, no fag packets and, regretfully, no fires. But then you know the routine better than I.

If, despite our precautions, we are discovered form landward, it will be your task to keep them away from the ship for as long as it takes us to get her safely out to sea."

The corporal nodded again, "How long would that be, sir. I mean how long would we need to hold them off for? In your estimation."

"Hard to say, practice will speed things up, of course, say an hour, hour and a half." The marine grimaced.

"Corporal, I want to stay a thorn in the side of Jerry's coastal shipping for as long as is humanly possible. If we are discovered I want to escape intact to carry on the work from the second base. Your job will be to hold the enemy off while we retire… It may be that we need more time than you can spare…It may mean you and your men being killed or being taken prisoner, but the ship must come before everything else…. All I can offer is that we may be able to pick you up from the second inlet the next night, if the worst should come to the worst."

"If the worst comes to the worst there won't be anybody to pick up," Bushel said grimly.

Barr looked away from the corporal's unblinking eyes, "I've the lives of two hundred and nineteen men to consider, corporal…Anyway… get something down on paper as soon as you can, all going well, we will hold another briefing here, same time tomorrow. Any questions?…No?… Good. Carry on please."

* * *

Down the forward seamen's mess deck, a long supper time argument was in progress over which of the gun's crew had shot down the German fighter the day before.

The outcome was a stalemate, with Leading Seaman O'Neill, by virtue of being in the Gunnery Director, and so controlling all the guns, claiming the majority of the credit.

O'Neill won most of the heated discussions entered into at tot times due more to his own weight than to that of his arguments for O'Neill was a man of huge proportions everything about him was large.

He was a big drinker, fond of saying that 'too much is just enough'. He could down twenty pints of his beloved Guinness at one sitting and was ready, though seldom able, to ask for more. Once he had won, outright, the coveted 'Prick of the Far East Contest' held spasmodically in the dockyard canteen in Singapore. He was, indeed, a man of legendary proportions in every respect.

As the disagreement had become more heated it was, as usual, Wilson who stepped in to calm matters with a change of subject.

"Is that a crucifix round your neck, Nervous?"

"Of course, my mother gave it to me at my confirmation."

"You ain't religious though are yer, I mean you don't go to Prayers or anything?"

"Too many bloody officers there for me."

Wyatt, who had led the opposition against O'Neill over the question of the German fighter, was still up for it, "Religion! It's a load of rubbish invented by the rich to hoodwink the poor. I don't believe in God."

Nervous leant on the hammock netting, "Bejappers! Won't he be gutted when he finds out?"

Wilson waited until the laughter had died away but before the verbal cudgels could be picked up again, said. "I remember some writing on a wall somewhere, one of the railway stations in 'Smoke', I think it was. It said 'God is dead'.

"Now, that could be true," said Wyatt theologically

"Yeah, but underneath, in that fancy writing you find in the bible, someone had wrote, 'Oh, no I ain't'."

* * *

Lieutenant Grant pointed over the starboard bow of the sea boat, "That looks a good spot."

O'Neill leaned forward, "Oars!" the emphasis on the word made it sound more of an insult than an order. The four oarsmen jerked their blades clear of the water and the boat slid in relative silence towards the craggy face of the rock.

Deep under the overhang a series of caves could be seen burrowed deep into its stony face. "Hold water." the heavy ash oars dropped as one and the boat instantly lost way.

They lay there, still in the water, bobbing in the sheltered cathedral-like grandeur of the inlet. All around the rock face rose sheer to a neck-arching height, claustrophobic in its immensity.

"Right you two," said O'Neill pointing at the two nearest oarsmen, "Boat yer oars and grab a hold of this little beauty," he slapped the heavy warp anchor at his feet, the noise echoing around the rock walls like a gunshot.

Between the three of them they wrestled the anchor up onto the gunwale, the boat listing alarmingly.

At a nod from Grant, it was eased over the side until it hung fully submerged, held in place by a stout rope attached to a warping bollard set in the pointed stern of the whaler.

"Lower away," ordered Grant.

The anchor sank slowly through the green blur of the

deep to settle on the bottom.

"All right, coxswain, "I'll take her in, you take charge of the warp…Give way… together".

The final stage of the approach up to the treacherous rocks was made with understandable caution. The warp pulled taut, rising from the clear waters, the boat only feet from the rock promontory.

O'Neill made fast at the stern and called, "Over you go, 'Tug'."

The seaman scrambled onto the gunwale, paused a second, finely balanced, and then stepped almost gracefully across onto the rock ledge. The sea boat backed away.

They repeated the manoeuvre farther along the cliff face, again choosing a site with a ledge and an adjacent rock outcrop to which they, would later, secure the destroyer's mooring.

The boat turned back towards the inlet's entrance, the men leaning back into their oars as she gathered speed. As they moved out they made the soundings dropping buoys to form a marked channel deeper than the 'Nishga's' draught. They worked swiftly, for as long as there was sufficient water there was no need to record the exact depth. They needed to save time in any way they could for already a dawn-blue light glimmered in the eastern sky.

* * *

As the 'Nishga' nosed her way slowly in towards Olaf's Inlet, Grant climbed the bridge ladder two at a time. Barr sat huddled in his chair, he gave a quick salute.

The channel's marked, sir. Basically we'll need to keep her over to port all the way in. There's a shelf of rock to starboard at around one fathom but apart from that, the Inlet's deep enough." He turned and pointed," There's the first buoy, it marks the beginning of the shelf."

"Right you are, Number One, good job. You'd better

get for'ard and check the Bosun's arrangements".

"Yes, sir, I've briefed the coxswain of the sea boat he's ready to lead the way in."

"Very good," Barr leaned over a brass voice pipe, his breath misting the painted brass "Port five, both engines slow ahead."

He listened with half an ear to the acknowledgements from the wheelhouse as he watched the flagstaff swinging rapidly left across the rock face. He could feel the eyes of the bridge crew boring into his back. He couldn't blame them; it was an unsettling pastime, watching that unforgiving rock draw closer and closer. He deliberately turned away, "Any Kye left?"

* * *

Grant arrived on the fo'c's'le as the ship lost way and started to roll lazily in the easy swell. He looked up at the cliff, now noticeably nearer; but for the 'Skerries', as the islands were known, their task would have been much more difficult, perhaps impossible.

The fo'c's'lemen had been on deck for over an hour laying out the necessary gear, now they stood by stamping their feet, amid grey clouds of frosted breath. The petty officer in charge of the fo'c's'le, Petty Officer Stone, straightened up from his task and saluted.

"Just about finished here, sir… The sea boat lying off the port bow".

Stone, 'Rocky' to his few friends, was forty years of age, a saintly age amongst a crew whose average age was twenty. He was well named, his face rock-like, chiselled features above a square jaw. His huge arms were covered in an indistinguishable blue haze of tattoos that gave his skin the appearance of blue veined marble. He had been due for retirement in the September of '39, the very month that war had been declared, his retirement had been deferred by a

Navy hungry for experienced seamen. If the truth had been known, which it wasn't, he had been relieved when they'd stopped his discharge he had not been looking forward to a life ashore, the Navy and the sea were all he knew. Experience he certainly had in plenty. He had joined the Navy at fourteen, as a boy seaman, and was proud that he knew more about his trade than any man aboard the 'Nishga'. The younger officers were glad to have him, not only relying on his prowess as a first rate seaman but also on the tact he used dealing with their inevitable blunders in front of the men. It was, however, tact that was noticeable by its absence in his dealings with the men. That he was a bully there could be no doubt, the lower deck lived in constant fear of his quick wit and his proficient and ready use of nautical adjectives. It was said he could have made the Devil himself blush.

Grant gave a thumbs-up to the bridge and took up his post in the eye of the ship. The destroyer inched slowly ahead following the fragile sea boat thirty feet below her raked bow.

The 'Nishga' nosed cautiously around the rocky headland with dawn's light clipping the snow on the cliff tops above the masthead, forming a halo of blue light along its ragged edge.

* * *

O'Neill took the sea boat out of harm's way while the long warship manoeuvred using her twin engines until, turning in a half circle, her bows pointed back out to sea.

When O'Neill saw the eye of the first mooring wire snaking down the destroyer's side he took the sea boat close in under it. The boat's crew coiled a few fathoms of it in the bottom of the boat and secured the bight to the boats wooden bollard.

While the seamen on the 'Nishga's' fo'c's'le carefully paid it out the sea boat pulled away and ferried the end to the first mooring point. Finally they rowed carefully towards a cold Wilson and the end of the destroyer's stern mooring wire was passed to him. With the wire safely secured he jumped back into the boat.

At last, after thirty minutes hard graft the 'Nishga' was able to use her powerful winches to warp carefully in towards the weathered rock.

Seamen, spaced at intervals, along the length of the ship, lowered unwieldy basketwork fenders over the side, positioning them between the sharp rocks and the ship's vulnerable side.

Towering fifty feet above the top of the mast the rock overhang gradually cut the ship off from the grey sky. To the men on deck it looked as if the cliff was toppling slowly over to engulf the ship.

Barr looked at his watch, the one his wife had given him on his last leave; it had taken ninety-four minutes to manoeuvre the ship into her new berth. They would have to do better than that.

* * *

Corporal Bushel leant to his left and looked down the crevasse he had just ascended. Fifty feet below he could see Stilson climbing steadily, fifty feet below him Blake, head craned back, watched the progress of his two companions.

Scattered about Blake's feet lay the huge amount of gear they would need over the next few days. He could just see the lights that were to be used to mark the Inlet entrance for 'Nishga' when she returned from her planned night raids. In the other bundles were the means to defend the inlet along with their food, tents and other personal kit. Every item was vital to the task ahead; the loss of any one thing could mean failure or worse.

Bushel looked up; he still had a way to go before he reached the top of the sheer face. He wedged himself deeper into the fault in the rock and blew onto his cold hands. He smiled at his unspoken pun, time for a blow. He gazed out across the inlet, six maybe seven hundred feet across the still waters of the Inlet, the 'Nishga' lay snug under the overhang, her icy reflection mirror-clear beneath her camouflaged hull. Her decks swarmed with duffel-coated seamen doubling up on her mooring wires and laying out the massive camouflage netting.

He looked at his watch; within the hour he and his men would have to be up there, above the ship, ready to hoist the netting into place. He needed to get a move on; he shifted the coil of rope on his shoulder until it sat more comfortably and resumed the climb.

* * *

Captain Barr sat at his desk, his pen poised at the end of his signature staring at a photograph on his desk, it was of his wife and eight- year old son, taken on his last long leave that had been before the start of the war.

When he pictured them in his mind's eye, as he often did during the long night watches, it was always this photograph that he saw. Sometimes it seemed as if they were frozen in time, somehow preserved in the frame to await his homecoming. A knock on his cabin door brought Barr back to the present with a jolt. He looked up to see his steward standing in the doorway.

"Chief Petty Officer Graves to see you, sir."

"Very good Jenkins, show him in please."

Chief Petty Officer 'Spooky' Graves entered, his battered cap under one arm, his new Chief's buttons shinning in splendid contrast. "You wanted to see me, sir."

"Yes, Chief, I want to discuss some arrangements I have in mind for camouflaging the entrance to the inlet, take a seat," he indicated a padded chair next to his desk.

The Chief sat uncomfortably on the edge, holding his cap in both hands as he looked about him.

"Cigarette?" asked Barr offering Graves one from a

box on the desk.

"Thank you kindly, sir, I don't mind if I do."

Barr lit both their cigarettes with a table lighter and settled back in his chair. "We need to disguise the entrance to this Inlet and at the same time discourage enemy patrol boats from entering."

Graves scratched at his bald head with the hand that held his cap, "I can see why, sir…"but I can't, for the life of me, see as how you can do that."

"I've been thinking about it for some time. I've an idea, but it's only an idea, I'm hoping you can tell me if it is possible or not, put some meat on the bone, as it were. We could construct a raft to block the entrance." He reached into the back of the desk and pulled out a notebook. "Here's a rough sketch of the inlet. "I thought to place the raft here, where the entrance narrows."

The Chippy dragged hard on the cigarette cupped in the hollow of a horny and nicotine stained fist. "But I don't understand, sir, if we put it there it'll be seen by the very patrol boats we want to discourage. At the very least it's going to make them curious surely, sir?"

"Not if we make it look like part of the landscape, a landslide to be precise. "Barr turned the page of his notebook and revealed a sketch of a raft. "We pile it up with rocks, like this, there's enough of them around, God knows. This step under the raft's waterline carries more rocks, hiding the wooden beams of the raft. It will have to be loaded carefully to keep it stable. To look right the rocks will have to slope down from the landward end… that may cause problems with the trim though. What do you think?"

"A larger rock at the other end might balance her up, keep her level… or we could construct a framework in wood at the landward end. We could load the rocks on to that, make it look as if it's all rocks, if you see what I mean…That would be lighter than a pile of rocks."

"Excellent! Exactly what I was hoping to get from you." Barr paused and pretended not to notice the glow of embarrassed pleasure on the Chief's face. "We tow her into place and then just swing her open, like a gate, when we need to enter or leave, like the boom at Scapa Flow."

Graves a pulled a face, "Let's hope it does a better job," said Graves remembering the 'Royal Oak' sunk by a German submarine inside that boom.

"Hmm, perhaps that was a bad example… but you get the idea, Chief. What do you think, can it be done?"

"I can't see why not. We've got plenty of wood…"

"That's my next point; I don't want you to use our wood, there's no telling when we would be able to replace it, we may need it for damage control. I want you to cut it from the plantations ashore."

"What lower it all the way down from the top?… big job… can be done, of course, but erh…"

"No, I thought to take the sea boat along the shore and cut it from sites near the water's edge and tow it back here, floating behind . I want it done as soon as you can and, of course, without drawing any attention."

"It would be better to cut it inland and drag it to the water's edge so you couldn't see the felled area from the sea."

"Right, see the Chief Bosun's Mate, tell him from me to give you all the men you need and the boat, of course."

* * *

Lying flat on their stomachs in the frozen snow the two marines peered cautiously over the cliff edge. More than a hundred dizzy feet below they could see the starboard side of the 'Nishga'. The netting stretched from a point just below them to the iron deck fifty feet below that. They could see seamen hauling the bottom end out towards the ship's side.

"Looks alright. Let's cut some branches to place over these blocks and tackles. Cover the lot with snow and we're done."

Ten minutes work and they were ready to leave. Bushel rammed his entrenching tool into its hanging strap. "That's about it; we're losing the light now. We've got a lot to do tomorrow."

They had spent the whole day moving their equipment and hauling the heavy net into place.

They walked backwards down the slope raking over their footprints as they went. They had stepped out of their skis where the thick snow gave way to the windswept fringes at the cliff's edge and set off at an easy pace, east towards where Stilson lay up watching the only path inland through the dense plantation.

Stilson rose out of the snow at their approach, he had been invisible in his white ski suit until he moved. The snow was even thicker here, sheltered from the worst of the winds by dense conifer.

"Everything all right?" asked Bushel. Stilson nodded. 'Snake Stilson' was a man of few words.

"Good, we'll rig the other tent and get some shut-eye; I'll stand first watch, two on four off. You're next 'Snake'. As soon as it's light enough we get back to work."

* * *

Slowly the cold red sun rose, spilling a pink light across the grey surface of the sea. The 'Nishga's'' sea boat sliced through the calm, ripples of liquid silver fanning out from her stern.

Chief Shipwright Graves crouched against the cold, a woolly hat pulled down over his shiny red ears.

Standing alongside him O'Neill steered, using his legs to move the tiller bar, hands deep in the pockets of a stained duffel coat, his chin buried in its collar, his hat rammed down behind his ears. Five seamen bent to the oars, rowing awkwardly wrapped thickly in their foul weather clothing.

"Beautiful day," said Chippy, when he received no

44

reply from O'Neill he added, "Wouldn't know there was a war on."

"Too bloody cold for me, Spooky!" said O'Neill, squinting at the rocks to port; he suddenly touched Graves on the shoulder. "We could get in there pretty easy," he pointed to a small beach, thick with storm blown seaweed.

They had been looking for a landing site since leaving the ship at first light.

"Looks alright from here, take her in closer."

O'Neill took a half step to one side, pushing the tiller bar hard over with the outside of his leg; "Oars, port!"

The men on the port side lifted their oars clear of the water and the boat swung swiftly round.

"Give way together!" they bent to their oars and pulled towards the craggy shoreline.

* * *

Bushel

The inside of the tent glowed with an eerie green light as the rising sun filtered through the canvas. The marines were already awake, their breath condensing on the tent's sides dripping ice cold drops onto their down sleeping bags.

Bushel crouching at the open flap turned his watch towards the sun's glow. "We'd better make a move. Stilson you wet the tea, Blake see what you can do with the eggs. No smoke, we ain't supposed to be having fires, use the driest wood from well into the plantation we'll light it there so the branches disperse any smoke. If I see one puff of smoke from here out it goes and that means a cold breakfast, got it? I'll make a start laying out the gear and camouflaging the camp. After breakfast we'll rig up a few little welcoming presents just in case Jerry decides to drop in. After lunch we'll set up the lights at the entrance ready in case the 'Nishga' does go out tonight."

"Do yer think she will, Corp?" asked Blake.

"Weather's perfect for getting in and out, flat calm hardly a breath of wind and there's no moon tonight,"

"I heard there was a small one for Sergeants and Corporals only," said Blake straight-faced.

"I heard different," said Bushel, "no moon tonight, but there's to be two moons tomorrow night," his unsmiling face disappeared through the tent flap.

* * *

"Call the Hands… Call the Hands…Call the Hands, the quartermaster's voice droned its dirge through the ship. "Heave-oh…Heave-oh…Heave-oh. Lash-up and stow…Cooks to the galley has gone long ago. Don't turn over…turn out!"

A few blankets stirred in the forward seaman's mess as the starboard watch demonstrated their lightening reflexes. The hatch crashing back on its stop stirred a few more; the metallic clatter of the mess ladder a few more and then the booming voice of the Petty Officer of Port Watch woke the remainder.

"All right! Who told yer you could sleep? Feet on the deck my smelly little cherubs! Hands off cocks, on socks," he added pleasantly, punching the nearest hammock. "Anyone still in their pit in three seconds will be buried in it! One!…Two!…Three!… That's better!" he said to the assembled mess as they appeared, as if by magic, alongside their hammocks wearing a motley assortment of sleeping attire, topped off with the same bloodhound expression. They stood arms hanging down their sides as Petty Officer Stone retraced his footsteps back up the ladder and dropped the hatch back down with a wince of a crash.

"Another day in fucking paradise," moaned Wyatt.

"That'll do me all right," said Wilson, taking out a packet of 'Duty Frees'.

"I wouldn't mind a day in 'fucking paradise'. I ain't seen a woman in yonks."

He held out his packet of 'Blue Liners', anyone want one? He paused while a few hands reached out, "Well, fucking well buy some!" he said snatching them away...relented, held them out again and ruefully watched them disappear.

Gradually the ship and her tired crew came back to life. At eight the starboard watch took over at defence stations and commenced the checks on the equipment that would be in their charge for the next four hours. Guns and torpedo launchers were trained round, ammunition in the ready-use lockers checked, tests run on the Asdic and radio sets, aft the depth charge launchers and ramps inspected and secured. Below, the stokers dipped the water and fuel tanks, checked gauges and oil levels, and re-greased everything that moved.

By nine o'clock the ship was ready for anything, in perfect working order behind its thick camouflage.

* * *

By nine the marines ashore had also completed their preparations, the tent and other equipment had disappeared from sight beneath a blanket of snow.

It had taken them longer than Bushel had thought to erase all the footprints and ski marks from the tree line back as far as the cliff edge. He skied out to where the path emerged from the trees to take a last look round.

He nodded his satisfaction. There was no sign that the site was occupied even though he knew exactly where Stilson lay concealed in the observation hide.

He sidestepped into the trees and drawing a saw-toothed knife from its leg strap, reached up and cut a fresh conifer branch, rubbing the cut mark with moss to conceal it. With his ski sticks under one arm he slid slowly down the track, back towards the camp, using the branch to carefully remove his tracks as he went.

Back at the camp he and Blake helped each other into

their backpacks and set off across the snow field towards the inlet entrance.

A bitter wind had come up out of nowhere, gusting from the northeast sending a dusting of fine snow swirling in front of them as they skied. Beyond the cliff, out to sea, milky green waves had begun to appear leaping and dancing to the wind's call.

They set up the first of the lights on the south side of the entrance, positioning the shutters so the lanterns, once lit, would only be visible from a limited sector. When they had finished they covered them with small rocks and a thin dusting of snow. After a short rest they skied back into an icy wind that conveniently obliterated their tracks as they went.

They passed the invisible camp and veered out around the eastern end of the inlet to put the second lamp in place on the north side.

* * *

O'Neill

In the trees, to the south of the marines, the ship's logging party worked, felling the timber for the raft. Chief Petty Officer Graves and his men were sheltered from the wind, but it swayed the tops of the trees and sent snow and cold air tumbling down to settle about them as they worked.

Deep in the tree cover it was surprisingly dark. Chippy had chosen the site where, as he had put it, the branches were 'thin and far between'.

He had chosen well, there were fewer branches to remove and those dead were easy to deal with; consequently the work was progressing well.

They soon had a routine going, Chippy cut out the 'gob', as he called it, that directed the fall of the tree, while the rest cleaned the trunks of side branches and dragged them away to the water's edge. Graves cut the 'V' of the 'gob' with the care he usually reserved for cutting a dovetail joint back in his workshop on board. It had to be right; he explained, so once the back-cut was made the tree would fall clear and not get hung up in the other trees. The trees fell slowly, almost gracefully, like a ham actor in a death scene.

All morning they worked, systematically felling and dragging the trees to the water line. By ten o'clock they had cut half the wood they needed and O'Neill broke off from the felling party and with Goddard in tow, made his way back to the shore to begin lashing the trees together to form the raft.

After a further hour's work they took a rest in the cover of the trees.

Goddard blew on his hands his gloves tucked under one arm, "My problem is I can't tie bloody knots with me gloves on," he stared at his hands, "me fingers look like a string of sausages."

"Don't mention food, I've a terrible hunger on me. You wouldn't be having a bar of 'nutty' about your person, now would yer?"

Goddard was renowned for his sweet tooth, spending all his spare cash buying chocolate from every source, legal and illegal. He reached deep inside the warmth of his duffel coat and pulled out a bar. He broke off a few squares and passed them over to O'Neill.

O'Neill stuck the chocolate between his teeth while he pulled his gloves back on. "Cheers decent of yer I'll..." he broke off as he heard the snarl of a revving diesel engine. " Shite! That's a Jerry!" He grabbed Goddard by the sleeve and dragged him unceremoniously into the cover of the trees.

"Put that fag out." he whispered quickly, crushing his own into the snow.

* * *

The two marines had reached the northern side of the inlet and were about to set up the second lamp when they too sighted the German E-Boat moving slowly in from seaward. They dropped down behind the ridge out of the line of sight.

"Blakey get back to the ship warn them we've got company... Leave the Bren. Keep below the skyline... Get moving!"

While Blake's white clad figure skied rapidly away in the direction of 'Nishga', Bushel crawled carefully forward on his elbows until he reached the cliff edge. Laying out full length in the snow he set up the Bren. As he worked he noticed movement out of the corner of one eye. Off to the southwest he could see the 'Nishga's' sea boat, a half-assembled raft and what looked like a pile of conifer branches that seemed to be moving slowly towards the boat. "Bloody Matloes!" he hissed, "they're going to give the game away."

Chapter 4

Surprise

Olaf's Inlet, 1040 hrs, Tuesday, 16th April, 1940.

From his position, high above the entrance, Bushel studied the E-boat as she clawed her way across the sheltered water, gulls wheeling and planning in the sky above it. It had been modified at some point for although it still had its original crosstrees mast its torpedo tubes had been boxed in, streamlined to replicate the high fo'c's'le of the more up to date versions.

As she drew nearer he could hear that all was not well with the sleek craft. The animal purr of its powerful engines did not sound quite right, the revs were dying away and then picking up again. He couldn't be sure at first; it might have been a trick of the wind. If she was in trouble and perhaps coming in to carry out repairs it would make life very difficult. He thought of reporting the possibility straight away but quickly abandoned that idea. Blake would give an initial warning, far better to wait and watch, see exactly what she did and where she made her landing.

* * *

From his hiding place in the trees Goddard watched O'Neill crawl across the frozen ground towards the boat and the half-finished raft, behind he dragged a huge bundle of conifer branches.

Goddard sniffed and slowly shook his head the way he'd seen his mentor Able Seaman Wilson do on many an occasion. They should have hidden the boat when they first landed. He knew what Wilson would have said, 'Leaders of men eh? I've shit 'em.' He popped another square of nutty into an already chocolate smeared mouth.

* * *

O'Neill was sweating, that in spite of the freezing snow he was crawling through. He couldn't see the E-boat from where he was, had no idea what sort of progress she was making towards the shore. He expected any minute to see it tower above the rocks in front of him, rocks that hid him from view for the time being. His plan was to use the branches to break up the outline of the boat and the raft.

Crouching at the side of the boat he peeped cautiously over the gunwale.

The E-boat didn't seem to have made much progress. Curious; in his experience E-boat skippers like the 'Andrew's' gunboat skippers, mad bastards who liked to charge about everywhere at a rate of knots.

He crawled flat-bellied over the gunwale and into the boat. Keeping one eye on the still distant E-boat he eased the branches into place one by one.

Satisfied he peered over the gunwale of the sea boat and studied the other vessel, ugly looking things, more like the barges he seen on canals; but they had a fearsome reputation. They said they were better fighting boats than the British equivalent …bigger anyway.

He sneaked silently back over the boat's gunwale and

belly-crawled back as fast as he could to the shelter of the tree line.

* * *

Blake skidded to a halt in a shower of powdery snow. Across the cold expanse of water the 'Nishga' lay quiet behind her camouflage netting.

He was searching for his torch to signal her when he heard a thump below him. Leaning out he could see the ship's cutter unloading gear on the rock shelf below the cliff.

"Below!" he called; half a dozen red faces looked up at him. "Get back to the ship; tell them there's a Jerry E-boat coming this way."

The coxswain of the boat cupped his hands around his mouth," You coming back with us, 'Royal'?"

"No, I'm getting back to me mate," he waved and turning quickly dropped back down the slope as fast as his skis could carry him.

* * *

"Is that all he had to say?" asked Captain Barr.

"Yes sir, he seemed in a hurry to get back." said the cutter's coxswain.

"Very Good, thank you, Leading Hand, carry on…" he stayed exactly how he was, deep in thought. After several moments he turned to Grant who had been patiently waiting beside him.

"Number One, go to action stations… quietly, no alarm, no pipes, use the gangway staff to call the watch below. Train all the guns that can bear, out to starboard in readiness. If she comes round that corner I want her blasted out of the water before she can get a signal off."

"Aye, Aye sir, shall I get the men on the depth charges to man the tackles on the nets, we don't want to set them alight… if we have to open fire."

Barr nodded, "Good point, Number One, what would I do without you."

"Warm yourself at the fire, sir?" But Barr hadn't heard him he had started pacing the day cabin, hands clasped behind his back, chin on his chest.

* * *

O'Neill

The E-boat was now spluttering her way pass O'Neill's hastily camouflaged sea boat, "'erh engines don't sound too healthy, 'Nervous'."

"No, you're right…If she breaks down now, she'll be between us and the bloody ship!"

"She's turning in towards the shore".

They could see a man, in a white jumper, working his way for'ard coiling a rope in one hand as he went.

"She's going to tie up…Look!

"Bloody hell, she's got between us and the 'Nishga'. We got to get word to them."

"She's too close to us for my liking. Only wants someone to take a stroll…"

"You get back to 'Spooky' and the rest of the mob, tell them what's happened and tell 'em to keep quiet and stay where they are, out of sight, you got me?"

* * *

Bushel

"You see what's happened?" whispered Bushel, as Blake crawled to his side. He was pointing to the E-boat, now almost directly below them on the far bank. "She's got engine trouble by the sounds of her, and she's pulled in there, right next to our bloody sea boat. She's probably going to make repairs, or worst still, wait for help"

"Blimey! What are you ganna do, Corp?"

"I'm going home to me mum, I don't know about you"

Blake grinned, "Thought you were too old to 'ave a mum, Corp."

The thirty-year old chose to ignore the remark. "You stay 'ere; if they get wind of us, or those silly bastards in the sea boat, do the best you can with this," he patted the Bren, "Aim for her bridge, get the officers and knock out their wireless so they can't let on to their mates. I'll get back to the 'Nishga', let them know the latest. I'll probably have to stay there for a bit, wait for the 'salts' to make up their minds, that bit could take some time."

"Something's got to be done and quick, the E-boat's between the sea boat and the ship… and between the ship and the sea."

* * *

"As I see it", the Captain was saying, "we have two options, the easy one… do nothing and hope they'll go away… or take her by boarding her.

If we do nothing and she leaves, we won't know if she knows we're here or not. She might come back with more friends than we can handle. Mind you, if we board her and she manages to get off a signal… same result."

"We could just blow her out of the water, sir," said the Navigating Officer.

"Two thousand tons of destroyer creeping up on an E-boat, I think not."

"There's only one option really, sir," said Grant. "We'll have to board her and make sure she has no chance of raising the alarm."

"And how do we do that, Number One?"

"Surprise, sir"

"What shout boo!" laughed the Navigator.

"No, we board her tonight or early tomorrow morning

using our marines"

* * *

The corporal stood at ease in front of the Captain's desk, staring straight ahead his eyes riveted to a photograph of a 'Nishga' leaving Portsmouth harbour.

"I'll send Stilson in, sir, there is no better at that sort of work, at least no one I've met."

"What if there's more than one sentry?" asked Barr.

"We'll be with him, sir, if needs be we can take out three. If there's more than that, which I doubt, it's a non-runner anyway."

"Is that what you think?" said Barr surprised at the certainty in the corporal's voice.

"It's not what I think sir, it's what I know. There's not a man alive who can surprise a mob."

* * *

Behind the German sentry's back, a minute grey shadow moved, indefinable, even in the glowing white of the snow. When he turned he saw nothing, nothing but the snow and the swaying shadows of the trees.

Matrose Alfred Becker had been looking at the snow and the trees for three hours now, so long that the only thing he saw was the cold hour he had left before his relief arrived.

Marine Stilson waited while the young German sentry turned again, waited while he walked to the other side of the bridge. Only then did he move, when he moved it was slowly, imperceptibly. He had been in full view of the sentry since the man had come on duty. He expected to be there for another half-hour. Thirty minutes of cold and pain before he reached the E-boat's bridge. He smiled; in fact he expected to be there for the rest of the young sentry's life.

Stilson moved like a snake, he thought of himself as

one in these situations, it was the secret of his success, why the men in his section called him 'Snake'; 'Snake' Stilson. He was proud of that and of the way Bushel always chose him for a job like this. He was the 'someone' to guard the camp, the 'someone' to take out the sentry or to stalk the stalker. He believed in himself, he was good, dedicated for, to him, killing was an art; the hardship, the cold, the cramp that assailed his limbs, they were all part of what he was. It was foreplay; anticipation, the mother of delight. The real art was to create the 'Snake' to truly believe you were it. He had become addicted to his calling, the danger, yes, but something else, the power. At times like this he knew the future; he knew that the sentry was going to die. He would only die when he, the 'Snake' wanted him to die, die, the way the 'Snake' wanted him to die, the three ways; 'The Snake's' holy creed.

* * *

Sloth-like the white shadow moved on the bridge ladder.

The German sentry was leaning on the screen; he ducked into its shadow to puff at the illicit cigarette cupped in his gloved hand. He never straightened up. He died in the shadow and by the shadow. As he dragged at his cigarette the 'Snake' dragged at his throat with a serrated knife. Even as his lifeblood drenched the snow at his feet and he instinctively tried to turn to face his assailant, 'Snake' broke his back and his neck. He was smiling behind the white face mask as he eased the thrice dead man tenderly, almost lovingly, to the bridge deck; as gentle as if he were a baby. The white figure turned quickly wrenched the wires out from below the radio aerial and raised an arm above the bridge windscreen before merging once more into the background to wait and to gloat.

* * *

The crouching and silent First Armed Guard, saw the raised hand from the boat's bridge, and moved swiftly and quietly across the snow and up the darkened gangplank.

No one spoke, there was no need, they each knew what had to be done. All the possibilities had been covered. The Navy had been covering possibilities for hundreds of years; nothing was ever left to chance because nothing was new. Contingency planning was the thing they did best. At each of the upper deck hatches, a group of Balaclavaed men quietly assembled. From the group on the bridge one figure emerged, his hand reached out in the darkness and pressed a brass button.

The silence was abruptly shattered by the jarring beat of the Schnellboote's alarm system.

Below the crew woke, wrenched from their deep slumber, scrambling from their bunks, falling over each other in a fully-clothed rush for the ladders. With a much practised and automatic reaction they charged still half asleep to their stations.

At the top of the ladders, one by one, they were suddenly lifted, swung clear of the hatch and knocked unconscious. The next in line had no time to think. No time for a sleep befogged brain to register surprise that the man in front had gone through the hatch so quickly. As he reached the top he only had time for amazement at the ease with which he had cleared the hatch. By the time he realised he had help; it was too late. The crack of the pickaxe handle and the exploding pain heralded the dark that enveloped him.

It had taken minutes, no cry of alarm had alerted the men still below. They knew nothing until cork-blackened faces suddenly appeared from nowhere.

* * *

On the wing of the destroyer's bridge the Yeoman of

Signals raised the Aldis lamp to his forearm, signalled 'received' and turned to the Captain.

'Signal from the First Armed Guard', sir, relayed from the marine lookout post, 'Mission accomplished'."

Barr's automatic response hid the acute anxiety he had been feeling. "Very good, Yeo."

* * *

Barr and the Gunnery officer, Lieutenant Grey, who had been second in command of the First Armed Guard, stood on the E-boat's tiny bridge.

"Well done, Lieutenant, we are now the owners of one E-boat and who knows, with luck, a few weeks worth of recognition codes."

"Not to mention her collection of slightly concussed crew members," said Grey, indicating over one shoulder with a thumb. "Good news from Macdonald, the Leading Stoker, he's checked the engine and repaired the fault; it was a blocked lubrication pipe on one of the bearings. They would have had to stop the engine to work on it, obviously why she came in here. Macdonald has fallen in love with the engines he hasn't been out of the engine room, even had his food brought down."

"What does he find so fascinating?"

"The Daimler Benz engines."

"Nasty oily things engines," said Barr absentmindedly looking across to the trees where the 'Nishga's' sickbay attendant administered to the bunch of rather dejected looking prisoners.

"She has three of them, driving three shafts and a Siemens auxiliary for manoeuvring and silent running."

"Hmm," breathed Barr, " More importantly how much ammo has she."

"Magazine's full, so are the ready use lockers. She hasn't fired a shot this trip. Fuel tanks are full as well, Eight thousand litres of diesel. According to Macdonald that's

59

enough for two thousand miles."

"Now that is interesting." Barr was frowning in concentration, very interesting.

"Wouldn't like to pick up her fuel bill, that works out at about a mile to the gallon."

"We'll ferry the prisoners back to 'Nishga' and drop them off at the Flow as soon as we can, preferably before they eat us out of house and home."

"What about the dead chap, sir, bury him here or later, at sea?"

"Later, I think, have him put aboard 'Nishga'. I want you to collect some 'wreckage to scatter when we go out tonight, we'll float him off with it, thrown in some oil…it might fool Jerry and stop them cancelling their recognition codes. They might not even bother to mount a search; with the invasion in full swing I think they have their hands full at the moment."

"Does that mean the operation is definitely on for tonight, sir?"

"I think we're ready, we'll be leaving the marines ashore. We'll give them a stoker and a couple of good seamen to work this beauty for them; he patted the metal in front of him. "That way if we can't get back, for whatever reason, they'll have a chance of getting home under their own steam. Lady Luck seems to be with us this trip, Number One."

* * *

The marines stood by the light on the headland, looking down on the 'Nishga' as she singled up her moorings. She had darkened ship, but hooded torches gave enough light for them to see the wires dropping with an audible splash into the icy water. A burst of iridescent foam suddenly piled high at her stern.

She began to move slowly astern, two thousand tons of metal pulled at the one remaining wire, the after spring it drew taut singing its protest while her sleek bows swung out from the cliff face.

The foam dropped away to an urgent ripple of white water, the after spring hung in a great bight, then slipped into the glassy water and was hauled quickly inboard. The warship trembled briefly as her powerful engines first stopped her and then moved her slowly ahead, free of the land and into her natural element.

Barr called from the blackness of the bridge wing, "Yeo, make the signal for the lights to be turned on and for the boom to be opened."

The Aldis chattered out four dashes of light, startlingly blue-white in the almost total darkness. Instantly green and red lights glowed high above them.

"Well done the 'Royals'," offered the Pilot as he took his bearings.

"Must admit," replied the Captain from somewhere in the dark, "I'm glad they're on our side and..." The bridge team waited for him to finish, he had stopped in mid-flow. Something had just occurred to him; they knew the signs and remained quiet.

* * *

It had begun to rain as they left the Inlet, a sudden downpour drifting across the ship from the north-west, battering the choppy waves down into a submissive thick oily swell. Each heaving wave lifted her momentarily before rushing away to the southeast. There was an edge to the wind as they made their way north, constantly changing their course amongst the maze of scattered islands and lethal rocks.

Visibility had dropped drastically to just a few cables by the time the ship's engines finally died away and the 'Nishga' lay in a narrow channel between two islands.

The rain increased its tempo further reducing the visibility drifting out of the darkness in sheets, sweeping across the deserted fo'c's'le and vanishing into the gloom out to port,

Barr leant over the chart table, squinting into the weak glow from the hooded light, rain dripped from the peak of his cap splashing on the chart waterproof covering in blue blobs.

"I made a note of this position as we came south, Pilot. It should be ideal for our purposes, if we keep this island," he stabbed a wet finger at the chart, "between us and the deeper channel, here. It will give us some cover, but allow us to fire across it into the main shipping lane.

"It is a good position," agreed Lieutenant Usbourne, "The dark backdrop will make it very difficult for them to see us, at least until we open fire. I see one snag, sir, enemy convoys could use either of these passages between the islands or they could just as easily stand farther out to sea."

"They could, that's true; but I don't think they will want to use the narrower passage; not for convoys. If they chose to keep out to sea they'll lose the cover afforded by the islands. Time is on our side…We can afford to wait, if I'm right the pickings will come to us and they will be well worth the wait."

The bridge ladder rattled, and the shadowy figure of Grant appeared out of the dark.

"Ah, Number One, have you and the midshipman managed to work through those captured recognition signals yet?"

"I've just come from the wireless office now, sir. It was quiet easy. Mr Hogg seems to understand German very well, I must say. I've forwarded the codes to the Admiralty, repeated 'Warspite', we should be able to put the cat among the pigeons all the way along the east coast with this little lot," a paper rustled in the dark as he tapped it.

* * *

Lady Luck wasn't with them that night, no coastal

convoys, no sign of enemy shipping at all. Nor for the two nights that followed in wet and dreary succession.

They returned tired and empty handed to the inlet each morning before first light. Barr began to doubt his judgement.

The fourth night was a clear moonlit one with a stiff breeze nipping in from the west. Barr sat, as he had on all the previous nights, huddled in his bridge chair, running through his plan over and over. He stirred only to drink 'Kye' or to consult the chart.

He was still there when the watch changed at four and Grant began his spell as officer of the watch.

After the change over briefing, Grant paced the deck, one weather eye on his Captain. It wasn't like Barr to be so quiet. Determined to engage the Captain in conversation he edged closer with each crossing of the bridge.

"Bit warmer tonight sir, have to keep an eye on this wind though, lee shore and…"

The lookout's cry interrupted his efforts at small talk.

"Red one seven five! Ship! Near! "The two officers spun round together, binoculars already raised. The excited lookout was pointing. "There sir! Port quarter!"

Grant lowered his night glasses, "She's just come out from behind the far island, sir… Well spotted lookout."

There, less than a mile away across the sheltered channel a warship was moving swiftly into open water. She was illuminated by the moonlight as if it was day. The silver light dancing on her grey paint work, her bow wave flickering, a phosphorescent blur as she cut neatly through the black water.

"Action Stations, Number One, if you please…And hoist the Battle Ensign."

Grant leant across and stabbed at the button,

The Chief Yeoman turned from his binoculars shouting above the dim of the action alarm, "German all right, sir, F Class escort, by the looks of her." The Yeoman had the best eyes on the ship, honed by twenty-two years squinting into all kinds of weather. "Astern of her... I see two...no three coasters."

The ship's communications had sprung into life, every part of ship reporting in its turn. Grant, who had been ticking them off in his mind, saluted, "Ship closed up at action stations, sir."

"Very good, Number One... Pilot; bring the ship round to port, broadside on to the convoy. I want all guns to bear on the target... Oh and before you go to your action station tell 'Guns' I want the for'ard four point sevens to engage the lead ship, the escort. Our after guns are to fire at the aftermost coaster. With a bit of luck we'll trap the other two ships in between and in mid channel." He looked at the bow, swinging rapidly now. "Tell him to fire as his guns bear. Without waiting for a reply he lifted a sound powered telephone from its cradle, whirled the handle and spoke briefly. Abruptly 'A' and 'B' turrets erupted simultaneously in a blast of noise and shooting flame, the sea flickering and flashing a pale green in the stark glare.

Grant had a clear view of 'B' Gun as he made for the ladder. It was a hive of disciplined activity as shell after shell roared from it's blackened barrels towards the distant target. It was a fiery demon belching forth a billowing cloud of acrid cordite fumes. The crew were its companions answering its every call in fiendish servile haste. In the flashing light they moved at the jerky pace of an old movie. Duffel-coated and tin-helmeted they laboured like slaves to sate the insatiable hunger of their terrible master.

On the bridge, enveloped in clouds of choking smoke, men strained streaming eyes as they tried to gauge the results of the satanic activity around the four point sevens. Across the water in short spells of clear visibility the terrible damage could be seen. Massive explosions and great swelling clouds of black smoke, enveloped the target; clouds that were aglow from the flames licking and flaring from the doomed convoy. The lone German escort lay dead in the water, aflame from stem to stern, listing heavily to starboard like a wounded sea bird. Taken completely by surprise, at point blank range, she'd had no chance to return fire.

'Nishga's' after guns shifted target to the next merchantman and almost immediately she swung out of line and stopped in the water; bludgeoned to a halt by the continuous, devastating and rapid fire. Suddenly she exploded, her placid heart ripped out, as her cargo of ammunition ignited. The massive fireball rose rapidly into the sky illuminating the remaining ship, a tanker, aft men could be seen wrestling with her flag, dragging it unceremoniously to the deck.

"Cease Fire," yelled Barr, from behind his binoculars. Above the fearful noise; the gongs sounded at each of the 'Nishga's guns and they fell silent; their crews falling exhausted to the cold decks.

* * *

The sea boat pulled slowly back to the German tanker, weaving its way amongst the flotsam through oil streaked water.

The oarsmen were tired; their blackened faces illuminated by the glow from the two fires still burning; they had spent much of the night crossing backwards and forwards between the two ships.

It had been they who had ferried the First Armed Guard out to pick up the pitifully few survivors from the water. The cutter had collected the survivors from the escort, twenty-five men in all. There had been none from the ammunition ship.

The prisoners were a sorry looking lot, wide-eyed and dejected, their faces and clothes covered in oil.

Only one, a crop-headed rugged looking individual, had been defiant, shaking his fist at the boat's crew as they drew near. Another, coughing oil had died in the boat. They had simply slipped him back into the water like an unwanted fish.

Then there had been the trip with the two Petty officers. The 'Jack Dusty', to supervise the commandeering of useful stores and a stoker to dip the fresh water and fuel tanks of the enemy vessel.

The prisoners were ferried across to the tanker. The enemy tanker was carrying aviation fuel, there were no volunteers to crew it; no one, as Wyatt put it. Before adding, 'anyway, the 'Flow's' a lousy run ashore anyway, more life in the body they had just put back in the water'.

* * *

Astern of the two ships the first inkling of morning wove the eastern horizon with slender pink ribbons. The German tanker was making a healthy twelve knots, the 'Nishga' slowly circling her at twenty, shepherding her home.

On the bridge of the warship the ever-present and all-invading ping of the Asdic speaker formed the background to the watch's routine. The bridge lookouts scanned the empty horizon their dark silhouettes stark against the dawn's glow. The officer of the watch studied his chart, occasionally crossing to the compass platform to check a bearing or the ship's head. The bridge signalman had his eyes on the tanker's bridge wing where, in the growing light, his colleague could be seen peering sleepily back.

The morning was passing peacefully by in the well-oiled rhythm of naval watch keeping. Below decks, the morning jobs were well under way, the galley fire was lit, the ship's cook and the duty cooks from each mess began to prepare breakfast. The hands off watch were shaken and climbed ladders to wash and shave.

At six-thirty the decks were scrubbed and hosed down with salt water from the fire main then the hands went to their breakfast.

"Jesus!" exclaimed Wyatt, "what this? Cabbage for

breakfast?"

"It tastes ….weird." said Stubbs.

"That's because it's ain't cabbage," replied Wilson, smugly, he was cook of the mess and had prepared the 'dish', as he insisted on calling all his 'creations'. Confiscated it from that Jerry tanker, the cook reckons yer Jerry eat it all the time."

The men wordlessly poked the sauerkraut around their plates. The action moved Wilson into further defence of his cooking. "Well, it was free…There ain't a lot left in the mess funds…I thought we oughta give it a go."

"That's what it'll do, all right…make you go," remarked Wyatt, prune faced.

"Cook said it was sour sommick or the other." Wilson added, with a vain attempt at enthusiasm.

Another short silence followed provoking Wilson once more, "If you don't like it stick it on the side of yer plate and eat yer German banger."

"German!" said Wyatt, "Gawd Almighty!" he pushed his plate away with an expression of disgust, "I don't know about you blokes, but if this is what we're fighting Jerry for, I reckon we oughta let him win."

* * *

They escorted the tanker until the drone of aircraft engines, from the west, announced the arrival of the air cover they had radioed ahead for.

Before parting company with their prize, they heaved to and transferred several drums of aviation fuel pumped up from the tanker's hold. The rumour spread that the wardroom had run out of gin.

They turned south then, signal lamps flashing. Barr hoping that the westerly course would again fool any spotter planes.

A thankfully uneventful day followed; there was time to rest after the rigours of the night, time to recharge their batteries and time to clear up the chaos above and below decks.

For the first time in weeks, they went into four watches instead of two. It meant three-quarters of the men had an afternoon off, a 'make and mend'.

It didn't please everybody.

"You know I ain't had a dry stitch on me back in yonks." said Wyatt, moaning to no one in particular whilst arranging his overalls over an adjacent warm pipe.

"'Ere! Look at that will yer," exclaimed Goddard, staring at the naked beauty in his borrowed 'Esquire', "That's what I'd like my girl to look like."

"If you had a girl you wouldn't know what to do with her." said Wyatt.

"I wish my misses had breasts" commented Wilson peering over the reader's shoulder.

"What's she got instead?" inquired Stubbs.

Wilson feigned memory loss, "I can't remember it's been so long."

"How long has it been since the last leave, Blur?" asked Wyatt.

"Christmas... four months now... I wish you lot would stop calling me Blur!"

"No one uses their proper name in the Andrew," said Wyatt emphatically.

"I know that! 'Tug' started calling me 'Blur' and now everyone does."

"Wyatt finished hanging out his washing before adding, "Well, yer stuck with it now, you'll never get rid of it. Even when yer change ships it'll dog your every footstep, I've had mine for yonks."

Wilson smiled looking up from darning a sock, "Shouldn't loaf when there's work about... Should pull yer weight, like the rest of us."

"Yeah! Bloody yeah! said Blur in a rare show of temper. "One sodding time, that's all it was... and...and I weren't feeling all that well, either was I?"

"You got away swift enough for one so sick, as I remember it," accused Wilson. "There was this blur and yer was gone!"

As darkness fell they turned, unobserved, heading east once more, back towards the Norwegian coast.

* * *

The darkness descended over the Norwegian Sea with the wind strengthening from the west, the sea livelier; cold grey waves marching in, rank upon foam topped- rank as far as the eye could see. The forecast looked bad for the next twenty-four hours at least.

At the change of the watch Lieutenant Grey came up onto the bridge to relieve the First Lieutenant.

Barr was back in his bridge chair following a short, but welcome, spell below. He was the only seaman officer who kept no set watches but his standing order, that he should be informed of any sightings day or night, meant he got very little rest. As a consequence of his own order he found it more convenient to doze in the bridge chair than to struggle into foul weather clothing and come up onto the bridge every time there was a sighting.

He stared out at the horizon as he waited for the usual exchanges between the incoming and outgoing officers to end.

"Number One, before you go below for your well-earned, I'd like a word, if I may."

"Certainly sir... I not in trouble, I trust."

Barr smiled through his stubble, "No, no, everything's fine, you're doing a great job" he paused his eyes automatically searching the horizon as he assembled his thoughts.

"Do you remember the other day, when we were leaving harbour; the day we boarded the E-boat."

"Yes, sir."

"Well, it occurred to me how we were completely

relying on those lights the marines were putting out for us. That made me think how Jerry must be doing exactly the same thing; all along this coast…relying on their lights I mean. Now…Just supposing the lights they were relying were not in the right place. What if we were to move them inland?"

Grant frowned, "You mean…like the wreckers on the coast of Cornwall in the eighteen-century?"

"That's it, precisely. Of course we have no idea when the enemy convoys are coming at the moment. What we need is recognisance. I see a role here for the E-boat. A crew, led by you and the German speaking Midshipman, what's-his-name, as your second…"

"Hogg, sir."

"What? Yes… yes… Hogg, that's the chap." Barr was in full swing now, Grant couldn't remember when he had seen him this animated, he was speaking faster and faster thinking on his feet. "He's a reliable chap…speaks good German, as you said yourself…You could scout along the coast. Take a couple of marines with you. Watch out for lights marking rocks, headlands, shallows, that sort of thing.

Ideally you'd be after full convoys supplying northern Norway, rather than empty ones returning. They'd be sailing north, that means…" he walked over to the chart with Grant following. "You'll be looking for somewhere like… "His gloved finger moved to a headland on the chart." …this… of course it's only an example, you'll be better placed, on the spot, to choose exactly where. I mean look at this its runs east west and looks as if it would prove a formidable hazard at the best of times, but on a dark night, or a foggy one…Once you have chosen your site… move back along the coast south and find your convoy, get back to your headland at a rate of knots, ahead of the slower target, land your marines, they move the light inland." He paused, leaning back, suddenly aware of the ache in his back and the sudden sapping tiredness.

As Grant remained silent Barr felt obliged to offer some encouragement, thinking perhaps he was lukewarm to the idea. "I've always considered myself a good judge of character. I think you've got what it takes to make this sort of thing work.... At your age I would have given anything for an opportunity like this. Your own command, more or less independent it's only temporary at the moment, of course, but, make good and I'm sure it can be made permanent. What do you think?

"I'm flattered sir... It's all a bit sudden...After all I've only held this appointment for a month... at this rate. I'll be in charge of the war by the end of the year"

Barr laughed out loud, a rare event, taking Grant by surprise.

"One step at a time, Number One, one step at a time. I'll speak to Grey he can act as First Lieutenant in your absence. That's settled then! I'll get the writer to get something down on paper and then we'll discuss it in more detail. In the meantime you can draw up a list of your requirements, crew members that sort of thing"

* * *

"You got some of my best men here Number One! He ran a finger down the list... Petty Officer Stone! Leading Seaman O'Neill!...Hmm! Macdonald, well, you're welcome to him; the man's a load of trouble; always in fights, ashore, on board, it seems to make little difference to him. The man's an annoyance. I see him, on defaulters, more than any other man on this ship, with the possible exception of your leading hand."

"He knows his job inside out, sir... used to be a Chief Stoker on a carrier"

"I know, that's what I mean. Been demoted twice since then... always through the same thing, drunken brawls, in my judgement not a suitable candidate for a small boat."

"As you said yourself, sir, It's an independent

command, I'll need the skills of these men, it'll be no use to me having a nice chap who doesn't know a wheel- spanner from a grease-nipple…I could change him for your Chief Stoker?"

"No, you bloody well can't… He threw the list of names across his desk at Grant with a grin. Approved!...With reservations."

Chapter 5

Operation Daphne du Maurier

Norwegian coast, Saturday, 2200 hours, 20th April, 1940.

The E-boat's engines snarled into life, the sound echoing back from the cliffs. A seaman on the tiny fo'c's'le slipped the painter and the craft moved slowly out into the deserted Inlet.

Grant jammed his borrowed German cap down tight around his ears as the wind snatched angrily. He hoped he'd remembered everything, there would be no chance of supplies for a few days; a week even. He had to admit to just a touch of apprehension. He hadn't been his own boss for some time, not since before the war. The yacht-skippering job in the Med in the spring of thirty-seven. Halcyon days indeed; with a struggle he forced his mind back to the job in hand.

"Slow ahead, steer south by west, belay that steer one nine oh. Blast! His first order! He would have to get used to these confounded giro compasses. Now where was he, he ran through the list in his mind for the umpteenth time. He had carried out an inventory of the E-boat's equipment;

they were well supplied. He had the light checked, nice job the 'Nishga's' Chief 'Lecky' had made converting the portable signal lamp. They could now adjust the flashing sequence to mimic any shore side light. What's more two men could manage it easily.

"Starboard ten"…The two marines had their kit stowed below in the boat's tiny magazine, too small, by far for the extra gear they had on board.

Interestingly, among the equipment onboard the captured boat they'd discovered three of Jerry's new magnetic mines. German mines were more reliable than their British equivalent and had been for some time. In fact it had been a Hertz horned-mine that the British had copied to produce their first contact mine in the last do.

"Midships… Steer east…" These magnetic mines were deadly things; six foot long… they were the first he'd seen. He remembered when Jerry had first used them, blowing the old 'Gypsy' in half in Harwich Harbour and then of course the 'Belfast'. He'd seen firsthand the damage just one had done to her hull. It would be a sweet revenge if the opportunity to use them on Jerry came up this trip.

He snatched a quick look at the compass. "Starboard ten… steer north,"

Darker shadows, the islands protecting the entrance, scrolled across the bow as the boat turned broadside on to a stiff westerly and began to roll like a drunken man.

* * *

Corporal Bushel's cork-blackened face turned slowly towards Stilson. He was checking to see if he was still there and closed up; too bloody easy to get separated when it was this dark.

It was Stilson who carried the fifty pound lamp strapped to his back. They were moving at a snail's pace, checking beneath each foot before letting it take their full body weight. In the darkness, this close to the enemy it was the only way to move. He eased a twig away with the side of one boot.

They had spent nearly an hour moving past the cliff-top sentry post, time they could ill-afford if they were to reach the lighthouse before first light. He turned slowly to look in the direction of the enemy position; it was barely twelve yards away. Almost past it; about two hours of darkness left. Another two hours and they would have to lie up whether they had reached their target or not.

Grant and his 'new toy' might return as early as sunset tonight. They needed to know the ins and outs of the target by then. They just had to be in place by dawn.

Time and the cold were his main worries. The Germans used pretty low-grade troops for garrison duties... Suddenly, to his left, a loud voice broke the silence. Thick guttural German accompanied by the sound of boots skidding on icy rock.

He sank slowly to the rock floor gesturing for Stilson to do the same. His hand inched towards his knife. The man was moving directly towards them. A second voice, full of banter, rose mockingly from the guard post.

'Voice One' replied with a short and sharp. "Arschloch!"

Bushel's hand reached the hilt, gradually, inch by inch; he eased the knife from its greased sheaf. 'Voice One' stopped. The sound of leather and the rustle of clothes now only yards away.

'Voice One' farted, a ripping rolling sound that drew a cheer from the enemy position, more mocking words from 'Voice Two' a cloying smell filled the Englishmen's nostrils.

The crouching man was barely three yards from the two marines. Luckily he was in a hurry; the freezing night did not lend itself to things leisurely, especially when it involved exposing vast quantities of tender German flesh.

'Voice One' pulled at his trousers, Bushel could hear teeth chattering as the man turned his back and hurriedly retraced his steps.

*   *   *

It had been seven long hours since the German sentry had pulled up his trousers; seven long, cold hours in which they had moved unseen past the post and carefully circled the darkened lighthouse.

They were now in position to the south of the target. They lay under a snow-covered ground sheet, their chilled bodies wrapped in down sleeping bags. Stilson dozed while his corporal watched. Their heavy packs were hidden under the sheet behind them in a hollow in the ground. To their right a rock rose steep and sheer against the grey morning light casting a faint, but welcome, shadow over their position. This wasn't an ideal spot, too bloody cold for a start, but it would have to do in such a barren bleak-white landscape.

Something moved by the target. He eased the sheet up a touch. Someone had opened the lighthouse door. A man, heavily wrapped against the cold, emerged from the building. He was making his way to the pile of snow-dusted wood to the right of the door. Bushel checked his watch; the last load of wood had lasted him two hours. The man turned and walked back towards the unlocked door; Bushel slowly lowered the flap of the groundsheet.

Darkness came quickly, no lingering twilight like further south. Bushel nudged Stilson and folded back the groundsheet…Darkness…and a chance to get the circulation moving in cramped frozen limbs.

*   *   *

Lieutenant Grant signalled for slow ahead and took the E-boat in a gradual slow turn that took them around the island putting it between them and the convoy.

There were seven ships in all, including the escort,

heading in just the right direction; it all looked perfect.

He waited until the convoy disappeared from sight, behind the looming bulk of the island then he leant to the voice pipe and ordered full ahead. The E-boat's bow rose sharply and she planed across the water like the true thoroughbred she was, her powerful engines quickly taking her up to her top speed. At thirty knots the eight-knot convoy's position was soon hull down below the horizon.

They had spent some time watching the German lighthouse, timing the sequence of the light, studying the courses steered by passing ships and the areas they avoided noting both on the chart. Grant was acutely aware of the possibility of minefields.

"She certainly can move, Mr Hogg."

"Yes, sir." called the diminutive Midshipman, ducking as a sheet of ice cold spray hissed across the fo'c's'le and hit the bridge windscreen with a noise like frying fat. "Quite exhilarating if a trifle damp, don't you think, sir?"

Grant smiled in the darkness, he had come to know and like this youngster over the last few days. "What part of the country do you come from Mr Hogg?"

"West Country sir, mother has a place there, I was away at school when the war started."

"Where was that?"

"Wellington, sir."

"So you had planned to join the service anyway?"

"That was the idea sir; most of the chaps join the forces from there. But...well after my father died, mother thought I should take over, run the estate. She sort of stood in for me while I finished my schooling. But the war changed all that. And you sir, where do you hail from?"

"Originally the south coast, my father has a boat yard at Yarmouth. He repairs coastal stuff for the 'Andrew' now. But... well...I sort of drifted around a bit... bit of yacht minding... bit of coastal work before that, got my ticket working colliers out of Newcastle... Hang on..." he placed a cautionary hand on the Midshipman's shoulder, "that's sounds like the mines moving about."

A dull thump sounded from aft as the boat slammed into another wave. "See Petty Officer Stone; get him to check the lashing."

Grant turned back, leant heavily on the vibrating windscreen and checked his watch, he hoped he had allowed enough time; the whole thing relied on good timing. He had carefully gone through each phase of the operation. It seemed to work on paper…but then so did the Pools, that didn't mean you were guaranteed a prize.

* * *

Grant ordered slow ahead and peered into the night. Somewhere out there, the rocky headland waited but he could see no sign of it; nothing. The conditions were perfect for his purpose but made navigation damn difficult. A light flashed, a loom of ghostly silver sky dead ahead.

"Stop engines!"

They had no time to search for the target, his dead reckoning had to be right first time; every second that convoy was getting closer.

"Lookout! Any sign of the land?"

The lookout snatched a quick look through his powerful binoculars before replying, "Nothing in sight yet sir."

He inched the boat in another cable towards the unseen shore. Were his tired eyes playing tricks or was that something.

"Lookout, bridge… There's the headland, sir… fine on the port bow."

"Very good… Signalman…standby…O'Neill, stand by to gun the engines."

* * *

The roar of the E-boats' engines shattered the quiet

night. As the noise died away, German voices could be heard raising the alarm, cursing as they stumbled over each other in a rush to their stations.

The gun emplacement's searchlight stabbed out a sword of light, cutting through the dark, straight to the source of the alarm, pinning the E-boat to its watery backdrop like a grey moth to its mounting. In the harsh light every detail stood out even the broad grin on the face of the E-boat's skipper as he lifted his cap in a sardonic salute.

"Damn Kriegsmarine, playing silly buggers," said the searchlight operator while at the same time he admired the fine lines of the boat caught in the beam.

A hundred yards away, to the north, Bushel heard the engines and, averting his eyes from the blinding light that followed, checked his watch. The Navy would have to wait a bit, another thirty minutes. According to his calculations that would be when light house keeper would run out of wood for his fire...

Or could it be keepers, they had only seen one man, the same man, during a day's careful watch, a soldier in his mid forties. There could be others; the tightly closed shutters had kept that piece of information from them. Only one man had been relieved at eight that morning, but there was no telling what rota system they worked. To find that out for certain would have taken several days of clandestine observations; time they just didn't have.

He placed a hand on Stilson's shoulder, gaining his attention he pointed to the lighthouse and drew a gloved forefinger across his own throat. Even in the dark he saw the flicker in the unblinking grey eyes. Excitement? Possibly but there was something else, something he had noticed before, something that made him uneasy. A hint of pleasurable anticipation, it was more intense than that... madness? He couldn't be sure. Whatever it was, it was only there for a split second, but it was there all right and it would bear watching.

* * *

There was no light from the building, no noise, no sign of life as Stilson drew close to the woodpile, his slow, careful and silent movements eerily imitating those of his mentor. He slid pass the stock of wood, paused momentarily by the plank door, listening, his tongue flickering over blue-cold lips. Then his dim shadow slipped into the dark recesses beside the door.

* * *

Bushel had moved his position. He was now between the sentry post and the lighthouse. Nothing left to chance, that was his saying and it had served him well so far. Cover every eventuality and you'd done all you could, the rest was the luck of the draw.

Twice, during the day, the fat NCO from the sentry post had crossed the three hundred yards to the lighthouse. If it happened again he wanted to be in a position to ensure it would be a one way trip.

From where he lay he could see both the path to his right and the lighthouse to his left. He settled down, hidden by his white ground sheet.

* * *

The lighthouse keeper was in a hurry. He'd put off going out into the cold to the last possible moment he had fallen asleep in the dying warmth of the fire. Now it was barely alight, urgently in need of more wood, not much time, the convoy was due at eight, he had to put the light on at seven, and he hadn't prepared his supper yet. He reached for his greatcoat, cursing his own stupidity; he hastily banged an old lidded pipe out on the stove's cast iron lid.

* * *

The sharp metallic sound the pipe made on the stove was the first sign of life Stilson had heard since arriving at the door. He curled back in against the wall, deeper into the shadow. The door's bolt drew back onto its stop; he heard the rusty creak of its hinges.

The shaft of yellow light flaring from the lighthouse's warm interior illuminated the frozen snow and reflecting in the white of Stilson's wide staring eyes.

* * *

Grant replaced the cap on his head, a fixed smile playing to his audience, He knew they would be watching him from the cliff top and he knew what fine instruments German binoculars were, after all he owned several pairs himself.

He gave one final wave and took the E-boat in a broad curve back out to into the sea's darkness.

* * *

Bushel saw the beam of yellow light from the opening door, watched as the silhouette of a man paused briefly and then moved off to the left, leaving the door slightly ajar. The steady light from the opening flickered momentarily as another, slimmer shadow moved swiftly across it. So swiftly, so silently, that you had to be expecting it to see it. A heart-beat later and the slim figure moved back into the light, the door gapped and then silently closed behind it. The darkness that descended was somehow blacker than before, the night somehow colder than before.

* * *

Unteroffizier Heinrich Altmann doubled over in pain,

rocking backwards and forwards, rubbing at his bloated belly with both hands. He cursed his stomach and the skipper of the E-boat for awakening him to such discomfort.

He scrambled awkwardly from the gun-emplacement calling to his men his intention to check things at the lighthouse. Not entirely a lie, he had to make sure that lazy oaf of a keeper was awake for the northbound convoy.

Of course he knew that his men knew that he was also going there to sample the 'oaf's' Schnapps and the warmth in front of his lighthouse fire. He rubbed again at his ample belly. That schweinhund of a company cook...the arschloch never washes his hands. It was a wonder the whole squad wasn't sick. He flapped his arms about his distended body, Gott it was cold, it didn't help that he had bared his backside in the wind ravaged latrine so many times during the night that it felt more like a block of ice than an arse.

* * *

Stilson wiped the slippery blood from his gloves, quickly removed and pocketed the fuses from the control panel below the great light. He did the same with the reel of fuse wire. Then, with the hilt of his knife, he smashed the connections for good measure. It would take a skilled electrician several hours to get the lighthouse functioning properly again; more than enough time for their purposes.

Silently retracing his steps down the spiral staircase he stepped out into the bitter cold night. At a trot, to get his circulation moving, he headed for the cliff top and the rendezvous with Bushel. He chose a route off to one side of the snow-trodden path, but within sight of it.

* * *

Bushel saw the willowy figure that was Stilson leave

the lighthouse and moved the ground sheet slowly to get to his feet; suddenly he heard soft footsteps coming from the opposite direction. He sank back down looking quickly in the direction of the lighthouse, too late to warn 'Snake', he could be anywhere. He'd have to deal with this alone. Let the man pass and then...

* * *

Heinrich Altmann trudged on, head down holding his rumbling belly in one hand and the strap of his machine pistol in the other. Suddenly the griping pain cut through him again, ten times worse than before. He staggered to his left and fell to his knees in the snow with a groan... there was another groan; not his. He must be hallucinating with the pain it was if the snow was moving under him. Mein Gott! He was hallucinating the snow had a foot, the foot hit him in the face, more pain. He rolled his twenty Bavarian stone onto the top of the flailing mass that was Bushel and his groundsheet, pinning the corporal firmly to the ground, he began to bellow at the top of his voice.

* * *

The German emplacement sprang into life for the second time that night men running in all directions pulling on greatcoats and boots. Once again they scanned the blackness out to sea.

* * *

Stilson stopped dead in his tracks that noise would alert everyone for miles around, what the hell was it? It sounded like a pig squealing. He started to run, moving with the ease of an athlete. The knife flickered from its sheath as he sighted the fat target. Without pausing he slid pass the yelling figure, a flickering white silhouette against the pristine snow. The knife flashed fleetingly, the Bavarian's second mouth gapped soundlessly as he toppled slowly back. Stilson's pace did not falter carrying him on towards the cliff top.

Twenty short seconds after the first cry of alarm Stilson struck for the third time that night. Two grenades arced through the night over the sandbagged walls of the sentry post. They ignited as one, the explosion seizing the sentry post in a blast of light and flame.

* * *

Lieutenant Grant stood at the back of the bridge; his officers and NCOs positioned around him wherever space allowed.

The E-boat, dead in the water, heaved beneath their feet to the long slow swell from the west.

"This operation is going to be difficult, no two ways about it. There are three stages, the diversion, the mine laying and the attack itself. Our principle task will be the mine laying. It will take place here in this narrow neck of shallow water we're in at the moment. We are between the headland and the island group on our port quarter. My intention is to draw the escort away from the convoy into the mined shallow water. If this proves successful we will then be free to attack an unescorted convoy at will. I intend using the….." Two explosions ripped the night apart.

"Full ahead all engines… port twenty! Action Stations!"

* * *

Bushel threw the enveloping mass of the groundsheet to one side, gagging for breath. The tremendous, pinning, suffocating weight on his chest had gone. He had no idea why and did not waste time wondering. He gasped another lung-full of ice cold air and tried, shakily to stand up. He

84

staggered to his feet wrapped in the groundsheet. A flash of light blinded him, then two explosions close together. He searched frantically for his weapon realising, for the first time his whole body was a sticky mess. Kicking his legs clear of the sleeping bag he discovered the source of the blood that covered him.

The German's body lay spread-eagled, the snow around it black with blood. Then he found his gun and he was up and running.

* * *

"That's put the cat in amongst the pigeons sir." Hogg lowered his glasses. "Do you think the convoy would have seen the explosions?"

"Undoubtedly, they can only be about three miles astern. We'll just have to go ahead as planned and hope the 'Royals' are still able to do their bit. Better get yourself aft and stand by to lay those mines"

* * *

"OK, lads get the lashings off these bastards, look lively or Jerry'll 'ave our arses for target practice. PO Stone stood, legs braced apart, leaning over to absorb the violent turn the boat was making to port.

Wilson and Wyatt had left their guns to help with the heavy mines. They removed the lashings, fumbling in the dark on the steeply inclining deck. Each mine was now held in place only by a stout metal bar, once this was removed the mines would be free to roll down the ramp and into the sea.

Midshipman Hogg appeared by Stone's side, "The skipper wants to know if you are ready. We are coming up into position now." As he spoke the lean to starboard eased and the engines died away to a deep throaty rumble.

"We're ready, sir."

"Right! Stand by," ...I'll give you the word from the bridge when we are in position"

* * *

Bushel was running flat out for the enemy emplacement. It had gone eerily silent following the explosions and he feared the worse.

The sandbagged perimeter appeared out of the dark, there was no challenge, no warning shots. Without pausing he leap-frogged over the bags. They were all dead, nothing moved. Silently, cautiously he advanced towards the emplacement itself

He burst through the door and found himself looking down the barrel of Stilson's Tommy gun. The marine held his gaze for a second before returning to his check of the bodies. He poked the point of the gun behind the bloody ear of a German private and turned him over with one booted foot.

"Did you get the lot?" gasped Bushel.

"Yeah, you were a lot of use."

Bushel scratched the top of his head, embarrassed, "Sorry about that, I couldn't move a bloody muscle under that fat bastard. I assume it was you that copped him?"

The wiry marine nodded once.

Bushel turned away "We'd better get on...that light should be in place by now!"

* * *

Hogg's young and high pitched voice waxed and waned in the stiff breeze, "Right PO slip two mines, keep one in reserve."

Stone lifted an arm in acknowledgement. "Alright lads, you heard the officer... Wyatt, get the weight off the pin before you take it out, you ain't going to move it like that."

"Bloody thing's jammed... tight as a duck's arse, PO."

86

"Get for'ard to the locker and get me a lever, a cable jack anything... whatever you can find." He turned calling after Wyatt's hurrying figure, " and look sharp about it. Jerry's peering up our hawse pipe!"

"What's happening down there? What's the delay?" called Hogg.

"Jammed, sir, I've sent Wyatt for a lever, here he is now... Gis it 'ere",

Stone snatched the wooden pole from the AB and rammed it in between the mine and the metal ramp, throwing his huge weight behind it, "That's it! Now get that fucking pin out.

The pin slid free, Stone pulled the jack clear and the black bulk of the mine rolled sluggishly forward... and stopped.

* * *

The two marines dropped the reins of the improvised sledge allowing its own weight to bring it to a halt.

"Gis a hand to turn it round to point out to sea...that's it, let's hope the bastard works! Some sodding thing's gotta go right tonight...Get ready to make yourself scarce, we make tracks for the laying up position when I throw the switch, I don't fancy sticking around in the light from this bastard and keep your eyes averted otherwise you'll be as blind as a bat." He threw the switch: nothing happened.

They looked at each other.

Bushel exhaled, "Fuck...You any good with electrics?"

Stilson shook his head.

"I'll try the little I know." He placed a well aimed kick at the body of the light.

* * *

Stone yelled into the wind, "Bridge there! Can you

87

turn her into the wind, sir? This rolling's jamming the mine against the sides of the ramp"

Grant bent down and called through the wheelhouse door, "O'Neill, slow ahead all engines, starboard twenty."

Suddenly the rocky outline of the cliffs to starboard lit up, a sequence of two long and one short split the night and then blinked abruptly out.

"There's the light, sir. At least the marines are on time!"

Grant covered his eyes with one hand as a second sequence flashed forth. "Trouble is that's going to light us up like Blackpool Tower on a Saturday night. They'll be able to see us for miles."

"Not only us, sir, look," the eerie silver light from the new lighthouse flashed again, on the port beam the sleek grey bows of an enemy escort, She was about a mile away and closing fast.

Slowly the boat came round into the wind and the roll changed to a pitch

Almost immediately there was a wallowing splash from aft as the first mine was consigned to the deep.

Then the German's signal lamp flashed into life.

"It's the Kraut interrogative, sir. She's challenging us, sir," Shall I give her the recognition signal?

"Unless you have a better idea. Add, 'Enemy destroyer in sight, follow me.' "

"We haven't got the Jerry code for that, sir."

"Send it in plain language... German of course!"

The splash of the second mine came from aft.

Grant cupped his hands and yelled, "Secure from there! Back to your action stations!" He twisted round on his heels, "Hard aport, full ahead all engines."

The powerful diesels coughed black smoke as the E-boat turned back onto her old course and began to pick up speed, spray hissed across the deck as, broadside on; she bit deep into each wave.

Very quickly they drew ahead of the slower German

and she faded into the blackness astern.

"Open fire with all guns Middy!"

"What at sir? There's no target visible?"

"Target's right ahead.... and drop a depth charge for good measure."

"This is the diversion you were about to tell us about..."

"Yes, get on with it Middy... I want to draw the bugger away from the convoy and onto those mines."

* * *

On the German escort's bridge the strange behaviour of the E-boat had thrown her captain in a quandary. What to do, stay with the convoy or follow this capricious Schnellboote Kapitan. The sound of gunfire followed by a loud explosion made up his mind for him. With a sense of relief he rang down for maximum speed. After all an officer could not go far wrong if he headed for the sound of gunfire.

The magnetic mine had just reached its designated depth when the activated sensor picked up the escort's magnetic field. The explosion, triggered as the force field amplified, cut the three thousand ton ship in half, the fragmented bow section settled rapidly. The after section still afloat canted over, debris washed from her shattered compartments as they rapidly filled with water. With her propellers still madly churning the air, her stern reared upright. She bobbed there like a monstrous cork, her metal plates moaning and rattling; steam bellowing from her crippled steam pipes. The propellers slowed and then stopped as the engine and boiler rooms filled with water. One by one her compartments succumbed to the hungry sea, finally, she sank reluctantly beneath the waves.

* * *

The six remaining ships of Convoy AX23 alarmed by the turmoil on their port bow shied away from the explosions like a flock of sheep from a wolf's howl.

No orders were given, but each captain surreptitiously altered course a few degrees to pass closer to the familiar lighthouse and farther away from the horrors unfolding out there in the blackness of the night.

* * *

The sky, astern of the speeding E-boat, lit up with bursts of orange and red light from the escort's exploding ammunition.

Grant had to yell to be heard above the thunder of the detonations and the ragged cheer from his bridge team. "Port thirty!" He pointed ahead, "Middy, we're going round that island to come in astern of the convoy and give Jerry one mighty kick up their arse by way of encouragement."

"Amazingly effective those magnetic mines, sir," shouted Hogg gripping the windscreen as the stern sea lifted the speeding boat.

"Midships...port twenty...steady... I was on the 'Belfast' when she got hers."

"I didn't know you were on her, sir. She survived alright though didn't she?"

"It was in November...she survived, but her back was broken. They drafted us all off anyway...except for some of the gun's crew... It'll be months, if at all, before she gets back in commission."

"Was she your first ship sir?...the 'Belfast'?"

"Yes, joined as a subby...straight out of training...Eighteenth Cruiser Squadron based at Scapa."

They talked on in bursts, yelling above the roar of the engines, as they bounced their way south with the velvet black of the island looming to port.

* * *

"Ship fine on the starboard bow, sir!"

They slowed to a sedate ten knots, only slightly faster than the enemy convoy as it crept along, hugging the coastline like a child with its comfort-blanket.

"That's the arse-end Charlie, Middy, shouted Grant from the for'ard screen. We'll pass her well to port and see what's happening up front."

"There's the lighthouse sir," he pointed at the loom of a light flashing its sequence across the black sky ahead of the convoy... looks real enough doesn't it."

"It seems to have fooled them anyway, no one's altered aw, if anything they're closer inshore than we estimated."

"Seems a bit of a shame really", said Hogg, "sinking all these ships, I mean."

"They're doing murder to our lads in the Atlantic...At least the crews of this little lot will have a chance to get ashore, they won't be treading water hundreds of miles from anywhere."

"I didn't mean that sir, what I meant was it's a pity we couldn't take the lot back, help the war effort."

"And our pockets, I got a nice little sum from the prize we took on my last ship. Mind you that would be nothing compared to what this little lot would be worth... I think that's the lead ship... stop engines."

Their speed fell abruptly and the engine noise dropped to a soft purr, the bow sinking back down as the way came off her. They drifted slowly onward watching the enemy ships through their night glasses.

"Right, Yeo! Make to the convoy, 'Keep closed up, enemy ship to port'."

"Plain language?"

"Affirmative."

* * *

A burst of iridescent white foam spurted from the stern of the nearest merchantman as it blindly obeyed Grant's order. Only two ship's lengths had separated the vessels in the convoy, now it was down to one.

Suddenly the lead ship began to turn sharply to port.

"She's seen the land ahead of her," yelled Grant, "But she's too late, I'll wager!"

She began blaring out a warning on her steam siren, her screws stopped and then started again as her captain desperately tried to stop her headlong rush to destruction. Her manoeuvring and the wailing of her siren seemed to cause more confusion. Ships were turning to port and to starboard in frantic attempts to avoid running into the ship ahead.

The convoy leader had turned to port, the next in line found himself heading straight for her. He put the wheel hard over to starboard trying to go round her stern. Then he too must have seen the headland. The screws stopped turning and then burst into life again as her engines went full astern.

The grating, booming sound of metal plate on unforgiving rock filled the air. The rest of the convoy, now visibly slower, began an emergency turn to port, signal lamps flashed urgently as they realised the dangers ahead. Some were managing the turn faster than their fellows, but this only caused more problems in an already congested channel. Collision followed collision like a skittle alley from hell.

Two ships, helplessly locked together, drifted down onto the two columns slowly and inexorably ripping and tearing their way through their battered ranks.

The last two merchantmen, weaving and twisting from in amongst their fellows, managed, somehow, to get through the nightmare, but found themselves heading straight for the island. The smaller vessel, to seaward, was too late in her turn away; with the tide and wind against her she was driven broadside-on into the shallows, her for'ard mast ripped from the deck by the impact, fell over the port side trailing the entangled entrails of her rigging.

The sole survivor of the ill-fated convoy kept to windward in her turn, heading for the gap between the island and the headland. She made the narrow channel and began to pick up speed. Suddenly there was the scream of metal on metal from her direction and she listed crazily to port.

Grant and Hogg, watching through their binoculars, could see her deck cargo, lashings parted by the impact, dropping into the sea.

"What's happened there," asked Hogg, "I could have sworn she was well clear of the shallows."

"Grant lowered his glasses, "You're right, she's clear of the rocks. I think she's hit the wreck of the escort."

"But she's on the bottom by now, surely."

"It's probably one. Or both halves are only half submerged…it happens; neutral buoyancy. Many a would-be rescuer has met her end on the half submerged wreck of the ship she was meant to rescue."

"You mean the escort hasn't completely sunk."

"Precisely, there could be enough air trapped in her compartments to keep her bobbing about, just below the surface, at least for the time being."

* * *

Bushel

Bushel and Stilson had stopped to listen to the racket emanating from the doomed convoy, "That's our cue to bugger off 'Snake', let's get that light".

* * *

"We are going in to finish them off sir?" asked Hogg unable to take his eyes off the mayhem all around them.

"No, I think not, we've done enough damage for one night and I want to retrieve the marines before first light. Besides if we stay out of it there's a good chance they might think it was all a terrible accident."

Hogg nodded in the dark, "I see what you mean. That will leave us free to play another day."

Chapter 6

Fuel and Ammunition

Olaf's Inlet, 0730 hrs, Tuesday, 23rd April, 1940.

Lieutenant Grant waited while Wyatt and Wilson completed rigging the gangway across to the 'Nishga'. The E-boat had made it back to Olaf's Inlet before first light, but only just.

Across on the iron deck of the destroyer Lieutenant Grey arrived hastily, still straightening his cap to join the gangway staff already manning the side. Grant was entitled as captain of one of His Majesty's ships to full gangway honours. He should have been piped aboard the 'Nishga'. It would have been the first time he had been afforded the honour, but it was not to be, the clandestine nature of the operation and Captain Barr's direct orders forbade such noisy displays of tradition.

He climbed the gangway and saluted the 'Nishga's' quarter deck and grinning, shook Grey's hand warmly. The two men walked quickly for'ard towards Captain Barr's day cabin. As they chatted Grant was aware of just how much bigger the 'Nishga' now seemed after spending the last few days on his tiny command. He stopped and turned aft to watch his boat bobbing gently at her moorings. She was only slightly longer than the destroyer's quarterdeck.

"Bit of a poisoned dwarf alongside the 'Nishga'," remarked Grey, "how did she perform."

"Amazingly well, she managed to bag a few of her former comrades, if that's what you mean." Grant had snapped out the last part, irritated by Grey's derogatory reference to his new charge's lack of stature. For the first time he realised how attached he had become to the E-boat. "Sorry old chap, tired I suppose."

"Think nothing of it, old boy," replied Grey; "it's the relief… I expect it's been a hectic forty-eight hours."

* * *

Grey knocked on Barr's door, swung it wide to grandly announce Grant's arrival.

"Lieutenant Grant of the…the E-boat sir."

"That's one of the things we need to sort out Grant…a name for your new command," said Barr advancing hand out-stretched, a welcoming smile on his face.

"The crew have already done that, sir."

"I can imagine."

It was Grant's turn to smile.

"No, sir, they have nicknamed her 'Eddy'."

Barr appeared shocked to his regular Navy core. "Eddy indeed… That will never do for one of His Majesty's warships."

The 'Eddy's' captain nodded his agreement, "No, sir… but the men seem to find it amusing…'Eddy the E-boat', to give her full title."

"Of course in these stringent times she would normally only rate a number, but, you know me, I have enough difficulty remembering names let alone numbers!"

Grant sensed a new intimacy, the destroyer's Captain

was treating him differently, their relationship had subtly changed. Could Barr be thinking of them as equals, even though their commands were so very different, they were, after all, fellow captains with the same responsibilities, the same problems, if on a somewhat different scale?

"We need something with a bit more dignity than that." Barr was saying.

"Edward sir?"

"Hmm… Edward… HMS Edward, that'll do nicely."

There was a knock at the door and Barr's steward entered carrying a tray of coffee, placing it on Barr's desk he quietly withdrew. The two captains lit cigarettes and sipped their coffees while Grant briefed his superior on the events of the last few days.

"Well, I knew you would do a good job…but I didn't expect this! All I can say is you seem to have been formidably successful with your first command. Well done…"

"Thank you, sir," said Grant, pleased with such a compliment from an officer he so admired.

Barr saw the effect he had had on the young officer and diplomatically changed the subject. "We carried out one raid in your absence much along the lines of the first one. I kept it to the north of here, so as not to interfere with your operation to the south. I think that should be policy from now on, don't you? At the very least it'll keep the buggers guessing."

"I agree sir; otherwise we could end up stepping on each other's toes. You said 'from now on' so am I to assume your intentions are to carry on as we are?"

"I've had no orders to the contrary and, in view of our successes so far, I can't see the Admiral issuing any. Especially as Flag Officer he stands to get a tidy little sum in prize money. The 'Nishga's' last raid produced two ammunition barges, they surrendered as soon as we trained our guns on them… you couldn't blame them for that, I'd do the same thing in their shoes. Their cargo was of no use to us, all the wrong calibre, but I've some useful acquisitions for your command. We have them stowed in the 'Nishga's' magazine you can arrange for them to be transferred after this, along with your fuel."

"Are the barges on their way to the 'Flow', sir?"

"No I couldn't spare the men, especially with you and your men on detached duties; so I've had them taken to that hideaway Olaf found, to the south of here, we'll lay them up for the future. Sort of money in the bank, as it were."

"Sir, my chaps could do with some rest, they haven't had much sleep since we parted company with you on Saturday night."

"Of course, of course that's one of the things I hope to have sorted out by the time we have to refuel at Scapa. I've already requested reinforcements from the Flagship to replace you and your men on the 'Nishga' and to provide you with a full crew for the …for the…"

"The 'Eddy' sir."

"Hmm…Quite, for the 'Eddy', in fact I give you a toast," he raised his coffee cup... to HMS Edward."

"And all who sail in her! Have you had any ideas for future operations, sir?" asked Grant as Barr offered up the coffee pot.

"Now, it's funny you should mention that…"

* * *

Twilight.

The Germans had reinforced the old medieval watchtower at the entrance to Trunsholm Fjord with sandbags and barbed wire as part of General Nikolaus Von Falkenhorst strategic plans to use its sheltered waters as replenishment and supply base for his campaign in central Norway.

The sentries, from the second signal regiment of the 21st Army Corp, were cold, bored and due for relief when their searchlight picked out a Schnellboote rounding the headland.

In close company, and slightly astern of the patrol craft, sailed a motorised barge of the type that had been entering and leaving the Fjord, regularly, since the invasion.

The watch tower guard paid scant attention to the two vessels as it coincided with the appearance of the lorry which contained the relief guard.

The signalmen did exchange call signs as the two vessels sailed slowly under the guns of the watchtower, the sailors on deck waving to their comrades in arms as they passed.

The vessels altered course for the anchorage and their crews turned to preparing the ropes for coming alongside.

Their course took them straight out from the watch tower towards a group of barges already moored in the middle of the fjord well away from the main concentration of shipping around the old town.

* * *

Bushel, Stilson and the Norwegian guide, Kristiansand, watched the lights of the German lorry from the high ground to the south of the tower as the overloaded vehicle carefully picked its way back down the steep road.

In their lying-up position they had spent a bitterly cold day watching the tower and the harbour beyond it. Concealed under a thick canopy of compacted snow, they had an excellent view of the fjord and the target far below. The ammunition barges moored out in the fjord were being used to store huge amounts of explosives.

Twice during the daylight hours they had seen men working on board, swinging up ammunition boxes and loading them into fast launches for dispatch to the front. The workers, wearing civilian clothes and under armed guard were obviously prisoners of some kind.

The launches, once loaded, had made their way back out of the fjord in the direction of the main German army base at Trondheim.

The reconnaissance team had carefully noted the times that the watchtower's small garrison were relieved. They had signalled the 'Eddy' from the cliff top during the night and passed on the information.

Kristiansand lowered his camouflaged binoculars. "Clever of the Bosch to keep their ammunitions here, in this isolated fjord, away from the careful attention your RAF is paying to their main base."

No one replied and the long silence continued. He tried again, "It was lucky my contacts had seen the toing and froing." ...Nothing...He was seriously worried about these two. He knew that the English weren't known for their conversational abilities but these two were something else... and Stilson! He shivered despite his warm skiing overalls and duck-down sleeping bag: Stilson gave him the creeps.

* * *

Grant stopped engines, and allowed the wind and tide to take the boat crabwise in towards the darkened ammunition barges.

Twilight had been short, night falling with its usual swiftness as they crossed the fjord. The moored barges appeared suddenly from the edge of the darkness. Two German seamen armed with machine pistols rose from the bollards they had been sitting on. He beckoned Hogg forward and retreated into the shadows at the back of the bridge.

Hogg waved and shouted something in German, whatever it was, it seemed to work for the two men shouldered their arms and waited, in the icy wind, to take the mooring lines. Hogg again engaged the two seamen in conversation as O'Neill and three of his seamen arrived on the fo'c's'le.

The E-boat bumped gently alongside. Grant stepped for'ard smiling and waved. At this signal O'Neill and his seamen leapt across onto the barge. The outnumbered Germans were wrestled to the ground, gagged, tied and unceremoniously bundled onto the E-boat.

The barge, skippered by Petty Officer Stone appeared out of the night, bumped alongside and was quickly secured.

Grant jumped aboard, "Well done Captain Stone. Start the timer and then get your men back on board the 'Eddy' as quickly as you can."

"Thanks for the promotion, sir; I'll try not to let it go to my head."

Grant laughed, but then abruptly held up one hand commanding silence. "E-boat?"

"They could be coming here to re-ammo," whispered Stone.

Grant nodded in the dark, "Wilson! Wyatt! If they come alongside take their lines... Mr Hogg stay on the jetty, we may need your German... How long have we got left on the timer P.O.?"

Stone looked at his watch, "Twenty- two minutes sir."

"In that case you'd better switch the thing off until we know what Jerry's intentions are. Get the rest of the men back on board and tell them to clean their guns...anything to look casual and no talking!"

* * *

Hogg and the small impromptu berthing party, now wearing Kriegsmarine caps and carrying the recently acquired machine pistols waited as the noise of the German's engines drew nearer.

"I reckon we could get a job on the stage sir, whispered Wilson, "after all the acting we've had to do this trip. I can see it now, 'The Eddy Repertory Company..."

"Quite, Wilson…" hissed Hogg," Her she comes."

The grey nose of an E-boat emerged from the gloom, on her fo'c's'le a German seaman held a bow line curled in one hand.

"They're coming alongside alright… stand by to take their lines."

The English seamen shouldered their machine pistols and moved to their places by the barge's mooring bollards.

The enemy bowman said something to Wilson as he threw the rope over the rail.

"You there!" shouted Hogg, "Keep silent! We have no time for idle chat. Get on with your work."

Oberleutnant Kaleun, commanding the German boat, looked up from the clipboard he was studying," Thank you, Herr Stabsoberfeldwebel, but I am quite capable of giving my men any orders they may require"

Hogg managed to look shocked at the reprimand and the hastily hidden grins from the German seamen. A long and awkward silence followed the telling off. Which suited Hogg to a tee it was exactly what he had hoped for; his quick thinking had stopped the Germans discovering his men couldn't speak the language.

A working party of four Germans jumped across onto the ammunition barge and began clearing away the lashings of on the tarpaulins covering the holds. The wordless assurance with which the Germans worked showed they had done it many times before. With the tarpaulins turned back they formed a chain and began to move ammunition.

On the bridge Kaleun was writing on his clipboard. He looked up from the paperwork with some surprise at yet another outburst from the young second Lieutenant directed at his men.

This time the irritable Stabsoberfeldwebel's own captain laid into him, he couldn't hear what was said, but it was clear from the expression on the youngsters face that his captain was not, to say the least, pleased with his subordinate's conduct. Suddenly the captain grabbed the youngster by the elbow, and frog-marched him in Kaleun's direction.

Kaleun, standing with one gloved hand on his hip and a smirk on his face, enjoyed the spectacle. It must have been a common occurrence, for the crew on the other boat took it all in their stride, hardly looking up from their work.

Kaleun turned as Grant propelled a sheepish looking Hogg up the ladder to Kaleun's bridge. Grant smiled and shrugged apologetically and held out his hand. The German Captain took a pace forward and held out his. Suddenly, he found his arm twisted up his back and the barrel of a pistol thrust into his ear. The man holding the gun spoke in English, English which was immediately translated by the young Stabsoberfeldwebel.

"Stay still, keep quiet... Tell your crew, all of them, to muster on the jetty... now!"

* * *

With the ammunitioning completed by the German seamen, two British seamen moved quickly along the line tying the hands of their prisoners. With the heavy machine guns from both vessels trained on them the Germans offered no resistance.

"We've done it again, sir," said Hogg awkwardly climbing the bridge ladder with a fat folder under one arm. He dropped his burden onto the chart table and opened it out.

Grant peered over his shoulder, "Done what?"

"A month's worth of recognition signals and... look at this," he drew out a buff envelope. "The skipper's orders, signed by an Admiral, no less... can't make out the signature; but they make interesting reading. Tonight, they were going to Trondheim to collect a group of Norwegian politicians and high-ranking officers, along with their Gestapo interrogators. They were meant to take them back to Germany. Looks as if we've spoilt a spot of home leave, for them; no wonder they look so glum."

Grant crossed quickly to the port side and leant over the lowered windscreen. "Petty Officer Stone, you've been promoted again, take charge of the 'Eddy', divide the prisoners in half and share them amongst the two boats lash 'em down on the fo'c's'le ...it's going to be a rough ride!"

"Shall I reset the timer?" asked Stone.

Grant hesitated; he had noticed something earlier, "No... Wait one... Have you noticed the tide and the wind are in the same direction?"

"Westerly, yes sir, from us to the old harbour."

"And the big fat German merchantmen alongside," added Grant. "How far away would you say they are?"

The big P.O. turned to face east, "About a mile, sir, I would say, perhaps a little less."

"See what arrangements the Germans have on the trot's anchors fore and aft... see if you'll be able to split the cables."

He turned back to Hogg, "Sorry but I have to give command of the 'Eddy' to Stone instead of to you, but you can see my dilemma."

Hogg held palms out in front, "Erh...That's perfectly alright, sir. It's your decision... if I may say so; you do underestimate your own German. Why do you need me, I thought we were on our way back."

"Because we're not, at least not straight away, I'm going to need that German of yours again."

Hogg tapped the folder with one knuckle, "Anything to do with this, sir?"

Petty Office Stone appeared beside them, interrupting the conversation.

"They use the same sort of gear as us on their anchors, sir, nothing we can't handle. I can take the weight off the cable with their bottle screw and then take out a joining link and slip the lot, if that's what you want."

"That's exactly what I want, Petty Officer. You slip one anchor and get O'Neill to do the other. You can take half our men with you to crew the 'Eddy'... I'll set the timer, I don't see why Jerry should be sleeping while we're working, do you?"

"You're going to give them a rude awakening, sir."

"That's the general idea."

"Do we wait for you to give us the all clear before we break the cable?"

"Yes...they need to be slipped more or less together."

"Aye, Aye, sir."

* * *

The two E-boats eased astern, backing away from the ammunition barges. The tide and wind caught the eight barges and, still tied together, they drifted rapidly away towards the dark shoreline.

Like well rehearsed dancers the two boats turned smoothly together and, with Grant's boat in the lead, Shot, at full speed, towards the fjord's entrance.

The sentry at the old watchtower recognised the snarl of the boat's Daimler diesels, rather than the boats themselves and let them pass without bothering to switch on his searchlight.

* * *

Wilson swung the heavy machine gun round on its mounting to let Wyatt by.

"Did you see the face on Bushel when the skipper told him he had to look after those prisoners until we got back."

"Royals! Never could understand 'em, if that had been me, I'd be well chuffed to be left behind. The skipper's going to need more flannel than a Pusser's blanket to get away with this... Is that the town ahead?" he nodded towards the black outline of buildings silhouetted against snow.

"That's it," Wyatt pointed, "and that, over there to the right, is the jetty where we are going to pick up the passengers."

"Ain't worth you going below, we'll be there in no time."

As if on cue the engines died away and the boat's raked bow sank slowly down to reveal more of the coastline.

* * *

"I think that must be the building at this end of the jetty, I can see two guards," Grant lowered his binoculars. "You'll be on your own once you're ashore Middy. If it seems matters aren't going well, make some excuse to get outside, go for a pee, tell them you've forgotten some papers, anything. Then get back here, we'll be ready to give you covering fire should you need it. If you pull it off and those guards come with you, use the same tactics you used on the ammunition barges to stop them talking to our men, inspirational stuff that, by the way."

Hogg smiled as Grant continued, "Try to make the guards see we have no need of them and that we'll be responsible for the prisoners once they step foot onboard. Plead lack of space, that might work. Last thing we need is a bunch of Jerries swarming all over the bloody…"

Suddenly, on the port beam, a blinding flash of orange light lit up the sky. Moments later, the thunder of a huge explosion reverberated around the fjord echoing back from the tree-covered mountains. Before the noise of the explosion had completely died away, a volley of smaller explosions sent rockets of light and flame soaring skyward. The whole northern sky lit up like day. The inferno grew in its intensity, from the midst of the blazing light a huge mushroom of smoke rose into the sky reflecting the flashes from the explosions beneath it.

On the jetty, German soldiers were spilling from the

huts to stand open mouthed staring at the huge firework display that was erupting just beyond the mountain's black silhouette. Indeed the whole town had been awakened; people were running from their houses to line the shoreline.

Almost unnoticed, the E-boat bumped alongside, before any lines could be passed, Hogg, clutching his wad of German papers had jumped the gap between the deck and the jetty. Not looking to right or left he marched swiftly towards the hut, stopped, showed his papers, spoke briefly to the guards and went inside. The door had hardly closed when it swung open again. Hogg emerged followed by two men in black leather jackets. He pointed towards the explosions and the three men stood watching for a few moments before, turning, they went back inside.

As Grant waited the explosions slowly died away and the darkness returned. A welcome darkness that crept across the fjord until only the water on the far shore reflected the glow of the flames. Convoys of vehicles and escorting motor cycles began to leave the town, passing along the shore road in a seemingly endless stream. Grant began to worry that he had created too much of a diversion; he willed the door of the hut to open again.

It was a long five minutes before it did; a helmeted guard was first out, followed by a file of six men chained together by their ankles. Even in the poor light Grant could see the caked blood on faces. The two men in the leather jackets and one other uniformed guard followed, close on their heels, to Grant's intense relief, came Hogg.

The prisoners and their escort had just reached the bottom of the gangway when, worryingly, Hogg and the two Gestapo men became embroiled in a heated discussion. Grant, although too far away to understand a word, could detect frustration and anger in their voices. Hogg seemed to be losing the argument; finally he shrugged dramatically and turned away as he did so he glanced up at the bridge, there was a worried expression on his face. A second later Grant realised why. The prisoners were pushed towards the gangway and the Gestapo men followed.

Grant walked casually across to the unmanned machine gun and flicked off the safety.

Below, Hogg motioned to Wilson and Wyatt and they began dragging the gangway inboard. It was then that Wyatt tripped on one of the ropes. He must have said something for suddenly the two Gestapo men swung round, shouted, reaching inside their jackets.

Then everything seemed to go into slow motion. The guards on the jetty hauled their machine pistols from their shoulders, the Gestapo men pulled revolvers from their coats. Wyatt kicked out and one of the Germans dropped to the deck. Wilson delivered a blow to this head with the butt of his gun. Feet away Hogg wrestled with the other man.

On the bridge Grant swung the gun round and, aiming at the guards still on the jetty, fired one long, sweeping burst. The men took the short-range fire full in the chest jerking rapidly backwards like discarded puppets. Immediately he hauled the heavy gun round to cover the jetty yelling for the ropes to be slipped. There was a long burst of fire from aft and Grant saw a leather-clad figure hit the port guard rails his body almost cut in half by Wilson's Schmeisser.

Ashore the door to the interrogation hut slammed back against its hinges, a group of men burst forth. Grant opened fire, lifting the men from their feet, twitching and jerking they were thrown back against the side of the hut.

"Wheelhouse! Full astern starboard, full ahead port! Wheel hard a starboard." With a roar the powerful engines screamed into life swinging the bow out from the jetty.

"Stop starboard. All engines full ahead, steer west!" The length of the jetty had suddenly filled with the bobbing, weaving figures of more soldiers. Grant opened a withering fire. Flashes of tracer arced back and forth between the wooden structures like angry fireflies. The opposition took cover and returned the fire. Splinters and sparks flew from the stern rail.

* * *

Slowly he regained conscience; the back of his head was splitting from the blow from the butt of Wilson's gun. The Gestapo man opened one eye. He could see the bottom half of the man who had posed as a German Officer. He grabbed at a foot and jerked it viciously to one side; with a crash Hogg hit the deck. The German scrambled to his feet kicking out at Hogg's kidneys, the youngster jerked into a pain-filled ball. The boat suddenly leapt ahead turning rapidly. The deck sloped, the German, caught off balance staggered backwards, arms flailing the air, trying desperately to regain his balance. He fell through the gap where the gangway had been, turning a half somersault into the froth, he had time for one scream before he was sucked down into the three whirling thrashing screws. The white foam turned momentarily pink as the E-boat trailing lines of tracer, roared away into the night.

* * *

The shore batteries spaced along the fjord had been on a high state of alert since the massive explosion and were waiting to join the fight. Their barrels trained quickly round onto the renegade E-boat. As she came into range orange-tongued flames flickered from a score of the deadly eighty-eights.

All around, the fleeing boat, water spouted high into the night sky. The E-boat bucked and jumped as she ploughed through, her bridge inundated with water.

Suddenly another E-boat appeared from out of the dark, roaring in towards Grant's boat, her heavy machine guns firing wildly her Reichskriegsflagge snapping from her mast. Flak rounds from her after gun screamed across the rapidly closing gap, passing within feet of the renegade's bridge.

One by one the crews of the shore based eighty-eights were forced to cease fire only able to watch impotently as the newcomer crossed between them and their target.

Grant's boat had, somehow escaped damage, but it could only be a matter of time. The two boats danced and pounced at each other, their giant bow waves and powerful engines churning the water into a maelstrom. The frustrated shore gunners could not believe their eyes, neither boat had scored a hit on the other and the renegade E-boat was now almost clear of the harbour mouth with the other boat in close pursuit. The flashes from the heavy machine guns disappeared behind the headland as the two charged out through the entrance to the fjord all their guns blazing.

* * *

The two E-boats lay hove to, side by side, gently bobbing their bows to the waves.

Grant lifted a megaphone to his lips. "By God. You had me worried there for a second or two, Petty Officer Stone…but well done …quick thinking."

"That's a pint you owe me, sir!"

"I'll buy you a bloody crate as soon as we get back, and that's a promise. For now, get your chaps looking for anything we can use as 'wreckage'; we'll be doing the same. Clothes, lifebelts anything you can spare. Throw the lot overboard. We've a dead German to get rid of as well. I'll drop a depth charge as we leave, with a bit of luck, the explosion may fool the Germans into thinking there's been a collision and both boats have sunk here. The PO waved an acknowledgement as the 'Eddy' dropped astern of her prize.

Within ten minutes, and amid the dying echoes of the depth charge explosion, the two boats were once more in line astern and picking up speed. Astern a balding leather-clad figure bobbed violently in the wash from the two boats, its eyes staring at the clouds rushing across the moon.

* * *

Wilson and Wyatt lifted the edge of the 'Nishga's' camouflage netting high above their heads. The E-boat inched slowly ahead and the two men 'walked' the net aft, over the heads of the prisoners on the small fo'c's'le, climbing on winches and wash-deck lockers to clear the bridge and gun positions. Reaching the stern they threw it into the water clear of the slowly turning screws. As the prize tied up to the grey bulk of the 'Nishga' the 'Eddy'' in its turn, crept under the netting and into the dappled shadow of the hideaway.

Quite an audience lined the decks of the destroyer. A great cheer erupted at the appearance of the second E-boat; she emerged from behind the thick curtain like a Prima Dona taking a well-earned curtain call. A grinning Petty Officer Stone gave a Royal wave and bowed deeply from the waist to more cheers.

* * *

"Welcome back!" said Barr as he clasped his fellow captain's hand. "I thought I was seeing double there for a moment. If you carry on like this you'll soon have your own Navy and won't need to work for His Majesty's."

Grant gave a tired smile, "It's good to be back, sir, A bit like coming home. He looked around the, now, familiar cabin.

Barr's ever attentive steward had anticipated their requirements and the coffee pot and cups were already arranged on the tidy desk.

"It's funny you should mention home," began Barr. Grant stiffened as he recognised his senior officer's standard preamble to important news, "It appears we all have a spot of unexpected leave coming up."

"Really!…Bit sudden isn't it, sir, why now?"

"We've been having a spot of engine trouble on and off for the last week or so, the Chief seems to think it's because the boilers weren't cleaned on schedule. As you know that's a dockyard job, so while we are having it done we should be able to fit in five days leave to each watch. We need fuel anyway and you've managed to give us half the Kriegsmarine as prisoners so we'll be calling in at the 'Flow' en route. Now you're back, we can leave tonight. From there we'll go on to Liverpool where, apparently, there's a vacant dock."

"Well, that's splendid news, sir. I know the men will be over the moon. What about the remaining ammo barge, are we taking that."

"No, that stays where it is for the time being. It's a sparsely populated area and I plan to leave the Norwegian what's his name…?"

Grant smiled, "Olaf, sir."

"Yes, yes Olaf. He'll stay and continue to gather information, his home and village are near enough for him to keep an eye on both berths and he can warn off the locals if necessary."

Grant handed Barr a wad of papers, "Here's my report, and the German boat's papers."

While Barr read his way carefully through the report and the translations, Grant poured a second cup of coffee while his mind drifted around the prospects of shore leave. He hadn't been home for some time, he tried to remember exactly when, but his tired mind could not get a grip on the dates. It seemed like a lifetime. God knows they had been lucky so far, there had been no one killed, but all of that could change, would change probably. All in all a rest would be a fine thing recharge all their batteries. The men had certainly earned it.

"This reads like a Boy's Own adventure story." Barr said at last, as he threw the thick wad on to his desk, "You certainly deserve a rest after this lot. Truly, Robert, there's some stirring stuff in there. I see you have mentioned Hogg and Stone. This will almost certainly mean an oak leaf cluster for both men. Grant's eyes went to Barr's medal ribbons and the cluster he had won when he had been 'mentioned in dispatches' last year.

"I had thought of that, if it was up to me I'd recommend far more."

"Well, Stone, as a Commanding Officer of one of His Majesty's ships, however temporary, could certainly be in line for more. We will have to see... I think it no bad thing that we're going back, we've stirred up such a hornet's nest it won't hurt to give things a week or two to calm down."

Grant rubbed his forehead with one hand, "As I mentioned in the report, sir. We tried to make it appear as if both boats had come to grief outside the fjord. But, we have no way of knowing whether they took the bait." He drained his cup, "Before we sail tonight, sir, I'd very much like to have a closer look at those caves."

"You mean the ones under the cliff overhang?"

"Yes, sir, I was thinking that we might be able to put them to some use."

"It won't hurt to take a look, Robert. We might be able to store extra fuel and ammo for your boat or boats I should say."

Grant noted the use of his Christian name again with some pleasure, "I'd like to explore the possibility of using them to berth the 'Eddy' and if we keep her, the 'Ethel'."

"The 'Ethel'! I can imagine what the Admiral will think of that name. I suppose it's that crew of yours again, is it?"

"Yes, sir, but I took into account his strong objections to 'Eddy', sir and took the liberty of dignifying 'Ethel' into 'Ethelred' sir."

"As in 'The Unready' you mean, "Barr, rubbed his chin, the hint of a smile playing at the corner of his mouth. "Well, I suppose that could be acceptable for the time being, but I live in dread of what the Admiral will have to say on the subject."

Chapter 7

Caves and Wooden Pillows

Olaf's Inlet, 0845 hrs, Thursday, 25th April, 1940.

Guided by Wilson, with the aid of a powerful torch, the 'Nishga's' sea boat inched slowly into the biggest of the caves. The shaft of light showed a cavern much bigger than the entrance suggested.

"By the mark ten fathoms," called Wyatt, his voice echoing off the rock had a strange metallic edge to it.

Ahead his torch picked out a rock ledge stretching away into the unfathomable gloom.

Grant turned to O'Neill, "Bring her a point to starboard, coxswain".

They edged slowly up to the blue-grey rock forming the shelf.

"Rocks ahead!" yelled Wilson, grabbing his boat hook.

"Hold water!" barked O'Neill.

The four oarsmen thrust their blades into the water.

"Back-water!... Lively there!"

The oarsmen struggled against the forward motion of the heavy boat. Wyatt's boat hook slipped on the submerged rocks and the stern swung sharply round to present the boat's port side to the rocks.

"Fend her off!" yelled O'Neill.

There was a horrible grating noise and the boat staggered to a halt.

"She's sprung a leak," called someone.

O'Neill clambered for'ard atop the thwarts reaching down between the oarsmen he felt the planking; it was wet to the touch.

"Shine that lamp over here, Tug." by its light he could see the water trickling down onto the bottom boards.

"It's not too bad, sir," he called, "stressed a plank or two is all, nothing Chippy can't fix…We not going to sink…"

"No survivor's leave then, Hooky?" asked Wilson, straight faced.

O'Neill grinned in the dark, but chose to ignore the remark, "'Blur', keep your eye on the bottom boards, if the water comes over the top get to work with the bailer." He scrambled back to Grant in the stern, "It's nothing to write home about, sir."

Grant stood up in the boat and squinted into the dark water out to port.

"I want to take a closer look at these rocks… Wilson! Pass that light down here."

The beam of the lamp flashed about the walls of the cavern as it was passed from man to man.

"This looks promising; it could be what we're looking for. It's deep enough and then there's this."

O'Neill looked over his shoulder at the rock ledge a foot or so under the surface. "And what might we be doing with that, sir? Apart from springing a few more planks on it, that is?"

"We could build it up to the same level as the ledge behind it that would widen the shelf enough to give us the headroom we'll need to bring the 'Eddy' in here."

"Arh! I'm with you now, sir; it's a landing jetty you'll be making. Well, there's enough rocks over there to build ourselves two of the buggers."

"Where?" asked Grant.

"If you pass me the light, sir; I'll show yer."

O'Neill shone the light to the far end of the cave. "Now where the fuck are they?... begging your pardon, sir... Arh! There they are!" The torch had picked out what appeared to be a rock fall. "I saw them as we came in. We could ferry some of it over here easy enough."

"Some of them look a bit heavy for that."

"The big ones we could sling over the side, keep them underwater. They're not so heavy that way. We could rig a jackstay from that wall to this one and pull the boat backwards and forwards on that, save time not having to manoeuvring her."

"Pull over there, coxswain, we'll take a closer look."

The pile of fallen rocks towered above them for twelve feet or more. "Plenty there," said Grant, "We'll return after 'stand easy' and make a start."

"Aye, Aye, sir, it'll be near high tide then, it'll give us a better idea of the headroom we'll be having. But it looks to me as if we'll have to unstep the 'Eddy's' mast to get her right in as far as the shelf."

* * *

Ordinary Seaman Goddard stepped over the hatch coaming and clattered down the metal ladder holding on with one hand and carrying the steel teapot deftly in the other. The rest of the mess had already arrived and were seated around the table.

As he set the huge teapot down the talk was of leave. It had been the only topic of conversation since the Skipper's broadcast at nine that morning. The men manning the sea boat hadn't heard the news until they arrived back on

117

board.

" ...I'm looking forward to a decent night's sleep," Wyatt was saying.

"You had an all-night-in the night we left the tanker, bloody second part of starboard dipping in again! The one night we weren't closed up at steaming stations in weeks and it was you lot that got the whole night in yer pits. That was two on the trot; remember that time in 'Cripple Creek'."

"It's in recognition of the hard work we put in compared to the rest of you loafing bastards!" said Wilson, straight faced.

"Yeah, bloody right!" said Wyatt, above the groans from the rest of the mess, "I'm taking about night after night of uninterrupted kip." He lay back luxuriously, "I'm talking 'ere of every bloody night for five bloody lovely nights... Anyway all-night-in on board with you lot don't count, who can get a full night's sleep 'ere, when the watches are changing at midnight and again at four. I swear blind, every bastard who gets up bumps into my bloody 'ammock."

Stubbs blew cigarette smoke down his nose, "That's because your 'ammock's slung right by the bloody ladder."

"Yeah, well that ain't my fault is it?"

"'Cause it bloody well is! I can remember when we first come aboard; you said I'm slinging my 'ammock nearest the hatch so I can be first out if this bugger goes down."

"It's being so cheerful that keeps Earpy going, ain't it Earpy." said Wilson.

"Ere, talking of sinking," said Wyatt, watching Goddard pour out the last of the 'wet' of tea to make sure he got his fair share. "How about our 'rum bosun' very nearly sinking the sea boat."

"Sure! It was only a tap," said O'Neill, There wasn't even enough water to fill this cup."

"Arh! Ignore 'im," said Wilson dismissively. "He's

only trying to wind you up."

O'Neill stood up to reach for his cap and banged his head on the overhead fire main It was as well the news of the impending leave had put the Irishman in a good mood. "Be God!...I'll be putting in for an aircraft carrier, once Jerry has sunk this bastard!"

"Funny, ain't it?" mused Goddard. Heads I mean; you think we would have had a bit more protection for our heads really wouldn't yer. You know, what's his name? That bloke who reckons we were all apes a long time ago." He looked around the table for an answer, but could see by the expressions on his messmates faces that he wasn't about to get one. So he continued in his ignorance. "Anyway he thought that we are what we are now was down to nature getting rid of the weak. You know the slowest runners in a tribe would have got eaten by a dinosaur, sort of thing. So you'd think, bearing in mind how many people get killed being hit on the head, that those of us what got this far would have more than a thin bit of skin and bone to protect our heads, after all it's where our brains are."

"Or, in your case, where they should be" said Wilson. "I see what you mean though. It's a wonder we ain't got a big flap of fat on top of our heads for protection."

"Suit you that would, tug. You'd have a beer head to go with your beer belly."

* * *

It was close on tot time when they found the tunnel. They had been steadily moving the rocks across the cavern and had just returned for another load.

Wilson and Wyatt levering at one large rock, sent it toppling forward onto its face. A bright shaft of sunlight suddenly beamed through into the cavern.

Wilson got down on his knees to investigate, "'ere there's a sort of tunnel under 'ere."

Slowly they cleared the rocks around the opening, moving them across to enlarge the shelf. Impatient as they all were to explore the tunnel Grant, conscious that they would have to leave very soon, insisted they complete their main job first. The work was hard and it was a tiring, but it was still an enthusiastic boat's crew that eventually began the climb up the tunnel. The sides were smooth and dry.

Part of the way up, they were surprised to find a sizeable cavern, it ran off to the south, they pushed on without exploring it fully. After ten minutes hard climbing they saw a pale blue circle above and with renewed energy pushed rapidly on towards it. The strange colour of the light was explained when they found the exit blocked by a considerable quantity of compacted snow. Working in relays with the boat hook they broke through and found themselves on the plateau above the destroyer much to the surprise of the marine sentries stationed close by.

Grant saw that with a few alterations, a rope handrail and maybe some steps cut into the rock in places, the tunnel would make the job of guarding the inlet much easier. Now there would be no need to scale the cliff face to reach the top.

* * *

The dawn spilled pink across a grey sea, to port the west coast of Scotland stretched low and dark along an indistinct horizon.

The 'Nishga' dipped into the curling waves, submerging her wet nose with the enthusiasm of a terrier burying its snout in a rabbit burrow. Each time she emerged she lifted tons of green water up with her, spewing it back into the sea from her overflowing scuppers.

The men were stood to at dawn action stations, those exposed to the elements, hunched deep into their duffel coats, deep into the womb-warmth of their own bodies.

Below the ship was battened down, hatches screwed

tight, the metal deadlights clamped over thick glass scuttles produced a dismal half-light that made everything look tired and dirty. The pitching of the sea and the sealed airlessness made for miserable conditions in which to pass a long day.

If the sea conditions made life squalid below decks on the destroyer, on the two E-boats astern of her, it made life intolerable. The two tiny warships climbed the steep sided waves, clinging to them like camels ascending sand dunes. Dwarfed by the vast seas, they took onboard impossible amounts of water, tilted to impossible angles, smashed with impossible force into towering walls of water.

The hulls of the patrol boats were shaped for speed, shaped to ride on top of the water, to skim across the surface like water boatmen. They were essentially coastal craft and made bad foul-weather boats. In any sort of sea they bucked and bounced, launching themselves from the wave tops like unbroken stallions. Consequently the E-boats, capable of forty knots, could not operate above ten. With the real chance of an attack by friendly forces, as well as those of the enemy, it was vital that the 'Nishga' stayed with them; so she too hobbled her way south at the same snail's pace. It was seven hundred and fifty miles to their destination it would take more than two days.

On the 'Eddy', Grant had been continuously on the bridge since leaving the Norwegian coast; his whole body ached from the unrelenting strain put upon aching muscles by the merciless pitching and the rolling.

In view of the clandestine nature of their operations Barr had timed their

arrival to coincide with darkness. His future plans depended on the existence of the captured German ships remaining a secret. The men had been warned about loose talk and how their very lives depended on anonymity.

The two E-boats parted company with the 'Nishga' at a secret base on the east coast of the Isle of Man where their crews were transferred to the 'Nishga' for the short trip across to the mainland.

*   *   *

The dry dock rang with sound of hammering, echoing and clanging off the high walls, jarring the nerves of the men still aboard. A bored bosun's mate stood by the quartermaster's desk flicking lethargically through the pages of a tattered magazine he had found on his rounds.

Wyatt, who was acting quartermaster for the leave period, looked over his shoulder "Where you get that from Blur?"

"Wardroom… I didn't know officers went in for this sort of thing," he pointed at a scantily clad female form.

Wyatt leant on the desk, "It's a great leveller, we're all the same when it comes to that sort of thing," he waved at the page, "But you were right to lift it, I don't agree with them looking at things like that, it might give them ideas… We don't want them reproducing, there's enough of the bastards as it is."

"You don't like pig's much do you, Earpy?"

Wyatt rubbed his tired eyes, "Arh! Don't talk to me about pigs, lazy lot of bastards. You've seen 'em. When we're in 'arbour they 'ave even less to do than when we're at bloody sea. Worse than the bloody dockyard maties," he pointed at some dockyard workers who had been standing at the end of the gangway for over an hour, "and they get more time off then the Unknown Warrior."

*   *   *

"What's so interesting about that particular merchantman, sir? asked Midshipman Hogg. "Troopship isn't she?"

They were both working on the bridge, Hogg updating the Admiralty charts and Grant attempting to get to grips with the intricacies of the Watch and Quarters Bill. The latter had lit a cigarette and was leaning on the bridge screen, studying the troopship with great interest.

"She's the 'Empire Trooper."

"Doesn't the Empire bit of her name mean she's an ex-German?"

"That's right," said Grant, peering intently through his binoculars. "As far as I know all, well, nearly all, captured enemy ships carry an 'Empire' prefix. She was the 'Cap Norte' before. When I was serving aboard the 'Belfast' we captured her as she was returning to Germany from South America."

"When was that exactly?"

"Oh... October last year. She was trying to get back to Germany disguised as a neutral."

"Did you get prize money," asked Hogg, his eyes lighting up.

"They say we will, someday," smiled Grant, "and, if we do, it will be enough for the first payment on a yacht of my own after the war."

"Is that how you intend to pay the bills when it's all over, go back to yacht minding?"

"Haven't really decided yet, but something like that. Preferable something that doesn't involve blowing things up anyway."

* * *

Barr had, unusually, taken the first five-day leave period, normally he would have let his Number One have that privilege, while he stayed on to see that the start of the refit was trouble free, but he had complete trust in Grant's abilities and was happy to leave the ship in his hands. This coupled with the fact that he had several vital appointments to keep in London allowed him, with a reasonably clear conscience, to board the Suffolk bound train...

As the soot-stained trees slipped hypnotically by his window, he dozed. The clickerty-clack of the wheels became a Bren gun firing and the rhythmic sway of the train carriage became the 'Nishga' in the Norwegian Sea. The hiss of steam and the squeal of the train's brakes translated into a diving aircraft that woke him as the train jerked to a stop at Ipswich. He'd slept through the entire journey. It had grown dark. He straightened his cap and tie in the cracked carriage window before pulling his holdall down from the string luggage rack.

The ticket collector had a shaded hurricane lamp propped in the corner, its orange glow illuminating his plump Pickwickian face as he clipped the ticket.

Barr stood in the station concourse feeling like a truant from school. Nothing to do for four whole days. He smiled as he walked to the taxi rank. Nothing to do… it wouldn't last; his wife would make sure of that.

* * *

The mess radio was playing a Carol Gibbins' number.

"Deep voice for a bird," commented Stubbs.

Wilson laughed, "I always used to think Carol was a girl's name."

"Course it is… ain't it?" asked Wyatt.

"Well 'is name's Carol and he's a bloke," said Wilson, jerking a thumb over his shoulder at the speaker on the bulkhead.

"You can be called Carol if you're a bloke?" said Wyatt, his voice rising in disbelief.

"Not in my fucking book you can't." growled O'Neill from his slung hammock.

"What about Gene Kelly?"

"He's a dancer, enough said?"

The nightingale sang no more in Berkley Square as the clattering of the metal ladder drowned out the music. It was Goddard.

"How'd you get on," asked Wilson, as he arrived at the bottom of the mess ladder.

"They failed me again."

"What!" exclaimed Wyatt, "after all that revising you did while we were watch keeping on the gangway!"

Wilson grimaced to hide a smile. "I told yer, you should have been revising from yer seamanship manual and not those girlie magazines. You carry on like this, you'll never make Able Seaman, you'll go blind from all that revising."

Goddard said nothing, a picture of gloom.

"Well, what was it you got wrong?" asked O'Neill, "When I tested you the other day, you was all about."

"Yeah," ribbed Wyatt, "All about like shit in a hurricane fan."

"Yeah well! I don't think it was fair really."

"What'd 'e do ask you a question on seamanship?" said Wilson.

Goddard ignored his mentor, "Jimmy the One asked me if you was at anchor, how many times you would pipe the side for a visiting Admiral."

"Twice," answered O'Neill. "And you knew that the other day when I asked you," he added, accusingly.

"Yeah… Well I said, 'Four'. He said, 'Wrong! The answer is two… What made you think it were four?' "

"I said, 'I thought it was a trick question, sir. It's four times if you count when he leaves as well. You pipe once as he approaches the ship, again when he comes up over the side and the same again when he leaves, that's four."

"He's right enough there," agreed O'Neill.

"Yeah, well Jimmy the One didn't think so. He says 'Quick Goddard, but not quick enough.' He thought I was being clever, he failed me!"

* * *

Barr sat in his favourite armchair smoking and watching his son playing.

"This is your ship, Dad," said the boy pointing to the

largest, it's my best one, the one you bought for me for last Christmas, remember."

"I remember, that's a battleship though, son, the 'Nishga's' a destroyer."

"I know that, Dad, but my only destroyer's in refit."

Barr smiled at his son, only eight years old and already he wanted to go to sea. But then, he'd been that age, perhaps a little older, when he'd first shown an interest. His son was attacking his tiny fleet with an aeroplane in each hand imitating the bombers they watched at the cinema the night before. He pushed the ships round on the lino-covered floor with one foot.

"See this, Dad; they're all turning out of the way."

"They'd have to turn the same way though otherwise they be colliding with each other and they'd have to turn together and to port so as to bring all their guns..." his voice tailed off. He knelt down beside his son and started to rearrange the toy ships on the floor, "Can I borrow one of your aircraft a minute, son."

The boy handed it over and watched for a few minutes while his father, squinting from the smoke spiralling from his cigarette, moved toys enthusiastically around the living room floor. The boy soon lost interest and wandered off, flying his other aeroplane, peering into the tiny cockpit. He heard his father call to his mother for a note pad and a pencil.

* * *

On Saturday, port watch returned from leave and the starboard watch clattered down the gangway to begin theirs.

Grant left the ship just after eleven, delayed by a meeting with Barr concerning the progress of the refit.

After a long train journey south punctuated by long and frequent mid-station stops, Grant found himself with forty minutes to spare before catching his connection for the coast.

He wandered over to a tired looking cafeteria and, putting his half empty hold-all under a window table, bought a cup of steaming tea from the chain smoking be-turbaned woman behind the counter. He sat drinking and smoking, watching people hurrying pass the grimy window.

He had a good view of Platform Number One, from which his train was due to leave. He watched as a train arrived, small clouds billowing across the platform, shouts of steam spouting noisily from beneath the engine. Doors banged and soon people began to move in and out of the steam, appearing and disappearing like ghosts in a cemetery mist. An initial trickle of passengers soon turned into a continuous stream, flooding through the gates past the portly ticket collector.

Leaning on the oilcloth covered table, chin in hand, he stared numbly through the window seeing the bustle, but not really registering it in his thought-filled mind. He had been kept busy over the last few days despite the fact that boiler cleaning had more to do with the Chief than him. He had worked on the complicated watch bills for all three vessels. The extra men had arrived on the Monday after they had docked; most of them were raw recruits. 'Hostilities Only' as the Navy called them, straight from the training ships.

Abruptly he was yanked back to the present where a figure had appeared at his side. He leant back in the bentwood chair and looked up. A woman in her twenties looked back down at him,

"Is this chair taken," she asked. Completely unnoticed by Grant the place had filled with people from the train, all desperate for a cup of tea after the long journey north."

The woman was very pretty, her brown hair curling down from a jaunty black hat worn at a fetching angle. Her smiling face moved abruptly to one side to be replaced by another that Grant recognised instantly.

He jumped to his feet "Benjamin, old chap! What a lovely surprise! How are things on the," he whispered, "'Belfast' and who's this!"

"The girl laughed, "This… is Ben's sister Charlotte."

"Sorry, I didn't mean to sound rude, it was such a complete surprise."

"Don't mind her, Robert; she's used to bad-manners with me for a brother."

"That's the truth," added Charlotte, "Look you sit here, Ben, then you two can swap salty sea-lies while I get the teas."

Sub Lieutenant Benjamin Crosswall-Brown slumped down into the chair opposite his friend, with the air of a man used to taking orders from the opposite sex.

"So how are you, old man, still on destroyers?"

"Sort of, I've been on detached duty for a while; on five days leave at the moment."

"So am I! Only I've only got four days, Charlotte just met me off the train, she intends to shepherd me quickly onto the next, south bound. I think she fancies herself as my chaperone; protecting me from the flesh pots of London."

"She'll have her work cut out if she does. I remember you on the 'Belfast'," he dropped his voice, leaning forward over the table. "Are you still…?"

"No, old chap." whispered Crosswall-Brown inches from Grant's ear, "Not from today, drafted to Harwich… M.T.B.s."

"You have always been a lucky sod, just the job… How was everyone on the 'Belfast'?"

"Most of them have been drafted off;" he dropped his voice even lower, "The rumour is it's going to take two years to get her sea-worthy."

"As long as that! That's one hell of a refit; I didn't think things were that bad."

Crosswall-Brown lifted an eyebrow, "It doesn't look that bad, I agree but, we were right at the time, you remember we thought she might have broken her back."

Grant pulled a face, "Hence your draft, I suppose."

"That's right old man…It's an ill wind…The buzz is they're going to keep some of the gunnery department on board. No need for the old eight- inch or the bods who manned them, so here I am. Can't say I sorry I was getting a bit…"

Charlotte arrived with three piping hot cups of railway tea.

"Here, let me pay for those," said Grant.

"Wouldn't hear of it, old boy!" said Crosswall-Brown, "this one's on the old girl. She's no one else to spend it on."

"Not so much of the old. Just remember you're still my little brother. Keep your place. Little boys should be seen and not heard."

"Yes miss!" grinned Crosswall-Brown, "See how she bullies me, Robert, she only follows me around so that she can cramp my style."

"What style?" laughed his sister.

"You two musical-hall turns catching the train for Pompey?" asked Grant.

"Yes, are you going on to Yarmouth?" asked Crosswall-Brown.

"Only to visit, I'm be spending my leave near Pompey."

"Where abouts?"

"Southsea…a boarding house I've used before."

"Did you say boarding or bawdy?" teased Charlotte.

"Leave him alone, you pest…We wouldn't hear of it, old chap, you must stay with us… right old girl? Stacks of room, you know, in the old pile."

"Well, that's awfully good of you, but…"

"I hate to admit to my brother having a good idea… but he's right, he's not much company, as you must know, so I for one would enjoy having a house guest with some conversational skills."

* * *

Nuneaton Station

Goddard's right eye was streaming he'd been looking out of the train window waiting for his first sighting of Nuneaton Station when he got the piece of grit in his eye. He'd tried blowing his nose, tried pulling his eyelid down over the, by now, bloodshot eye, nothing seemed to budge it. He peered through the good eye into the speckled mirror of the empty carriage. He sighed. He looked a right state one red eye, tears running down his cheek and his face all screwed up. Just his luck, here he was the returning hero, and he looked like a sprog with the screaming hab-dabs.

The train slowed, he hastily grabbed his case and the bunch of flowers. For a second he thought of stuffing the flowers into the case. It had seemed a good idea to buy the flowers when he was having a few pints with the lads, but now he'd sobered up a bit...

He jumped down from the slowing train and slammed the carriage door behind him. There was no one at the station to meet him; the fact that he hadn't really expected anyone did little to ease the disappointment. He had thought that perhaps they would surprise him, a banner or two, even a small cheering crowd. The station was empty, apart from the old ticket collector who stared at his sore eye as he stood blinking, waiting for the man to punch his ticket.

* * *

Central London

O'Neill punched the copper on the nose while he was still fumbling for his whistle, the policeman fell back and his tin helmet rolled noisily across the cobbles.

O'Neill, grinned, his head nodding, as if in total agreement with his fist, he swayed drunkenly and took another swig at the bottle of black market rum. Hiccupping grandly, chin on his chest, he attempted to focus on the prostrate form before him, failed and said to the blurred image, "Get some sea-time in you bloody Englishman."

Seemly satisfied at this incoherent rendering he slid loose-limbed down the wall.

* * *

Lower Road, Rotherhithe.

The rain stopped as the bus neared the corner of Maynard Road. Able Seaman Wyatt jumped off, tipped toeing to avoid the puddles on the cracked and pitted pavement.

The bus continued, splashing its way up the main road, towards the underground station, spraying the pavement with muddy waves as it progressed.

He hoisted his bag onto one shoulder and sprinted across the road and round the corner by the doctor's; a dog-eared notice in the window proclaimed it was 'Closed until we've beaten Hitler'.

Their flat was at the far end of the road, only a few houses between it and the dockyard wall. A group of kids playing 'stick and fuggel', yelling as they splashed through the wet after the fuggel', socks down around dirty ankles.

He recognised, Terry Rawlings, from the flat next door, one bare knee grazed and bleeding. The youngster gave the piece of firewood a good whack with the stick and it flew into the air high above the heads of the fielders.

Wyatt paused for a moment watching the game he had played himself so many times when he had been their age.

Nothing much had changed, beneath his feet the pavement was marked with the kids chalk drawings and the dockyard wall had a lopsided goal chalked on it in the same place where there had been one for as many years as he could remember.

He walked pass the screams and the laughter and in through the gate to the flats. Out the back, in the courtyard, a long line of washing flapped tiredly, stark and crisp-white against the mossy walls.

He ran up the draughty stairwell, impatient now to get indoors, up he climbed, through the faint smell of urine to the top veranda and along to the end flat. It was bag-wash day and bulging pillowcases, full of dirty washing, lay piled up outside each of the front doors. He remembered how, on bag-wash days, he and Terry's brother, Roy, had used the bags, just like them, as cover while they had shot at each other with their Winchester repeaters.

Roy was dead now, killed over Norway early in the war, he'd been on Wellington bombers. He remembered how proud he'd been when he told him of the posting. Tail gunner….they'd both become gunners…all that practice on bag-wash days.

The bottle-green door opened before he could use the knocker. His mum grabbed him in one of her bear-hugs crushing the breath from his body rendering him incapable of speech.

His sister, Susan, black pigtailed, hung to his leg in a pale intimation of his mum's death-hug.

"Welcome home son." she said, as she dragged him in through the front door. He kissed her on one fire-flushed cheek and patted his sister's head as she clung to his leg. She held on while he hobbled stiff legged along the dark passage to the kitchen.

A fire burned orange-red in the black cast iron range, a clothes stand of 'airing' stood beside it, his dad's rack of stained clay pipes on the mantle-piece. He felt for a moment as if he hadn't been away, as though the past few months had never been.

"Where's the old bastard? Working?"

" Spect so…he never came back this morning so I

suppose he's gone and got a day's work in one or other of the docks... Hope so, it's been 'ard going lately, not much work about...and yer know what 'e's like when 'e ain't got nothing to do. Thank Gawd for the fire-watching... keeps him busy."

"And out from under your feet?" he added.

His mum laughed, the years dropped away from her tired face, she was, in that short moment, a young girl again.

"How'd you know that?... never mind I don't wanna know, cheeky sod...The kettle's on the boil, I'll make us a nice cuppa and you can put your feet up, I expect you're worn out after that journey." She moved to the fire. "Where you've bin son, anywhere nice?"

* * *

Silvertown

"It needs to be done proper, or not at all, you supposed to do it on one knee."

"Which one?" asked Able Seaman Wilson.

"It don't matter which..." began Maude, then she saw the twinkle in his eye. She pulled a face, "No! Don't play the silly bugger you'll spoil it."

"What me knee?"

"Look if you ain't gonna behave your..."

"All right; all right." Wilson took up the classic pose, hand on heart.

She pulled his hand away, "Don't overdo it!"

"Blimey, make yer mind up."

"What am I going to do with yer?"

"Do yer want a list? I'm game for anything," he started to giggle... Maude joined in.

"Look, you sure you wanna do this, or not?"

"'Course I do." he said.

"I mean, what's the difference, you know? We've been together all these years. It ain't mattered before."

"Well...you know the blokes were talking onboard..."

"Surely that don't bother yer!"

"Nar!... Not about us, let me finish. They were saying as 'ow they... some of 'em anyway, thought there could be problems with wills and that if you ain't married proper... You know if something was to 'appen to somebody."

Maude's eyes glistened, "You can 'alf be a morbid bugger when yer want," she sniffed.

"No! No!... It's only right... So, anyway, I got permission off the skipper, and asked about a license and that."

"You were sure of yourself, weren't yer!"

"'Course I was."

"Well...at least you can ask me proper."

"Maude, will you be my wife."

"No."

"What yer mean?"

"Oh, all right then," she said, laughing at his face, "you've talked me into it, but I want you in a proper suit when we get married."

"I thought I could get married in the rig."

"You know what thought done."

"No."

Neither did Maude, but she wasn't going to let on. "Like I was saying, if we're going to do it, I want it done proper. I want us to be able to forget about the war, just for a while...and we can't do that with you're in uniform."

"I ain't got no suit, you know that."

"You got that money your uncle left yer. Every man should have a suit anyway."

"Well... I suppose I could use Uncle Tom's money... Seems a bit of a waste though."

She laughed, "It could double as a laying-out suit, when the time comes."

"Yeah, you could get someone to row it out to me, afore they sew me up in me 'ammock."
"Don't!"
"You started it!"
"Yeah… well, now I'm ending it."
They fell silent.

* * *

Central London

The wooden pillow wasn't meant to be comfortable; in fact O'Neill thought the whole cell left much to be desired in that particular area, but, looking on the bright side, at least he had more room to himself than he had on the mess deck. He put his hands behind his head as a cushion and wondered what the 'beak' would give him.

He only had three days leave left and he hadn't even reached home yet, odds were he wouldn't make it back again this trip. The little woman would go daft. He shouldn't have told her he was coming home. Could have surprised her, come to think of it, it would have been a surprise for him as well, if he had managed to get home for once. He reached for a cigarette…either he'd smoked his last one or them thieving coppers had nicked 'em.

* * *

Silvertown

" 'Course I wanna special price! Didn't we go to school together for crying out loud." said Wilson.
"Business is business, me boy, I gotta make a living, and this is quality gear, feel the width."
"It's thickness, Goldy; thickness."
"Yeah?" said the tailor, looking up. "Feel the thickness? Yeah? Don't sound right somehow, still

whatever, my son… it's still ten bob."

"Ten bloody bob!"

"It's a good price."

"Yeah, for you maybe, not for me it ain't."

"All right, all right, for you the special price, after all, as you say, we went to Silvertown Road together, no… Nine and six."

"All right," said Wilson resignedly, "Nine and six it is."

"Done!" said Goldy, spitting on one hand.

"You don't 'ave to tell me, I know I was," said Wilson.

Chapter 8

Cider and Charlotte

Hampshire

They waved as the London train moved off. Benjamin Crosswall-Brown's grinning face ducked back inside the window of the last carriage just in time as it disappeared into the tunnel. Charlotte gasped, "He's always doing that, I wish he wouldn't."

Grant looked down at her, surprised at the sudden show of concern for her brother; it was in stark contrast to her usual laughing apathy. He saw tears on her cheek and it suddenly dawned on him that it was all a front to cover up the real love she felt for her brother. He felt a twinge of jealousy. Which he forgot the instant she put her arm around his waist and leant her head on his shoulder.

* * *

Able Seaman Wilson and his wife sat in the snug of the 'Pig and Whistle", in the centre of Silvertown. They were having a quiet drink and watching some of the regulars playing darts. He still wore the new suit and she still had the flower in her hair.

"So is it one or two days we've got left, Luv?"

"Two ain't it. It'll be like our 'oneymoon, what made yer ask. Fed up with me already, counting the days are you?"

"No!" she said, digging him in the ribs with her elbow. "You are terrible, 'onest, you twist every little thing round."

"That's what the actress said to the vicar."

"See what I mean?" She laughed out loud, startling a pensioner at his darts causing him to miss the board altogether.

"'Ear do yer bloody well mind… this is the finals, a bit of quiet, if you please!" He turned back to the board, "No respect youngsters nowadays," he mumbled to the rest of the team as he lined himself up for the throw.

"Well, sorry, I'm sure," said Mrs Wilson stifling another chuckle and digging her husband in the ribs again.

" 'Ear pack it in. You'll 'ave me black and blue in a minute and you know they're colours what don't go with me 'air."

"Blimey, what you talking about, you ain't got no 'air."

"Yeah, well," said Wilson, stroking a hand over his pudding-basin haircut, "That's the bloody coxs'n again ain't it? Took me station card off me and told me I wouldn't be getting any leave until I'd me 'air cut. I'd to run around like a blue-arsed fly to find the bloody ship's barber before he disappeared on his leave. Cost me 'alf me tot and all."

" 'Ear, he did that to you last leave and all, you remember, missed your train that time. I reckon he's got it in for you." She rapped her knuckles on the table, "You oughta complain."

"Fat lot of good that'll do; 'e'll 'ave me getting it cut

twice next time!"

"Why don't yer come out of it, after the war's over, Luv…ain't you 'ad enough of it, you been in it since you were a boy."

"After the war! I 'opes I'm out afore then, the way the wars going, if I'm into the finish… I'll be as old as that silly old bastard," he nodded his shaven head in the direction of the darts team.

"Do yer reckon we'll win in the end though, Luv?" asked Mrs Wilson, suddenly serious.

Wilson took a long pull at his ale before replying, "Only if they put me in charge, Luv."

* * *

Hampshire

Grant crouched down by the rear wheel of the sit-up-up-and-beg bicycle.

"Bad?" asked Charlotte.

He rubbed his nose, leaving a smudge of road grim, "How old did you say these bikes were?"

"Oh, I don't know, donkey's years I suppose, I remember them in the garage when we still had a nanny, she used to use one, this one I think, to go into the village."

"Well, they are old…but the tyres aren't that bad, they're not perished or anything. Strange getting a puncture out of the blue this is a pretty decent road." He looked up at her, "That's interesting what you were saying about your nanny. Surely when you were that sort of age the wheel hadn't been invented, had they?"

She cuffed his ear. "There's nothing else for it," she said resolutely, "we'll just have to push them home."

"What do you mean 'we'!… Mine's perfectly alright." It earned him another cuff.

The country lane stretched endlessly, and unnoticed, as they walked, glorying in each other's company; sometimes chatting and joking, sometimes in companionable silence.

He had forgotten the old thatched inn at the crossroads. They had passed it on the way out. By the time they reached its rose covered door they were both tired and ready for a drink; but it was still closed.

An old man sat on a chestnut bench beside the door, puffing on the end of a broken clay pipe, a scruffy dog lay at his side. "Ain't open yet," he said, revealing teeth like marinated dog-ends.

"Half hour, I reckon," he said, looking up at a watery sun and answering the unasked question. "Do a nice bit of cheese," he added, as an afterthought.

"I was just going to ask you if they had food," said Grant.

"I know," replied the old man, banging his pipe out on an upturned boot.

"How did you know what I was going to say?"

"We, all like to think we're different, don't we ay? But there's nothing new under the sun," he said, pointing at it with his pipe as if he thought Grant too young to know where it was.

Charlotte petted the dog.

"Good dog that," the old man said, knocking out his pipe, "catch a rabbit in his seat."

* * *

Nuneaton

Goddard found himself wandering in the direction of the cattle market; the harsh aromas on the west wind reminded him it was market day. He waited at the corner while an army convoy passed by, heading south, nose to tail at least as far as the distant bend in the road. He sighed; quite a few people were waiting, on both sides of the road. They were already looking impatient. It was a long convoy.

"They can't stop for you, you know, they're not

allowed," said a voice at his side.

He looked down; a pretty girl of about his own age looked back up at him.

"They're not allowed to get separated." she added.

"It's like that in the Army," he said, "they're not allowed out on their own."

She laughed, looking up at the young sailor, "You're Peter Goddard ain't you?"

"That's right...I don't know you, do I?"

"You don't remember?...Jennifer Mott... I was in Miss Irving's class when you was in Mr Hardy's."

"Blimey! You've got a good memory; I can only just about remember what happened yesterday."

"Oh, all the girl's at school remember you!"

"Really!" he said, surprised and visibly pleased, he never knew he had a reputation with the girls.

"Yes... you always had a dirty neck".

* * *

Silvertown

Able Seaman Wilson bit into his bread and dripping, "Nice bit of dripping Luv, where you get it from?"

She stopped pummelling at the dolly tub, "From mum...she had a bit of brisket... saved up her coupons... here you save me some of that...I ain't had any yet."

"I've saved you the nice brown stuff at the bottom of the bowl."

"You better not have ...you're pulling my leg...you know I 'ate that bit."

"You 'haven't 'ate' it... it's still here," he called in his officer's voice.

She appeared at the back door, arms full of wet washing. "If you don't stop taking the mick I'll give you such a cuff."

She went out again and shortly he heard the big

141

wooden rollers of the mangle begin to turn, the metal cogs grinding like giant's teeth.

"Oh blast the sodding thing!" she suddenly yelled.

"What's up?"

"It's jammed again."

He popped his head around the door jam and peering into the whitewashed back yard. "Let's 'ave a gander."

"Look it's this adjuster thing-a-me-jig on the top." Wilson looked at the ancient contraption with a seaman's distaste for all things mechanical. "Blimey you need an engineer's ticket to work this lot, do you understand it?"

"A bit," she said.

Wilson was genuinely impressed, "Blige me, I reckon I could get you a job as a Chief Stoker, no trouble."

* * *

Rotherhithe

Wyatt's sister, Susan, walked into the corner shop in the Lower Road, before the bell had stopped ringing the familiar smell of spices and dried fruit had assailed her nostrils. She hated that smell, burying her stubby nose in the sleeve of her mackintosh.

'Old Drew', behind the counter, handed over the usual loaf of freshly baked bread and she got out as fast as she could. The bread was nice and warm. Using her front teeth she nibbled the tiniest hole in the crusty underside.

She hated shopping for her mum. There was that time with the eels when her mum was busy…she scooped another bit from the doughy inside of the loaf…It was the first time she realised her mum bought eels from the fish shop while they were still alive. She could feel them now, sliding wetly around inside the damp newspaper… horrible! She shuddered; on the way back one of them had gotten free, squirming and slithering around in the gutter, it was like a wet snake! She had somehow plucked up the courage to put it back in the paper with her bare hands. Ugh! She squirmed now at the thought of it and wiped her hands on her Mac. Just one more mouthful, mum wouldn't notice through that finger- size hole in the crust.

* * *

Rotherhithe

"'Ear my girl! What's a matter with this bread?" said Mrs Wyatt, holding up the loaf.

"It was like that when I bought it mum…honest," lied Susan.

"You telling me old Drew sold you it like this?" her mum held up the evidence one finger pointing at the hole in its bottom.

"Yes, mum… honest."

Her mum squinted disbelievingly over the top of her thick glasses and was that an evil smile playing with the corner of her lips?

"Well you just take this back to Mr Bloody Drew and tell him, from me, he's got mice and didn't oughta be selling his customers bread what's in this state.

"Oh!…Do I have to mum?…Couldn't you take it?… You'd be much better at it than me."

Her mum thrust the loaf at her and pushed her towards the front door. "Get on with it, my girl!"

The door closed reluctantly slowly behind the dejected girl. "That'll teach the little cow to lie," she whispered to her son.

"That bread ain't as good as I remember it, mum, how's that?"

"Different baker; we had to change to old Drew when they took Mr Fricke away."

"What yer mean, took him away?…What the coppers?"

" Yeah… he was interned, like the rest of 'em…taken

away to some camp in Surrey, so they say. Shame, really, he was such a nice man."

"Made nice bread and all, what they intern him for? He's been here for as long as I can remember."

"Still an Austrian though, ain't he?...he's been 'ere since the Great War. He was a prisoner up at the 'Big House', when it were a prisoner of war camp. He never went home after the War, stayed on and married Ethel May. She's dead now, you wouldn't remember her. She used to play the piano at the 'flea pit', before you was born'... 'Ere, there's an idea, why don't you go to the 'flicks' tonight, do you good to get out for a while, might meet a nice girl!"

"Thought it was closed… It was the last time I was home."

"They've opened it again, but it closes early on account of the blackout."

"I don't know…" said Wyatt, screwing his face up, "I was thinking of listening to the wireless for a bit and having an early night."

"Early night at your age, indeed! I've never heard such a thing!"

"Mum, early nights is all I've been dreaming of for yonks."

* * *

Magistrate's Court, Central London

"You are a disgrace to the uniform you wear." the magistrate was saying his voice falsetto with indignation. "If it wasn't for the fact that your comrades would have to do your duties, as well as their own, in your absence, I would give you a much longer custodial sentence. As it is you will jolly well spend the remainder of your leave in police cells. I therefore sentence you Patrick Benjamin O'Neill to …to."

"Three days," whispered the clerk of the court.

"Three days," piped the magistrate, "and I hope you'll use the time to contemplate the errors of your ways…after all there is a war on you know!"

* * *

Hampshire

They sat in comfortable armchairs in front of the inn's roaring log fire, feet outstretched, drinks in hand. Alongside the dancing flames their shoes lay in an untidy, steaming heap.

The room was empty apart from the old man and his dog. He sat by the sash window that served as a bar, through it, the owner could be seen moving backwards and forwards busy preparing their lunch.

If Grant could have frozen that moment in time he would have, He took a long and leisurely sip at the pint of cider. He was pleasantly tired, the kind of tiredness that only came with physical exertion and alcohol. He hadn't felt like this in a very long while. He observed, with almost scientific interest, the glow as the alcohol spread around his body, numbing the ache in his legs and neck. What was it he'd overheard O'Neill say once? 'Booze was God's way of showing he still loves us'…something like that anyway.

"What did you say?" asked Charlotte, she too sounded tired.

He realised he had spoken out aloud. "Oh, nothing I was only thinking of something someone had said."

"What was it?"

"It was nothing much."

"Well, I want to know everything anyone has ever said to you."

"That'll take a lifetime."

"I know," she said.

* * *

Nuneaton

Mrs Goddard removed her carpet slippers, the ones she seemed to live in, and shuffled one foot into a scuffed garden clog. Crossing to the back door she picked up the garden fork.

"Bit late for gardening, mum, ain't it? It's getting dark." said Goddard.

"Feeding the chickens, son,"

"What's with the fork? What're feeding 'em, sides of beef?"

"No, you're daft as a brush you are, the fork's to keep that bloody cockerel away from me."

"What's fancies yer, does 'e?"

"Don't you be crude, you know I don't like it. Sailor or not, you're not too young for me to wash your mouth out with soap, like I used to… you remember?"

"I remember mum," said Goddard, almost tasting the soap as he spoke.

His mum was half way out of the door, a determined look on her face. "He's a blighter that bird. I can't wait for Christmas to come so he gets the chop."

"That ain't like you mum," he called, rising from his chair.

"Well… that's as maybe… all I know is that he's a right bugger. Every time I go in the hut he gets behind me… and then he jumps. Yer Dad's right, he's always say's the brighter the colour the fiercer the bird and they don't come any brighter or fiercer than that there Rhode Island Red, I'm here to tell yer. He ain't managed to knock me down yet, but it ain't for the want of trying."

Wyatt wandered out after her, cup of tea in hand. Leaning on the door jam, he watched her make her way down the long garden with her a brimming pail of peelings and meal. The sun was setting behind the Chestnut tree, as she past the row of vegetables. She spoke to his dad, who was bent double, weeding rows of tiny greens. He looked up and said something, his mum laughed. The wire compound, where they kept the chickens, included the big tree. Goddard could see the birds flapping down from it as they saw her nearing the gate.

The neighbours donated their left-overs and , once a year at Christmas, they each got a chicken in return. His mum had been telling him how well it was all going. It had put a stop to the neighbours moaning about the noise the cockerels made. It all sounded a bit illegal to Goddard, bit of a black market really, what with rationing and that.

Her back was towards him, but he could she was having trouble with the bent hook on the gate. She put down her pail and swung the rickety wire gate back wide, lifting it over his Dad's pile of weeds. It was just then that the Rhode Island Red struck. Flying at her in a flurry of feathers and talons. She screamed and made to close the gate, but it stuck fast on the pile of weeds. She dropped the pail and the fork and ran screaming back down the path amid a fluff of feathers and foul oaths.

Seeming inspired by all her swearing she was a good two feet in front of the cockerel by the time she reached the cement post, the one that held up the washing line. The cockerel chose that moment to launch his attack; he flew at her head down and neck outstretched.

But…he was on unfamiliar territory, and hadn't seen the post. Goddard's mum dodged aside and the bird hit the post head on. He fell pole-axed and unmoving.

Goddard's mum didn't stop, she was still swearing when she reached her back door.

Her eldest was leaning on the doorframe, holding a long bar of Sunlight soap in one hand and her best scrubbing brush in the other.

"Open wide mum," he said smiling.

* * *

Hampshire

The remains of their lunch lay before them; a pleasing debris of cheese rind and tomato pips, the amber liquid in their refilled glasses catching the light from the fire.

The innkeeper appeared at his side smelling faintly of pickled onions,

"I hope you enjoyed your meal, me dears," he said before he began to clear the table.

"It was excellent, thank you very much."

"Thank you, sir," said the man, as he turned to leave, "Oh! I almost forgot. Your room's ready, sir."

"Room? ...What room?" he asked, bemused.

"Your wife said..." began the innkeeper.

"Oh! You've spoilt my surprise!"

"Oh! I am terrible sorry, Mrs...I didn't mean..."

"That's all right, what's done is done," said Charlotte magnanimously, waving a trivializing hand. The innkeeper backing away, withdrew, a trifle red in the face.

She glanced at Grant across the fire's glow, its light reflected on the room key hanging in one hand. "It took careful planning you know," she said. In her other hand she held up a penknife and shrugged at the stunned silence coming from Grant. "True, I underestimated, miscalculated the distance back to this inn, but..."

* * *

Silvertown

Wilson tucked the blanket back in behind the curtain wire and got down off the chair. "That's better, won't do to break the blackout a second night, old Bill Gatsby'll blow his top proper."

"Arh! You don't want to worry about him...don't know what he frets about, we ain't seen 'ide nor 'air of a

German round here since the war broke out. His wife pointed at a bucket by the grate. "Stick some more coal on, while yer up, Luv there's a dear."

"What's you last servant die off?" asked Wilson, bending to the coal scuttle.

His wife smiled, but didn't look up from her mending, "You want these socks darned or not?...How long you been walking round like this?"

"Since birth or a little after." he said, resuming his seat by the range.

"I'm talking about these," she held up his navy blue socks. "There's more spud than sock."

"Give over... no one bothers with that sort of thing now...'sides I always wear two pairs at sea; as long as the holes is in different places it don't show."

She shook her head slowly, "Men!"

Wilson leant forward and switched on the wireless, it sparked into life like an angry cricket. The static suddenly cleared giving way to a brass band playing a march, the station drifted in and out.

"Nice bit of music; bit faint though ain't it?"

"It's the accumulator, needs changing."

"I'll pop over to the newsagents tomorrow. Ted Ray's on tomorrow night, don't want to miss him, do we?"

She smiled, "I've been putting it off, they're so heavy." Her tussled head bent once more to her work. Nice to have a man about the place again, she thought, even if it's only for a little while.

* * *

Nuneaton

"No, it's no good, it's gotta go, son," Goddard's dad was looking up the garden. "The bloody thing's a menace, it nearly had your mum that time... she's livid, spoilt her best pinny."

"How about Christmas, you'll be one short… when it comes to the share out, I mean."

"Bugger the share out, I ain't having no more of it, he's for the chop, could've had yer mum's eye out." Mr Goddard senior turned and headed down towards the netted enclosure. He disappeared through the gate and seconds later all hell broke loose for a second time. He emerged from the compound with the cockerel suspended upside down from one fist. Ignoring the bird's screeching and attempts at pecking, its triumphant captor carried it straight to the back wall and the two nails over the drain.

The condemned bird was trussed feet first to the rusty iron nails. His Dad's hand disappeared into his pocket and pulled out the knife that was always there. Goddard remembered from a boy.

But the cockerel wasn't finished yet, as if sensing his impending doom he burst into life. It was all his Dad could do to hold the thrashing bird still with both hands, "Give's a hand 'ere son."

Goddard bent down and retrieved the dropped knife. There was a flash of silver in the dying sunlight, a spurt of red, and mum's torment was over.

His dad looked him in the eyes, "You couldn't have done that a few months ago, son," he said.

He stared back at his Dad as they crouched together, the cockerel's blood running river-red between them. There was no need for a reply, Dad had been in the Great War, he knew what war did.

* * *

Central London.

His wife was getting into full swing, O'Neill snatched a glance over her shoulder… the copper behind her was loving it, the sadistic bastard.

"It's taken me all this time to find you," she was

yelling, "and if it wasn't for the placard outside the newsagent…And the disgrace of it!"

That word again…

"I've never been so embarrassed, I've been after asking everyone if they've seen you and then I find out like that. Not just headlines in the newspaper, oh no! I had to have the newspaper man yelling it out for all to hear, 'Local Irishman jailed for assault on policeman!'… I knew it was you, I just knew. Be Jaysus! Last leave I never saw you… you were on another of yer drunken binges and now this."

O'Neill sighed.

"And don't you sigh at me! I'll put your bloody eye in a sling, so help me I will!"

The copper had company now; it seemed as if the whole station had turned out to watch his chastisement.

* * *

Nuneaton

When he came into the room Goddard's mum was sitting down in her favourite chair. She was painstakingly wrapping the wool, salvaged from one of his Dad's old pullovers, around a cardboard milk bottle top.

"What's that you making , mum,"

"Handbag dear, you string 'em all together, like this," she pointed to a pile on the chair next to her.

"Oh nice… Look mum, I'm all packed… I'll be off in a bit."

"I'll make you a last cuppa shall I?"

He looked down at her, something in her voice, her eyes were full to the brim.

His eyes were stinging now, "You stay there, I'll make the tea."

* * *

Silvertown

"Ear it comes, Luv," said Maude, as the Number Ten rounded the corner. He kissed her quick and picked up his bag. The bus slowed, stopped and started to empty.

"One last kiss," she offered him her lips. He kissed her again, she held him very tight.

He took her shoulders and held her away at arm's length. Jumping up onto the platform he turned. "Bye, Luv!" he yelled above the revving of the bus's engine. " 'Ere afore I go, what's it like to be an 'onest woman?" A few heads turned in their direction.

Maud ignored them, "It's daft, after all we've been together all these years, but I do feel different."

"What'd yer mean different?"

"Oh, I don't know how to say it, I ain't got the words…I feel like I belong to someone."

"Who?" he called as the bus pulled away.

Chapter 9

Birth of the Killer Whale

Admiralty, 0930 hrs, Monday, 6th May, 1940.

  Vice Admiral Sir Walter Mackenzie, KCB, DSO, Head of Special Operations, put the folder he was reading down and came around from behind his desk. "Arh! Barr just been rereading that report of yours, inspiring stuff."
  Barr shook hands, "Thank you sir." he stood to attention while the old Admiral resumed his seat with a grateful sigh. The yellow Labrador in the corner of the room rose to his feet and wandered over to the desk. The old sailor pulled absent minded at the dog's ear, "Have a seat…The Minister was particularly pleased with your work. He's ex-army of course…horses and all that… had the gall to say that all this charging in knocking them for six and charging out again was in the best traditions of the bloody Army! Anyway it looks as if you may have given him a few ideas, for a start there's this," he threw a piece of foolscap paper across to Barr's side of the desk and raised one bushy eyebrow. The expression of inquiry slowly

153

changed to a smile as he watched Barr's face.

"Well, I don't know what to say…"

"Thank you could be in order… Commander, but I'd think, in your recently promoted shoes I'd wait to hear the rest before I ventured any thanks. That's what I should have done when they took me off half pay and gave me this bloody job. I realised, too late, that they only gave me the post because no one else wanted to sail this dammed desk…Mind you, there are some that say I got it on merit, cloak and danger stuff coming naturally to a scheming old bastard like me!"

Barr smiled, "I am grateful for my promotion, thank you, sir."

"Arh well, there's always a price to pay for promotion, my boy, especially when it's out of turn like yours, and in your case it's a practically heavy one…here it is." He lifted a thick folder and passed it to Barr.

The newly promoted Commander only had time to glance at the cover, before the Admiral continued. Stamped on it, in large red letters, were the words 'Top Secret'. Under that, in black, was the title 'Special Operations Group'.

"In a nut shell, what that 'desk-banger' says is that, as of now, you are the leader of an independent group, code name 'Orca'. It will comprise the 'Nishga', the two E-boats that you captured, in addition you will have two of our own motor torpedo boats. You will, under my command, carry out special operations against the enemy held coast of Norway." He paused to pull furiously at his pipe, from the midst of a cloud of acrid smoke, that would have done a First World War coal-burner proud, he continued. "Now, as you know the land war is not going… at all well, is probably the most diplomatic way of putting it. Between you and me it won't be long before the army has its back to the sea. Doubtless it will be the Andrew that has to get them out of the soup they've managed to get themselves in. Now, you are probably thinking, what's new, we've done that so many times it's a wonder the British Army hasn't evolved webbed feet. And you'd be bloody right. What is new, however, is the First Sea Lord, Churchill. It's refreshing to have ministerial backing, for a change.

You will form part of an operation that is set to grow in the weeks and, who knows, even the months to come. If we evacuate, or rather when we do, France will not be able to stand alone for long. It's only a matter of time before Hitler's little lot will own the whole bloody coast from Norway, south, to the Iberian Peninsula. That's three thousand bloody miles. Jerry will be able to launch attacks on our shipping from any of a dozen ports. He will be able to launch attacks by U Boat, E-boat and surface raider. He will have full use of these port's facilities to repair and replenish.

Remember the Hun very nearly crippled us with just a few U Boats in the last do and from nowhere near the number of ports he'll have available to him this time round."

"That's a pretty grim picture you paint, sir. But, we've been there before with the Kaiser and with Napoleon and neither of them made it across the Channel. I believe Hitler will have his work cut out, remember what you were saying works both ways. Three thousand miles is a hell of a lot of coastline to defend it gives us a wide selection of targets."

"You are nothing if not confident, I'll say that for you, personally I've no doubt we will prevail in the end. What I'm trying to get across to you is the magnitude of the task. It will not do to underestimate the enemy, the next few months will be crucial. If we can show him the Navy's not beaten ... even if our 'Pongoes' have had their arses well and truly kicked. There is still a good chance the Hun will think twice before launching an invasion of this country and unless he invades he cannot win and he cannot invade without first beating the Navy and nobody has ever managed that.

If we can hit Jerry where it hurts, prevent or seriously

disrupt his building an invasion force, sink his ships in their harbours, give him a bloody nose. Really, what you've been doing in Norway over the past few weeks, only on a much larger scale. Assemble a whole network of Olaf's gathering information about Jerry's plans, hit him not only with your group, but with others too…everything available. If we can make him realise that crossing the channel will be too risky… that the Royal Navy is still a force to be reckoned with, he'll back off… and then he loses."

"He who hesitates is lost, is that it sir."

"Barr… you know…That'll do nicely for 'Orca's' motto."

Chapter 10

Preparation

The two M.T.B.s turned gracefully, entering the peaceful harbour in line ahead. It was a beautiful May evening, a star-buttressed sky reflected in the mirror-calm of the bay.

The base had been chosen well, tucked away from the main shipping lanes that crossed and criss-crossed this part of the Irish Sea. The small bay lay between the Isle of Man's eastern ports of Douglas and Ramsey to the north.

Lieutenant Benjamin Crosswall-Brown's M.T.B. led the way in towards the heavily camouflaged 'Nishga'. His men lifted the netting with their boat hooks and feed it aft hand over hand as the three huge Isotta-Fraschini engines purred at slow ahead. A hooded torch moved about the destroyer's sea boat's davits pointing the way to where they were to berth.

While his men tied up the second M.T.B. Crosswall-Brown studied with interest the two E-boats moored to the destroyer's quarterdeck.

He had met them several times before both on the east coast and in the Channel, but it had always been at night, fleeting glimpses by the flickering light of battle.

He knew the German's called them Schnellbootes, S Bootes for short, he had no idea why the British called them E-boats.

Unlike the Royal Navy's M.T.B.s and M.G.B.s they were fitted with diesel engines, they were a lot longer and at least half again wider in the beam. They were fast, capable of forty knots, as was his own M.T.B. The difference lay in their respective armament. He looked with special interest at the twenty-one inch torpedo tubes and the twenty millimetre cannons. He paid particular attention to the Flak 28 on their sterns. It was this gun that had been the telling factor in many an encounter in the Channel, easily outgunning the British M.T.B.s machine guns.

The RAF were having the same trouble pitting the Spitfire's Browning machine guns against the Messerschmitts cannons, with their exploding shells. He shook his head, it was like fighting with your bare hands when your opponent was wielding a bloody great sledge hammer.

A shout from the 'Nishga's' deck broke into his thoughts.

"Fine evening Lieutenant Commander Crosswall-Brown."

He peered up into the dark.

"Well I'll be buggered. Robert, by all that's Holy…what are you doing here?"

Grant smiled, I might ask you the same thing, I work here. This is the detached duty I told you about."

"You mean we're working together… how absolutely, bloody, splendid!"

"Watch your head, sir!" called a seaman from the destroyer's deck. The man kicked at a short rope ladder, unrolling it down the destroyer's rust streaked side. Crosswall-Brown grabbed at it eagerly and scrambled up.

Grant saluted formally and shook hands warmly, gripping his friend by the elbow as he did so. "Ben, I can't tell you how nice it is to see you again. The 'Old Man'... Commander Barr... you've met? No, not yet, well, he told me about your promotion and that you were to command the M.T.B. side of things."

"This is a turn up for the books, you wait 'til Charlotte hears. What a bloody coincidence!...I say you've made an impression there, what? Every time I speak to her on the phone she manages to bring the conversation around to you."

"She made quite an impression on me, as well."

"So it seems! No accounting for tastes. Just what did you get up to after I left the two of you alone...I hope your intentions are honourable."

"As honourable as yours in your dealings with the fairer sex, old man."

"You bounder!" laughed Crosswall-Brown, "Never get to see the real thing much these days, these are my little girls now. What do you think?" He waved his hand the length of the two M.T.B.s. It was as if he was caressing them.

"Very sexy, Italian engines I read somewhere?"

"Yes, that's right. Isotta-Fraschini. Forty knots official top speed, though, between you and me I've got forty-seven out of the beauties."

"I didn't know they were that fast. She's a Vosper boat, isn't she?"

"The new ones aren't, retrograde step if ever I saw one. For some reason they put different engines in them, Hall-Scott's I can literally run rings around them. Twenty-five knots on a good day! I ask you, haven't we enough of a disadvantage against E-boats as it is? I can make twenty five knots using the old Ford V8 we are fitted with for silent bloody running!"

"What is she sixty five or seventy?"

"Seventy footer and strong as an ox, mahogany and birch. The frames are only a foot apart! Although in truth I'd have preferred a B.P.B. The 'Old girl's' not too bad.

She was built for the Chinese originally, but then along came the war and we nicked 'em, before they could be delivered to the Chinks."

"Come and have a look at my little command," said Grant. The two friends turned aft and walked side by side back towards the darkened and silent E-boats.

"That's new!" Crosswall-Brown said, catching sight of the blue and white ribbon on Grant's chest." Super, DSO, eh? I say, they're not giving them away with packets of cigarettes now, are they?"

Grant smiled as he climbed down the Jacob's ladder, "How did you find out…but it's still an honour, they don't give them to just anybody. You have to be a twenty-a-day man…That's new as well." He was pointing at a ramp welded to the 'Nishga's' quarter deck

Crosswall-Brown looked with interest at the framework. "Bit like a depth charge ramp, bit bigger I suppose?"

"It's one of the 'Old Man's' ideas, fitted recently, while we were having a boiler clean. You'll find him full of ideas. It's to hold the spare fuel for your M.T.B.s as a matter of fact. The idea is you can dump it overboard in a hurry, if needs be."

"Wise precaution, highly inflammable stuff. So it's just 'out pins' and over she goes into the hog-wash? Good idea."

"And then there are these," said Grant jumping deftly across onto the E-boat's stern, he pulled off a canvas cover. "The first on any operational boat."

Crosswall-Brown was looking at another metal structure; this one was mounted on a turn table. "What on earth is it?"

"This, old boy, is the new depth charge launcher, shortly to be fitted to the fleet, the swivel bit is the 'Old Man's idea… that makes it even more experimental. When the launchers are eventually fitted to escorts they won't have the swivel. They have enough room on their arse ends for one each side so there'll be no need for the 'Old Man's modification. Of course it's a different story on our cramped quarter decks. To tell you the truth I don't think the Admiralty even know about the turntable. I think the 'Old Man' bribed the welding foreman with a bottle or two. With this little beauty we can drop two-hundred and ninety pounds of Amatol right in Jerry's jolly old lap and this bugger," he patted a depth charge fondly, "will blow a hole in any hull as long as it lands within twenty feet."

"How do you get on for ammo, old chap? I suppose you're all right for Bofors' ammo, but these other guns, hardly standard Navy issue."

"We keep what little two centimetre stuff we have for this chap." Grant patted the machine gun. "The for'ard one we never bother with under normal circumstances." He shook his head, "Jerry doesn't bother with it either."

"I know why, I've come across them on the East Coast. These high fo'c's'le rise up out of the water at high speed, consequently they can't depress the gun far enough to engage surface targets. Bit of a design fault if you ask me. The earlier boats S fourteen to S twenty-five had the lower fo'c's'le no problem. Different story with these though."

"Of course, I forgot I was talking to an expert. Personally, I still have it manned at low speeds or when there is a risk of attack by aircraft."

"My knowledge is confined to that gained by bitter experience on the wrong end of the barrel," boasted Crosswall-Brown, a smile on his face. He pointed to the stern mounted Bofors. "No design fault there though, those blighters are terribly deadly, old man."

"Bit of a rum deal having our own guns turned on us."

"The Bofors? Not strictly ours, old boy... Swedish made, I think. Most of the E-boat's skippers have managed to have them fitted now, captured during the first few months of the war, not always from us though... Jerry knows a good gun when he sees one."

161

*   *   *

Captain's Day Cabin, HMS Nishga.

"Good morning gentlemen, sorry about the early start, but there is a lot to get through… lots to plan. I trust you all enjoyed your leave."

Barr paused while murmurs of assent and a few jibes passed around the packed day cabin. Unlike many captains he was always glad to hear it. He saw it as an important 'barometer' to gauge his ship's company's morale, a happy ship was an efficient ship.

He pulled aside a white cloth covering an easel, as he did so the overhead lighting reflected on the untarnished gold of the new third ring on his outstretched arm. He found himself staring at it, he saw his wife sewing it on, sitting by the coal fire in their cosy parlour… with considerable mental effort he pulled his attention back to the present situation.

"Those of you who have sailed with me before may recognise this particular chart,"…again the laughter. We are returning to our old hunting grounds on the Norwegian coast. Only this time we go there with a larger force and with larger responsibilities.

But, I'm forgetting myself; before I go into details, I would like to take the opportunity to welcome Lieutenant Commander Crosswall-Brown and his men. Motor torpedo boats 34 and 35 are very welcome additions to our merry band." He smiled, "I believe they are better known as the 'Dirty Four' and the 'Dirty Five'," he paused briefly before he continued. "As, I think, most of us foresaw, the war on land has taken a turn for the worse. If… or, as seems more likely, when Jerry takes Norway, he will use her ports to threaten our sea lanes all the way from the north of Scotland way out into the Atlantic and up towards Iceland. The whole of Norway could well become a giant launching pad for his U Boats, his surface ships and his aircraft. It will be vital that we get information on the movement of his forces. We want to know when his ships sail, when his aircraft take off, we want to know in what direction they are heading and in what strength.

Collecting this information is one of three main tasks we have been entrusted with. "He flipped the chart up and secured it with a clip, underneath was a short list. "First, 'Gathering Information'... When 'Orca' ceased operations on the Norwegian coast we already had an embryo network of information gatherers in Olaf..." Grant noticed Barr's eyes dart to a prompt sheet in his left hand, "...Kristiansand and his friends. Now, while we have been enjoying all the comforts of home and hearth, he has been, out there, adding to this list of 'friends'. He has gone about this in rather an ingenious way. Each new recruit was required to recruit one other person, that person is known only to the person who recruited him or, indeed, her. I'm sure you can see the advantages of this method of enlarging the 'Network'. No one person will have knowledge of the whole organisation, not even Olaf himself. Now, our part in this is simple, we will be there to pass the information on to our intelligence people. In the first instant it will go to Lieutenant Grant's E-boats who will rendezvous with Lieutenant Commander Crosswall-Brown's M.T.B.s. They will carry the information to the intelligence services based at the 'Flow'." He raised a hand to silence the murmur from the men in front of him. "I know... I know, it is long winded, but it is the way Mr Kristiansand wants it. His people have no training in Morse code and he will not allow any of our agents into his organisation. It's early days yet and I'm sure he will grow to trust us more."

Barr paused, "Now I come to the second of our three tasks. The whole force will harass enemy shipping along the entire length of the Norwegian coastline, wherever and whenever it is encountered... Now this is pretty much what we were doing, before we were rudely interrupted, by a spot of leave. I hope, by now, those of you who were not with us last trip have been given copies of the operational reports that we submitted at the time. You should be able to get some idea of the sort of work we were engaged in and how we went about it from them. It's basic stuff... As Nelson put it, you can't go far wrong if you put your ship alongside one of the enemy's. Or as I hear Petty Officer Stone puts it. 'When you're in a fight, be first... be fast... and be furious."

When the burst of laughter had died down Barr continued, "Third, and final task, is that of 'Supply'. Jerry has complete air superiority over Norway. This means it would be unrealistic to rely on slow merchant ships to supply our troops; it's a job for fast warships capable of completing the crossing in one night. For these 'shopping trips' we will be using the 'Nishga'. Those of you brave enough to venture out onto the upper deck this morning will have noticed we are already busy loading stores. This is equipment urgently needed by a company of the 24th Guards Brigade at a place called, "he glanced at his sheet of paper, "Mosjoen."

He eased the clip and the chart fell back into place. "A battalion of the 24th landed at Mosjoen, a little over two hundred miles from Narvik on the 10th of May. Now, by coincidence, Jerry put men ashore at Hamnesberget... here... to the south, more or less at the same time. This has cut off our men from their mates and severed their supply line. That's where the 'Nishga' comes in. After we've delivered the groceries we will be playing things very much by ear... the situation ashore is, to say the least, fluid. "Our side may need some help from our four point sevens or they may need more supplies; we'll find out from them once we get there...That's about it gentlemen... Questions please!"

Chapter 11

Mosjoen

It was Sunday the 12th of May before the flotilla was fully ready and the 'Nishga' was able to lead the line of warships north, her boiling wake making a straight foam channel for her consorts to follow.

The passage through the Irish Sea was uneventful and Barr took the opportunity to put 'Orca' through their paces. It was the first time they had all been at sea together. The set of drills and manoeuvres he had first worked on, using his son's toys now had their first airing. He had run through them, but this was their first chance at full sea trials. On the whole Barr was pleased with Orca's' performance and said as much to the flotilla before the force split up, south of the Shetland Isles. The M.T.B.s hurried on towards the Shetlands, the E-boat's turned east towards Olaf's Inlet, and the 'Nishga' headed north east to commence her 'grocery run'.

The destroyer entered harbour at first light after a very fast passage. They anchored off Bodo after receiving re-routing orders from Scapa Flow, events, ashore, were changing rapidly. Now the whole of the 24th Guard's brigade could only be reached from the sea.

The Germans, with their air superiority and use of 'Blitz' tactics were sweeping north and already threatening Mo to the south.

To add to an already chaotic situation the Commanding Officer Major General Mackesy had been replaced. The newly appointed CO ordered Mo to be held as long as it could be supplied by road and for Bodo to be held at all costs. The 'Nishga's' cargo was quickly unloaded into barges and by late afternoon she was ready to sail.

The bombers arrived at a little after four. The crew were already at their action steaming stations, already closed up on full alert. All guns were brought to bear and opened up on the Heinkels as they swooped into the attack. Light anti-aircraft artillery, ashore, added their fire to the barrage.

The captain of 'A' turret took two men and ran for'ard to raise the anchor. In the lulls between blasts from the four point sevens, it could be heard clanking and clanging its way slowly inboard.

As soon as the men had signalled 'clear anchor' the destroyer got under way and quickly began to pick up speed, turning through the wind in a tight circle, making a run for the open sea. Astern, the sky above the docks, to the south of the town, blossomed with deadly black flower-heads criss-crossed with the tracer from pom-poms and heavy machine guns. Somehow the flight of Heinkels emerged unscathed from the barrage, seemingly immune from a terrifying display of firepower. Other aircraft followed in waves, like migratory birds, they swept in, wave after wave, dropping their bombs into the smoke that soon enveloped the docks.

As the last group of bombers came onto their target one peeled off in a graceful lazy dive to port and headed in towards the 'Nishga'. She came in low, rapidly overhauling the speeding destroyer from astern, volleys of fire from the ship's close range weaponry stabbed at her, tracer whipped and lashed across her nose bucking her from her line, but still she came on. She started to return the fire, her own tracer joining in a deadly dance with the destroyer's, ripping through the sky astern of the racing warship in white-hot bursts of light.

The pilot was good, he had positioned his aircraft for a textbook attack, one that could not possibly fail, he opened the bomb doors.

* * *

HMS Edward, Olaf's Inlet.

Lieutenant Grant edged the pointed bow of the 'Eddy' cautiously into the rock boom. Wilson leapt across the gap. Wyatt quickly passed a basketwork fender across to him before leaping down himself. They clambered across the uneven surface of rocks and untied the mooring wire. With the 'Eddy' inching ahead and the bulky fender in place, to protect her vulnerable hull, the boom was slowly, gently, pushed to one side. The two seamen held the raft in place while the 'Ethel' too slid quietly into the inlet.

The rest of the forenoon was spent unloading stores at the newly constructed stone jetty, deep in the womb-like cave.

Shortly after sunset Grant and Bushel climbed up the tunnel and set off on skis for Kristiansand's house where, over piping hot coffee, the Norwegian supplied them with some very interesting information.

The Germans were amassing a convoy of small boats in a bay only an hour along the coast. It was thought that they were loading supplies possibly for a large party of German infantry who had landed from the sea at Hamnesberget a hundred and seventy miles to the north. Coincidentally these were the very men threatening the 24th at Mo. The very same people the 'Nishga' had been dispatched to help.

* * *

HMS Nishga, Bodo Harbour.

Commander Barr stood feet astride, watching the Heinkel as she sped in seventy feet above the 'Nishga's' bubbling wake. He waited quietly, one hand on the array of voice pipes.
He lifted the lid on one, "Ready 'Guns'? You know the drill?"
"Yes, sir."
He flipped the cover closed and bent over another. "Ready Coxswain, just as we practised!"
"Aye, Aye, sir."
All the while his eyes had not left the approaching aircraft, close enough now to see the bomb doors opening, he fancied he could see the pilot's faces…Whites of their eyes…Time… "Hard astarboard!"
"Hard astarboard….thirty five degrees of starboard wheel on, sir."
At thirty knots the destroyer leant over to a seemingly impossible angle as she cut to starboard, taking the corner in a racing-horse-turn throwing a wave of green water tumbling away to port.
With deadly accuracy the stick of bombs fell from the screaming aircraft, black dots, diving like cormorants. They dropped right on target. Right where the destroyer should have been, right where, with any other captain, she probably would have been. Broadside on to the turning destroyer and at point blank range the Heinkel took the full blast from the stern mounted Pom Pom. She was quite literally torn to shreds. She flew into the stream of rapid fire intact; the madly jerking barrels of the gun spewed the forty millimetre shells casings out like popcorn, viciously ripping into her frail frame. She flew out the other side in

bits, great chunks of metal fell into the churning sea. When her fuel tanks flew into the line of fire an explosion ripped through the remains of the aircraft. In seconds she was no longer an aircraft, just a mass of blazing debris plummeting into the quenching sea.

The warship continued her turn, completing the full circle she sped out of the harbour entrance.

* * *

0200 hrs, Tuesday, 14th May, 1940. Vikjord, Norway.

The two E-boats lay offshore of their target bobbing and dancing in the long westerly swell. The sea reflected black and silver, as clouds tumbled across the white face of the moon.

Inshore the darkness hung heavy with fog, its skirts moving slowly to a fitful breeze. It had been seven hours since Kristiansand and the marines had been put ashore, bobbing into the night in their rubber dinghy.

The weather forecast had predicted a westerly wind, increasing to force five by dawn. Ideal conditions for what Grant had in mind.

A little after two the inflatable was spotted returning with part of the reconnaissance party. By a quarter past, Kristiansand and Blake were onboard and being debriefed. Their news was good. Nothing had changed ashore all was exactly as Kristiansand's spies had reported. At the southern end of the fjord the Germans had moored some fifteen assorted barges and coasters, along with their escorts. To the west, near the entrance to the fjord and a half- mile from the convoy, there was an oil storage facility. It was close to here that the 'Nishga's' landing party had left Bushel and Stilson lying up, awaiting zero hour.

Grant paused, looking from face to face. "So that, in a nutshell, is the plan. This will be no picnic. We will need to go in bloody fast and out… even faster. Jerry has chosen the site well. In fact he couldn't have chosen a better place to assemble a convoy. Steep sided, well concealed, impossible to spot from the sea and difficult to bomb from the air. The passage in is narrow, made even narrower by German minelayers a week before they began assembling the convoy. We can only pray the wind does what it is supposed to do and holds steady, otherwise our ace in the hole could prove to be a joker." He rose to his feet, "Now if there are no more questions…. Good, then we've time for a few hours rest before the off…" He held out a hand towards the door, "Gentlemen."

* * *

Grant lay on his bunk unable to sleep, thinking of the coming operation, going over and over the plan in his mind. If one thing worried him above all others it was the minefield, probably because of his experiences on the Belfast. He tried to tell himself it would not be like that. He'd read somewhere that it was difficult to find a hero at two in the morning. Whoever wrote that could well have added that the same went for optimists.

He told himself that he should be one of them. Thank God for the 'Network'. It had managed to provide him with a pretty good idea of where the swept channel through the mines was. While the German minelayer had been busy placing its deadly cargo, the 'Network' had been just as busy mapping it from the mountains above. Grant delved into the spinning depths of an already tired mind. If he remembered correctly from his training days on the 'Alfred' it took seven pounds of pressure on a mine's horns to detonate it. He could remember his instructor, Chief Poppem, holding up a sledgehammer and saying all it took was to rest this on the horn and…

It was going to be a nerve- racking few hours for them all.

* * *

A bitter cold night had splintered into an icy morning. It was still dark, a few minutes to five: Zero hour. Grant and Hogg stood side by side on the tiny bridge peering into the dark. They spotted the flash of light at the same time.

"There, sir!" cried the midshipman, "There's Bushel's signal."

"He saw us easily enough," said Grant, "Let's hope Jerry isn't as alert." They were still half a mile from target. "Signalman!... Make 'Execute'."

* * *

Bushel lowered his hooded lamp, concentrating on the light as he read the reply. He could feel, rather than see, Stilson coiled just behind him, ready for the off. The man's blood lust was almost tangible. As he turned, to give Stilson the nod, he felt like a handler releasing an attack dog. The marine showed his yellow teeth in a fierce grin and loped off towards the oil dump. Bushel followed, at a slower pace, weighed down as he was, by the heaviest of the equipment. He saw 'Snake' drop to the ground at the crest, remove his skis and start his slow careful approach to target.

Two minutes later Bushel stopped; easing the heavy pack from his back he dropped to his belly and inched carefully forward until he could see over the crest.

Below was the camouflaged compound. It was piled high with the twenty-gallon oil drums. The moon abruptly appeared from behind its cloud cover and revealed the helmeted sentry blowing into his hands, his machine pistol slung over one shoulder.

With difficulty he picked out 'Snake' below him, he was moving slowly around the back of the compound, keeping it between him and the German guard. Bushel would have been the first to admit, he was watching a master at work, it was classic stuff all right. When 'Snake' reached the corner of the compound he disappeared, as if by magic, into the thin blue shadow cast by the wooden end post. Unless you knew he was there…and even then. Bushel shook his head in wonder. He did not like the man, but his admiration had nothing to do with like or dislike…Stilson was making no attempt to get nearer. They had watched this particular sentry from a distance. He was a creature of habit, not a good characteristic in a sentry. He rubbed his hands together, pulled at his belt. Bushel almost said aloud 'Now straighten your helmet'…There he goes… yeah a creature of habit all right. The corporal of marines felt almost sorry for him. He was looking at a dead man; there was a morbid fascination in watching him. He swung about on one jackbooted heel and trudged slowly back through the snow towards the concealed 'Snake'. He turned once more, paused momentarily, as usual, and died.

'Snake's' trade mark, what he called his 'three in one overkill', break the neck, break the back and slit the throat.

* * *

Even before the sentry was gently lowered to the ground, Bushel was up and skiing fast downhill. One minute later and his bolt cutters were slicing through the wire compound fence. Stilson dragged the body of the sentry through the hole and dumped him unceremoniously on the oily slush.

Bushel drew a marlin spike from his belt and stabbed into the nearest drum, black oil spouted out forming a pool at his feet. In the lee of the drums he reached deep inside his ski-suit and pulled out a wad of cotton waste. He lit it, pushed it into the puddle of thick oil and watched it slowly catch and then roar into bright life. Then he was up and running for his skis, following in 'Snake's' shallow footprints.

He caught Stilson up at the crest just as the first drum exploded, a deep throated roar that turned to a ripple as its neighbours joined the conflagration shooting a ball of flame and black smoke rolling high into the night sky. The west wind lifted the oily cloud and sent it billowing off across the southern end of the fjord.

* * *

Grant looked over his shoulder at the signalman poised ready at the foot of the stubby mast. "Hoist Battle Ensign… Make to 'Ethel' 'Follow me with all speed'." He crouched over the compass repeater… "Full ahead. Steer east by north."

The E-boat's diesels roared into life, sparks flew from the triple exhausts and the boat's fore ends lifting gracefully as they gathered speed. Within seconds they were cutting through the water like a sharp knife through hot butter, each boat lifting a bow wave of clear white water as high as their bridges before it was allowed to dance away and settle into a broad avenue of incandescent frolicking foam.

Ahead the entrance to the fjord appeared out on the edge of the darkness. They eased round to port and shot through the entrance at forty knots, their combined wash sending waves crashing and clawing up the rocks to port and starboard.

The fjord widened abruptly and they saw the huge pall of black smoke, from the burning oil drums. It covered the entire south side, completely obscuring the target. Grant altered course to run down its edge. Hogg's boat, on the quarter followed suit. Tips of masts could be seen poking above the foul acrid fumes.

He waited until the first of the mastheads were abeam and bawled "Open fire!" The depth charge launcher coughed and the canister flew up just as, with a deafening roar every gun on board opened up.

Astern Hogg played follow-my-leader as he too

opened fire, adding to the general and noisy mayhem. The terrifying cacophony from the guns and exploding depth charges were soon drowned by the explosions from the target itself. Shells stored deep in the holds of the enemy coasters ignited, sending projectiles screaming into the air in a deadly firework display. Great belches of red-hot flame soared up above the target. Both speeding boats managed to fire a second depth charge before they reached the end of the run. Still at full speed they carried out a racing turn to port. Suddenly the water around Hogg's boat spouted columns of water. An eighty-eight at the harbour entrance had opened fire. The sea around both boats became alive, spray sweeping across their bridges in drenching sheets of icy water. Undeterred they completed their long turn and raced in towards their target for a second time.

Their objective looked like a scene out of Dante's Inferno, massive explosions were ripping the thick smoke apart, sending pillars of flame and smoke spurting into the sky. Between the billowing smoke clouds they caught brief glimpses of the havoc they were causing, figures running, flames everywhere, a writhing man of fire, mouth open in a soundless scream.

* * *

The German crew of the eighty-eight worked frantically at their smoking, jumping charge as it rapidly trained right following the racing Schnellbootes. Their fleeting targets were impossible to anticipate. At times the great waves of spray shooting out from their sides hid them completely. The gun aimer had to find them with the naked eye before training the gun back onto target. Their concentration was intense... too intense to see the two white-clad skiers approaching fast from the south... out from the source of the swirling black smoke.

The two figures shot past bent double over their skis, they bobbed straight in turn, two black dots sailed lazily

174

through the cold air.

*   *   *

Grant realised, too late, that the second run was unnecessary, the target was completely destroyed. He signalled 'cease fire' and turned the boat early to fool the enemy gun. It was then that he realised the eighty-eight had stopped firing. As they roared on out to sea, he looked up at the gun emplacement, high on the cliffs above them, but he could see nothing to explain the welcome lack of activity.

Elated with their success they emerged from the fjord and raced out into the swept channel.

He slowed his boat as they approached the mine field. Suddenly the white-hard flash of a signal lamp pierced the gloom ahead. Seconds later a ghost-grey shape resolved into the unmistakable silhouette of a German destroyer. It was straddling the only navigable channel. Either side, just beneath the surface, the spiked menace of the mines waited, astern the furious wasp nest they had just stirred up.

*   *   *

The German Destroyer. 'Wagner'.

Freggatenkapitan Linz stamped back onto the 'Wagner's' bridge, "Will you look at those… those mad misstuck Schnellbootes! They think they are the new cavalry. Will you look? They are blocking the channel with their, their rowing boats!"

Leutnant Ankar, his First Watch Officer, hid a smile as he watched the bridge signalman replying to the flashing light from the lead Schnellboote. Linz's fiery temper was well known throughout the squadron probably the Kriegsmarine, almost as well known as his dislike for young officers of the Reconnaissance Force and their commander Kapitan zer See Hans Butow.

* * *

HMS Edward

"Jesus! Where did she come from?" exclaimed one lookout.

"A shrewd guess would be Germany."

The shock of suddenly seeing the enemy so close, no more than three cables ahead of the two E-boats, threw Grant for a moment…. The bridge team turned towards him… In that split second he felt, maybe for the first time, the full weight of command fall on his young shoulders and how, oh how, he wished he had someone to turn to…

"Hold your fire, Middy, hoist the German colours, lively there!" He turned grabbing the signalman by one shoulder, "Make to the 'Ethel', 'Hold your fire, pass fast and close down the enemy's starboard side.'… O'Neill! Take us down the enemy's port side, watch your steering, remember the mines."

"Middy, make to the enemy destroyer 'Enemy seaborne force attacking fjord suggest you remain here, to cut off their retreat. God's speed'… Send it slow as you like now… the longer it takes the better."

* * *

'Wagner'.

The signalman was calling from the wing of the bridge.

"The Schnellboot report enemy boats are in the fjord… her capitan suggests we stay here to…

"Suggests?…Suggests!" screamed Linz his face turning a brick red, "The blasted cheek of the young whelp…He makes suggestions to me!"

The Schnellbootes were now almost on top of them and seemed to have increased speed they were going to pass one down either side.

"What are they doing!" Linz yelled to nobody in particular. "What are they doing! Don't they know we are in the middle of a minefield?" He broke into a panicked run across the width of the bridge. Leaning out over the side he raised his fist and shook it in the direction of the two boats. "Dummkopt! Dummkopt! Slow down, slow down!" he was screaming now, completely beside himself with rage.

* * *

HMS Edward

"Bunty!" bawled Grant, pointing to the swastika flapping madly at the stern. "Stand by on those ensigns now, on my order get that bloody rag down, and hoist our own colours. Full ahead all engines!"

* * *

'Wagner'

From his vantage point, on the wing of the bridge, Litz was now looking right down into the speeding boat as it tore pass him at forty knots. A young grinning gunner, on the E-boat's bridge, was looking directly up at him, an insolent look on his bearded face. The man raised two fingers in an unmistakable sign. Litz blinked his astonishment. Flags suddenly fluttered from the tiny masthead… Litz blinked again, this time in disbelief. "Mein Gott! White Ensigns!"

"Open fire! Open fire!" he screamed at the top of his lungs as he darted back into the bridge. He tripped on the step and staggered on at a furious pace, before regaining control… "That…that man," he blustered," He put his fingers up to me!"

Ankar hesitated... Open fire? That seemed a strong reaction even for Litz.

The lean shanked destroyer had began to roll madly in the huge wash from the two E-boats as they disappeared into the drizzle-grey of a Norwegian Sea dawn.

Chapter 12

Pontoons, bridges and bluffs

Norway, Wednesday, 18th May, 1940.

Farther north, the situation was deteriorating fast, the 'Nishga' found herself in the thick of the fighting. Now, due to the enemy's overwhelming air superiority the 'Grocer Runs', were having to be carried out under cover of darkness.

As the situation steadily worsened, Barr signalled the rest of his flotilla, ordering them north, to rejoin the 'Nishga'. She had spent the whole of Tuesday in hiding, with enemy aircraft almost constantly overhead. The increase in air activity had coincided with another attack on the Guards battalion at Mo.

The day after the attack the Guards began their withdrawal through prepared positions. The same night the two E-boats entered the part of the vast fjord that the 'Nishga' was using as a base. Later, at 2100 hours, they were joined by the two M.T.B.s, following their fast and uncomfortable passage from Scapa Flow.

As soon as the M.T.B.s had secured alongside, all four captains were called to a briefing in Barr's day cabin.

"Good evening, Gentlemen, nice to see you all here, alive and well. Although I suspect Jerry will be doing his damnedest to change that. I know you haven't had much rest I intend to be as brief as I can. I'm sorry to tell you we have an op scheduled for 0400..."

There were a number of groans.

Barr smiling and nodding held up his hands. "And that's the good news" He picked up a pointer, propped in one corner of the cabin and crossed to a chart on the bulkhead. "General Auchinleck has ordered that the town of Mo, here, be held for as long as possible. The army has prepared a number of positions on this road. At these they plan to fight a series of rearguard actions to delay Jerry's advance.

Today the Twenty-fourth began withdrawing towards us here at Bodo... Jerry will be hot on their heels. They are, at this very moment, building a pontoon bridge across this fjord." He pointed to the chart. "As you can see, if he is allowed to complete the bridge and cross the fjord he will cut the coastal road that the Guards are using for their withdrawal. Our task, tonight, will be to get to this bridge before he can complete it and destroy it.

It's one hundred and seventy miles to the pontoon bridge and by a strange coincidence, discovered by our own flotilla's Navigating Officer, the same distance back." He paused for the expected laughter and an embarrassed grin from Usbourne. "There is a good chance that the destruction of their bridge will annoy Jerry, and I expect he will be after our blood as soon as it is light, hence the early start.

Obviously torpedoes will be of no use against shallow drafted pontoon bridges, so we will be taking the opportunity to try out the new depth charge throwers. The usual pressure detonators are being replaced as we speak, they will be of no use, our torpedomen have been busy adapting fuses to work on a simple timing mechanism. We will need all four boats if we are to stand any chance of success. There was a murmur from his audience, "I know, I know the M.T.B.s will stand out like sore thumbs… So my plan is this…"

* * *

Heereskustenartillerie emplacement.

Leutnant Klaus Westlich, Commanding Officer of Number Two battery, Heereskustenartillerie, grinned his pleasure as his men cheered to the echo their comrades in the Kriegsmarine. There was no denying it was a glorious sight. In the dying light, not one, but two captured enemy motor torpedo boats were being towed ignominiously back along the fjord, under the guns of the battery. Through his powerful Zeiss binoculars he could see the enemy sailors were subdued and downcast hanging their heads sitting on their battered boat's decks. The German sailors, by contrast, were magnificent, proud in victory, cheering and waving as the two boats sounding their klaxons.

He smiled indulgently. Those men of the E-boats were indubitably exhibitionists but it was all good for morale. He had heard of their approach from his colleague, downstream at Number Three battery. Apparently it had been the same along the entire length of the fjord, wherever the little flotilla had passed with the glorious Reichskriegsflagge fluttering proudly above the cursed Britisher's flag.

He raised the glasses once more and closely studied the four boats in the little armada. It must have been quite a fight, he could clearly see the damage that the vastly superior German Schnellbootes had inflicted. The English dead and wounded littered their decks.

* * *

"I never gave us much of a chance at pulling this off," said Wilson as he squeezed past Wyatt at the helm, "another twenty minutes and we'll reach the target."

"Oh yeah! But the journey back will be the crippler though, won't it? What are we supposed to do on the way back, eh? Tell me that. Even bloody Jerry's going to catch on once the fireworks start, ain't 'e. You mark my words we'll cop it on the way back. Up the bloody fjord without a bloody paddle, that's where we'll be."

"Silence you men," hissed Midshipman Maurice.

* * *

The German field engineers were working by floodlight, lashing the barges together broadside on to the bank and laying heavy bridging timbers across them. They were already half way across, with no fear of attack from the air, or a retreating British Army, they could afford to be complacent and so they were.

The four boats bobbed gently in the dark centre of the fjord, away from the loom of light that enveloped the work site. The tow ropes were slipped and stowed below decks. The correct flags, broken out and hoisted, hung limp in the light airs.

Grant watched the engineers at work through his powerful binoculars. It looked as if 'Orca' had arrived not a moment too soon. At the rate the enemy was working they would finish the job by daylight.

He looked around, they were ready he raised his cap above his head, "Line ahead, gentlemen… let's go!"

The four boats' powerful engines coughed and thundered into life, the roar of five thousand break horsepower revving up and echoing in the confines of the fjord assailed the eardrums.

They shot forward as one, in seconds, they were in line astern, their combined wash engulfing the sides of the fjord as they roared towards the target. Complete surprise was theirs. The captured E-boats' cannon wrought havoc on the closely packed barrages. Explosions ripped the night into searing day, tracer swept the enemy decks clear of life. The machine guns on the M.T.B.s joined in, opening fire at point blank range. Within forty-five seconds of flashing up, all four boats were past the pontoon bridge and turning sharply to port, engine revolutions dropping as they turned to negotiate the narrowing fjord. They lined up for the second pass like racing cars at a staggered start. One by one they shot forward, leaping and bounding across water that now churned and leapt like a live thing. Ahead their old wash had swelled in across the low barges, sweeping the German soldiers from their feet as they madly scrambled for the safety of the shore.

On this pass they fired the depth charges sending them high into the fiery havoc they had created on the first run. As each boat passed the pontoons its launcher thumped once, the grey canister flew up and into the tidal wave from their wash as it crashed once again across the bucking decks of the barges.

The explosions followed each other rapidly, one after the other, ripping the bridge into fragments, throwing the debris high into the air to crash back into the maelstrom created by the careering boats.

Inside of two minutes the attack was over and the four boats were lunging back down the fjord, flashing by open-mouthed the German gunners of Number One emplacement and onwards towards the distant safety of the open sea.

Grant strained to see his watch in the dim light from the compass. The fjord was forty-six miles long... That meant a little over an hour, if they could maintain their top speed. They still had enough time and fuel to get back to base before enemy aircraft could begin their search; but that was only if they could manage to get by the other enemy gun emplacements. Grant suffered a moment of doubt; that was a very big if. On the way in, he had counted three batteries, anyone of which was quite capable of blowing the four tiny boats to hell and back.

* * *

Grant looked astern, he could just see all his charges in place, Hogg's boat brought up the rear. They were in line ahead, their, by now, standard formation.

His wasn't the best German, Maurice, 'Eddy's' new middy, was streets ahead. He turned to him now, "That knocked ten bells out of the bastards Middy."

"Is it always like this, sir," Maurice yelled.

"Like what?" yelled back Grant.

"So bloody terrifying, sir."

Grant smiled reassuringly, "Only most of the time, the rest of the time …well, it's a damn sight worse."

"You all seem to cope with it pretty well, sir."

"We learnt the secret from Able Seaman Wilson."

"Really, sir?"

" 'If you can't take a joke you shouldn't have joined'. That about sums it up, don't you think."

"Some joke, if you don't mind me saying, sir."

"Exactly… Some bloody joke."

* * *

The German artillery were ready, communications along the length of the fjord were good; more than enough to convey the acute embarrassment and anger felt by the men manning the emplacements. They found it hard to believe that they had actually cheered the enemy past their guns. There was to be no more of that, the Britishers would pay, must die.

Powerful one hundred and fifty centimetre searchlights probed the narrow fjord, illuminating it as if it was day. Itchy fingers hovered over trigger guards. Mein Gott, they were ready for the Britishers this time. This time it would be a different story. They would not pass…they could not be allowed to pass; it was a matter of the honour.

* * *

It was the lookout, Wilson, who sighted the second German anti-aircraft battery first. The loom of its searchlights glowed forebodingly above the mountains that obscured a bend in the fjord. Grant immediately cut the engines, the boats, astern, followed suit as the distance between them shortened alarmingly. The boats danced in their own wakes ,as Grant called for the marines and the handling party for the rubber dinghy.

* * *

Bushel and his men had luck on their side, even so, it had taken them an hour, an hour they could ill afford if they were to reach base before first light. Using the adjustable spanners in the dark and the numbing cold had been easy. One slip with the spanner would have been enough to alert the whole emplacement.

* * *

At the emplacement, so recently visited by the marines, the German gunners crouched beside their eight-eights. Leutnant Klaus Westlich paced backwards and forwards regularly checking his watch, fiercely determined that the enemy would pay a price for their earlier audacity. But where were they? If they had crept along the fjord at a snail's pace they would have been here by now. He switched on his torch and shone its bright beam over the guns in his charge. Everything was in place. He was completely unaware that they were a certain item of kit short.

Abruptly from upstream an air raid siren moaned its

ominous warning.

"Action aircraft!" yelled Westlich.

The gunners worked furiously at the crank handles. The muzzles of the eighty-eights trained quickly skyward and they waited.

"Get those search-lights out! They'll be following the fjord, using the glistening water like a pointing finger indicating their undoubted target, the new bridge. No need to telegraph the exact position of the guns.

The fjord plunged into darkness.

* * *

"What do you want me to do with the Kraut air raid siren, sir?" asked O'Neill. It's taking up a lot of room down in the wheelhouse. It's a bit cramped down there at the best of times."

"Dump it overboard?" suggested Maurice.

"Good Lord no," called Grant, "Not after all the trouble the 'Royals' had stealing the bloody thing, besides it might come in useful again, you never know…Stow it below for now."

"Aye, Aye, sir," said O'Neill.

* * *

The schedule for the raid had been tight now, as a consequence of the marines 'run ashore', they had some time to make up. The delay, however unavoidable, meant they would have to spend an extra hour of daylight exposed to the attentions of the Luftwaffe.

The four tiny craft sped north as fast as they could. The swell heaving its way south was against them, not much by Norwegian sea standards, but enough to slow them down to thirty knots and more than enough to make sure they would not make it in time. So first light found them closed up at action stations and still fifty miles short of the base.

The aircraft came in from the south-east, three Messerschmitt 109s peeling off one after the other, line ahead, swooping in from the heavens like avenging angels.

The flotilla was also in line ahead, the young skippers avidly watching the blue and white of Grant's 'execute' pennant as it snapped urgently in the slipstream. Grant, for his part watched the attacking aircraft.

"Execute," bringing his raised arm down to his side. The pennant was whipped down from the masthead into the waiting arms of the signalman. Instantly, the boats put their helms hard over. Odd numbered boats cut to starboard, even to port. The resulting fan tail of fleeing patrol boats provided no easy target. The manoeuvre, first carried out on the carpet in the comfort of Barr's front room in Suffolk, brought all the flotilla's guns to bear at the same time. The fighters flew straight into a vicious spray put up by the fourteen machine guns and the two Flak 28's of the flotilla. Miraculously, at two hundred knots, the aircraft screamed past unharmed. Turning to starboard, bombs still in their racks, they climbed rapidly into the grey dawn.

Their long turn completed they swooped back in from the east. The boats had reformed heading north and presented a broadside target moving at thirty knots left to right.

The 'execute' pennant flew high at 'Eddy's' masthead once more. The boats held their fire and their course, guns trained fore and aft. The flag flashed to the deck, this time all the boats swerved to starboard, leaning hard over as they did so, their for'ard guns were brought onto the target by the turn and they opened fire immediately. A withering screen of tracer arced up towards the approaching aircraft. The boats, now stern on, presented very small targets for the aircraft. The aircraft tore in, fifty feet above the waves. Hogg's boat took fire, heavy rounds of tracer punching holes in the wooden deck. The Messerschmitts screaming in over their racing targets flew straight into the fire of the little flotilla's stern guns. The lead plane was hit in the tail, immediately oily black smoke poured from it, its port wing dipped and touched the sea, the plane skipped and somersaulted on its wingtips, water spinning from it at a tangent like sparks from a Catherine Wheel until, shattered, it disappeared from sight completely in a welter of spray. The two remaining planes turned sharply and came in from astern.

This time, when the pennant fluttered to the deck, the boats turned, hard aport, twenty degrees, again bringing all guns to bear firing over their port quarters. The enemy planes had time to alter course away from the withering fire only to find the boats turning fast in the opposite direction, their guns swinging madly round to give another full broadside. The tail end aircraft visibly staggered out of line and leaving a writhing trail of smoke, both pilots clawed their aircraft round in a tight turn and made off to the south-east. The boats turned, as one, back onto their northerly course and reduced speed as Hogg's men fought to bring a small fo'c's'le fire under control.

* * *

It had grown colder, the sun had passed behind the high cliff face throwing the destroyer and her small consorts into its deep blue shadow. The four patrol boats nestled against the destroyer's side like suckling pigs at a sow's belly. The sheltered water, glass-calm, reflected the sheer sides of the fjord doubling their height. Here there were no convenient overhangs, the camouflage nets were hung straight out from the cliff. A wire strung between the 'Nishga's' two masts held them clear of the deck and superstructure.

Below decks 'Up Spirits' had been piped and the sailors waited in crowded mess decks for their rum to arrive. The seamen's mess deck was even more packed than usual, for in addition to the destroyer's own complement, they were catering for the seamen from two of the four patrol boats.

O'Neill was in a foul mood. Fresh from Captain's defaulters, he sat silently at the mess table. Usually, as the senior rating he would have been up top, drawing the rum ration for the mess and licking his lips at the thoughts of all the 'sippers' that would come his way when he dished it up. He was still finding it hard to come to terms with the severity of the punishment the skipper had metered out to him. It was nothing short of barbaric, so it was, flogging round the fleet would have been kinder. He could see the skipper now standing behind his desk…

Barr was saying, 'I'm sure you don't need me to tell you what these continuous appearances at my table are doing to your chances of promotion.'

Well, fair enough, he couldn't give a damn about promotion anyway, but then a surprised looking skipper had added, 'It's not a matter to smile about, O'Neill.'

It had been his turn to be surprised. Surely to God wasn't that up to me, he'd thought.

Barr referred to his notes saying, 'Perhaps, bearing in mind your previous record, I should have said the chances of re-promotion. I see here that you have held the position of Petty Officer once before."

Now you would have thought that someone of the skipper's undoubted abilities and education would get things like that right. 'No sir, that's not correct' he'd replied, staring straight ahead.

Barr had looked bewildered, 'What do you mean? Here it states clearly that you held the grade of Petty Officer on your last ship.'

He had nodded his agreement, relieved that the Ship's Office had something right, "That's correct, sir."

'Arh, that's right enough as well…'

The skipper had looked even more confused, 'So are you now saying the record is correct.'

'Yes and no, sir.'

'What do you mean, yes and no, O'Neill? It's either

correct or it's not.'

Now he'd never heard the skipper raise his voice before except maybe in the teeth of a gale. He'd hurried to explain, 'Well, sir, it's like this, you see,' he'd shown, as he remembered, a good deal more patience than the man himself, 'I'm sure you'd agree that records aren't of much use unless they're a true record. If your records say that I was a Petty Officer once, then they're wrong.' He'd paused there while his chest swelled with pride. 'I've been a Petty Officer three times in all.' There had been a long silence while he'd stood ramrod straight and why, to God, shouldn't he have been proud. After all it didn't it take a special type of man to get promoted three times.

Standing there, at attention, staring over the skipper's shoulder, he could see the Coxswain, his face was screwed up in a rare expression for a disciplined man such as himself. If it had been anyone else, at all, he would have sworn the coxswain was trying not to laugh.

The skipper looked down at his papers, leaning over the tall table, arms straight like a vicar giving a Sunday sermon from his pulpit. He feared that he must have angered him for he could see the skipper's shoulders were shaking uncontrollably. Here it comes, he thought, it's back down to able seaman for me...

Without looking up, the skipper had slowly shook his head. 'O'Neill, O'Neill,' he'd said, a catch in his voice, 'With a mind like yours, if you'd stayed off the drink, you would have outranked me by now and then, who knows, I might have been standing where you are and you where I am.'

'If that was the case, sir... then, sir,' he'd hastened to say, 'I'd be after letting you off with a caution,' it had been said with all sincerity and with true Celtic generosity.

It was then that O'Neill realised he'd gone too far. The skipper's head had gone down and his shoulder's had begun to shake again. When he raised his head, apart from the tears in his eyes, he seemed to have regained control for he said, 'Well thank you, O'Neill, but I am not inclined to be that lenient.'

So he had misjudged the man, he had not regained his composure at all, he must have still been angry for it was then that he'd uttered those terrible and damming words. Sure, they still rang in his mind like the death knell at his own funeral.

'One week's stoppage of rum'. The tears welled up now, as he relived that horrible moment. Sure the English for all their education and fancy ways could be a cruel race when they wanted to be.

* * *

The stand in rum bosun, Leading Seaman Thompson, clattered down the metal ladder, rum fanny in hand.

Leading Seaman Reginald Thompson was part of the new draft of 'hostilities only' ratings, brought in to replace the regulars drafted off to man the patrol boats. Besides being an H.O. Thompson had one other built in disadvantage. He was in the accelerated promotion scheme and was on his way to becoming an officer 'through the hawse pipe', as the lower deck called it.

Now O'Neill hated all officers as a matter of course, but what he thought of officers promoted from the lower deck he could not have put into words, a terrible thing for an Irishman as he would have been the first to acknowledge. It only made matters worse that Thompson had gained his, it had to be said considerable, knowledge of seamanship sailing daddy's yacht in the waters off Cowes. Taken all in all these factors were not calculated to gain respect from the fiery Irishman and had earned him the nickname of 'Regatta Reg'. Now, to cap it all, he, as the next senior rating, was dishing out the rum. O'Neill now hated the younger man with an intensity he usually reserved for those of the Catholic persuasion.

For his part Thompson looked on O'Neill as an

uncouth Irishman who should never have been put in charge of men, especially when those men were better educated than the stormy O'Neill. In the mess deck jargon they had long since 'parted brass rags' and it was the opinion of the ship's company that there could only be one outcome.

* * *

Thompson had difficulty making his way through the crowded mess and stumbled over one man's outstretched feet. There was nothing more calculated to upset the volatile O'Neill.

"Watch that rum 'Regatta' you clumsy bastard. You spill one drop and I'll have your guts for a signal halyard!"

"Look O'Neill. Mind your tongue on my mess deck. There's not enough room down here to swing a cat you should have brought your chaps down later."

"Well, dish the stuff up and we'll get out of your way with pleasure, now won't we lads." O'Neill turned, for support to his mates, "Sure he makes you as welcome as a dose of clap to a couple of newlyweds."

"I'm sure I don't have to remind you I am the Leading Hand of this mess. If you don't moderate your language I'll have you off the mess deck altogether. You are under stoppage as I understand it, you shouldn't be at the rum table at all."

This inflamed O'Neill even more, for it was the truth. Under stoppage the only rum he would get for the next week was what he could cadge as 'sippers' off his mates. He rose up from the mess bench, "Put down that rum fanny I'll not have it said I spilt the rum."

Thompson turned round to face the Irishman, "Am I to understand that this is in the nature of a challenge?"

"I know you're not been in this man's Navy more than a dog watch, but I would have thought you would have been in long enough to know that."

"If you want a 'grudge fight' you'll have to go through the proper channels."

"Well, ain't you the lower deck lawyer, It's a hurry I'm in, it's tot time and I've no time for all that shite...now put 'em up."

"Look. I don't want to hurt you O'Neill, I feel it my duty to inform you I was an Oxford Blue and I am quite capable of defending myself should it be necessary."

Now O'Neill had no idea what an Oxford Blue was and if the truth be known he cared less, "Oh it is necessary." He turned to his mates, "Don't worry lads, this won't take long, I'll not be keeping you from your rum for long."

"I have no reason to fight you."

"Now, is that the truth... try this for size," said the big Irishman, swinging a pile-driving right that would have floored a horse.

To the surprise of the mess deck this 'horse' ducked neatly under the swing and stabbed out with his left, a short sharp blow that drew blood from the Irishman's top lip.

O'Neill stood there wiping the blood away with one huge fist, staring at Thompson in disbelief that quickly turned to amusement when he saw that Thompson had taken up a classic Queensbury Rules stance. A lopsided smile creased O'Neill's face as the two began to move around in the circle that had cleared around them.

"Yourself being an educated man I'm sure you will appreciate my taking the opportunity to teach you a few things. I'm a religious man, so I'm thinking I'll teach you about faith, hope and charity. He stabbed with a lightening left... CRUNCH! Thompson staggered back, one hand to his split lip. "That was to give you faith... the faith you'll never get hit harder than that in the rest of your life."

Again the left stabbed out... CRUNCH! Thompson's eyes glazed over either side of an already swelling nose. "That's to give hope, hope that you'll never see me in a bad mood again ... and now charity... because," this time it was his right that shot out… CRUNCH! "That's the last time I'm after hitting yer."

'Regatta Reg' sank slowly to his knees, his arms straight down at his side he fell ungracefully forward onto a battered and bloody face.

* * *

Relaxing in the wardroom, his feet on the coffee table, Grant sipped at the pink gin, it was his second. He sniffed at the heady fumes, it smelt like perfume and put him in mind of Charlotte. She wouldn't have liked the idea. A shadow fell across his glass and he looked up into Charlotte's eyes. It was Crosswall-Brown. He hadn't realised how alike they were until that moment.

"Fancy a game of crib, old man?"

"Why not… Sound idea," said Grant.

Crosswall-Brown already had the board and cards in his hand. He placed them on the small oak table to one side of Grant's chair and pulled up another.

"Good to be back in civilisation?" he asked shuffling the dog-eared pack.

Grant nodded his head, "Too true. It's like a different world, Ben. I took all this for granted when I was Number One on the old bucket."

"Like it all back?"

"What the job?" He thought for a second, "No… well, at this moment…" he laughed, "… possibly yes." He took a deep breath and looked deep into the glass. "I like the excitement of my own command…the responsibly, I suppose, certainly the independence. But you know what I really appreciate, what is even more important to me, is to be master of my own fate, at least as much as one can be in this day and age. If I'm going to risk my life and other peoples I want it on my terms … Don't get me wrong the 'Old Mans' the best… But I have served with some right…well… dangerous idiots, in my time. Mostly people who are someone's son and heir and who don't know their ear holes from their...Well, you know the aperture I have in mind. People who no idea how to do the job and are put in charge of those who have."

"People like me you mean."

"No! God Lord no. You're the exception that proves the rule."

"That's a relief."

"Sorry, you know what I mean, don't you, old chap? To take command, it's the hardest things any of us can be called upon to do, certainly not everyone can do it, it's not something you should have as a right. When men's lives are at stake old school ties shouldn't count for anything. We British do have a tendency to put some right dunderheads at the top. Look at Haig in the last show. We put that man in charge of thousands of men and he slaughtered them. He simply did not have the ability, not an original bone in his whole body. He was more dangerous to our troops than the bloody Germans. Pure waste; pure murder, if the truth be known." He stared into his glass. "Sorry I'm going on a bit. I've probably had too many of these... I know I'll never have the kind of responsibility that that old man had. By God, I don't think I'd want it. I've enough... more than enough!" He leant forward over the table. "I'll tell you what, old chap, I'm going to use every ounce of grey matter I possess, to bring the few I have under my command through this one safely."

"I'll drink to that ... Steward, bring two 'Horse's Necks'. He laid a seven of hearts, "Fifteen two."

* * *

Commander Barr rubbed his smooth, recently shaved chin and turned back to the map of Norway, "Jerry is using this coastal road to supply his troops at the front. Not surprising really, this is the only usable road. It crosses the river Landola... here. As you can see it is very near to our old base… here, at Olaf's Inlet. The plan is to carry out a night attack and spend the following day hiding up at the Inlet. This will also give us the opportunity to gather any information the 'Network' have accrued since our last visit. You all have your orders in writing. That's about it Gentlemen… unless are there any questions?"

Barr pointed at Grant's raised hand. "Robert?"

"It might be a good idea to contact Olaf before the attack, sir, rather than after, he may have more up to date information on the target."

"Good point…but that will delay the operation by twenty-four hours…"

"Not if we contact Olaf early enough sir, it's only two hours from the Inlet to the bridge."

"True… that's what we'll do then. Any more for any more?…No …Suggestions?…No. Well, thank you, gentlemen, I know you all have lots to do, carry on please."

* * *

As soon as it was dark the four boats slipped south, making good progress in a stern sea, they were off the Inlet three hours before first light. The 'Eddy's' dingy was lowered quietly over the side and Bushel and his men paddled in along the length of the Inlet, under the high overhang and into the cave. Since they had abandoned the idea of a permanent presence they had to check for signs of the enemy before they entered. Grant had given them thirty minutes to search the cave, tunnel and cliff top.

The three men secured the dinghy and moved slowly and gingerly along the rock ledge. Bushel was in the lead, using the canvas sling of his Lanchester to check for trip wires. He edged forward, half a step at a time the gun held out in front, its sling dangled to the cave floor.

It was surprising how much warmer it was below ground. Bushel had, almost, come to think of the place as home. They had constructed a sleeping gallery halfway up where the tunnel widened. Nature had done most of the work for them, they had simply levelled the floor and fixed mountaineering spikes into the hard rock walls to take their hammocks.

Bushel climbed on pass the gallery, all seemed as they had left it. If it weren't for the cold the task of guarding the Inlet it would have been a quiet number, even more so since the construction of the 'HQ' around the tunnel exit at the top. It had taken them two nights to roll and drag the trees into position and to carefully arrange them to look like a natural fall of timber. Inside they had rigged one of the 'Nishga's' canvas awnings, suspending it from the tree trunks forming the roof.

The HQ was the first of his 'Thoughts', that's what he called them, his little play on words... his little joke... too little to tell the others. 'Thought One' was the HQ at the top of the tunnel, 'Thoughts Two and Three', had yet to be started, they were to be machine gun positions constructed in a similar manner to the HQ that would give flanking fire, should the need ever arise.

With the thick snow cover the construction was invisible from the air as well as from the ground. Not invisible, no that wasn't the word, undetectable no... indistinguishable, yeah that was it indistinguishable from the other piles of wood in the plantation. He remembered how he had spent moonlit nights meticulously covering everything with a dusting of pine needles only to have it snow shortly after completion.

The work had made the position on the cliff top better for their purposes, but there was still room for improvement... as his school reports used to say.

Before the discovery of the tunnel the position had been a death-trap. He had realised that the first time he'd laid eyes on it. It would have been impossible to withdraw under fire with their backs to the cliff, even if the boats had waited... and Barr had made it bloody clear that they wouldn't be doing that.

He climbed on...He'd spent a lot of time trying to figure out an escape route before the tunnel had been discovered. Now if the worst came to the worst they could all climb down into the sleeping gallery and hide up, with all their supplies, for months if need be.

He reached the hatch into the HQ and switched off the torch. He shut his eyes tight for a few seconds to regain some night vision.

Even if an attacking force took the HQ, they would be hard put to find this hatch. No one would dream that there could be anything but solid rock here. He remembered his alarm when the matloes had suddenly appeared from the tunnel that first time. Silly bastards nearly got themselves shot.

After the 'Nishga's' Chippy had fitted a hatch 'Snake' had camouflaged it. He had some patience, that bloke, you had to hand it to him...he had individually chosen the small rocks, from among the same type that had littered the ground around the immediate area of 'Thought One'. The rocks fitted into the existing floor like a jig saw; not a straight line anywhere, it was difficult to find even though they knew where it was.

He eased a shoulder against it now, inching it open the tiniest fraction. It was dark out there, he felt around for any wires.

Everything seemed in order, as quietly as he could he scrambled through, checking behind the hatch cover before lying it gently back onto the floor. Suddenly something cracked to his right. He dropped to one knee swinging his gun round. A rodent of some kind rustled away into a dark corner. He listened for a few moments, his finger poised on the trigger, taking the first pressure. You could never be too careful, he smiled to himself, there could always be more than one rat.

At the observation slit in the wood wall he listened for several minutes. Hearing nothing he returned to the tunnel entrance and whispered,

" 'Snake' take the main path… Blakey, the cliff tops. Look for footprints in the snow and remember where you've trod I don't want any false alarms over our own footprints."

* * *

The marine scouting party found plenty of reindeer prints, but no sign of human visitors. 'Snake' stayed as lookout at HQ while the others climbed back down the tunnel to the dinghy. It took only minutes to give the waiting boats the all clear.

As soon as they were alongside Sub Lieutenant Hogg, accompanied by Bushel, climbed to the surface and putting on skis, set off at a fast pace to make contact with Kristiansand as planned.

* * *

On the 'Eddy', below decks there were different priorities.

"Earpy, you know any Germans?" asked Wilson.

Wyatt thought for a moment, "No, Why?"

"Just thinking."

"What about?"

"Arh…You know…I mean what's so different about 'em, that makes 'em do all this," He was indicating a dog-eared, month old, newspaper.

"Arh, you don't wanna take any notice of that, that's all a load of bollocks. They dream all that up just to sell newspapers, everyone knows that!"

Goddard put his darning aside to join in the conversation. "I knew an Austrian lived near us, baker, he was all right." said Goddard.

O'Neill rubbed his blue veined nose, "It's not your ordinary man that's the problem now is it? It's the bloody politicians. Aren't they the ones that are responsible, they make all the troubles of the world. By rights it should be them that should sort the bastard out. When I'm in a bit of trouble ashore I don't go asking Chamberlain to sort it out for me, do I? They cocked it up, they should sort it out, not drag every other bastard into it."

"Not a bad idea that 'Nervous'." said Wilson, "Rig up a ring outside the 'ouses of Parliament and get 'Itler and Chamberlain to fight it out. Grudge Fight that's the way we sort things out in the 'Andrew'; works all right. Clears the air, like."

"Can't say I'm fancying Churchill or Chamberlin in a punch up . I wouldn't be after putting my money on either of them. You English would have to change your Prime Minister if you wanted to win anything."

"Get a bigger bloke in," added Goddard.

"You could be Prime Minister, Nervous," said Wilson warming to the idea... "Now, come to think about it...That's it, whoever is the Heavy Weight Champion of Great Britain gets to be Prime Minister as well... Yer Middleweight Champion gets to be Minister for War...We could do away with elections and all that crap, have boxing tournaments instead. Charge an entry fee and do away for the need to tax every bastard."

There was a companionable silence while the mess deck thought about the revolutionary idea.

Ordinary Seaman Goddard, deep in thought, had not been listening to the conversation. "Whose side are the Austrians on, anyway?"

Wyatt pulled a face, "Fucked if I know."

"Did you say Austrians or Australians?" asked Wilson from his seat close to a noisy donkey boiler.

"Austrians!" yelled Goddard, Austrians. I know whose side the Australians are on."

"Well, sprog, you know more than I do," said O'Neill. "Sure, I've had more fights with Australians than I've had with Austrians."

"That's because the Austrians ain't got a Navy. Land

locked ain't they?"

O'Neill thought about the likelihood that any country could do without a Navy and dismissed it as unlikely. "Sure, if they ain't on our side they must be on the other side."

"Nah" said Burton, "'Itler conquered yer Austrians before we got into the War, ain't that right, Tug?"

"Don't talk daft," said Wilson, 'Itler's an Austrian, everyone knows that."

"I didn't," volunteered Goddard.

Wilson shook his head, "Why am I not surprised?"

"If you're right, said O'Neill, "they managed to keep that quiet."

"Wouldn't you if he was Irish?"

"He'd make a good Irishman," ventured Wyatt, an evil smile playing at the corner of his mouth, he's a stormy bastard all right."

O'Neill refused to bite.

Wyatt tried again, "Are they right, what they say about the Irish?"

"And what would that be?"

" That Irish arse is poisonous."

"And isn't it like yourself to lower the tone of the conversation."

"What's that supposed to mean?"

Wilson had a question before things could deteriorate any further. "Do you speak from personal experience when you say it's poisonous, Earpy?"

"I wouldn't touch one with a barge pole," said Wyatt.

"As I remember the saying, it's Scotch arse that's poisonous," continued Wilson, on a more scholarly line of thought.

" 'Ere ain't you a Scotsman, Tug?" enquired Burton.

Wilson shook one finger smiling, "Oh no yer ain't going to get me biting, you know damn well I'm from Silvertown."

"I thought as much," said the South Londoner, "North

of the Thames, that's Scotland, in my book."

* * *

Olaf's night visitors returned to the Inlet as dawn splintered through the grey of the eastern sky.

"It's as well we came in here first," reported Hogg, "according to the Kristiansand there's a whole nest of Panzers, resting from the front and parked right beside our bridge. He was there the day before yesterday he said that the whole area is a hornet's nest."

In the silence that followed Grant lit a cigarette and offered the pack around. "A lot could have happened in two days... We'll take a look ourselves tonight, We'll have to delay the raid; I want to be sure what we're taking on, if we take it on at all."

* * *

The moon shone down on the parked German tanks, by its ghostly light they had an appearance not unlike massive silver crabs. There were eleven of them, assembled in a tight circle, nose to tail. Five were the older PzKwIII's the remainder were the heavier PzKwIV with their long-barrelled seventy five millimetre gun.

A gap had been left on the bridge side of the laager through which soldiers in the green uniforms of the Waffen SS moved continuously. Two sentries patrolled the outside perimeter; another guarded the gap checking papers.

The south side of the defensive ring was only yards from the bridge and its sentry box. There had been no attempt at concealing the parked vehicles from the air, no camouflage netting, no cut branches, nothing. The Germans, obviously, felt secure from attack by air.

Above the enemy tanks, a road wound its way up to the top of a steep incline. Half way up and almost level with his own position Grant could see an empty lorry, with

SS markings it was waiting outside a barbed-wire compound, its engine running, exhaust fumes swirling in its headlights.

The wire gate was opened and it passed through and parked just inside. The compound, unlike the tanks, was draped in camouflage netting. Grant assumed it to be an ammunition or fuel dump.

Below, the main road was jammed with enemy traffic, its earth surface churned to a glutinous brown slush.

Across the bridge, on the far bank of the Landola River, Grant could make out three eighty-eights their muzzles pointing skywards. That side of the bridge had its own sentry box, manned by two members of the Feldgendarmerie checking papers.

Grant was about to crawl back from the ridge, to where the marines waited, when he noticed a group of soldiers on the bridge. They were waving, looking down at the river. Crouching low he carefully moved to his right and looked down into the swirling waters of the fjord. A hundred feet below an E-boat was passing slowly under the bridge.

A Naval patrol, it was only to be expected, he was a fool not to have thought of it before. The bridge must be one of the most important in Norway right now.

As he considered the implications of his discovery he caught sight of the lorry, on the slope opposite, it was weaving its way back down to the crowded road.

He would have to leave his marines here to time the E-boat's movements ready for a possible attack on the bridge the following night. Suddenly a tank engine roared into life, making him start. The revving of its powerful engine drowned even the drone of the convoy passing along the road. The tank, nearest the small opening, was moving to allow the lorry, he'd seen descending the mountain, to pass into the ring of tanks. As soon as it had passed the tank moved back into place and switched off its engine. Grant watched as men began to unload the lorry's cargo, fuel and ammo, stored together, The Germans were getting

203

complacent.

* * *

Grant decided to take Bushel back with him after all. The corporal's particular brand of expertise might come in useful when it came to drawing up the finer points of a plan. It left Blake and Stilson behind on the ridge with orders to keep watch and taking note of the times the sentries changed, the E-boats patrols, enemy movements in general and anything else that might be of use.

Back on board the 'Eddy', Grant and Bushel, fortified by a couple of cups of thick sweet tea, set about drawing up a detailed map of the enemy positions from the notes they'd made on site.

By lunch they had finalised a plan for the raid that evening. There was, however, one problem. It called for good communications between the three separate groups that comprised the raiding party. It would, almost certainly have to be used within sight and hearing of enemy soldiers. So whatever method they used it would have to be short and sweet as well as silent and meant they could not use wireless or lamp. They pondered the problem over more tea.

Grant offered round a packet of cigarettes.

"Cigarettes" cried Bushel, banging the table top and making them all jump.

"There's no need to sound so surprised, anyone would think…" began Grant.

"No, don't you see…" Bushel paused, holding up his hand for silence, while he thought about his idea. "We can use cigarettes," Grant stared open-mouthed at Bushel fearing the corporal had gone completely mad.

"The Germans are not bothering with a blackout, right?"

Grant nodded, still confused, "Don't you see, there's no smoking restrictions. I remember everybody lighting up

204

while we were on that ridge."

Grant's face showed he hadn't.

"Well, I did, continued Bushel, "I was gasping for a burn all night…Anyway what I'm saying is, we work out a series of signals using cigarettes and matches. Jerry will assume it's one of their men and be none the wiser."

Chapter 13

Of Hairy String and Hairier Deeds

Near Landola, Norway, 2300 hrs, Thursday, 23rd May, 1940.

Grant studied the damp paper for the twentieth time. The only pattern, observed by the marines, seemed to be that there was no pattern.

It did seem, however, that the E-boat never visited the bridge more than twice in any four-hour period. If they moved in directly the patrol had passed, allowing for them to get out of earshot, it might give them the time to launch a river borne attack and get away safely. Time was a critical factor any delay would jeopardise their chances of getting back to base by first light.

* * *

"How about over there, sir, that looks like a likely spot." said Maurice, Hogg had been right the diminutive midshipman was nothing if not keen, too keen; perhaps. So far he had spotted six 'likely spots' in the space of thirty

206

minutes.

There had been quite a bit of toing and froing of kit as well as men before they were able to get under way. Midshipman Hope had joined one of the two shore teams, he was one of the few sailors who could drive, it was a skill that few of seamen possessed.

That particular team, led by Hogg and guided by Marine Blake, had to cover almost a mile of torturous mountain paths before they could reach their objective, the lookout point on the ridge above the target.

* * *

'Snake' Stilson straightened and lit his cigarette, at his feet the still form of the German sentry had, horribly, acquired a second gaping mouth, one that grinned back at the marine, blood red.

He pulled deeply on the cigarette; the glow illuminated his face momentarily before he moved its glowing end in the shape of a tick.

One hundred yards away Hogg, Blake and Jackson emerged from the deep shadow cast by a stack of ammunition boxes. Hogg moved quickly across to a row of parked lorries while the other two began rolling oil drums to where the ground fell away steeply.

"How many of these do you want moved, sir? asked Blake, as he arrived at the cliff edge with the first drum.

"Hang on..." grunted Hogg, as he rolled his drum up alongside Blake's. "It's a case of the more the merrier I suppose... say thirty."

"That'll take some time, sir, do you think we've got it to spare?"

Somewhere behind them an engine coughed and spluttered before revving noisily into life. It appeared out of the dark, moving slowly towards them, it stopped with a jolt and Midshipman Hope jumped quickly down from the cab. "I can't believe our luck, sir, all the vehicles have their keys in their ignition."

Blake jerked a thumb in the direction of the lorry park. "That'll be in case of a fire, sir. They're all loaded with either ammo or oil drums."

"Oil drums!…That will save us some work. Mr Hope back one of them over here. Then go back for one with ammo aboard and pick me up at the top of the road."

* * *

Hogg and Hope had the heavy bonnet of the ammunition truck propped up and were working industriously on its engine. Parts lay scattered on the ground at their feet. Neither of them had any mechanical knowledge whatsoever, both worked on the principle that if it had bolts you could undo, then it joined the growing pile. As they worked, they kept a weather eye on the fjord below the bridge and on the queue of heavily laden German lorries slowed to a trickle by the ammunition truck parked on the narrow road.

* * *

Marine Blake, binoculars raised, watched the young officers hundreds of feet below him. Stilson was somewhere behind him, watching the road that led down from the supply dump, in case of problems there.

From where he lay Blake could not see the water in the fjord, only the steep side of the opposite bank.

In the circle of his binoculars, the magnified figure of Hogg, straightened from his labours and gave a cigarette to his young companion before lighting one for himself. Blake waited to see what the signal would be. Hogg yawned and stretched both arms above his head as he did so the red end of the cigarette made a distinct tick in the gloom.

Blake jumped to his feet, standing well to one side, he opened the tailgate of the lorry. Nothing! The cargo hadn't budged an inch. He swore out loud and scrambled quickly up onto the curved and slippery surface of the drums, bracing himself against one he pushed with his feet against the first in the line. Nothing!...He yelled for Stilson.

* * *

Hogg stretched again, his cigarette making the signal for a second time. He waited... Nothing! What the hell had gone wrong? With the 'Eddy' already in place any delay could prove fatal... He looked casually around; all it wanted now was for someone to ask for their non- existent papers.

* * *

The two marines were dragging the heavy, oil-soaked beam of wood behind them. It was difficult going, their feet slipping on the hard frozen snow. Reaching the front of the lorry they dropped it into place. Blake straightened. "Right drive the front wheels of the lorry up onto it, that should give us a slope to get the drums moving,"
Stilson looked doubtful, "I can't drive." He looked at Blake's blackened face, until it dawned on him, "Don't tell me..."
Blake rubbed his chin with one oily hand... "Shit!"

* * *

"You two men!" a harsh voice called from the direction of the tank park. The two young English officers flashed a quick look at each other. They ignored the remark, hoping it wasn't directed at them... It was... an angry looking Jager Oberst had appeared at their side.
"Am I talking to myself!" he yelled, above the drone of the passing convoy
The two sprang to attention, "No, Herr Oberst," replied

Hogg,

"What do you think you are doing? You are taking up half of the road with this heap of shit!..." his eyes dropped to their naval overalls. "Kriegsmarine? What are you doing here? What unit are you with?"

* * *

The two marines rested after another attempt at getting the drums moving. Blake jumped down and sat on the beam they had dragged there. "It's no good, the bloody things haven't moved an inch." He pointed, his breath white against the dirty snow. "We'll never move this lot... over that edge... might 'ave...but for the slope ... One of us'll have to have a go at driving the bloody thing up on to this," he slapped the beam.

He placed a hand on each knee and pushed himself to his feet, "I'll take a shufty."

The cab was huge, the controls a bewildering maze of dials, switches and levers.

"Right, the first thing's got to be to start the engine." He picked at a tooth contemplatively while he studied the dashboard. The key was in the ignition, where Hope had left it... "All right! 'Ere goes'...Nothing! Blake worked his way systematically along the line of switches and buttons, the lights came on, the windscreen wipers danced madly backwards and forwards... suddenly he found the starter button. The powerful engine roared into life and, in gear, jumped back towards the waiting abyss. Blake gave a yell of alarm and jumped out head first. The lorry hit the wooden beam and stalled with a mighty jerk. He heard a rumble followed by the scrape of metal on metal and, alarmingly, the lorry began to jump up and down. The jolt of the engine stalling had dislodged the oil drums and, one by one, the drums were dropping off the back of their own accord.

"See!" gasped Blake to his grim-faced audience of one,

"nothing to it really."

* * *

Behind the German officer the surface of the mountain had suddenly come alive, a seething, heaving mass of drums, leaping and tumbling down the slope.

The German colonel swung round, his voice trailing off in mid sentence.

Hogg, seeing his chance, flicked the switch on the timing device taped to the petrol feed, grabbed Hope's arm and half dragged him out into the slowly moving traffic, unceremoniously he pushed him down the bank, into the darkness.

Turning they and ran along the line of army trucks, yelling, jumping on and off the cabs, pointing up towards the landslide of drums. Lorries stopped, drivers wound down windows, staring in horror at the oil drums plummeting towards them from the mountain above.

The drivers began to abandon their vehicles, leaping to the ground and running for their lives. Ahead the remaining convoy continued in complete ignorance of the drama unfolding behind them.

Again Hogg seized the moment. Jumping into the abandoned cab of the lead lorry he whipped out the keys. In seconds he was back down onto the road and running back to where Hope waited.

Then all hell broke loose. The first of the drums had reached the tanks, leaping and bouncing over the laager and into its centre. Many of the drums had split and were cascading oil in glistening black Katherine Wheels. One after another they smashed headlong into the unyielding metal of the tanks and soon a river of oil began to flow out from the laager across the road and under the stalled convoy.

* * *

Grant peered up at the bridge, the headlights of the vehicles cast surreal shadows onto its heavy metal girders. The rumble of lorries crossing, which had drowned the noise of the E-boat's engines, had stopped. It had been replaced by the yells and screams of men in flight and in fear of their lives. In the background an unidentified rushing, booming noise grew rapidly in its intensity.

The boat moved into the shadow of the bridge. He craned his neck back. The structure was now directly above, an oil drum bounced suddenly into view soaring out, falling like a depth charge. The column of water that shot into the air had barely settled when two others shot out from the road above. With considerable effort he turned his attention back to the diving team assembling on the cramped fore-end of the E-boat.

The frogmen, Dirty-Four's diver, Burton, and the marine, Bushel, were poised outboard of the guard rails looking back at him. Burton, bulky with rope and tackle, Bushel with a rope wrapped around his middle. Aft of them two men steadied a drum, packed with explosives, balanced precariously on the gunwale.

The 'Eddy' eased slowly forward, under the bridge they had been in deep shadow now as they passed out from under it they were barely making headway, Grant was gauging the speed of the water hissing past, adjusting the revs to stem the racing current. At last he was ready to give the signal and the heavy drum was dropped to the waterline. Alongside it the two frogmen slipped soundlessly into the swift flowing water and were rapidly swept past him towards the stern. They struck out frantically for the steep banks of the fjord the light grass line squirming snake-like in their wake.

The two swimmers had no sooner reached the shore when a gigantic blast of light and sound ripped the night into shadow less day.

212

* * *

The German colonel, Luger pistol in hand, cap now missing, bent double, gasping for breath. He had outrun the drums, the avalanche of oil drums had stopped; of the two 'mechanics' there was no sign, but they were the least of his worries, he turned back towards the convoy and broke into a staggering lurching run along the line. Thick black glutinous oil squelched under his running feet, the smell rank in his flaring nostrils. It was everywhere, his convoy sat in a volatile inflammatory lake of diesel. He had to get it under way, get it clear of this section of road.

He reached the first lorry, the one that blocked the road, he threw his gun up into the cab and hoisted his exhausted body after it.

He had time to realise there were no keys before a searing flash of soundless light ended the rest of his days.

Hogg's ammunition lorry vanished in a ball of howling orange and red flame that shot to an incandescent column of white hot flame that soared hundreds of feet into the night sky. Then the oil lake ignited, erupting outwards, from the exploding truck, in a fiery dome of burning oil that encompassed the entire convoy and the bridge. Liquid flame spewed over the edge of the bridge like molten lava, a hundred-foot cascade of flame that quenched itself in a hissing, boiling river.

Grant reduced the revs and the boat sank swiftly back into the inferno into the dancing flickering shadow of the bridge. Amid the rip and roar of further explosions his men worked quietly and quickly, floating the drum across to the waiting divers.

Once the frogman had the drum, bucking and bobbing at their feet, they attached Burton's purchase to the rope that encircled its fat belly and hoisted it clear of the water. Leaning out they grabbed it and swung it in among the supporting girders of the bridge. As they worked both men snatched nervous glances upwards at the blazing inferno a mere hundred feet above their heads. At last the drum was secured under the iron buttress that supported the eastern end of the bridge. They started the short, but perilous journey back to the E-boat, pulling themselves along the grass line through the surging waters. Floating debris smacked into their bodies threatening to pluck them away into the waiting darkness downstream. An oil drum, blazing fiercely, crashed into the water to their right. They were only yards from safety when they saw it, in seconds it was surrounded by a spreading raft of burning oil that rushed down towards them.

Wilson, on the 'Eddy's' deck, saw the danger, grabbed a boat hook and leaning out attempted to push the drum clear, but it spun round, slipped by him and again headed for the men in the water.

Desperately the divers reached out for the hands of the men leaning over the stern. Bushel was dragged clear with only seconds to spare. The men grabbed for Burton, the heat from the burning drum searing their bare faces. He was in mid-air, suspended by his wrists, when the drum hit his flailing legs. The drum spun away as he kicked out at it. The legs of his water suit were in flames. Two seamen dunked him back in and, mercifully, the flames were snuffed out by the icy water. He was dragged aboard. The two divers lay, side by side, exhausted, mouths open gasping for air like wet and very oily fish.

Grant cut the engine revs to virtually nothing allowing the 'Eddy' to be swept clear of the bridge and to disappear rapidly into the gloom downstream.

* * *

The second massive explosion ripped through the fjord ten minutes after the 'Eddy' had shot out from under the bridge. It blew one leg, of the towering structure, away from its supporting rock bringing down hundreds of tons of rock that had loomed above it.

The effect was staggering, the tremendous weight of falling rock, crashing down on one end of the metal structure, bent the roadway into an impossible bow. It snapped and sprang back twisting the bridge into an impassable, Chinese puzzle of metal hanging by its one remaining leg.

* * *

The third explosion that lethal night was by far the biggest. The ammunition dump exploded. Blazing oil from the stacked drums spewed out with the force of an erupting volcano. It turned the mountain top into an inferno to rival the devil's own bonfire.

Forty-gallon oil drums shot into the sky, arcing away like great fiery rockets. Exploding ammunition sprayed the mountain with great showers of sparks that flickered the high terrain into dancing light. It illuminated the trotting figures of Hogg and his men as they chased their long shadows west towards the fjord.

* * *

The mess sat drinking their rum and staring in amazement at the lemonade bottle that Wilson held in one grimy hand.

They had secured alongside less than an hour before and their rum had been waiting for them. The irrepressible Wilson had produced the bottle from amongst his kit with great reverence. Inside was a metal shackle that was so big it touched the sides of the narrow necked bottle.

"There you are, I told you I could do it that's 'alf a tot you owe me Nervous." He reached out for the Leading Hand's of the mess's rum.

"Will you hang on a minute," said the Irishman, snatching his rum out of harm's way as quick as any mother would her threatened child. "It's a trick you're after playing…That's never the same bottle…"

"What d'yer think I did … made a bottle around the bloody shackle, I ain't no glass-fucking-blower am I, of course it's the same bottle, you crud. Come on cough up…." He leered lecherously at his Leading Hand while adding, "Put your rum where my mouth is!"

"Arh!…See half it off then, I suppose," said O'Neill, begrudgingly handing a grinning and victorious Wilson his precious tot." Come on then, how did you do it? You sponging bloody rum-rat you!"

"Ha! Ha!" cried Wilson, one finger alongside his crooked nose, "I ain't letting on, am I?" He swigged back lusciously, seeing off half of the Irishman's rum and handed back the rest. "It's for me to know and you lot to guess at. That little trick's won me more rum than a cow's got udder."

"Well," said the Irishmen, his voice full of cunning, "You might as well tell us, 'cause you ain't going to get any more rum out of us, are you now? Not seeing as we know you can do it." He held the remains of his rum up to the light to make sure Wilson hadn't taken more than a fair share.

"Yeah?… Well that's true," conceded Wilson, feeling generous as the rum took effect. He stroked his beard thoughtfully, "Tell you what… a 'gulpers' off the each of yers and I tell yer."

" 'Gulpers'? …Sippers," bargained O'Neill, already half a tot down.

"Sippers!…You got to be bloody joking, I tell you the secret and you use it to get extra rum for the rest of your naval career and for this you're only willing to part with a bloody 'sippers'. You can bugger off the lot of yer!"

"Gulpers seems fair to me," said a voice from the far end of the tot table.

"Now!" slurred Wilson, "There's a man that knows a sound investment when he sees one!"

"Alright then," said O'Neill after a long pause for

sober thought.

" 'Gulpers' it is …if everyone agrees…?" There were nods around the table.

"Right, away you go," ordered O'Neill.

"Oh no!… bloody rum first," said a still cautious, but grinning, Wilson.

"Sure, you're a trusting soul, Wilson do yer know that?" mournfully O'Neill handed over his rum for the second time. Wilson took a generous gulp, and followed it up with, an equally generous gulp from each of the drawing members of the assembled mess.

"Right you bloody rummy, now tell us; before you become incapable of speech."

"All right, all right. But I'm not sure if you lot 'ave the necessary intellect to take it all in…" He bit his lip, looking doubtful, "…but, a deals a deal. You do it with a belt, a locker door knob and a piece of 'airy string… oh and a bucket of cold water; so there you 'ave it."

"And…?" asked O'Neill.

"What'd yer mean, and?"

"And?… And!… fucking and!" half screamed a, by now, incensed O'Neill…Have I to spell it out for you…what… do… you… do… then!"

"What? You mean you want me to show you how to do it and all."

"Bugger off, Wilson," cried Wyatt, "I've sussed you…you robbing bar- steward you ain't getting your hands on no more of my rum!"

"All right!…all right…only joking," said Wilson, grinning and getting unsteadily to his feet. "Where's the bucket of water I used," he reached behind the lockers. "Arh! And there's me 'airy string," he held up half a fathom of ginger sisal. " There's me locker door knob and there…"

"Alright! All fucking right!" yelled O'Neill, "enough of the Houdini shit; get on with it will yer?"

"And 'ere" persisted Wilson drunkenly, "is what you

do. Tie one end of the string to the locker door knob. Stick yer bucket of water 'ere, nice and 'andy and take a lemonade bottle..." He peered around until his eye fell on one with a drop in the bottom, he unscrewed the top and downed the contents.

"Oh, fucking thanks!" said Wyatt, "that was mine, that was, I was fucking saving that."

"Donated to sightific research," slurred Wilson dismissively. "Now you tie the udder end of the string to your belt, sweat back on it like this." He leant back, "... so it's nice and taut, catcha turn around the bottle, so it in the middle of the string like this. Then you push and pull the bottle up and down ....up and down... See that, with the string round it, the bottle's getting hot. You do that until you smell the string burning," He worked away like mad until smoke, from the friction of the string on the bottle, snaked its way up towards the deck head. "And then," he said breathlessly, "quick as a flash... you whips it out of the string and plunge it in the cold water...thus. "There was a crack and one half of the bottle floated to the bottom of the bucket. The men crowded round, Wilson reached into the bucket and retrieved the bottom half of the bottle and carefully fitted the two halves back together again. "You can put what you like in there now." he said, a look of drunken triumph on his plump face.

* * *

Olaf Kristiansand arrived on board shortly after lunch with important news. The situation ashore was changing hour by hour, but he had discovered that following their successes against the British the Germans were moving aircraft, supply and naval bases further forward.

Later, in his tiny cabin, Grant studied the information in detail. Olaf had supplied him a comprehensive list of the new bases. He sat back in his chair, wondering what effect the changes in enemy troop concentrations would have on their operations.

Some of the new bases were closer to 'Orca's' forward base. The inevitable increase in traffic would certainly go hand in hand with an increase in the risk of detection. On the other hand 'Orca' would be that much closer to their targets and that would mean less time spent getting there and back and that might actually reduce the risks.

New bases meant new defences. Possibilities there, new bases took time to construct and it was then that they were at their most vulnerable. Minefields for instance, always a thorn in clandestine operations, they took time to put into place.

A pre-emptive raid now, before Jerry had an opportunity to build adequate defences would have a very good chance of success. Grant leant forward studying the list and carefully plotting their positions on his chart.

There was a new airstrip being constructed at Trondheim. Now there was a tempting target if ever he'd seen one. Large areas by their nature were harder to defend.

If he held a war council straight away it might be possible to mount a raid tonight, delay would only increase the risks. He could see a mountain of difficulties to overcome, foremost in his mind was the little problem of transport. The partially constructed base was several miles from the sea…

* * *

Scharfuhrer Engelbert Baum swore, "Pull over, pull over!" his driver, quickly signalled right and came off the accelerator, in his mirror he saw the two road tankers behind breaking violently.

Ahead a man, caught in the two powerful headlights, was fighting to control two horses as they reared and backed away from him towards the centre of the road.

The farm cart they had been pulling had lost a wheel. The accident had blocked the narrow road completely.

Extracting his ample body from the close confines of his Panzerspahwagen Baum shouted angrily at the carter. "Clear the road immediately."

The sudden and noisy outburst only served to upset the already nervous horses even more. He gestured angrily for his men to lend a hand and clear the road.

The Scharfuhrer waited impatiently, hands on hips, legs astride, the very picture of anger. Clearly this dummkopf of a Norwegian peasant knew nothing of horses, his inept attempts at controlling his animals were only making matters worse.

Already he was behind schedule now this important supply convoy would be further delayed by this incompetent rustic oaf! He drew his pistol, advanced and pointed it first at the man then at his wall-eyed horses.

"Clear this road now, or I will shoot your damn horses and then you! Do you understand me!"

The man almost certainly knew no, but Baum's furious features and the pointing gun had the desired effect and the man renewed his efforts to drag the reluctant horses off the road.

But what was this? He hadn't noticed the peasant women before, two of them standing there behind the cart. In his experience these Norwegian women could be quite beautiful; he stroked at his heavily waxed moustache and stepped out eagerly in their direction. The women were buxom, big breasted, just his type, for was he not 'big boned' himself. He had no objections to the same attributes in his women, in fact he preferred it. Tantalisingly hidden behind those flowered headscarves it was difficult to see if their faces matched the promise of their ample bodies. As he drew near they kept their eyes averted, but he knew they were watching him he could hear them giggling. Of course they were shy! Only to be expected in his presence... So much the better; he liked his women big and shy. He smiled at the charming creatures, curling his lip and raised one enquiring eyebrow, an expression he had practised much in his shaving mirror. He gave his short self-assured laugh.

One turned her head in his direction: she had a large ginger beard. Baum stepping back in surprise, caught a movement to his side, two men clad in white overalls jumped down onto the road, for a second he thought they were German Alpine Troops. Then he heard the shouted commands, British! He looked quickly, over his shoulder back towards the vehicles. His men were being dragged from their cabs. He lifted his hands slowly above his head.

* * *

Midshipman Hope popped his head up through the hatch of the Panzerspahwagen.

"This could come in handy," he said, swinging the heavy machine gun round on its mounting.

Grant leant on the bonnet, MG34, good weapon, but with luck, you shouldn't need it. Remember the plan, park up on the north side of the airfield, we'll meet you there as soon as we can. You have the recognition signal?"

"Yes, sir," said Hope, locking the machine gun into place as Grant sprinted back towards the tankers. "Wilson! What are you doing? I told you to get in the truck."

"I'm 'aving a spot of bother trying to get out of this dress, sir."

"No time for that, man. Get in as you are."

"Easier said than done in this lot, sir" said Wilson hitching up the heavy woollen skirt, exposing his black boots and legs. "Did you notice the legs, sir. I think they're better than the wife's."

"Will you get in!" cried Hope, looking with understandable distaste at the seaman's hairy legs.

"I am , sir." said Wilson as he sat down heavily on the seat, "Just remember I'm spoken for."

Hope grimaced as he turned the key in the ignition and the eight cylinder Horch roared into life. He drove back onto the road and, with headlights blazing, the convoy resumed its interrupted journey.

Behind them some distance from the road, eight, bound and gagged, German soldiers shivered in their long woollen underwear.

* * *

The sentries hastily dragged the temporary barrier from between the newly erected gateposts urged on by the young and foul-mouthed Scharfuhrer in the Panzerspahwagen.

The armoured car pulled over to one side and the two Opel Blitz tankers accelerated past, through the gate and onto the tree-lined avenue that lead to the airstrip.

The older of the two sentries stood with his hands on his hips, shaking his head slowly as he watched the red tail-lights of the lorries swerving erratically away down the slush covered perimeter road.

"Ha!,,, S.S! Did you see that arschloch, barely out of nappies, uniform didn't even fit him, and already he's a Scharfuhrer!"

In the lorry Hope laughed excitedly, "I don't know about you, Wilson, but I'm beginning to enjoy this."

Wilson raised his eyes to heaven and the cab roof, saying nothing. Shortly their headlights blinked out.

* * *

Grant's wheel-spanner moved an inch and then slipped violently so that he rapped his knuckles on the outlet valve. Swearing, he yanked on the spanner once more and the aviation fuel spurted out in a fine mist. He jumped to one side, finding he could now turn the handle easily, he adjusted it so the highly inflammable liquid poured out from the tank at a steady rate.

A few feet away Blake was having no such difficulties with his valve. Grant gave a thumbs up in his direction and they both ran back to their cabs.

The two tankers shot off in opposite directions, fuel gushing down onto the concrete runway beneath them, it spread its way out across the apron and under the neatly parked aircraft.

Grant had been driving for less than two minutes when the engine suddenly spluttered and died. He tried the ignition. The starter motor whirled, but the engine failed to start. He pumped at the accelerator and tried again, with the same result. He turned to a silent Wyatt in the seat alongside him, "It's no good, I think we are out of fuel, but the other tanker should be along in a bit to complete the circle. That's the plan anyway."

"No need to worry then," grumbled Wyatt, "there'll be another one along in a minute…unless, of course, they get into trouble. For all we know they could have run out of fuel and all."

Grant thought for a moment, he knew Wyatt was a cheerful soul, but that didn't stop him being right. "Do you know how to set the timer?"

"No idea, sir," said Wyatt, helpfully.

"I'll do that then…you collect up our gear and…" A sudden blazing white light illuminated the darkened cab.

"Christ!" yelled Grant, "get out quick. We're sitting smack in the middle of a bloody bomb waiting to go off."

They jumped down from the cab with an audible splash; they were ankle deep in aviation fuel.

"Walk round to the back, keep the lorry between us and the light."

Wyatt, still in his peasant women's clothes, lifted his skirts clear and followed Grant. To their initial surprise, no one called on them to halt. It could be the guards thought it was just a tanker in difficulties or it could have just been the shock of seeing a bearded man in a woman's skirt alighting from the cab. Whatever it was, they kept on walking, past the end of the vehicle, keeping in its shadow as much as they could until they emerged once more into the white light. Their luck was not destined to last. They were only yards from the edge of the darkness, when a challenge barked out and a burst of machine fire kicked the tarmac up in their faces.

* * *

"Nein Nein!" screamed a panic stricken German voice from the darkness, "cease firing! Cease firing! The whole area is swimming in fuel! One spark and we are all finished!" The firing stopped as abruptly as it had started.

Grant recognised Hogg's voice immediately and even understood some of what he was shouting. With Hogg clinging to its running board the other tanker appeared in the pool of light and screeched to a halt. The midshipman jumped down and pointed his machine pistol at Grant's belly. "Let's get out of here, sir."

Grant lifting his hands in the air, gesturing for Wyatt to do the same, "Bugger it, Middy! I've just remembered, I haven't set the bloody timer... I'll make a dash for my lorry, you shout for them to hold their fire and then give chase. Don't catch up with me until I'm out of sight around the back of the tanker; that'll give me a chance to set the timer."

He turned running into the blinding beam of the searchlight, feeling terribly exposed despite hearing Hogg behind him doing his bit in German. Thankfully no shots rang out; it appeared to be working. In the cover of the truck at last, he leapt up into the cab and quickly set the timer on the explosives. Hogg arrived close on his heels and waved his vehicle in. Out of sight of the guards Grant crammed himself into an already packed cab and, with Hogg on the running board waving to the searchlight operators, they drove off into the night.

* * *

The headlights of the armoured vehicle flashed twice. Hogg, back in the driving seat once more, stamped the accelerator to the deck and they shot forward like a bat out of hell. They hit the perimeter wire between two line posts ripping them from the ground as they careered on. There was an explosion as one tyre disintegrated, ripped to shreds by the barbed-wire. The tanker crashed on erratically, dragging with it a jumping occasionally airborne section of fence complete with posts.

Clear of the field, they skidded to a halt, leapt down and sprinted across to the waiting armoured car. Barely had they obtained a handhold when it, it began to move, accelerating across the grass as they clung to it for dear life. Suddenly there was a huge explosion behind them and the night sky erupted into light.

Chapter 14

A Change of orders

Swept Channel, Firth of Forth, 2215 hrs, Wednesday, 22nd May, 1940.

"Do you hear there? This is the Captain speaking. As you have probably realised by now we are heading south and not north. Shortly after leaving harbour I received a signal from the Admiralty ordering us to the French port of Boulogne. Our orders are to assist the Dover Patrol in the evacuation of army personnel cut off by the advancing German Army. We will enter harbour at oh eight hundred hours tomorrow morning. That is all."

* * *

Morning Watch, Approaches to Boulogne Harbour, Thursday, 23rd May, 1940.

It was a beautiful spring morning, fresh and clean, already warm with the promise of a hot day to come. The sea oily smooth, sparkled with reflected sunlight. The warship's raked bow cut through the still water sending an arrowhead of tumbling foam hissing down her sides.

Despite the deep beat of the destroyer's engines and the sharp cry of the seagulls overhead it was strangely quiet. The beauty of it all, made the horror that was to come the more bizarre, the more senseless. Its prelude was a deep rumble, rushing in from the distant shore, rolling over them like thunder. The once clear line of the horizon smudged suddenly with drifting smoke, billowing listlessly eastward.

The seamen settled behind their gun-sights preparing themselves like nervous batsmen before the first ball of the over. Every sense stretched taut, trigger fingers tensed, sweating hands gripping tighter. Tired minds began to imagine the worst, the tumbling wake hid a torpedo's track, a distant seagull became a diving aircraft, a breaking white capped wave a periscope.

"Do you hear there this is the captain speaking. We have had another change to our orders. We are now proceeding to a point five miles north of the harbour to give close support to our troops on the ground. We will be carrying out a bombardment in company with elements of a French destroyer squadron.

In addition, the port authorities have requested our assistance with their docking arrangements for the Dover Patrol, who will be entering harbour sometime today. I intend to drop the sea boat with a berthing party under the First Lieutenant at the harbour entrance and then to proceed to the rendezvous point with the French destroyers. That is all."

* * *

As they sailed closer, Boulogne seemed to be completely ablaze. Black smoke, that hid most of the town, rolled out across a debris-strewn harbour.

Barr scanned the installations with his binoculars. Judging by the gunfire the Germans were already in the town. He ordered the sea boat to be lowered.

As if to confirm his worst fears, sniper fire began to rip in above their heads. Through his glasses, he could see puffs of smoke coming from a building on the port beam. He used the ship's engines to quickly swing the 'Nishga' around so as to put her between the snipers and the men working on the sea boat.

The 'Nishga's' four point sevens opened fire with a bark that rumbled off the walls of the old warehouses like a roll of thunder. A full broadside slammed into the second floor of the building turning it into a dense dust cloud. The dust slowly settling, like a falling curtain, revealling the desolation wrought by the four hundred weight of explosive. It had demolished the entire floor; blown clean away as if it had never existed. The sniper fire had ceased, immediate proof, if proof had been needed, of its source.

While the over-laden sea boat began its lonely crossing to the nearby jetty, the 'Nishga' turned sharply to starboard, her screws thrashed into life as if in a fit of temper. She surged forward flashing across the harbour, rapidly working up to full her speed. She cleared the entrance doing twenty knots and began a long lazy turn to starboard.

* * *

The sea boat bobbed madly in the departing 'Nishga's' wake.

While his men leant to their oars, every man anxious to reach some sort of cover, Lieutenant Grey watched the destroyer race away with feelings of acute trepidation, he felt abandoned and very much alone. Ashore, he could hear screams, shouting and the rattle of small arms. The jetty, they were making for was full to overflowing with soldiers, many on stretchers. There appeared to be no discipline some of the men even appeared to be drunk. Standing in the stern, peering through the swirling smoke, he caught fleeting glimpses of another jetty, one that appeared to be deserted. He pointed it out to Petty Officer Stone, standing beside him at the tiller. "Take her in there."

Although they were not receiving any direct fire, spent rounds of ammunition where falling in the water all around them as they nosed their way through the now dense smoke.

Suddenly they were there, seaweed covered wooden pylons towered above the sea boat.

"I'll take her right in, sir, get her under the jetty, she'll be out of sight there and it'll give us some cover."

They bumped gently into a cross strut and quickly passed the stern line around it.

Petty Officer Stone worked his way forward stepping on the thwarts, "It's near enough high tide, lads, so leave plenty of slack on those lines, we don't want to find her hanging down the jetty when we get back."

Fastened to pylon, a rusty iron ladder led to the jetty's wooden decking ten-foot above their heads, pushing off from strut to strut they 'walked'' the boat across to it.

Stone pointed, "I want two men to remain with the boat, keep her in cover, out of sight." You'll do he pointed out his two men. "It'll better be here intact when we get back you got yer rifles use them if you need to, don't let anyone and I mean anyone ,friend or foe, take this boat from yer, understood."

Stone gripped the bottom of the ladder, "The rest of you, up you go."

He held tight to the ladder, the boat rocking as the men made their way for'ard.

* * *

'Nishga'

The French liaison officer climbed the short rope ladder up from the sea boat and stepped onto the 'Nishga's' quarterdeck. He saluted and wished the Officer of the

Watch 'a good day" Together they walked along the iron deck to the break in the fo'c's'le and passing through the Wardroom Flat climbed two more ladders before they reached the bridge.

The four French destroyers were fine on the starboard bow steaming on the same northerly course and running parallel to the coast. The nearest was less than a cable's distance and as the two officers reached the bridge her broadside rang out.

They had arrived unnoticed; all eyes were trained on the shore watching the fall of her shot with professional interest. The target, a line of advancing German tanks, was in plain sight, less than a mile away so the explosions, when they came, could be easily seen with the naked eye. The target was momentarily obscured in a cloud of smoke and dust as the French shells exploded. The tanks, Panzer IIIs, judging by the fifty millimetre guns, trundled out from the other side completely unscathed.

"Bloody Frogs, still can't shoot," remarked the Navigating Officer, without taking his eyes from his binoculars, "you'd think they would have learnt something since Trafalgar."

"Perhaps, monsieur, you would like the opportunity to show us your skills, said the Frenchman, I think it is, 'ow you say in English, your turn now?"

Lieutenant Usbourne went bright red, " I...I do apologise," he stammered. "It was just a joke."

"Ah, yes!" said the French Lieutenant coldly, "the famous English sense of 'umour. I was warned about it before I left my ship."

Barr hid a smile, amusing, but not really the start he would have wished for. He trained his glasses on the distant cape watching the swell marching on the lighthouse at its point. He turned abruptly and walked to the Gunnery voice pipe, his direct line to the Gunnery Officer high above them in the director.

"Engage enemy tanks, green two oh, range two

thousand yards."

He could hear the orders being relayed to the four point sevens.

"Main armament to follow director; target bearing green two oh; range one thousand seven hundred."

"Shoot!"

The full broadside shook the whole ship, the enormous recoil physically pushing the two thousand tons of destroyer sideways. The smoke billowing aft from 'X' and 'Y' turrets shrouded the bridge in its acrid folds before the following wind cleared it away over the bow.

The smoke, however, had not managed to obscure the view from the Gunnery Director. He heard a ragged cheer from above.

" Hit by God!"

"First bloody salvo!" said another voice.

"Bloody wonderful!" came from another.

The French Liaison officer turned his back and walked swiftly to the other side of the bridge. Barr concealed his pleasure behind a harsh.

"GDP control yourselves this isn't a cricket match." The yelling stopped as if a tap had been turned off.

* * *

Lieutenant Grey reached the top of the ladder and peered along the wooden planking that formed the floor of the jetty. At its shore end, less than fifty feet away, stood a ruined brick warehouse, he immediately recognised it as the one 'Nishga's' four-sevens had damaged earlier. Scrambling up the last few rungs he joined Petty Officer Stone kneeling behind the disintegrating remains of a small boat.

"Best keep your head down, sir," whispered Stone, "There's someone in that building. I seen them moving around it might be more snipers."

Just then two men appeared climbing gingerly through

the rubble. More men emerged from the ruins until there were about thirty in all. Some were obviously the worse for drink, all were dirty, covered in brick dust.

"Pongoes, sir; Frogs by the looks of 'em."

"Could be Germans," whispered Grey.

A shake in his voice made Stone look round at him. He was shocked by how pale and drawn he was.

"They're Frogs, all right, sir, I can smell the garlic from 'ere."

Grey peered cautiously over the gunwale of the boat, "Looters do you suppose."

Stone shrugged, Deserters I'd say …most of them haven't got their bundles…I think they've seen the boat."

"My God do you think so."

Stone's assumption was confirmed seconds later when one of the advancing men called out in good English.

" English, we only want your boat, we want no trouble, give us the boat and you can leave.

"Shall I tell them to clear off, sir?

"Erh…I don't want to provoke them."

"Don't you worry, sir. I'm used to dealing with drunks and living with them. Leave it to me. He gestured to his landing party to follow him and rising from cover he marched smartly forward. In the middle of the debris-strewn jetty, he halted and about turned. Grey, still crouching behind the boat, could only admire the man, it was as if he was drilling recruits on the parade ground at Whale Island.

With his back to the advancing mob, he held out his arms. "Form two ranks in front of me, move yourselves!"

His ten-man squad fell in, picking up their dressing, reacting automatically to their training and the sound of his voice.

"Squad!… Wait for it, wait for it! Squad…Shun! High port, arms!"

Stone turned right smartly and marched to the end of the line, where he halted and faced front. "Front rank, one round only, over their 'eads…Present!…Aim!…Fire!"

The volley cracked out, echoing back from the warehouses, reverberating around the dockyard. The effect was as instantaneous as it was dramatic, the rabble froze, stopping dead in their tracks. Then, most turned on their heels and began running back down the jetty scrambling and falling over each other in their haste to escape. The rest, bolder or more foolish than their friends, took cover behind the metal bollards lining both sides of the jetty.

Stone looked across at his officer, he was still hiding behind the boat where he had left him. He hoped the men hadn't noticed.

"High port arms! Order arms! Prepare to fix bayonets…Fix…Bayonets!" The click as the wicked bayonets turned into their sockets was followed by an eerie silence. A silence that seemed to extend beyond the dockyard, it was as if all the fighting and the looting in Boulogne had suddenly stopped and the whole of the city was holding its breath.

Except, that was for Petty Officer Stone, "Squad! Shun! Slope… arms!

By the left… quick… march!

Eleven men stepped smartly off. The remains of mob rose one by one from cover staring at the advancing line of seamen.

"On guard!" Eleven rifles flashed in the sunlight, the seamen marched on, no break in their step.

The sight of the bayonets extended out to the front on the long Lee Enfield were enough. The remaining looters turned and ran.

* * *

Lieutenant Grey peered out from the sandbagged emplacement in which they had set up their HQ. There was a lull in the firing. He could see Petty Officer Stone and his men had resumed working at the shore end of the jetty.

They still had no contact with the port authorities.

Grey came out of cover into the open, looking to left and right he broke into a run out into the open ground. He could feel the fear rising like bile from the pit of his stomach, his hair prickling on the back of his neck. Reaching Stone and his men, he stared aghast at a huge hole they had made in the floor of the jetty.

"What are you doing PO! How are we to get to the shore, how will the troops reach the ships?... For crying out loud!"

Stone stepped in close to the distraught officer, his voice low, so it would not reach the men. "Keep your voice down, please, sir... You'll upset the men. We have to defend our position, that rabble could come back, perhaps with some of their friends, " he gestured over his shoulder towards the other jetty. "A lot of them still have their weapons. I've got the men to lift these planks so they can't just storm in 'ere at will."

Grey looked harassed, gazing at the planks and then at his PO.

Stone could see he wasn't getting through, Grey hadn't heard him. "I'll be our first line of defence, sir. It will make getting onto the jetty more difficult. Once the planks are off, if need be, a couple of men will be able to keep the boat safe.

There was still no response from Grey. "We'll use the planks that we remove to make a gangway, we'll be able to slide it across when we need it." Stone stared at his superior officer with a growing realisation that it was all too much for the man.

Grey nodded, his eyes flickering wildly he turned away and abruptly sat down on a stack of the wood his knees pulled up close to his chest.

"Perhaps it would be best if you returned to the emplacement, sir. I can take charge here."

Grey stood up and without a word walked off.

Stone remained where he was for several seconds,

staring after his superior. Then, conscious that the men had stopped working and were watching as well, he walked quickly after Grey calling out loud, "Where did you say you wanted the Bren situated, sir?"

* * *

Grey was sitting on the floor behind the sand bags, his knees hunched up to his chest, drinking from a canteen, Stone could smell the gin, he swore under his breath, that was all he needed, as if things weren't bad enough. "Good stuff that, sir, but it won't help the rest of us...You've work to do...the men are relying on us. There'll be a time and a place for this." He snatched the canteen from the officer's limp-fingered grasp, "But it ain't here and it ain't now." He crouched down beside Grey. "You'll be better off without it, sir." he added in a gentler ton.

Grey had made no objection, unable to meet the P.O.'s steely blue eyes, instead he stared at the floor. "Can't you see PO..."

Stone could see he was close to tears.

"I can't cope with all... I'm afraid, you see... I've been able to leave this sort of thing..." he swept an arm up and let it fall back down, he took a deep breath, "...to avoid this sort of thing...leave it to the others."

Look, sir, you're as good a bloke as they come, I know that, if there's one thing I'm good at it's judging blokes, you'll do. Take it from me. I know this job inside bloody out... Christ knows I've been enough years at it. Stick close to me, I'll help yer, cover for you if needs be. Take you under my wing, as they say... We're all afraid of something."

"Not Barr not Grant, they aren't afraid of anything," Grey spit it out as if he was accusing them of some monstrous crime.

"Oh they're good officers all right, sir; two of the best. But they're as afraid as the rest of us, take my word for it…either that or they're stark staring mad, one of the two…."

Grey shook his head despairingly, "No, not them!"

"Well, begging yer pardon, sir, I know better, it's all an act …we all do it…. for the sake of the lads and for our mates, but mostly we do it for ourselves, believe you me , we're all as scared as each other…The trick is not to show it."

Grey looked up for the first time.

The Petty Officer stared back for a few moments and then said gently " All you'll need to do is follow my lead, it's the way we all learn… bit by bit, poco y poco, as a Spanish bird I knew used to say. You were thrown in at the deep end when they made you up First Lieutenant, everyone knows that. You'll have to learn while you're doing the job, is all." Stone sat down on the wet boards. "I had longer than you to do it all in. I grew up with good blokes around me on the mess deck. I knew how to act the part even before I'd got my first stripe. You've had it thrust on you all in one lump, that's what's wrong, mark my words. You'll be all right, you see."

"Yes…yes… Thank you, PO."

"That's the stuff, sir…Let's start right away, shall we? Stone smiled the sort of smile you'd give a child on their first day at a new school. "Watch and learn, eh, sir? Watch and learn."

Stone stood up, gesturing to Grey to join him at his side. Loudly he answered an unspoken question. "I see them, sir," he said pointing, "So you want the lads to use them to build shelters at intervals along the jetty."

" Erh…Yes… PO… Carry on."

"Aye, Aye, sir!" Stone said out loud adding, "That's the stuff… sir." under his breath.

* * *

The extra sandbags had been a wise precaution on the

part of the Petty Officer, An hour of steady work had barely elapsed, the seamen were putting the last of them into place when the German snipers returned. Bullets kicked up splinters from the wooden boards, thwacked into the bags, zipping over their heads like angry bees. It would have been impossible to move on the exposed jetty without the hastily erected cover.

The puffs of smoke from the windows of a hotel clearly marked the enemy's new positions. The Bren, returning the fire, managed to keep the snipers occupied while the seamen ran from shelter to shelter with the last of the sandbags. Grey's visual signalman noticed his sandbag getting lighter and lighter. When he reached the end shelter he found a sniper's bullet had slit open one end of the bag and a trail of sand ran back the length of the jetty. He threw it to the boards in disgust and flopped down, his back against the sandbags. He looked out to sea. "Sir!"... he called, "Two warships... just off the headland, to the north!"

Grey's head appeared from the adjacent shelter as the signalman fumbled in his pack to find binoculars. "Destroyers...I think, sir..." He raised the glasses to dirt ringed eyes. That's a 'B' Class leading them in."

By now Grey had his binoculars trained on the distant ships, "By God! Petty Officer, he's right, It's the Dover Patrol! That must be the 'Keith'."

"It's like the cavalry arriving in one of them Yankee pictures, called the signalman.

"Shouldn't we signal them, sir?" asked Stone, wincing as a sniper's bullet kicked up dust at their feet. Grey shuffled back into cover. The signalman, crawling on all fours, appeared dragging the portable signalling lamp. Mind reading was one of the attributes of a good signalman.

" 'Bunty', said Grey, "make the recognition signal to the 'Keith' ask her...ask her..." he fell silent looking at Stone.

"Sorry to interrupt, sir, but she could give us some support against the snipers up in those buildings."

"That's ...what I was about to say, PO."

The signalman nodded lifting his Aldis, he sighted it as if it was a rifle and its light began to dance on the sandbags. Almost immediately, an answering glint of light came from the lead destroyer. The signalman sent the message, fast, pausing only occasionally for the long flash from the warship which showed she was receiving correctly. "They're asking 'where away' sir."

"What was it you said earlier, sir? Something about using the Aldis to pick it out... Wasn't that what you said?"

"Erh?...yes."

" Right, you heard the Officer. Let the 'Keith' know what you're doing and then illuminate the snipers' position. But keep your bloody head down...don't want you getting a packet... my Morse ain't none too good."

The Morse lamp chattered out once more and then the powerful beam of light swung around and steadied on the hotel.

There followed a short silence, Grey watched the 'Keith' through his binoculars. Abruptly there was a puff of harmless looking smoke that drifted lazily away on the breeze. Then an anticlimactic crump, a whistling noise that built to a screaming crescendo as the sighting shot flashed by, high over their head. The explosion shook the old jetty as if they were at the epicentre of an earthquake. A ragged cheer went up from the 'Nishgas', cut short as they ducked to avoid the debris that fell like rain around their position.

* * *

Stone, arms crossed, stood alongside Grey, as the two destroyers crept cautiously through the harbour entrance. "Not that hard really is it, sir?"

"What isn't, PO?" asked Grey, a smile on his face for the first time since they had stepped ashore.

238

The big PO nodded slowly, smiling in return.

The moment did not last long, Grey suddenly grabbed Stone's arm, "Quickly PO! They're not coming alongside here, they're heading for the other jetty. Leave two men here, tell them to pull in the gangway once we're across, the rest to follow me at the double."

Stone's voice boomed out and the men scrambled to their feet, snatching up their rifles, shrugging hastily into their heavy webbing and rucksacks they fell in. Within seconds and at the double, they were moving off in the direction of the other jetty.

It was overflowing with men, dead, alive, wounded, French and British, civilian and military. The Nishgas pushed and shoved their way through, carefully stepping over the wounded and dying as they lay on their makeshift stretchers.

They reached the jetty's edge, just as the 'Keith' came in on her final approach. Here, what had been a cramped and chaotic situation had developed into a hysterical and potentially lethal push and shove to be the first aboard the destroyers. For it was here that many of the drunken, rebellious soldiers that they had encountered at the first jetty had ended up. They were determined to get on the first boat out of Boulogne and to make good their escape before the Germans overran the town. They resisted all the Nishgas attempts to clear them away.

The destroyer came running in alongside the jetty like a steam train entering a station. She slowed, shuddered and came to a stop a few yards out from the concrete side of the jetty. Before even the first lines were passed, men began to jump across the yawning gap, reaching desperately for the destroyer's guard rails. Before anything could be done several fell screaming into the churning waters below. Their heavy kit pulled them quickly under; dying almost unnoticed in the yelling and pushing.

Within minutes the iron deck of the destroyer was overrun with the drunken, hysterical soldiers. Orders were shouted from the bridge and, as if by magic, the mob began to scramble back onto the jetty. Quickly, an area, amidships, began to clear and the Nishgas saw a line of grim-faced seamen advancing bayonets fixed. Quickly, professionally and none too gently, they cleared the deck of their unwanted guests. In their wake other seamen appeared dragging a gangway between them, with Grey's men giving what assistance they could from the overcrowded jetty, it was dragged into place.

With the restoration of order, the destroyer's medical team began the task of ferrying the wounded from the jetty and taking them to relative safety below decks.

HMS Vimiera, rust streaked and soot-stained, glided silently in outboard of her consort. Lines snaked across between the two warships and within minutes she, too, began loading the wounded.

Suddenly shots rang out from buildings across the harbour near to the river mouth. Men ran for cover as bullets chipped sparks from the metal superstructure of the two warships. The fire was accurate and unrelenting. The stretcher-wounded, were still on deck, twitching and groaning as their inert bodies took the brunt of the merciless sniper fire.

The 'Vimiera's' two-pounder opened up in reply and great chunks of masonry flew like shrapnel from around the enemy position. The enemy and the fire faltered and then stopped. Immediately, men ran forward and the loading of the wounded resumed.

The enemy were now in the town in some numbers and remnants of the Guard's Brigade, who only hours before had been landed at Boulogne to protect it for use as an evacuation port, were engaged in fierce hand to hand fighting in and around the old warehouses.

French troops could be seen, on the far side of the harbour, pushing cars and lorries into the water to ensure they did not fall into enemy hands.

The news of the arrival of the ships of the Dover

Squadron quickly spread and numbers of civilians joined the hundreds of people already on the jetty. Men and women pleaded to be taken aboard. Grey's men were appalled to hear British voices amongst them.

During the afternoon, in the thick of renewed sniper fire, the Commanding Officer of the Guard's Brigade came aboard and the rumour quickly spread that the destroyers would be sailing before long.

A little while after the Guard's officer's arrival on board, men from the 'Keith's' crew carried the body of a Royal Navy captain across the gangway. Only hours before he had gone ashore as officer in charge of a demolition team blowing bridges and railway lines.

About mid afternoon, two more destroyers appeared in the approaches to the harbour. Shortly afterwards the short range weapons on the 'Keith' and the 'Vimiera' opened fire again; their target, a high-flying plane which was slowly circling the harbour. It must have been spotting for other aircraft for it made no attempt to approach the two ships and within minutes of its appearance, the drone of approaching bombers was heard. The two-pounder's rapid pom pom beat suddenly ceased. The Nishgas, looking up, saw a flight of Hurricanes had swooped down on the German aircraft, scattering them to the four winds. The fierce dog-fight continued while the men returned to their work. Minutes later the scream of Stuka sirens filled the air and again the seamen ran for cover.

The dive-bombers dropped from the sky, like stones, sirens screaming. The men looking up, could see the bombs, five-hundred pounders, slung beneath the aircraft's bellies like giant yellow eggs. The note of the wing-mounted sirens began to change as they pulled out of their dives. Alongside the 'Vimey', a gusher of water twenty foot high shot into the air. Miraculously the bomb itself failed to detonate, but elsewhere, in the smoke filled dockyard, whole buildings crumpled and collapsed in clouds of dust from direct hits.

Exposed as they were, to sniper fire and shrapnel, the gun's crews on the two destroyers were, inevitably, taking causalities and shortly after the Stuka attack the captain of the 'Keith' asked Grey for men to fill in as loading numbers.

It was a terrible sight that greeted these men as they arrived at the Bofors' guns. Taking advantage of a lull in the fighting, sand was being scattered over the decks where they had become slippery with the blood of the killed and wounded.

There was a sudden loud explosion and a mortar shell landed on the end of the jetty. The throng of people ducked as one. A second explosion tore through the air, even closer to the ships. Evidently the Germans had a spotter somewhere nearby. A third round landed in the water between ship and jetty. Water and stinking mud from the harbour bottom covered the men exposed on the upper deck. Thankfully, the mortar suddenly fell silent, no one knew why, perhaps the crew of the mortar had been hit or they had simply run out of ammunition.

The main force of Germans were very close now, they could be seen, running from cover to cover among the ruined buildings and on the hillside above the town.

Petty Officer Stone ordered the unemployed Nishgas to grab rifles from the 'Keith's' ready-use lockers and return the fire.

Grey appeared, ducking and diving along the length of the upper deck jumping over Kaki figures as he ran. He dropped down, panting furiously, beside his PO.

"Getting a bit close for comfort, Petty Officer."

Stone squeezed the trigger of his rifle and Grey saw a distant German soldier throw his arms into the air and roll slowly down the slope until his body came to rest in a bush. "Excuse me French, sir, but I think it's about time we got the fuck out of here." He licked one thumb and rubbed it across the rifle's foresight. "All our men are back from the 'Keith's' gun crews." He snatched the rifle to his shoulder and fired another round in the direction of the enemy held hillside.

"I'll go up to the bridge and see what's what. Stay here until I get back."

As Grey sprinted forward, intent on keeping as much of the destroyer's superstructure between him and the sniper fire, he heard Stones gravel-deep voice calling. "White, you horrible little sailor, don't bloody well waste ammunition, Mark your target before you fire… the Navy's not made of money, you know."

* * *

Lieutenant Grey climbed the bridge ladder two at a time and arrived to…"Get your bloody head down if you don't want it shot off."

Everyone on the open bridge was crouching behind the armoured screens. Grey could hear a noise like a clipping hammer at work on the exterior plating. Two of the bridge crew were dragging an officer across the deck towards the ladder he had just ascended. Grey recognised the destroyer's second in command. Both his hands were clasping his leg, blood pouring from between white fingers.

The bridge had become like a magnet to sniper fire. "Keep low," yelled the same voice, "They're after the officers, they already got the 'Vimiera's' skipper."

Grey crawled across to the only other officer left on the open bridge; a red-haired, fellow two-ringer. "I'm in charge of the berthing party what do you want us to do?"

"Unfortunately for you, the 'Whitshed' and the 'Venamous' are coming in now. They'll need a berthing party, they'll be taking off more of the Pongoes once we're out of the way. Take my advice and cadge a lift off them when they leave. This place isn't going to hold out for much longer." He shrugged, "But then, I'm not in charge of your chaps, you are old boy, the choice is yours, stay on board if you like, no one will notice in this bloody mess."

Just as a sound powered telephone shrieked suddenly, as a signalman called, "The 'Vimy's' leaving!" The Lieutenant reached cautiously up and pulled the receiver down, from its hook, by its cable.

Grey crawled across the few yards to the signalman's side. The 'Vimiera' was going out stern first, sparks flying from her bridge superstructure as sniper rounds ricocheted off her armour plate. She hadn't even bothered to slip her moorings; she'd gone full astern and snapped them in two, their ragged ends hung down from her fairleads like dead man's hair. As she came level Grey could see an officer hanging over the bridge screen blood pouring from a head wound.

The Lieutenant, now in charge of the 'Keith's' bridge, shouted across, " Our Skipper's bought it, sniper's got him, That was the Navigating Officer on the line. He's taking her out, conning her from the wheelhouse, if you and your chaps are going, you'd better make yourselves scarce."

"Oh!... I'm sorry... about your skipper, I mean... You're' right, we'll have to make tracks...Thanks." Grey crawled backwards towards the ladder as he added "See you in Blighty".

"By God, I do hope so, old chap...I do hope so...Good luck."

As Grey hit the iron deck running, he was already yelling to Petty Officer Stone. "We're leaving, PO, get the men together."

The 'Keith's' engines were already going astern as the 'Nishgas' leapt for the guardrails. As they ran for cover they could hear the berthing wires singing under the strain. There was a huge bang from forward and the remains of the fore spring shot aft, with the power of a bull whip. As the screws madly churned the harbour water to murky froth, another wire parted with a bang and the 'Keith' surged astern.

Grey watched from cover as the destroyer's fo'c's'le flashed by, her decks were still crowded with dead and wounded. The head of the 'Keith's' Navigation Officer bobbed in and out of the wheelhouse porthole as he gave orders to the helmsman. Whenever the helmeted head appeared the snipers ashore opened up and sparks and chipped paint-work showered down like falling snow.

* * *

Minutes after the two destroyers had roared out of the harbour mouth, the 'Whitshed' and the 'Venamous' appeared through the smoke, their guns blazing away.

"P.O!" yelled Grey, "Quick as you can get someone back to the other jetty. I want the men there to stove in the planks of the sea boat, sink her under the jetty."

"Aye, Aye, sir, understood. We'd better wait until the destroyers get alongside, they'll give us some cover."

Grey nodded; he should have thought of that, he turned his attention back to the rapidly approaching warships, now only yards from the crowded jetty. The leading destroyer's for'ard turrets suddenly belched fire and smoke and four rounds of H.E. crashed into a hotel on the water's edge. It was then that Grey noticed the tanks that were her target. The two steel monsters disappeared under a mighty avalanche of dust and brick rubble, the whole front of the hotel had collapsed on top of them burying them completely.

Now that Jerry had tanks in the town, he felt the old panic grip at his stomach, tight as a vice.

Petty officer Stone appeared at his side, "I've detailed the men to take the wires, sir, and I've sent Gordon back to get the lads from the sea boat.

"Good man…Volunteered did he?"

"Not exactly, no sir."

"What do you mean?"

"This is the Navy, sir. You won't get Jack to volunteer. Not unless you bribe them with a tot of rum and we ain't got any of that here, mores the pity."

"That's a very cynical attitude you got there, P.O."

"Cynical...me, sir, no sir...Realistic, maybe."

"So you just ordered this man...what's his name...Gordon to ..."

"Not ordered ...no, sir... You have to use, what's it called... psychology. His nickname's 'Galloping', you see, so I said. 'Galloping', 'You'll do nicely as a runner'. Once his mates laugh, Jack don't like to look as if he ain't got a sense of humour, not in front of his mates. You can get more out of your people with a joke or a bit of friendly abuse then a direct order. But no, you'll never get them to volunteer, sir. Not without the rum..."

* * *

"A lot steadier than that last lot, PO." Grey and Stone stood side by side watching another half platoon of the Guard's Brigade march smartly towards the Whitshed's gangway.

" 'Taffies' sir...Welsh Guards, talk the hind leg off a donkey your Welsh."

"The crew of the 'Whitshed' seem to know them."

"I think it was them what brought them here from Holland a week or so back...How long are we staying here for, sir, any idea?"

"I simply don't know P.O. Your guess is as good as mine."

"And what's your best guess, sir?"

"The way things are going... I doubt if we will be here tomorrow."

"Wouldn't let the lads hear you say that, if you don't mind me saying."

"What? ...Why?...We'll simply cadge a lift off the last warship, sometime today."

"Oh!..Right you are, sir. I thought you meant..."

"Meant what?"

"Oh...nothing, sir...it don't matter."

246

* * *

There were close to two thousand men left on the jetty, mostly Guardsmen with wounded from the rearguard arriving every few minutes. The 'Nishga's' berthing party were exhausted from a day of hard work and of raw fear. They hadn't been able to get away on the 'Whitshed' after all, instead, throughout a long night, they had been employed tying up destroyer after destroyer. A long procession of ships that entered harbour guns blazing and left loaded to the gunwales with men. The last one had sailed at around twenty two hundred hours. As night fell the fighting had died away to spasmodic sniper and machine gun fire, but, despite their exhaustion, they were unable to sleep for long. Fitful cat-napping would be interrupted by a fresh flare up in the fighting and they'd be wide awake again.

Grey had not slept at all; it had begun to prey on his mind that the ten o'clock ship had been the last. An officer on her fo'c's'le had called jokingly ' Don't worry, there's another one coming along behind," but that had been two long hours ago. He pulled his greatcoat up around his legs. It had got colder now, the wind had veered more to the west. He scratched at the stubble on his cheek, what he wouldn't give for a shave. Out the corner of his eye he caught a movement. Shadows were moving out there in the harbour itself. A flare suddenly burst in the hills above the town. There! The flare's glow reflected from something. He was looking at a ship's bridge window. He shook Petty officer Stone. "I think there's something moving out there…there see it."

"Wake up you lot," whispered Stone, kicking out to right and left, "Ship coming in. Get ready to take her lines and keep the noise down, we don't want Jerry alerted."

But the army had seen it too, "Guards! Stand To!" The 'alert' blared out across the harbour from the guard's bugler.

"Can you believe these Pongoes," said Stone. No point in being quiet now, sir."

Another German flare soared into the air, drifting slowly down, its parachute glowing a ghostly white in its trail. In its ghostly light a 'V" class destroyer could be seen edging in towards the jetty.

Two Jerry machine guns opened up from the ruins of the town, their hesitant beat echoing across the water. Around the destroyer's stern the debris strewn water churned into life. Men, standing by her mooring wires, dived for cover behind the fo'c's'le breakwater. A Lewis gun on the port wing of her bridge opened up, tracer ripped away from her and then seemed to slow, dropping onto one of the enemy's gun positions.

Suddenly there was a mighty crack and smoke and flame flashed from her for'ard turrets, lighting the harbour for hundreds of yards around her. It was followed immediately by an enormous explosion. Two-hundred pounds of high explosive, accelerating at 2500 feet per second, slammed straight into the shoreline. The four barrels trained slowly towards the second enemy machine-gun, trailing wisps of grey smoke like slow burning cigars. Ashore, by the dying light of the German flare, figures could be seen running in all directions abandoning the M20 to its fate and that wasn't long in coming. There was another crack and it too vanished behind a firewall of orange and red flames. As the noise of the big guns died away a thousand voices could be heard cheering the 'Vimiera' in alongside.

Three men, lead by Able Seaman Gordon, ran forward from behind the remains of a crane to take the warship's head rope. A heaving line snaked its way lazily through the air towards them.

There was a sudden long burst of machine gun fire. The three seamen started to twitch and jerk violently, in a gruesome and disjointed dance they staggered backwards before dropping to the deck like abandoned rag dolls. The destroyer's port Lewis gun opened up in reply and, too late, the enemy gun fell silent.

Petty Office Stone, even before the firing had stopped, was up and running towards the three still forms. He fell to his knees beside them, quickly he felt for signs of life. An ashen-faced Grey reached his side as the P.O. rose slowly to his feet. Sadly he shook his head to Grey's unspoken enquiry.

A sudden thump followed by a loud explosion sent a shock-wave of men rippling out from the explosions epicentre. A German mortar team had woken up to the arrival of the destroyer. Another explosion and a wooden shelter at the shore-end of the jetty disappeared in a spray of splinters, sparks and choking smoke. The third round was nearer, but fell in the water. The explosions were creeping ever nearer to the gangway where a mass of soldiers were scrambling on board the old destroyer.

"We'd better get aboard quick, sir, I'll get men to bring our dead."

By the red glow of the burning jetty, a duffle-coated seaman dragged Grey unceremoniously over the guard rails saying "Don't, worry, mate, the Navy's 'ere!"

"We've been here for some time," replied Grey dispassionately.

Again the mooring lines were sacrificed as the destroyer went full astern, chased by the explosions from the enemy mortar. The port engine stopped, the whole ship began to tremble, as if in fear. The port engine burst back into thrashing life and the 'Vimiera' seemed to spin on a sixpence. With her bows now pointing at the harbour entrance, both her screws biting deep into the oily water she shot ahead. Working up to her full speed, she roared out of the harbour mouth, trailing black smoke in her bubbling wake. The last the 'Nishgas' saw of Boulogne were the ghostly harbour walls as the final flare hissed itself into extinction.

* * *

Grey was still unable to sleep as the 'Vimiera' tore her way north towards Calais. He sat up on the canvas camp bed and looked around the darkened wardroom. Just about everyone seemed to be snoring it was no wonder he couldn't sleep. His throat was parched and he badly needed a drink. He stood up and picked his way through the mass of men littering the deck. He reached the pantry hatch and looked through, but even that small space was awash with sleeping men. He squeezed through the door and out into the wardroom flat. That too had become a temporary dormitory. He pulled the blackout curtain to one side and opened the watertight door leading to the boat deck. The wind snatched at it, almost dragging it from his hand. It was windy but warm, as he walked aft.

Because of the large number of casualties aboard, the boat party's deck locker had been requisitioned as a makeshift medical annex. Outside the bodies of the dead lay in neat rows. The dead soldiers and a few dead civilians were to be taken back to England for burial. The dead seamen, including the 'Nishgas', were to be given the normal burial at sea, it was due to take place before first light.

As Grey approached the sad line of dead men, the locker door swung wide and a seaman pushed aside the blackout curtain. Inside Grey caught a glimpse of Petty Officer Stone's craggy profile; someone else who couldn't sleep. He pushed the curtain aside and stepped quickly over the coaming into the brightly lit interior. The smell of rum hit his nostrils, Stone was crouched over a strip of canvas laid out on the deck. Palm and needle in hand he was sewing a round seam.

The 'Vimiera's' coxswain stood watching from a corner. "Evening, sir," he said.

At this Stone looked round, a strange expression on his

250

face. The overhead light reflected in his eyes; they glistened with tears.

"Evening, coxswain," said Grey, his eyes and attention still on Stone. "Don't you ever rest, PO, you must be ..." he stopped in mid sentence, through the narrow gap in the seam Stone was sewing, Grey could see the dead face of Able Seaman Gordon. He stood there his mouth open in shock. He had never seen a man being sewn up in a hammock before. It was like a door slowly closing never to be opened again. While a silent Stone continued his gruesome task, he watched mesmerised simply unable to turn his eyes away. The well known face of Gordon was stitch by painstaking stitch slowly disappearing leaving only the grey and featureless canvas.

"I thought you never volunteered, Petty Officer," said Grey strangely annoyed by the man's silence, "or doesn't that apply to Petty Officers."

"It applies to all of us," said Stone breaking his silence and sounding more than a little drunk. "You don't volunteer for anything for nothing. Me I get this." He lifted a chipped enamel mug from the deck beside his foot. "One for each of these poor buggers. Have a 'gulpers', do you good. Made from sugar that is. They're right when they say you can do anything on a tot of good rum."

Grey took the mug as Stone turned back to his stitching. He raised it to his lips, the fumes heady, strong, rich with the smell of fermented molasses. He sipped at it, coughing as the raw spirit hit the back of his throat.

It was as well that he'd taken something to fortify him, for the next stitch brought the bile clawing up into his mouth. Stone gave a grunt of effort as he pulled the three inch steel needle through Able Seaman Gordon's canvas covered nose. Grey downed the rest of Stone's rum in one swallow.

Stone took the mug from Grey's shaking hands and held it out to the 'Vimiera's' coxswain, "That's another one you owe me 'swain. The old sailor produced a wooden keg from the table behind him and splashed an unmeasured gill or two into the pint mug, shaking his grizzled head in silent admiration as he did so.

*　*　*

A lightship rose and fell gently in the westerly swell, her light waxing and waning with the crest and the trough. A faint light already painted the eastern horizon. The warship too rose and fell, mirroring the lightship's movements in a slow and rhythmic pas de deux.

Her lower deck had been cleared and her ship's company stood bare heads lowered. The chill dawn breeze lifting their collars, sending ripples of blue down their swaying ranks.

The captain, closed his prayer book and stood to one side. The last of the destroyer's own dead had passed shrouded into the deep. Petty Officer Stone stepped forward to take his place. Only the 'Nishga's' fallen lay there now, three lonely and silent bundles, like three canvas cocoons. Stone opened his prayer book and took from it a slip of paper.

"This is a very old seamen's version of Psalm twenty three, given to me by my father before he died. I read it at his funeral and I would like to read it over my shipmates now." In a low deep voice he commenced to read from the slip of paper as it flapped in the fitful breeze.

The Lord is my pilot; I shall not be lost.
He lighteth me across the dark waters. He leadeth me through deep channels.
He keepeth my log. He guideth me by the star of holiness for His name's sake.
Yea, though I sail through the storms and tempests of life I will fear no evil;
for He art with me; His love and His care shelter me.
He preparest a haven before me in the home port of

Eternity;
He quieteth the waves with oil; my ship rides calmly.
Surely sunlight and starlight shall be with me wherever I sail,
and at the end of my voyage I shall dwell in the port of my God for ever.

    The words drifted out over the swell, like the departing ghosts of the dead seamen, lost forever in the eternal sea.

Chapter 15

Confusion to the enemy

Abruptly the 'Eddy's' bridge team were jerked from their middle watch lethargy by the lookout's cry.

"Green one five!... Ship!... Near!". Binoculars shot to tired eyes as fast as a gun from a cowboy's holster.

To starboard of the lowered and lashed jack staff, the stern of a stubby coaster ducked in and out of the swell.

"Slow ahead!" Grant turned to check that the other boats, astern of him, had cut their speed in turn. The third boat in the line, Kendel's Dirty Five, swerved violently out of line, just managing to avoid smashing into the stern of Crosswall-Brown's boat. Kendel's crew would have to buck up; he'd have a word.

"There's two of 'em now," called the lookout.

He trained his glasses ahead... but the 'Eddy' had dropped astern with the speed reduction and both coasters had disappeared back into night's black shadow.

"Half ahead, Middy... And take the con, when we overhaul them, match their speed, knot for knot, keep station on them just in sight."

"Yes, sir; enemy coastal convoy?"

"Could be, or maybe stragglers from one... Signalman! Stand by with the hooded lamp, I'll be wanting you to make, to the flotilla, 'Desire to communicate.' But wait for me to give you the nod."

Ahead the ghost like sterns faded in and out of the darkness as the Midshipman kept station astern. "That's about it, sir," he looked at the rev counter. They're making a good fifteen knots."

Grant let his binoculars hang by their lanyard, "Fast for a convoy? Very good... Stop engines."

The sterns of the two boats ahead disappeared into the night. "Right signalman... make your signal." the signalman turned his duffel-coated back and there were three quick flashes of the red light.

The three boats manoeuvred in towards their flotilla leader. Grant tapped the top of his head and the four boats nudged even closer huddling together like a school of conspiratorial dolphins.

He cupped his hands around his mouth to call above the snarl of the twelve massive engines.

"It looks as if we have enemy shipping ahead of us. I propose to scout ahead, see just how many we have. Form line abreast, one cable apart, revolutions for fifteen knots course north twenty east. If you hear firing you'll know I need help, otherwise stay back and await my signal."

The three skippers waved their arms above their heads and Grant, his face illuminated by the faint light from the compass, called over his shoulder, "All engines full ahead... Steer north twenty east."

"Steer, north twenty east," called O'Neill, placing his thick sardine sandwich to one side and leaning closer to the glow from his compass.

* * *

Ahead of the 'Eddy' the coaster's sterns appeared once more, drifting into blurred focus out of the darkness. "

Revolutions for fifteen knots, Middy. Match their speed again and in a bit we'll swing around them, leave them to seaward and take a closer look ahead of them."

Ten minutes later the enemy boats, two fully laden coal burning coasters, were abeam of Grant's boat. They showed no signs of having noticed the E-boat against the black of the land mass. Grant took his time in a careful study of them through his powerful glasses.

"They're Jerry coastal stuff, all right, and heavily laden, but where's their escort?…Come to starboard Middy. Once they're out of sight increase to maximum speed, we'll get ahead of them and see what's what."

Twenty minutes later the signalman sighted a much larger convoy. In the vanguard, as escort, they had a solitary destroyer.

"Looks as if you were spot on, sir, the other two were stragglers trying to catch up."

The signalman closed his copy of 'Jane's Fighting Ships' with a satisfied snap, She's a Maas Class, five five inch, eight tubes and the usual AA stuff.

"What are we going to do, sir?" asked the Midshipman.

"I was thinking of playing a little game with Jerry convoys; this may be just the opportunity."

"Game, sir?" asked the bemused midshipman. "What kind of game."

"Hands, Knees and Bumps-a-Daisy," said Grant.

Midshipman Hope strained his eyes to see the face of his superior, and his brain to remember the exact wording in King's Regulations covering assuming command of one of His Majesty's Ship should her captain become mentally ill.

* * *

Crosswall-Brown, aboard M.T.B. 34, glanced anxiously at the clock above the tiny chart table. He drummed his fingers impatiently on the open chart, "The 'Eddy's' taking her time, can't abide this waiting." As he lifted his binoculars to the northern horizon the radio operator called from below.

"Message for decoding, sir. It's from the 'Nishga'. "

Crosswall-Brown lowered his glasses, "See to it, Middy, will you?--- Don't reply, maintain radio silence," he resumed his contemplation of the horizon. Come on 'Eddy' for Christ's sake!

* * *

The 'Eddy' was also waiting, engines stopped, crew listening for the enemy's engine noise. Their vigil was short, the deep throb of diesel engines washed in and out on the stiff breeze.

"Signalman! Hoist the German flag and stand by with our own ensign in case we need to open fire."

"There they are sir!", called Maurice. The two stragglers materialised, grey phantoms floating in a heaving black sea.

"Very good... Signalman hoist the international flags for, 'Stop immediately...follow it up with, 'You are standing into danger'." The yellow and black chequered bunting broke at the stumpy masthead followed by the red and white squares of the danger flag.

The two coasters lost way and stopped, a cable to the south of the E-boat, rolling heavily in the beam sea, a signal lamp flashed from the leading boat.

"She wants to know where the danger is, sir".

"Ignore her... Make to the M.T.B. 34, she'll be somewhere astern of the coasters, 'M.T.B. 35 and the 'Ethel' to board enemy vessels, Drill 3', add, 'Close on my position'."

* * *

On M.T.B. 34 Crosswall-Brown saw the flashing Aldis lamp at the same time as his eagle-eyed signalmen . "Full ahead both." He took an involuntarily step backwards as the powerful M.T.B. shot forward.

"Coasters…two of 'em…straight ahead."

"I see them…"

The 'Eddy' was signalling again.

Minutes later the signalman flashed a final 'T' . "From the 'Eddy', sir. 'Be advised large enemy convoy ten miles to the north of my position. Escort one Maas Class destroyer. Intend we both engage enemy destroyer, follow me'. Message ends."

"Signalman make to "Dirty Five" and to the 'Ethel' board the enemy coasters…. Port ten, steer North West, Full ahead all engines. Hoist battle ensigns….Drill Three eh Middy? Now this should be interesting."

"Should I know Drill Three, sir."

"You mean you don't know Drill Three… it's in Commander Barr's Flotilla Orders."

"Sorry, sir, no, sir."

"It's famous, you've got some reading to catch up on."

"Yes, sir, sorry, sir. But what so famous about it, sir, drill Three I mean."

"Drill Three is Hands, Knees and Bumps-a-Daisy."

The midshipman nodded once, an uncertain smile on his young face. He must really catch up on his reading of these Flotilla Orders.

* * *

'Ethel'

On Hogg's 'Ethel' another Midshipman's moment of glory had come. "Middy you have the command, I'm to take charge of the First Armed Guard, we're going in, starboard side to."

The midshipman's eyes lit up; speechless, he only just

258

remembered to salute before his Captain hurried away. In 'moments of glory' there is a marked tendency to forget the mundane.

"Fenders!" called Hogg, the fo'c's'lemen kicked them deftly over the side seconds before the two boats bumped gently alongside each other.

Sub-machine guns at the ready the 'Ethel's' seamen scrambled across on to the enemy deck.

The enemy crew offered no resistance, confronted with the heavily armed patrol boats, bewildered by the presence of the two E-boats and facing men who seemed to be everywhere at once, they could have done little else. Hogg took a long look at his new command, it was only then that he realised why there had been no resistance. A red flag fluttered at the foremast's yardarm, she was carrying something nasty.

It was a similar story on the other prize, no shots fired, no resistance offered.

* * *

The crews from the two German coasters sat, subdued, crammed shoulder to shoulder in their bobbing lifeboats, drawn up in the lee of the 'Ethel'. Hogg leant over the bridge screen and shouted down something in German, pointing ahead as he did so. Two English seamen threw the head ropes down into the boats. They slowly drifted away to windward. Then with a powerful growl, a shower of sparks from their triple exhausts the patrol boats raced off after the two coasters.

"Why have we taken the oars from the lifeboats, sir?" asked the troubled Midshipman.

"Don't worry we'll be back to pick our prisoners up later. We haven't the room or the men to spare for guarding prisoners. We don't want them to get away to inform the authorities of our presence. Keep the bastards guessing…always the best policy. Anyway I've a feeling they would rather be where they are than where we are about to be."

* * *

Hogg's Command

Hogg had always thought that Drill Three was a kind of joke, something Barr had thought up after a gin too many, never meant to be taken seriously. It just went to show how wrong you could be when dealing with a C.O. of Barr's calibre. It looks as if the time to deliver the 'punch line' was very near. He was now Captain of an enemy coaster, and had been for the best part an hour, and now, ahead of his new command, he could see the rest of the convoy.

"Coxswain!"
"Sir!"
"Steer for the stern of Tail-End Charlie."
"Aye, aye, sir."

He swept the horizon to their front, no sign of the escort yet, presumably she's still out in front leading the way home, hopefully she was oblivious to the mortal danger her charges were in; and long may it remain so.

He took a quick glance astern. Through salt-stained bridge windows he could see no sign of the flotilla. Out to port the other captured coaster was keeping station, under the steady hand of Petty Officer Stone. According to Drill Three she should be steering for the next to last coaster in the enemy convoy.

The convoy ahead seemed unaware of their presence; there was no sign of the crews, no sign of flashing lights. They could be under orders not to use lamps for fear of giving away their position, or it could simply be merchant seamen's legendary failure to keep a proper lookout astern.

"Coxswain are the First Armed Guard ready?"
"Aye sir, they're keeping a low profile, aft of the

funnel, as you ordered."

Hogg looked across at Stone's coaster, rolling lustily as she forged ahead. He could see a group of three or four men moving about just aft of her bridge structure; Petty Officer Stone's First Armed Guard were also in place. He peered ahead into the darkness, somewhere out there, Grant and Crosswall-Brown should be about to cross swords with the enemy destroyer, rather them than me, he thought, guiltily.

"I'll take the wheel now, Coxswain, you get down with your mates."

* * *

Grant and Crosswall-Brown sighted the enemy escort, almost simultaneously, it was a little before one o'clock. On the edge of the darkness, they matched her speed, biding their time, waiting for the diversion to begin at the rear of the convoy.

* * *

Hogg's Command

The bow of Hogg's coaster smashed into the rudder post of the enemy coaster, there was a grinding, tearing screech and the entire mechanism, wrenched from its fixings, dropped into the sea. The coaster's bow careered on, burying itself deep into the stern planking. Immediately the enemy coaster began to founder. The klaxon on her bridge belched forth and her crew made their first appearance on deck. Not to resist, but to panic, running for the lifeboat, shouting and pushing each other aside. Completely ignoring Hogg's coaster, they began frantically to cut the lashings away. Hogg could see there was no need to board her, her after decks were already awash. She was obviously going to sink unaided and very quickly. He shouted for his men to stay back out of sight behind the bridge.

Amid the scream of metal on metal and the crack of splintered planks, at full astern, the boat dragged her way astern and the two ships wrenched and tore themselves apart. He rang for full ahead and spun the wheel hard over. She gathered speed, clearing the other ship's stern they passed rapidly down her port side.

On a madly tilting deck, the stricken vessel's crew were labouring to launch her boat, they looked up as one. The hope of rescue on their faces was short lived, it turned rapidly to bewilderment as they caught sight of the White Ensign snapping at their consort's yardarm. Hogg felt a tinge of pity, they were not going to free their lifeboat from her chocks, not with the list that was already on her. It was a long, cold swim to shore.

But he was having problems of his own, the old coaster, initially handling well, was now sluggish, answering the wheel slowly. Something was amiss.

* * *

'Wagner'

Leutnant Ankar, had the watch on the bridge of the Maas Class destroyer, 'Wagner'. He jumped hastily aside as his captain rushed by and out onto the bridge wing. It was only then that he heard the wail of a coaster's klaxon blaring out from the starboard quarter. Under cover of the dark Anker pulled a face; Freggatenkapitan Linz had been in a reasonable temper only seconds before, now, he was his usual furious self.

"Now, what is the matter with these verdammt stupid merchantmen they have been a bloody nuisance ever since we left Bremerhaven. They are disobeying orders again! Standing orders clearly state that silence must be maintained unless we are under attack." He swept the horizon astern once more, dropped his binoculars onto their lanyard in a show of impatience and raised both hands, dramatically, above his head. "I see no signs of an attack! No explosions! No flares! They are like old women."

Back in the bridge he slumped into his chair, calmer now, he sighed wearily, "I suppose we had better go and see what the matter is." Reluctant resignation apparent in his shrill voice he added, "I expect one of them has run out of coffee! Come to starboard, Leutnant, we will circle these dummkopfs, that call themselves a convoy, and see if we can find out who is making that infernal racket... Signalman! See if any of the dolts can read Morse, make 'What is the matter now'."

Ankar passed the necessary orders and stayed at the compass as the warship began the fast turn, signal lamp flashing.

"Mein Gott! Herr Kapitan, Look flames!"

* * *

To the north, ahead of the German escort and her irate captain, the banshee wail of the siren was also heard on 'Eddy's' bridge.

Grant's gamble, that the escort would pass to seaward of the convoy to keep herself between it and the open sea, had paid off. He had positioned Crosswall-Brown's 34 to the south ready to receive the escort as she turned to go to the aid of her charges. "Switch on navigation lights, hoist the German flag, half ahead both engines."

* * *

Crosswall-Brown's 'Dirty Four' came bouncing in from the southeast, leaping the troughs between the waves like a steeplechaser clearing fences.

The 'Wagner' spotted her almost immediately. The two vessels were closing at a combined speed in excess of sixty knots.

With a roar like thunder the destroyer opened fire, a full broadside from her main armament. The extremely accurate first salvo fell about the speeding M.T.B., spouts of water twenty-foot high, adding to the watery turmoil about her. Still she came on, weaving in at high speed, sending great sheets of green water shooting from her glistening sides with every turn.

The destroyer was altering towards, changing her attitude to the attacking enemy, preparing herself for the expected torpedoes. Now bow on she was ready to comb their tracks, to present as small a target as possible. Her after turrets, unable to bear on the target, fell silent.

* * *

'Wagner'

On the bridge of the 'Wagner', Leutnant Ankar was truly amazed, Kapitan Linz was actually ecstatic. It was the first time in two years the Leutnant had seen his Kapitan show any emotion, other than anger that was. He knew what had brought about this abrupt change. This was Linz chance to get to grips with the 'accursed' Royal Navy since the acute embarrassment with that E-boat off Vikjord.

A signalman appeared at Linz's side, he had to shout to make himself heard above the crash and the roar of the for'ard guns, "Patrol Boat signalling to starboard Herr Kapitan."

Kapitan Linz tore his eyes from the fall of shot, a haunted look on his face, "Ours?"

"Affirmative, the S342, sir."

"Are you sure?…You'd better be sure! You understand me? Do you hear me! I don't want any repeat of that…that last fiasco." The Freggatenkapitan voice was ascending an octave with each clipped word.

"The call sign is correct, Herr Kapitan," said the young

signalman, a touch indignantly, after all the Kapitan's 'Grobe Scheibet', as it was known, had nothing to do with his branch. "We've double checked Fleet Movements, Herr Kapitan, she is part of the 5th Schnellbootflotille," he added reassuringly.

"All right, all right! What's the verdammt message!" Linz raised his glasses to watch the fall of shot. "Over! Over! Down one hundred! Not up! Must I do everything myself! Get me the Gunnery Leutnant!"

"Message reads..." started the signalman.

"Give me the gist of it, boy, the gist! Can't you see I'm busy here!"

The signalman took an involuntary step backwards, "She... erh... She offers us assistance, sir."

"Does she, well, tell her to get the hell out of my war!" ... He took a deep breath squeezing his lips together to regain control... "No, tell her to check out that fire to port."

He dismissed the signalman with one irritated wave of a gloved hand, his eyes still glued to the glasses. "That's better! That's better! No need for that, no need for that." He waved the gunnery telephone aside, "Good shooting! Good shoot..." The words died on his lips as the enemy boat shot clear of the curtain of water unharmed, springing from its saturated folds, like a glistening silver dolphin, its White Ensign snapping at the tiny masthead.

* * *

Hogg's Command

On the bridge, a bell rang abruptly and, above the voice pipes, a red light began to flash intermittently.

Hogg stepped across, unable to read the brass label under the light, he quickly raised the lids on all the voice pipes. It was the engine room.

"Sir, we're making water fast... permission to get out."

"How deep?"

"Over a foot now, sir."

"Very well...Get up on deck, leave the engine at full ahead, how long do you think we'll have power for?"

"Difficult to say...twenty minutes...less."

"Alright, get out of there, join the First Armed Guard abaft the bridge."

He looked quickly round. The nearest undamaged coaster was still about a cable away, on the port bow, she was low in the water, heavy with cargo.

He spun the wheel hard over and the bow began a sluggish turn to port. He eased the wheel as the swing increased and then rapidly put on opposite wheel to stop her. They began slowly to overhaul their new target. Suddenly, ahead of her, there was a massive explosion, it split the blackness apart in a vivid burst of light. In its dying after-glow Hogg could just make out Kendel's 'Dirty Five', under full helm, swinging clear of her blazing prey.

He put on ten degrees of port wheel, then had to increase it to twenty, she was very slow to answer, her head was noticeably down with the weight of water she had already taken onboard. He swore and hit the wooden helm in frustration; she had the manoeuvrability of a fat tired cow. He left the wheel, ran to the after bridge window and shouted down to the men gathered in the warmth from the funnel. "Prepare to board!...we're going in... starboard side to." He turned back to the spinning helm, grabbed at it and looked across at the target, his blood ran cold. In the light from the blazing coaster, he saw the target's swaying decks were crammed with enemy soldiers.

* * *

'Eddy'

Grant was gripping the bridge windscreen hard, teeth clenched as he watched Crosswall-Brown's heroic attack on the destroyer. "Signalman make to the enemy destroyer

'Do you need assistance?'."

The 'Eddy' was rapidly overhauling the enemy warship, coming up from astern, all going according to plan. It was all very well on paper, but would he be in position in time to save his friend from those terrible guns. The consequences of failure did not bare thinking about. He was the senior officer, it was his action... his responsibility...and it was Charlotte brother, of all people.

* * *

Hogg's Command.

Hogg rubbed at his forehead, desperately trying to think...A bloody troop carrier...he couldn't have chosen worse...but it was too late to change plans, if they didn't get off this old tub and pretty damn quick, they were going down with her. With the engine room abandoned, he couldn't even slow the old girl down, give himself time to think. He spun round looking for another target. There was nothing! Bloody nothing! There seemed to be coasters everywhere, but nothing near enough that wasn't either on fire or already sinking.

Counting the two men that had been down below in the engine room, he had eight men against, what appeared to be hundreds of soldiers on the target's deck. Impossible odds!

Shielding his eyes from the blaze of the coaster they were passing, he took another look at the troop carrier, as he did he caught sight of the red flag his own coaster was flying ...If only the new target had been carrying something else, even explosives anything other than bloody troops...it was then that it hit him, Ammo!...Blazing!...Of course! He yelled down to the men by the funnel. "Coxswain! Send two men aft with oil and rags, light a fire on the quarter deck, a big one, and then get up here at the double."

In less than a minute the burly leading hand appeared at his side, "Rummage through that flag locker, see if you can find a yellow and black striped flag...hurry man...that's it... and... that one," he pointed, "no that one, the red and white one!...now get them both hoisted quickly, as quick as if your life depended on it...because I think it does."

* * *

'Eddy'

The 'Wagner's' lamp was flashing its reply as the 'Eddy' steadily overhauled her. Range half a mile. Hopefully steering the same course would convince her skipper of his 'good intentions'.

"What are they saying now Middy?"

The middy looked up from his crib sheet. "They seem to have fallen for it, sir. They want us to check out a fire in one of the convoy's ships, told us to leave the 'English upstart' to them.... oh! And they bid us welcome!"

"Jolly nice of them! Let's hope we can repay their hospitality in a manner unbefitting their cordiality."

They slowly crept up the destroyer's starboard side, range about two thousand yards. The midshipman was taking compass bearings all the time and relaying them to Grant. He waited impatiently...Now, he thought... now's the time.

"Full ahead all engines. Hard a port!...Steady. Action torpedoes! Signalman! Pull down that rag!...Hoist our colours! The bow steadied, pointing directly ahead of the charging destroyer as the men rushed to their stations.

He took a quick bearing himself, squinting across the compass, bracing himself against the bucking of the madly accelerating E-boat. Just about right, with the turn to port he would be in the classic attacking position with a perfect, fat, beam-on target.

* * *

Hogg's Command.

The Coxswain bundled the flags under one arm and, running across to the ladder, began to climb quickly to the flag deck above the bridge.

Hogg looked aft, he could see black smoke already billowing across the water. He yanked on the whistle lanyard above his head and the klaxon on the funnel screamed its alarm.

A hundred yards ahead he saw the faces on the coaster turn sharply in his direction. He could see a figure on the bridge looking up at the newly hoisted flags; 'Dangerous cargo'… 'Keep clear'… You are standing into danger'.

On the other vessel's bridge he could see a man frantically shouting down to the soldiers. Whoever it was he knew his flags, men began to panic, there was a visible surge towards the fore end. The crowded deck became a death trap, men were trampled underfoot, suddenly a guard rail gave way, men poured from the gap in a human tide. Fifty yards to go and he could see that men were jumping over the side of their own free will, abandoning their fire arms, helmets, back packs anything that could weigh them down, some even struggling with their heavy boots. The water was alive with men.

Through his glasses he could see the looks of horror on their faces as the blazing coaster bore down on them, flying the flags that showed it was loaded with explosives, on fire and out of control.

The starboard side of Hogg's coaster ground into the port side of the troop ship, he ran from the bridge, calling to his men to follow him. He led them in a mad charge for'ard. Drawing his revolver, he jumped up onto the gunwale, balanced momentarily and then leapt over onto the enemy's deck. His men were not far behind.

A soldier appeared from behind a ventilation shaft rifle raised, Hogg squeezed off a quick shot, it missed and the man disappeared from view. The coxswain, at his side, put five rounds through the thin metal of the shaft and the man stumbled out from cover, crumpling to the deck.

With the engines still at full ahead, the ammunition ship, ground her way down the length of the abandoned troop ship, ripping and splintering the planking like a crazed chainsaw. Clear of the bow and still at full speed, she sailed on, her stern now completely enveloped in the flames.

Shouting orders at the top of his voice, Hogg split his boarding party into two sections. He sent one group, under the coxswain, forward and he took the rest in a sweep of the after deck.

* * *

'Eddy'

The two torpedoes belly-flopped into sea, their propellers already turning, churning the surface of the sea to lather, but all was not well, no sooner had the starboard torpedo cleared the boat's side, then it veered erratically to port. It was crossing their bow as they roared in towards the enemy destroyer.

Simultaneously the destroyer's 'X' and 'Y' turrets opened up, close range, accurate fire, cascading water across the entire length of the tiny boat, soaking the men at their guns, obliterating Grant's view of the rogue torpedo.

Near miss after near miss, denied Grant a sighting of the torpedo. Desperate, he yelled "Half ahead all engines." The last thing he wanted was to run down his own torpedo. Instantly the bow dropped and the boat lost way, hopefully the torpedoes were well ahead, but he couldn't be sure, but a new problem had raised its ugly head; the destroyer's gun layers now had a target moving at a fraction of its former speed.

Grant swore, this was no good, any second one of the enemy's rounds would find its target, that's all it would take, one round. He dismissed it from his mind. He could do nothing about that or the rogue torpedo except pray. He would have to take a chance, the torp should be clear and still turning to port.

"Hard astarboard... Full ahead all engines!" The diesels roared, jerking the boat forward. With luck he had slowed the charging E-boat just enough for her to turn in behind the torpedo. The trouble was now he was turning onto the same course as the enemy and would present a juicy beam target to their hungry guns. "Middy get aft, make smoke."

The Midshipman looked blank, "The smoke maker man! Ignite the smoke maker!"

The youngster turned, jumped down from the tiny bridge and began to claw his way towards the stern. The E-boat, turning through the swell, bucked like a mad horse at a rodeo, successive waves slammed into her side with the clap of thunder.

Grant snatched a look over the port bow, the sudden turn had thrown the enemy gunners and the madly churned water from their exploding shells was now way aft of the beam. At last he could see the destroyer, she was turning towards the surviving torpedo's track. God alone knew where the rogue one was. They had a few seconds respite as the destroyer's 'X' and 'Y' turrets fell silent, obscured from their target by their own superstructure. The silence lasted but seconds, for the enemy's 'A' and 'B' turrets swung round changing target from Crosswall-Brown's to Grant's boat. They were too late, before they could open fire, the E-boat completed her turn and with her stern towards the enemy, black smoke began to bellow from the smoke maker.

* * *

'Ethel'

Crosswall- Brown was soaked to the skin, water washing backwards and forwards across his feet, but it all went unnoticed because before him, to his utter amazement, the enemy destroyer was turning, until, beam-on, she presented him with the target of his dreams.

"Stand by tubes," 'he yelled ecstatically. He could see the reason for the destroyer's suicidal action. Grant's E-boat was rising on the swell, cresting a wave, she was directly ahead of the enemy, for a moment she seemed to hover there, perfectly balanced on the top of the wave, then, like a leviathan, she sank from sight into the cavernous trough. Grant was risking his boat to give him the target he wanted. Drill Three was no joke, that was for sure! It was bloody working

He yelled "Standby," Then…"Launch!…Launch!…Launch!" Even above the roar of the diesels and the crash of the destroyer's salvo. He heard the hiss of compressed air from the tubes.

* * *

'Wagner'

Kapitan Linz rushed out on to the bridge wing, the track of one torpedo was passing the stern, a transient band of ghostly white bubbles. Where was the second torpedo? The renegade E-boat had fired two. His eyes darted across the sea, panic building in his chest like an inflating balloon. Nothing! Mein Gott, the M.T.B.! Had he been concentrating on the wrong boat. He saw it now, the diversion… Fool! He charged across the front of the bridge to the other wing sending two sailors flying. There they were, two tracks running straight and true, one could pass ahead the other astern, or was he mistaken? They seemed to be converging, both would hit. He had to do something, to turn away now would be to take a hit in the stern, the screws! The rudder! Better to lose the bow than the stern. He ran back into the bridge screaming "Hard aport! Hard aport!" He spun round to look aft, the shearing light and heat of the explosion hit him, a split second later and the blast threw him across his bridge.

The whole forward end of the warship lifted out of the water. The released energy of five hundred pounds of Amatol shook the huge destroyer as if it were a toy, a mere model. A second later she fell back into the sea a shattered wreck.

* * *

'Ethel'

"Yes! Yes!... Yes!" screamed the Midshipman, water streaming from his oilskin as he leapt up and down like a possessed seal.

They were turning away, fast to port, away from the stricken destroyer, leaning away from the tight curve they sliced through the water at thirty knots.

On the beam a huge fireball was rising into the air above the enemy's fo'c's'le. Somehow, miraculously, her guns were still firing. Aft of the M.T.B. towering columns of water shot into the sky exactly where they had been only seconds before. The deck beneath his feet began shuddering under the strain of the fast turn.

Crosswall-Brown could clearly see the damage on the enemy boat, her entire fore-end had gone. Through the gaping hole he could see smoke-blackened watertight doors, electric cables and trunking hanging obscenely down into the water like the entrails of some huge beast. The bridge was still intact and the flicker of orange from her guns, told their own tale. Fatally damaged she may be, but by God, she was as dangerous as a wounded Goliath.

* * *

Kapitan Linz staggered to his feet, scrambled across to the shattered glass of the bridge screen. His hat flew from his head in the sudden gust of air rushing in to replace the huge fireball soaring into the air above his beloved 'Wagner'. Black smoke dispersed briefly, to reveal the colossal damage. What was left of the fo'c's'le bulged upwards in a hideous curve, at its summit one of the capstans hung over the hole where the bow had once been. "Stop both engines, Ankar! Phone down tell them to make smoke. We're a verdammt sitting duck."

* * *

Grant snatched a look aft, the enemy destroyer was completely obscured in clouds of thick oily smoke. He'd seen the massive explosion, at least one of Crosswall-Brown's fish had scored a direct hit. He searched the horizon for the M.T.B., she should be somewhere astern. Pray to God she was unharmed. The wind had risen unnoticed and the resulting swell could easily obscure the low profile of a patrol boat. "Lookout!"

"Sir!"

"Can you see the 'Dirty-Four?" He could hear the pleading in his own voice.

"Yes, sir... There..." he pointed a gloved hand towards the port quarter.

"Signalman, get up there with the lookout see if your Aldis will reach. Make to 34. 'Engage enemy convoy from the west."

"Middy, Starboard wheel steer north... We'll come at them from ahead."

* * *

Linz fit of smoke-induced coughing abated sufficiently for him to speak into the handset. The, fitful gusting wind had completely shrouded the 'Wagner' in her own smoke screen. Of the enemy, he could see nothing, but clung to the hope that it meant they could not see him either. They would not want to waste torpedoes on a half-mile stretch of smoke or enter it and face his guns at point blank range.

"Slow astern... let's see if we can take some weight off those forward bulkheads, before they collapse completely under the weight of water."

* * *

'Eddy'

Grant stood beside the port wing machine gun. On the bow a coaster, untouched by the turmoil around her, was heading for the shore. All around her ships were on fire, men swimming for their lives in the debris strewn water, smoke and cordite fumes filled the air. Occasionally a loud explosion would drown the otherwise continuous rattle of small arms fire.

The whole process was taking too long; they were very close to the coast, the alarm must have been raised by now and this was only their second coaster. He had allowed the crew of the first to take to their lifeboat before sinking her with the Bofors.

"Grisham, put a burst across her bows, as soon as you can and as close as you can."

The gunner bent to his sights and fired, his whole body shaking as the tracer blazed from the gun, arcing in towards the enemy coaster around her stem post the rounds kicked the sea into white feathers of irradiate foam.

It was good shooting particularly from this awkward angle, but the bugger wasn't stopping completely. He raised his binoculars he could see no one on her deck, the bridge was in darkness. Could she have already been abandoned, surely not while going at the rate of knots she was moving at.

They were now abeam, the distance no more than a cable or so. Suddenly a burst of fire came from her fo'c's'le. He ducked, something splattered across his face. Below him, the port gunner had slumped back, dropping into his harness. He hung there, rolling with the boat, blood running down from the exit wounds in his back.

The unhurried 'pom pom' of the Bofors aft filled the air, great chunks of the coaster flew into the air, her for'ard deck erupting into flying splinters, smoke and flashing light. Somewhere in the middle of all that, the enemy gunner and his weapon disintegrated and the firing stopped abruptly.

Grant vaulted onto the main deck and bent over the seamen gunner, his thin body was still twitching in its harness, his chest a mess of torn clothing and gore. His eyes were wide open as if with shock at the sight of the growing pool of his blood at his feet.

Maurice, the young midshipman, appeared at his side, a shell dressing in one shaking hand.

Grant unbuckled the harness and gently laid, the now still body, down on the deck. "Too late I'm afraid..." He swung the gun round on its pintel, crouched beside the torpedo tube and fired a long burst. The coaster's bridge windows shattered and the wooden structure splintered with holes as the heavy calibre bullets ripped into it.

The wardroom steward appeared and bent down beside him checking the gunner for signs of life. Grant grabbed the bridge ladder, "Bofors!" he yelled, "Aim below her water line. Sink the bastard!"

The steady unremitting beat recommenced and great smoking holes appeared in the coaster's black hull as the gunner trained slowly aft along her entire length.

"Half ahead both, starboard twenty," the Bofors aft ceased fire abruptly as the coaster crossed the bow. As the target reappeared on the port bow the gun recommenced fire, ripping into the coaster's other side. There was no sign of her boats, still no movement on her upper deck. Perhaps only one fanatic had stayed on board, perhaps more, it mattered not, one thing was for sure that was the last time he gave quarter. He would never again put his men's lives at risk that way.

The coaster was listing heavily to port now and the Bofors' aimer lowered his sights. Rounds ripped into the seaweed and barnacles covering the bottom.

"Cease fire!" A gong sounded aft and the gun stopped abruptly.

He had to look twice at the chart table clock. They had only been in action for three-quarters of an hour. He looked around the oil covered sea. All the squadron's boats were insight and intact.

The two M.T.B.s were still alongside enemy boats. Hogg's E-boat was off to the south east traversing rapidly from right to left. He shifted his gaze in the direction she was heading. Immediately he saw two coasters, survivors fleeing towards the shoreline. No time for them, the enemy destroyer would have signalled, called for help. Quite suddenly he was sick of it all, sick of the killing.

"Signalman make to the 'Ethel', 'Break off your attack'. Then general signal. 'Form line astern on me'."

* * *

Across the dark water Crosswall-Brown's signalman relayed the message to his captain.

The diminutive midshipman, his face black with cordite, wiped a grubby hand across his red rimmed eyes and surveyed the burning remains of the enemy convoy, the debris and the smoke. He waited while Crosswall - Brown gave the necessary orders to bring the patrol boat around onto a course to intercept the 'Eddy'.

"You know, sir, while I was in training, at 'Alfred', I often wondered what they meant at the Sunday church parade when they prayed for 'confusion to our enemies'."

Crosswall-Brown, wiped the lenses of his binoculars with the corner of the towel, he used as a makeshift scarf, "Scared, Snotty?"

The young Midshipman nodded in silent reply.

"There's one reassuring thing to remember at such times. You have to be alive to be scared….And anyway as someone, who was doubtless, famous, once said, 'Eighty percent of the things that you fear may happen, never do'."

"Then, sir, they may be famous, but it's my bet they've never been to sea."

Chapter 16

Almost Total Recall

HMS Nishga, 1300 hrs, Sunday, 26th May, 1940.

Barr lifted the brandy decanter and poured Grey a stiff one. His Number One looked as if he needed it. He looked that way a lot lately, nice enough chap, but he would not have been his first choice as a Number One if the circumstances had been different. Perhaps he was being unfair; perhaps they all looked that way these days. He handed Grey his drink. The First Lieutenant downed it in one.

Barr frowned, but refrained from comment, "There's some sort of flap on, Number One and 'Orca's' been ordered to regroup at the 'Flow'. He glanced at the clock above his desk. "They must be about half way between the Inlet and us, no sense in them coming all the way north. So we'll get a signal off and divert them there. We'll sail as soon as we're ready... Pilot, shortest and quickest route there, if you please."

Aye, aye, sir... What about the men at Olaf's Inlet, sir?" asked his navigator, "Aren't we picking them up first."

Barr turned his grey eyes in his Navigating Officer's direction, "They'll have to get by as best they can, until this flap's over."

"Have we no idea what it might be?"

"It's got to be something big that much is certain. It's my guess, that it's to do with getting the army out of France…but exactly what our role in it all will be," he shrugged, "only God and the Admiralty know."

Usbourne smiled, "I thought they were one and the same person, sir."

"No, Pilot. That's just a rumour… I think they just went to the same school."

Usbourne smiled down at his Wellington boots and then looked up at the 'Old Man'. "If you don't mind me saying, sir…There's more men, in France than you can shake a stick at. It may take weeks to get them across the Channel; surely we can afford to lose a few hours, picking up the three marines at the Inlet."

Barr put down his glass and sighed, "I have my orders. The situation is probably a lot worse than any of us realise. No… our chaps, at the Inlet, have enough food to last them to the end of the bloody war and water's no problem. I imagine they will be having an easier time of it than we will, over the next few weeks…God knows we may even be doing them a huge favour!"

* * *

Trondheim, 2130 hrs, 26th May, 1940.

The cold north-easterly had closed in around Olaf Kristiansand's home like a besieging army. His family had retired early leaving him alone, listening to the news. It wasn't good news, even from the British station. In France, Boulogne had fallen to the Germans. The British still held Calais and, with the help of the French, a smaller port called Dunkirk.

If you were to believe the Germans they had already taken Calais. It was all very confusing, but whatever way you looked at it, the British were losing the war.

The radio announcer had spoken of a National Day of Prayer for the trapped troops. Kristiansand had very little faith in prayer, it hadn't saved Norway.

He must have dozed off for a sudden noise jerked him awake. Someone was at the door he stood up wearily and made for the door, then remembered the radio and stopped dead in his tracks; quickly he hid it under the false bottom in the log basket.

"Whose is it?"

"A friend." said a female voice that he did not recognise.

When Kristiansand hesitated the voice added, "I have come about Jens…he has been taken…"

The Norwegian quickly slipped the bolt back onto its stop and swung the heavy door open. The snow swept in, driven by a wind that howled it around the living room. He stood to one side to let the oilskin wrapped figure squeeze in past him.

He closed the door against the snowy blast and turned his back to it. "Who are you? Who is this Jens you speak of?"

"My name Bendedikte Loevaas… Jens recruited me and you recruited him…correct?"

"Recruited…recruited you say, I am too old for the services, I do not…"

"And I have not the time for this! I have come here, at considerable risk to myself, so, please, just listen. They have him now… I am on my way to friends. If he talks he will give them both our names, the only two he knows…correct? What you do about it is up to you…I must go…" she made to leave. Kristiansand blocked her way.

"How do I know you are telling the truth?"

"You don't… and I don't have to prove anything to

you... Look...I came here to help you, I could have just left...I'm beginning to wonder why I didn't. I have risked my life...Get out of my way!" she pushed ineffectively at the big Norwegian.

Kristiansand stood to one side. The woman pulled her hood back over her blonde hair as he unbolted the door. She stepped out into the blizzard, paused and turned to face him." Think of your family, can you afford to take chances, to risk their lives?" Then she was gone.

Kristiansand stood in the open doorway, the snow quickly covering his shoulders. He shivered and it wasn't from the cold.

* * *

HMS Nishga

Heavy with static, the refined tones of the BBC announcer drifted in and out of clarity, "Storm; south, force 11, veering north-westerly, decreasing Force 10."

"Was that us?" asked Lieutenant Usbourne of the signalman. The man nodded.

The Navigating Officer looked above the moisture-obscured windscreen. The rain was coming in from the south east, drifting in dense lines across the bleak wind-swept fo'c's'le. "Middy!...better let the 'Old Man' know."

The Midshipman disappeared below, rattling the metal ladder in his haste.

Minutes later Barr, wrapped in his worn oilskins, appeared on the bridge; he stood, at the top of the ladder, hands clasped behind him, staring out at the southern horizon, "Better get Number One to secure the upper deck. Where is he, anyway?"

"I think he's in his cabin, sir."

Barr nodded as if he expected that as an answer, "Ask him to wait until the port watch have had breakfast and then get them to secure below first, there should be time."

As if by warning, a strong gust of wind cracked and howled at the signal halyards.

Barr stopped Usbourne, halfway to the ladder, "Better keep the close range weapons closed up. Use the men on the main armament to secure the upper scupper. I'll not take any chances, we'll still be in range of their fighters."

Something in his voice made Usbourne looked back, Barr was leaning over the chart table, he looked tired and drawn. Usbourne felt suddenly uneasy, the 'Old Man', they all depended on so, was becoming just that. Growing old before his time, before their very eyes. If he'd had a decent Number One, someone he could rely on it would help. He certainly shouldn't have to worry about which watch did what, that should be a matter for his First, he had enough on his plate, God knows.

* * *

The wind had veered right round in under an hour. Warming to its task, the gusts had become stronger, more malignant. The ship was still beating its way south, confused waves surrounded them on all sides, battered by the wind-change into colliding, leaping peaks.

By the middle of the forenoon watch, it had steadied from the south. The gusts replaced by a strong blow, force seven or eight, the sea-state maybe a little less, but building, like an over-stoked boiler about to blow its top.

Grey had gone to a late breakfast, along with the port watch. His relief paced a lonely vigil to port. Barr sat slumped in his chair, deep in thought, his eyes heavy from lack of sleep.

Jenkins, his steward, appeared silently at his side in his hands he balanced a silver tray of coffee and sandwiches.

"Just the job, Jenkins, thank you." said Barr, coming suddenly to life and rubbing his wet gloves together in anticipation.

"The cold sausage from your breakfast, sir, I thought

you might prefer it up here."

"Thank you, Jenkins, that's very considerate of you." Of course, breakfast, he'd completely forgotten, he had left it untouched in his cabin. He lifted the lid of the cover a crack, withdrew one sandwich quickly replacing the lid against the driving rain. The coffee was hot, laced with sherry, the way he liked it, he gulped hungrily at it, feeling the heat flow into his empty stomach.

They were still hours from Scapa Flow and the seas were piling up nicely. Eight-foot waves, stepping in from the south like a hundred white-haired chorus lines, ducking under the warship in perfect step and dancing away to the north.

Half way through his second sandwich, the port lookout shouted something, but the words were rushed away on the rising wind. The Officer of the Watch, nearer the man by several yards, snatched his glasses to his eyes.

Training his binoculars onto the same bearing, Barr glimpsed the stern of a small boat slipping into a deep trough. A split second later and she had disappeared as if she'd never been. Moments later and she re-emerged, lifted high on the crest of the following wave, her upper deck was embroiled in foam, her scuppers gushing streams of water, she was awash from stem to stern.

There was time enough for Barr to recognise her as a M.F.V. before she once again vanished from sight. A motor fishing vessel, foreign in design, but a M.F.V. all right, heading west. He sat tight-lipped for a second or two, deep in thought.

"Action Stations, if you please... and come to starboard ...steer south east, revolutions for fifteen knots. While the officer of the watch relayed his orders, Barr studied the boat through his glasses. She was rolling like a tub, empty by the looks of her and making hard going of it, as would be expected. There was something else...she seemed to be lolling, although it was very difficult to be sure, considering the conditions. Her roll was certainly erratic, not smooth and measured, as you would expect in a beam sea. At the end of each roll she jerked over sharply. She could have water in her hold, that would explain it, when she rolled, any water would rush to one side, jerking her the rest of the way over like that. She was on the wrong course if that was the case. Beam on to the sea she could easily flip over onto her beam ends.

The closing up reports began to echo up the voice pipes as Barr turned to his Yeoman of signals, "Challenge her, Yeo, find out who she is and if she wants assistance."

The shutter of the Aldis clattered for several minutes, to no effect. "She's not answering, sir."

Barr crossed quickly to the Gun Director's voice pipe. "Bridge, Guns... The Gunnery Officer's voice echoed back, ghost- like from the tube,

"Guns."

"Put one round across her bows... not too close, looks as if she's in enough trouble as it is."

Before he had even replaced the lid, 'A' gun barked out. Instantly a spout of water shot into the air sending a column of water to claw at the sky a half cable ahead of the target.

Barr lifted his binoculars, something white was being waved frantically from the boat's bridge window. It could be the shot across the bows had woken them up...it could be they were boxing clever.

" Pilot, take us in... hailing distance... take up station on her port side. I'm feeling generous, give her the benefit of our lee."

"Number One, I want you to head the boarding party." Grey's expression of sudden panic did not go unnoticed, so much so that Barr felt obliged to explain. "This looks more like a job for your damage control team than 'Guns' heavy mob. I don't think there'll be any need to knock heads together. But... no chances mind, I want your men armed. Better take Petty Officer Stone, he's a good man. You'll need a good Petty Officer Stoker and the biggest pump we've got by the looks of things. Oh and take a ship's diver. Have the sea boat manned and ready just in case, but I think I'll try and get up alongside her first… if I manage it, your chaps will have to be ready to jump."

* * *

"Half ahead both engines… Messenger tell the fo'c's'le, top and quarterdeck to be ready with fenders… Officer of the Watch make sure that Number One and his D.C. team are on the quarterdeck ready with their gear and get the sea boat swung outboard, just in case."

The 'Nishga' inched forward, steadily closing the gap between the two vessels. The M.F.V. was now less than a cable away, fine on the starboard bow and gradually drawing aft as the destroyer overhauled her.

"Slow ahead both engines."

The way dropped off the 'Nishga' and she began to roll. They drew level, from his vantage point on the wing of the bridge; he could look straight down onto the top of the fishing boat. White water swirled around her wooden deck in whirlpools, rhythmically emptying in a rush through her lee scuppers. The sea, squeezed between the two vessels, shot out astern like another wake. Every time the fishing boat rolled away to starboard he could see faces, white with fear, staring up through the bridge windows.

"Stop both." Only feet now separated the two as they rolled their way west. "Half astern both engines" The destroyer began to vibrate, astern a mound of water climbed into the air as the screws bit deep. "Slow ahead…revolutions for five knots."

A big wave rolled lazily in, lifting the two boats like toys it passed under them and they fell back in toward each other with tremendous force. The men positioned along the length of the warship, struggled frantically to keep their feet and to position the heavy basketwork fenders before the two collided. Then they came together, filling the air with the creaks and groans of the contorted basketwork.

"Over you go lads," yelled Barr, his voice was whipped away on the wind, but there was no mistaking his gesture. Men took running jumps, high over the dropped quarterdeck guardrails. Clear of the churning gap they landed on the sea-washed decks of the tiny fishing boat.

* * *

Lieutenant Grey landed squarely on the rolling deck, shouting for Petty Officer Stone, he made for the bridge.

The 'Nishga' was moving away already, like a slow train leaving its station. Clear of the smaller boat she listed heavily to starboard as, screws turning faster, she turned away to port.

Grey went quickly up the three steps to the enclosed bridge. Drawing his revolver, he swung the door open. The tiny bridge was crowded with oilskin clad figures, thick with cigarette smoke and reeked of vomit. Petty Officer Stone squeezed in alongside him, pushing for room with the butt of his Lanchester. There were five people in the tiny space, seven with the two destroyer men.

"Anyone speak English?" called Grey.

"I speak a little," the voice sounded young, northern European and came from the back.

"Right lad, come through here where I can see you."

The English speaking youngster pushed through the throng tugging at the hood of an overlarge oilskin.

"Now, who is in charge here?"

An unruly mop of blond hair had tumbled over the face and was pushed to one side with a decidedly graceful sweep of one hand.

"God Lord, a woman!" exclaimed Grey.

The slight figure said something in what sounded Norwegian to Grey's untutored ears, whatever it was it brought a laugh from the others.

"Keep quiet !" bawled Petty Office Stone.

They might not have understood the English, but they understood the big Petty Officer's tone and fell silent.

Stone spoke to the girl without taking his eyes off the four men "Tell the man on the wheel to lash it amidships, and then the lot of you can get your hands on your heads….Beg your pardon, sir, but it's better this way."

"Yes, of course," acknowledged Grey."

The girl repeated the order and placed her own hands as requested.

"Who is in charge?" the gravel in Stone's voice made it a threat rather than an enquiry.

The girl answered, "The captain was injured in a fall and is below with one other. This man is the only other seaman. She pointed to the man busy lashing the wheel amidships..

"Can you watch these, sir? Just while I send a couple of the lads below to search the others out."

Stone didn't bother to wait for a reply, but disappeared out onto the wind lashed upper deck.

Grey turned to the girl, "Who are you people?"

"We are all Norwegians." said the girl, she spoke perfect English with hardly a trace of an accent. "My name …"

Grey was becoming impatient with the girl's casual attitude. "Never mind that now. What are you doing on board this vessel, you are obviously not fishermen?"

"My name is Bendedikte Loevaas," she said evenly and with a touch of deviance. We, all of us, are fleeing from the Nazis, we were part of a network of information gatherers, we were betrayed. We are headed for the Shetlands."

"Why the Shetlands?"

"It is the nearest land that is free from the Nazis and most of us have family ties there, the islands once belonged to Norway you know."

Grey ignored the remark, "This network of agents, where were they based?"

"We had no specific base, we covered the coastline reporting the movement of enemy ships, aircraft, troops, that sort of thing. The information was relayed to you British."

"What is the name of your leader."

"We only know our immediate contacts, the leader is known only as Olaf."

Grey tried not to show surprise, "A common enough name in your country, I understand. Did you ever meet this Olaf?"

Before the girl could reply the door banged back on its hinges and a blast of cold air roared in. "Right, Foster, on the wheel. The rest of yer, Take this lot below, one at a time, search them first."

"Does that include the girl, P.O.?" asked a lecherous voice from out on the deck.

The grim faced PO his head held enquiringly to one side like a dog who hadn't understood his master's order.

"Certainly not!" said Grey, "She stays on the bridge."

The girl's mouth opened, "I object, you have no right to…"

Stone reared up in front of her, "I suggest, Miss, you speak when you're spoken to."

* * *

Grey rubbed the condensation from bridge window, through the running curtain of water could just make out the 'Nishga'. She was showing no lights and had taken up station to port and slightly ahead of them. From there it afforded them some protection from the wind and the waves.

Out on the deck, Petty Officer Stone was making his way aft pausing, legs astride, as the larger waves lifted the boat. He reached the bridge door, swung it open and stood just inside. "What do you want the men to do now, sir?…sir?"

Grey turned wearily round, Stone could tell instantly that he had been drinking again.

"Yes?"

Stone looked down at his feet, "Shall I carry on, sir?" Grey made no reply simply turning his back and resuming his vigil at the window.

Stone opened the door and slammed it to behind him. Bloody fool! A fat lot of use he's going to be. He shook his head slowly pursing his thin lips in though. He blamed himself, he should have done something about it after Boulogne, but, well, he couldn't help thinking that but for the grace of God... He just wasn't up to the job, but then, in Stone's book, few officers were.

His men were only yards away, even so he had to cup his hands around his mouth and yell at the top of his lungs I order to get heard above the roar of the storm, "Leading Hand!" Take one man, cut away the mast. Get the rest of them turned to dumping what they can from the upper deck. We've got to reduce the weight topside as much as we can, to lessen this loll. It'll reduce the weight of the boat at the same time ...which won't be a bad thing. Make sure you dump the gear evenly.

"What do you mean, P.O?"

"If you dump gear from one side of the boat, dump something of equal weight from the other, anchors for instance."

"Got yer, what about the life rafts?"

Stone hesitated...No life rafts no means of getting off if she founders. "Chuck 'em over, we will have to rely on our lifejackets. Anyway the 'Nishga' will be there for us if the worst comes to the worst, the 'Nishga won't be far off. I'm going below, if there's gear you're not sure about, I mean, gear you think we might need, stow it on the middle line and I'll sort through it as soon as I get back."

"Got yer."

"Got yer, P.O." reminded Stone.

He made his way aft, hanging on to the bulkhead

handrail, for dear life, as he went. The Stoker PO, a bearded Scotsman by the name of 'Jock' Sterling, was waiting by the engine room door. At his feet two stokers struggled with a heavy portable pump. A black hose ran from it to a ventilator.

"There's a foot of water in the engine room, she leaking like a bloody sieve from somewhere."

Stone nodded, " Leave Warren here to deal with the water in the engine room: The leading stoker crouched by the pump looked up in surprise, a seaman who knew his name.

"You come with me, Jock, we'll take a shufty at the holds, see what state they're in."

The pump rattled into life with a cough and a flying cloud of oily black smoke.

Sterling bent low, to make himself heard, "Warren, lash that pump down securely and then get yourself below, take charge of that civy in the engine room. Leave Seymour to man the pump." He turned back to Stone, " Right, Rocky, ready when you are."

* * *

The for'ard hold reeked of fish, Stone hung from a ladder rung and shone his powerful torch down into the gloom below. Only a few feet below him the rusty iron ladder disappeared into water, thick with oil. He looked for the light switch, found it and flicked it on with the corner of his torch, nothing.

"First job, get the 'Lecky' to rig up a portable light down here..." He paused as his words were drowned out by the crash and rattle of the anchor cable leaping its way up the hawse pipe from the cable locker. The Leading hand was hard at work dumping the heavy anchors and their cables.

He shone his light around the darkened hold, the water was deeper here than in the engine room...two, maybe three feet.

"Aye, this is where the water's coming from alright." called Sterling from somewhere above him. It was as if he was reading his thoughts.

"See that water-tight door, Jock." Stone shone the beam onto a rusty steel door in a fore and aft bulkhead which divided the hold into two. "Get it closed right away it will reduce the width of the compartment, reduce the free surface area and hopefully this bloody loll. Then get the pump up here as soon as you've got the water down to a workable level in the engine room."

"I've enough hose to reach both places at the same time. That way, if we have to, we can quickly shift back to the engine room without the bind of moving the pump and its hose."

"Good, anything that will save time," said Stone, climbing past the Stoker P.O. and out onto the deck. He leaned back over the open hatch and cupped his hands around his mouth. "Make sure you pump her out evenly, otherwise it'll make matters worse."

"Spare me, Rocky, I'm no yer grandma. Teach her to suck eggs if you've a mind."

* * *

"The pump's no holding its own," called Sterling, above the noise of wind and pump. "The level in the engine room's up six inches since we started pumping from the hold. It's up there too, but not by as much."

"All we can do is to keep pumping, Jock. I'll see if Grey's got any ideas."

"I've already tried that. You'll be wasting yer time there, man. He's as pissed as a bodger's handcart; again. I just come from the bridge."

"Well he's best kept out of it, then."

"You've no need to worry there. The lucky bastard's out like a light. You'll have to report him. You know that don't yer."

"We'll see," Stone replied, turning towards the bridge.

Grey was asleep, he tried to nudge him awake with the toe of one boot. He sighed and sucked at his teeth. "Bunty! Make to 'Nishga', 'Water level rising in hold and engine room, despite pumping, please advise'."

* * *

The 'Nishga' was slowing, dropping back, yard by yard, easing herself closer and closer to the fishing boat. Stone could see Barr poised on the starboard wing of the bridge, cap pulled hard down over his eyes, loudhailer ready in his hand. He looked around for his own, the signalman read his thoughts and handed it across.

Barr's voice drifted in and out buffeted by the freakish wind, "Has she sufficient steerage way for you to bring her alongside me."

Stone nearly blind from the spray, raised his megaphone. "I think so, sir, but she's very sluggish, handles like a pissed whale."

"Is that you Petty Officer Stone. Where's Lieutenant Grey?"

Stone momentary hesitation did not go unnoticed by Barr,

"He's indisposed…ill, sir." He saw Barr lower his hailer, a second later he raised it back up to his lips.

"Can you manage on your own, Petty Officer?"

"Yes, sir, I've Petty Officer Sterling to help. We'll be right as rain"

"Very well, I'll rig fenders and we'll bouse you in close alongside, Secure to two sets of bollards, if you can, just in case one lot are carried away. I'm rigging hurricane hawsers fore and aft to take the weight and absorb the shock. We should be able to keep her afloat that way, but I want as many of the men off as possible, keep Petty Officer Sterling, a couple of A.B.s, a stoker and the wireman with you. We'll need a half hour or so to lay out our gear."

Stone waved in acknowledgement and the destroyer began to claw its way ahead once again.

* * *

Barr turned back into the bridge proper and handed his megaphone to the bridge messenger.

"Guns! I know this isn't your part of ship, as it were, but the Bosun will know what's what, and what's where. Get him and Chippy to rig up two long baulks of timber as fenders; a couple of boat's booms should serve. They'll need to span at least three frames of the ship's side to spread the load. I want hammocks, complete with their mattresses lashed to them. I want two hurricane hawsers rigged in addition to bow and stern lines. Get the Chief Engineer ready with extra pumps and tell Chippy he will need his 'fishing boat repair kit', he's going aboard."

* * *

Barr studied the M.F.V. through his binoculars; her rolling had eased again, now that the destroyer had resumed her old position to windward of her.

Directly below the bridge wing he could hear two seamen in a shouted conversation

" 'Ere that's my bloody hammock, that is, look there's me name!"

Barr peered over the wing. It was one of the Pom Poem's gunners he couldn't recall the man's name. The two men were rigging the long boom fenders.

The captain of the Pom Pom had also overheard. "All right! All right! That's enough of the dripping. Pipe down and get on with your work."

"But that's me 'ammock, 'ooky, wrapped around that fender. What am I supposed to kip in tonight?"

"You've got two, ain't yer?"

"Yeah, but I scrubbed it this morning, it's still wet."

"Well, now… you got two wet ones, ain't yer!"

The seaman fell silent until the Leading Hand had moved on.

"It's all right for him, I bet his bloody 'ammock ain't down there getting soaked…"

* * *

When all the preparations had been made, the M.F.V. started her approach, wallowing along like a fat, drunken duck. Stone eased her slowly forward overhauling the barely moving 'Nishga'. Soon the two were rolling together, yards apart, making just enough headway for steerage purposes. Stone matched the destroyer's speed, revolution for revolution, easing her in yard by yard, till the heaving lines snaked across between them. Larger ropes followed and were quickly brought to the destroyer's capstans. The fishing boat was hauled in close, snug into the destroyer's side until only the breadth of the makeshift fenders divided them.

* * *

Stone, busy below, could feel the sea worsening. The two vessels, held together in their tight watery embrace, had altered course through ninety degrees. The huge seas were now strutting in from astern. The pumps were holding their own, but below all was chaos. The decks were awash, in every compartment rafts of debris were sucked from for'ard to aft by the pitching. He could hear the waves crashing and booming against her wooden sides. The noise was terrifying, diabolical. It was if battering rams, wielded by the devil himself, were intent on breaking through and dragging them all to a watery grave.

In the midst of the storm and with so many things on his mind, he had completely forgotten about the

Norwegians. He must get word to Barr. He would know what to do about the 'Networks' plight. He finished the extra lashing he was rigging and climbed the ladder to the upper deck. He hadn't been up on deck for a half hour or so. Even in that short time the fearsome primordial power of the sea had been hard at work. Now, as he clawed his way out onto the heaving deck, the wind-whipped spray cut at his face like sand, while the howling wind wrapped his foul weather gear around his shivering body like a second skin.

Huge seas were lifting the two vessels as one, like two dancers cavorting together in perfect step, wrapped in each other's arms in some nightmarish tango, they surged their way seaward.

On the destroyer, the helmsman was fighting hard to kept the two vessels within twenty-degrees of the course. Sometimes he failed, caught out by a freak wave or a heavier gust of wind. Then the bigger vessel's stern would submerge, dragged down by the sheer weight of water. When she rose again she became a great scoop, sending a green curl of sea plunging over the bridge to land with awesome force on her dancing partner.

Through all this Stone climbed steadily, clinging to the wooden dowels of the Jacob 's ladder slung over the destroyer's side. He held on tight when the ladder stayed plumb and the 'Nishga's' side fell away leaving him hanging precariously out over the fishing boat's bridge. On the opposite roll the destroyer's side rushed in towards him like an express train, and he'd smack into the metal with sickening force, driving the breath from his body.

* * *

The light had gone long before night fell. All day they had sailed through perpetual twilight, the sea white with spray the sky black with foreboding. The two vessels, locked together in each other's clasp, were also in the terrible embrace of the storm; a wild, mad embrace, that swept them relentless on to an unknown fate.

With the coming of evening, the darkness was total, there were no stars, no moon. For those Norwegians not use to the ways of the sea, the night was far worse than the day. In the twilight they had been able to see the power of the storm. In the dark, they had only their imaginations some possessed by them, lived a nightmare, spent the long night in fear, all hope gone, they sank into a seasick stupor. They didn't expect to see another day and cared less whether they did or not.

The destroyer's crew waited for the dawn to see what would be left of the two vessels. It was a long night for them too, sleepless, fearful, but above all exhausting. There were milestones to mark its slow passage. The time the life rafts were swept away, the time the thrashing anchor cables disintegrated into scrap metal, the time the Norwegian seaman was lost, swept away to windward wrapped in the awesome wave that was his only shroud.

A monstrous dawn finally appeared. Its first feeble light revealed the terrible seas marching in. Irresistible high, their roaring tops whipped off to leeward like long strands of ghostly white hair. The wind screamed its anger above the waves, lifting them over the two boats in great green and white sheets. Black clouds, piled high, moved across the sky like the smoke from hell's fire.

Somehow they had survived the night, whether it was God's will or man's tenacity none knew.

* * *

Only a few hundred miles to the east, it was a different story, almost a different world. When the 'Eddy's' crew fell out from their dawn action stations it was to a crisp cold morning, to such a day as never should have existed in war, one of light, of freshness and of colour, Turner-like in its luminosity. Men, at their stations stood in awe of its transient beauty, of its magnitude. The crimson glow of a still invisible sun flooded into distant clouds. On the horizon, the wispy remnants of 'Nishga's' storm captured and held the colour as the sun's light flowed across the sky, a crimson glaze, fresh from the divine artist's pallet. It touched the ship with pink, men glowed in its rosy overlay, its tint gently brushed the wave tops. All fear shrank from its cleansing light.

* * *

'Eddy'

The mess deck's hatch was open, letting the dry clean air into the freshly scrubbed compartment.

Ordinary Seaman Goddard, feet up on a bunk, stretched luxuriously and put down the American magazine he'd been reading while the deck dried. "Do you think the Yanks'll come in on our side Tug?"

Wilson straightened up from washing the last of the breakfast plates. "I bloody hope not, the war's dangerous enough as it is."

"Don't yer think they be any use then, Tug?"

Wilson pulled a face and shrugged a shoulder. "About as much use as a spare arse in a dysentery ward."

Wyatt, drying the last plate said, "They'll wait until they've made enough money from it, like in the last do, then they'll come in. You mark my words."

"Better off without 'em." said Wilson, "I remember one time, on the 'Nelson', when we were in the Med. joint exercises they called 'em…the cock ups they made! No idea, bloody dangerous to work with they were. We should try and persuade them to join the other side."

"Too much bloody chat," said Wyatt, "That's their problem. Too busy giving it all that," he added, opening and closing one hand in front of his generous mouth. " 'Alf the time they're not concentrating on what they're

298

supposed to be doing. Bunch of posers, walking the walk, talking the talk should try doing the bleeding job. They'll never make good seamen as long as their arses look downwards."

Wilson smiled in agreement, "They've got more badges than a cow got udder. Badges and medals for everything, Medals for getting shot, medals for not getting shot, badges for coffee making, badges for making one of them there highball things. You name it, they got a medal for it. Give 'em away like fag cards they do."

"Goddard looked at his one badge, "They look good though, all them badges I mean, don't they."

"You oughta join 'em if you like badges, Blur," said Wilson, "you'd probably have a couple of Long Service stripes by now."

"You're taking the Mick, ain't yer," said Goddard, unsure whether his mentor was joking or not. "I ain't been in a Dog's Watch yet."

"I ain't joking. Right how long you been in?"

"Nearly a year, now."

"There you go then, let me see," Wilson raised his eyes to the deck head in contemplation, they get 'em every three months, or so…so you'd be a three stripper, coming up for yer fourth."

"Where do they have 'em, on the same arm as your one?" asked Goddard pointing to Wilson's four year's good conduct stripe."

Wilson though for a minute, "Nar, They have 'em on the bottom of the sleeve, here, upside down."

"Would I have any others do yer think," asked Goddard with enthusiasm, " If I was in the Yank Navy, I mean."

" 'Course," said Wilson, looking the youngster straight in the eye, "On the other arm you'd have one to show when yer had yer nappy changed last."

Chapter 17

Doing the best they can

The icy wind snatched angrily at Corporal Bushel's clothing, snow had built up around the top of the sleeping bag. With the flotilla gone they were guarding an empty Inlet. Sometimes it seemed a waste of time, but deep down he knew Barr was right. It wouldn't do for the 'Nishga' or her consorts to arrive back to a German welcoming committee.

He carefully cleared snow away from the firing slot in the pine trunks.

So much for the 'Met' Boy's long range weather forecast, no snow they'd been that certain. A knock on the tunnel hatch made him start, must be four at last, the watch change.

Stilson reached out to his side and opened the hatch, Blake emerged. Stilson slipped back down the tunnel without a word, no by you leave, no wave, nothing. Blake scrambled into the still warm sleeping bag and wiggled closer moving with the grace of a fat white grub.

It was bloody cold lying here, but things had improved; at least the mess deck in the gallery was warm now. He wished he were down there, instead of up here, eight hours to go, eight on, four off.

He pulled his hood farther over his head. Tactically things were much better since they had completed the latest addition to the defences. Now the position was as good as the three men could make it.

The planning had kept his mind occupied during the long hours on watch. Working through an attack as though he was leading it in and then doing what he could to counter it. It was a bit like playing chess on your own. There were even the set moves, the text book stuff and then there were the unexpected moves. He hoped he'd covered the both, but you could never be sure. Well, you could, if Jerry found them then he'd know. Suddenly a dry twig cracked. He hadn't meant right now! He eased the safety forward on the Bren and nodded to Blake.

* * *

In single file, Olaf Kristiansand, his wife and two teenage sons moved swiftly down the path, their skis gliding smoothly over the compacted snow.

Suddenly, a few metres ahead, a hooded white figure rose out of the snow. The man held a machine gun; the barrel was pointed straight at Kristiansand's stomach. The Norwegian stopped in a flurry of snow. He was unsure who the figure was, but he was sure he had no choice in the matter.

"Bushel?" he asked tentatively. Blake shook his head and pointed over his shoulder.

Just then Bushel emerged from behind cover carrying the Bren. He pointed up the path the Norwegians had used. "Blakey, check, see if they were followed." He beckoned to the Norwegians to follow him.

When Blake returned Kristiansand was still talking, "...choice, I had to bring my family, I have them all, except for my father. He was not at home. I must return for him, now the rest of my family are safe."

Bushel turned his head from the lookout slit. "No chance! That's impossible. You're going nowhere. We can't risk you being taken. You're too valuable; you know too much…We'll be taking you away as soon as the flotilla returns…"

"I will not leave without my father."

"Alright, I'll just hold you here by force until the flotilla returns, it's no skin off my nose."

"You don't understand. If they take my father he will talk, he is old…"

"He can name names?"

"He knows the people I know; of course… they have been to my house many times… I cannot be sure what he knows. We have not talked of it…only he knows what he knows."

"Open the hatch, Blakey, take them below." He stepped close and added in a whisper, "And keep a close eye on the lot of them."

* * *

Left alone, Bushel considered his options: they were few. Kristiansand and his network had become more vital to 'Orca's' success with each passing day. They were more important than either him or his men, probably more important than the whole of 'Orca' for that matter. It they waited for the flotilla to come it could be too late. If Kristiansand's' father knew about this place and the Germans took him…

He shook his head resignedly. They would have to try; not for the Kristiansand's, the younger or the bloody elder, but for themselves. There was only the three of them; nowhere near enough and if they all went it would mean leaving the Inlet unguarded, if the Germans were one step ahead of them and had the old man already, they could return to a hornet's nest. There would be problems with

302

checkpoints, patrols. If they were challenged none of them spoke German, or Norwegian for that matter.

One part of him rebelled. Get on the radio. Let the bloody officers sort it out, they should be here, making the decisions that was what they were bloody well paid for! Officers! Never there when you wanted them, always there when you didn't.

Bushel dismissed the inner mutinous voice. The nearest British Officer was probably hundreds of miles away. He hadn't tried, but he doubted he would be able to reach anyone through these mountains. It was down to him, there was only him, his was the choice to go or not to go. Even now they could be too late.

He scratched at his head. Right! On the plus side we've, he thought for a moment, then exhaled air in a long sigh. There wasn't much. There was the Norwegian. He'd know the place like the back of his hand. There wouldn't be many Jerries who could speak the local lingo. Stick to Norwegian, with Olaf's help they had a slim chance of passing as locals.

An embryo plan began to form in his mind. It would mean relying on Stilson more than he liked. He was sure he was capable enough; problem was he was sure the bloke was cracking up. He'd seen it before, something in their eyes. The strange thing was it didn't seem to be effecting 'Snake's' legendary efficiency. If anything he seemed to be getting better. Cracking up or not 'Snake' was still the best there was. That was it then…but first things first, he must try and get a message to Barr. If they got the old man out then with him, a woman and her kids escape by sea was the only option.

* * *

Trondheim, 2300 hours May 27th 1940

Bushel held his camouflaged Lanchester to one side

and crouched at the street corner. Something or someone had most certainly put the cat in amongst the pigeons. The darkened streets were alive with patrols. It would be a bloody miracle if they managed to avoid them all. Stilson had done well, travelling ahead of them, sticking mostly to the rooftops, he had warned them of two patrols with just seconds to spare. 'Snake' and a strictly enforced blackout had got them through three-quarters of the town undetected.

He stood up, suddenly a two-man German foot patrol rounded the corner. They were as surprised as Bushel and friends, but, none the less, their machine pistols came off their shoulders in a blink of an eye.

* * *

The two Germans hesitated, pistols levelled at the three men. They looked at each other and smiled with relief. Not much to worry about then with these three, locals, breaking the curfew true, obviously betruckeenen. The one in the middle was the worst of the three his arms around the shoulders of the other two grinning like a hyena. Now he was shouting, something in his own incomprehensible tongue. He must have wanted to stand up unsupported, he was trying to anyway. Not that it would make any difference; they would still be going straight to the cooler. The two young soldiers lowered their pistols grinning... Now the three drunks were closer... something in their eyes... not the eyes of drunks.

. The indecision was a mistake, letting them get that close... was *another*... their last. There were two sharp, quick movements, barely seen by the soldiers and destined never to be remembered. The two buckled at the knees and sank to the ground. They were dead and their guns taken from them before they reached it. The two marines dragged the deathly still bodies into the deep shadow of an alleyway and returned silently, watchfully, to the Norwegian's side.

* * *

'Snake' had watched the scene unfolding in the alleyway below him, with professional interest. So far, he had only observed and warned, but there was a certain satisfaction in that, he had always taken pleasure in seeing and not being seen. Perhaps, later, there would be a chance to kill. A slow sneer moved through his top lip as he became excited by the thought. In spite of the cold, beads of sweat broke out on his forehead, his breathing became shallow and his long tongue licked at his nicotine-stained teeth.

He had sensed the foot patrol before the parties on the ground had even seen each other. Bushel and Blake were capable of handling that, no need for his help. He had watched the Germans die, a half smile on his lips that found no echo in the yellow eyes as he moved on.

It was at times like this, that he associated himself with the snake he loved to imitate. Times like this that he felt a snake's superiority, its proven power over others, it's confidence not only in itself, but with its environment, it was as one with the night. The snake and the others, so different. The 'others' moved and lived in the light, fearing the dark. Only the snake understood the dark, welcomed it as a friend.

When the 'others' were not there 'Snake' moved swiftly along the rooftops, but when they were, he moved slowly, silently. He could sense 'others' long before he saw them. There was pleasure in seeing, but not being seen, but not nearly as much pleasure as in the final act itself. They all tasted that pleasure, the hunter, the stalker, the snake. But the snake was the master. He never became a silhouette against light, never became a movement seen. He was a phantom, part of the darkness, part of the shadow, part of the night. If the hunted even suspected the presence, the game was lost, an end of the lethal game he loved, lived to play. It was why he lived, it was what gave him his passion for life; the taking of it that and the fact that there was no second chance; it had to be first time perfect.

*   *   *

There was no way around the crossroads. That's why the Germans had positioned the checkpoint there. It was well sandbagged, surrounded with barbed wire and floodlit. It looked impenetrable. The snake watched the position from high above. There were two guards, they were stopping and searching everyone, even their own kind. He sensed they were not just checking papers, they were looking for someone, possibly the Norwegian, Kristiansand.

He watched the two sentries, one fat, one thin, they had grown old in their trade, experienced, probably had seen war before. The snake sensed they knew every trick of their deadly profession for they treated every one as an enemy, treated everyone as if they were about to attack them. Now the two Germans had stopped a group of soldiers, halted them four yards from the post. Keeping their distance, they motioned the men to the wall. The Fat took up a position to one side, giving himself a clear line of fire. Thin walked along the line spreading the men's feet wide apart and pushing their bodies forward until they were off balance, kept upright only with the support of the wall. Always careful, He never put his body between the man he searched and the covering gun of his fat friend. Fat's eyes never left the men as the other searched them. Thin knew the game, his foot hooked around the feet of the man he was searching, ready to sweep the legs away. Unlike the foot patrol, these men were going to be a problem. It would be necessary to warn the others, very necessary. The snake sank back into the shadow.

*   *   *

27th May, Scapa Flow.

The door opened, a marine sentry entered, holding it back against its stop, Admiral Mackenzie followed like one of his own destroyers, firing broadsides of orders and questions over his ample stern, a thick plume of smoke trailing from his funnel of a pipe. In his wake, he towed a retinue of aides. He shifted his fire to a tall rheumy-eyed man... "Collins get 'Able Force' dispatched as soon as possible. Tell them time is of the essence, I won't stand for any delay." His head trained round and he opened fire on a new bearing, "Richards, I want 'Operation Klondike' underway as of yesterday, am I understood? Well, don't just stand there man! What are you waiting for... a blasted medal"

Lieutenant Richards retreated through the thickening smoke screen.

The Admiral's guns had detected a new target. "Arh! Barr!" he shot the words like two armour-piercing shells. "A moment please, gentlemen." He raised a signal arm and taking Barr under it, drew him to one side. I'm afraid I'm going to have to split your 'Orca Force' I want you, helping out at Dunkirk," he raised an eyebrow, "You've heard of course?"

"About the retreat? Yes sir."

The old admiral's eyes signalled a warning like a shot across the bows.

" 'Operation Dynamo' is not a retreat, Barr, it's a strategic withdrawal! Damn it almost a fleet action. Vice Admiral Ramsey has made an appeal for more destroyers, 'Havant', 'Anthony', 'Saladin', 'Malcolm' even the 'Harvester's' going and her crew are still under training! Unlike the other services the Navy does not do retreats, Barr!"

"No, sir, of course...But I've rather a lot on at the moment, I've still got men ashore in Norway. I've just heard from them that the 'Network' has been compromised..."

The Admiral signalled 'heave to' with one arthritic hand. "I know, I know... Grant will have to take charge of that...he'll have to do the best he can... under the circumstances...In actual fact we can't spare him either. You know the bloody Belgians have chucked the towel in?"

"I hadn't heard, no, sir."

"Today! Of all bloody days, their King... what's his name?"

"Erh...Leopold, I think, sir."

"Hmm! Whatever... he signed a bloody armistice, the blighter. His army laid down their arms and left a bloody great hole in our lines. Waterloo all over again. We're having to shift a whole bloody Division to fill the gap. If they don't get there in time we'll lose the bloody lot... Still might for that matter."

Barr wasn't to be side-tracked, "Grant'll need help, sir, it's not a one man job..." Surely the 'Dirty Four', sir?...Crosswall's boat?"

"You obviously don't fully understand the situation we're in, Barr. Calais fell to Jerry yesterday; they've been bombing Dunkirk for five days now, the place is a bloody shambles and we have over three hundred thousand men there. Ramsey's right...we will need every ship... Christ! Every blasted raft if we're to get them off those beaches. Nothing... Nothing can have greater priority... Can't you see...we are going to need those men in the months and the years ahead...And make no mistake, Barr, we are now talking years. This little lot will put set us back that long. Defending England is going to be our number one priority for the foreseeable future... Norway... the Network, every other bloody thing has to take second place to that." He took a deep pull at his pipe, it seemed to calm him. "No, Grant will have to do the best he can. I have every confidence in him." He thought for a moment, sucking slowly at the pipe, then sighed, a thin stream of smoke curling from his mouth, "Tell him he can have the other boat…in this bloody mess, I don't suppose one boat more or less will make that much of a difference."

Once the …erh… 'Strategic withdrawal?' is complete sir," asked Barr, he was trying hard not to appear too forceful, "Have I your permission to head north and help out?"

"Of course! But that could be days…weeks even. You have my permission…but!… only when the Admiralty call a halt to operations at Dunkirk… and hear me Barr…not a second before that…" He held up a warning finger as Barr went to speak, "Not a second before…I know they're your men. I know how you feel…Christ knows, I'd feel the same."

"Thank you sir." Barr saluted, turned on his heel and disappeared into the throng astern of the Admiral.

* * *

In the world in which it moved it shunned the light. Shadow and darkness were its only friends. It flowed into the shadow and it flowed out, merged and re-emerged, unseen, unheard. He had become it at last. He was one with his Mentor. Before the snake, all men walked in fear, wept with dread, sank to their knees in the filth of their own terror. At long last it knew who it was, and what it was, knew its power. Its prey was unaware of its presence, hidden in the deep shadow of the old apartment block, the snake slid to the roof's edge. Only inches below, the prey, the one with the corporal's stripes, moved out from the doorway, out past the sandbags. Then… slowly… slowly the snake's neck stretched over the roof's edge until it could see the other man through the window. He was standing at the desk writing in a book. The snake hung its long thin body from the roof and slowly slid to the floor. Unseen it slipped quietly into the hut… moments later it emerged and glided silently to the sandbag barrier. In the snake's trail, a river of black blood flowed from the doorway. It coiled, ready to strike, waiting; the time would come…for its prey would come to it, drawn by the Mentor.

* * *

Grant's E-boat bumped and bounced across the swell, heading east, fast to beat the sun, an all out race to get there before first light.

Astern the other boat, Crosswall-Brown's M.T.B., kept station. This time the race had a prize, Kristiansand; it was going to be touch and go. Grant looked to the east; pink had already begun to stripe the horizon.

He had no idea what the situation was ashore. There had been no second message from Bushel. They could have been captured, killed, anything. The lack of information made planning difficult, his mind ached with possibilities and contingencies. Somehow he had to allow for all and every eventuality. His first priority must be to reach the Inlet before first light. That much was clear. He checked the clock above the tiny chart table; they would make it unless there was a delay of some kind…an engine fault the other boat would have to proceed alone. If they met the enemy… then Crosswall-Brown would have to draw them off, deal with the situation, as best he could alone. Crosswall-Brown would have to buy him the time to disappear into whatever darkness remained. There never seemed to be enough of that. This war was one of dearth and deficits, not enough ships, not enough men, not enough information …not enough darkness.

* * *

Bushel crouched in the deep shadow cast by the stark white lights of the checkpoint. Stilson's warning had come just in time; another thirty seconds and it would have been too late. He was grateful for that, it was Stilson's manner that worried Bushel. It worried him more than being in a German held town worried him; and that was saying something.

It was in the look, it was in his movements, his smile, if you could call it that. Tonight he seemed to be worse. At one point he had put his hand on Stilson's shoulder... he went over the short conversation again in his mind.

'You all right, Snake.' he'd asked.

'What do yer mean by that!' he'd replied quickly; too quickly.

'Just that, are you all right?'

'We 'aven't time for this. We've work to do.'

'What I meant was...I don't know...I suppose what I'm trying to say is...Don't let it get to you.'

The marine had laughed a hollow empty sound, 'Killing always gets to you. Especially our kind.'

It had been the most words he had heard Stilson string together in a long time, but it wasn't the words, it was the way that he'd expressed them. The man was haunted, possessed, something. He had seen it there before, but now it was much more than just a passing mood. Those eyes, in that split second before he'd turned away. He'd seen it, putting a name to it was another thing. It certainly wasn't fear, eagerness? It was more than that, fanaticism? Signs of an inner struggle to control whatever it was that possessed him? Bushel was no doctor, but thinking about it now the bloke could be having a breakdown. If he was, he had chosen one hell of a time, they needed him and his unusual skills. For starters, he was the only one who could get them past that check point.

* * *

The German corporal heard the drunken laughter before he saw the three men stagger around the corner and enter the square. He looked in the direction of the sentry post, calling "Werner!" before turning back to face the drunken men, he couldn't handle this lot alone, where was Werner! Quick anger welled up inside him. He turned and marched rapidly back to the hut, past the sandbags. Suddenly his head wrenched back, his feet left the ground, He kicked and struggled, tried to call out, he could hardly breathe. His chinstrap was buried deep in the fatty folds of his neck crushing his windpipe and vocal chords. Something flashed in the bright light, stroked his exposed throat, warmth spilled down his neck. A terrible pain jerked at his spine. A loud crack echoed in his brain and then he saw an infinite tunnel of diamond bright light stretching back into an endless blackness.

Chapter 18

The Mentor

Bushel's breath came in quick gasps… cold air froze his lungs, exhaustion was draining his mind. For one crazy moment he thought the Germans could follow the steam of his breath. They wouldn't need to, his ski tracks in the fresh snow were enough. He snatched a quick look behind; they were still there, lights bobbing and weaving in the night.

All hell had broken loose as they'd left the village. The German patrol had shot out of nowhere, three tracked vehicles, for Christ's sake! They were still there, right up their arses and gaining, stuck to him like shit to a Pusser's blanket.

What a bloody mess… it couldn't be worse…It could; maybe enemy patrols were already ahead of them… if they were equipped with wireless. If only he'd had the men he had asked for, he could have dropped them off at intervals on the way in… they could have warned him of any patrols on the way back… A lot of 'ifs'…Frantically he swerved right…it was a job to see the bloody trees… They seemed to charge out of the dark… any darker and… The enemy were using their headlights… When they topped a rise, they shone out like searchlights, probing the sky before dropping back into the trees with a jolt. Suddenly he thought he could hear the sea...He listened as they crested the next hill...There it was again, or was it the sound of their skis, thrown back from the trees...No!...It was definitely waves... with a bit of luck... and they'd used up a lot of that tonight...

The old man was keeping up well...at least they had him... he must be fifty, if he was a day...probably born on a pair of skis.

He skidded to a halt in front of 'Fort One', spinning through a hundred and eighty degrees. Blake had dropped off; he was already at work frantically rubbing out their tracks from the tree line. Good man... no need to tell him anything. He'd have to be good...No 'Snake'...If they had been short handed before, now, with Stilson gone...He could already be here... He could be anywhere...He could be dead...The Norwegians would have to man one of the Forts... Would they have the nerve to hold their fire...he'd shoot the bastards himself if they fucked it up.

* * *

Jager Leutnant Wieland Sieg's helmeted head hit the butt of the MG42 as the speeding, bucking reconnaissance half- track jumped a bump in the dirt road. Cursing under his breath, he crouched lower. Through the forward gun slit, he could see the ski tracks clearly in the fresh powdery snow and the yellow glare of the headlights. They seemed to weave in and out of those of the half-track ahead of his. Who the hell were these men? They knew how to ski, that was for sure...but then everyone did in this verflucht country...Enemy Alpine troops...It was possible...Norwegians? Most definitely...If they were, then there would have to be reprisals... Unpleasant stuff...He didn't want to get involved in that side of things. He preferred to leave that to those who enjoyed it. There were enough of them.

He leant forward and shouted in the driver's ear. "If those ski tracks turn off sharp or disappear altogether brake fast, you hear me?"

"Jawohl, Herr Leutnant!"

Skiers could turn a lot sharper than this half-track, especially when it was driven by this dolt. If they disappeared completely it could mean an ambush. He had been in the Alpine Troop long enough to know that. He had learnt that the hard way from those sadistic sods of instructors in the forests of Bavaria.

His thoughts returned to the pursued, who where these people? Was there any sense in wondering? Whoever they were, they definitely weren't on his side, the blood trail proved that…he remembered the corpses …Oh yes, there would be reprisals all right.

* * *

Bushel shot back across the snow… his men were in place… the enemy headlights were cutting through the trees, sending ghostly shadows flickering and dancing in front of him. He seemed to be racing them as well as Jerry.

The first Jerry turned the bend in a flurry of snow and came crashing along the last stretch. He skidded to a halt; almost fell through the doorway of the HQ, his skis still attached to his legs. His tired brain fought to cope with the task at hand to remember the plan. Catch the first half-track… block the way, that was it. He struggled to control his breathing. Through the slit the harsh headlights muted to a warm red glow in his ski glasses.

Now! a blinding flash of orange light illuminated pieces of the half-track flying up in an eruption of white-hot flame. Behind the destroyed vehicle the other half-tracks swerved off the track to the left and right, soldiers leaping from them. Seeking cover, running, crouching low, harsh silhouettes against the white light of the flames and the snowy backdrop. A secondary explosion sent shadows jumping and dancing across the forest floor. The first fire had became a steady roar, exploding ammunition sending flying sparks bursting from its glowing centre.

He belly-crawled rapidly out of the emplacement and along the drainage ditch fumbling inside his ski suit, he drew the Very pistol and fired the signal. Even before it exploded, he was on his way back. The flare sailed high above the flames and exploded into white light. Immediately Olaf's machine gun opened up. A noise like mad static blended into the roar of the flames and exploding ammunition. Back in the HQ, Bushel waited by the firing slit. The Norwegian's Bren, opening up on cue, had sent the enemy troops wiggling and scurrying round to put the trees between them and the machine gun. The entire flank of the enemy troops now lay under the sights of his, so far, silent gun.

He moved his head slightly to peer along the sights, smelling the oiled metal rank in his nostrils. He squeezed the trigger, the figure in the sights twitched in time to the burst. He swung quickly to his right, another two-second burst, another twitching figure. He worked his way systematically from the enemy rear, killing as he went.

The gun was hot in his hands before they realised what was happening, then they began to run, at first in twos and threes that in seconds had turned into a rout. Caught between two murderous streams of fire, outflanked, nowhere to hide, they ran and they died in a slow-motion nightmare of deep leg-dragging snow.

The flare died, hiding the contorted dead, the bodies writhing in the snow and the tree cover that had been no cover at all.

* * *

Jager Leutnant Sieg thanked his God that when he had run, he had run to his right. The enemy guns, now thankfully silent, had concentrated their fire on the other side of the blazing half-track. He had been lucky to escape the secondary explosion as they exited their vehicle, his driver had taken the full blast, his body a tower of squirming flames.

There were two guns beautifully positioned, well thought out, too well positioned to have been a spur of the moment ambush. Light machine guns, probably Brens. He was looking at a professionally executed and pre-planned ambush, either that or a defensive position that had been in place for some time. The first thing he must do was to get the other Sonderkraft half tracks and all the spare ammo off that verdammt road. He waited for a loll in the firing before yelling, "Hofmann!"

Oberjager Hofmann lay some distance behind his officer waiting the expected call. He took another long pull at the second water bottle, the one half full of 'Hero's Piss'. He rose warily and began moving forward from tree to tree, crouching and ducking as he went. With a last sprint, he dived into the thick snow at Sieg's side.

"A nest of vipers we've stumbled on here, Herr Leutnant."

Sieg nodded, "We are going to need more men. Find me some drivers, if there are any still alive! Get those half-tracks back up the trail, reverse them mind, keep to the old tracks. The whole road could be mined for all we know. Inch clear, use the half-track's radios to call up reinforcements. And, for the sake of Christ, tell them 'no garrison troops' we don't want any careful old men, this is going to be work for heroes."

"Ya Herr Jager Leutnant." replied Hofmann, without enthusiasm he backed away on his beer belly, thinking it was as well he had brought the 'piss' with him; he was going to need it.

* * *

317

The snake slid silently from the path into the tree cover. All night it had kept the prey in sight. There was no need to move quietly, the roar of racing half-tracks drowned all other noise. It peered through slitted eyes; the defences around the HQ had given a good account. The two surviving vehicles were being reversed away from the blazing wreck of the lead vehicle. In a welter of snow they skidded to a halt fifty yards in front of it. Three men climbed down. They stood talking. One a, N.C.O, left quickly, one took guard by the wheezing hot vehicles and the third climbed on and into one half-track.

A burst of small arms fire from the right, the snake recognised the splutter of a German MG42. Tracer ripped through the trees. The snake attached his ski sticks in his pack. No need for them on the slope down to the half-tracks. He slid the safety on the Lanchester forward and pushed off. The skis slid silently over the compacted snow, gaining speed all the while.

The trooper on the ground took the short burst in the chest. The surviving man rose to his feet, reaching for his abandoned machine pistol. His headphones stopped him short. In a panicked filled second he had struggled free and swung his weapon towards the snake. These were vital seconds, seconds that could have saved his life, and didn't. The snake struck first. Miniature crimson volcanoes erupted across the man's heaving chest and he slumped back into his seat. The noise of the distant MG42 had drowned the noise of the snake's swift strike. It slivered to a halt, a bow-wave of snow covering the sentry's body. Removing the skis with quick glances to right and left, it opened the engines of both half-tracks and snatched out the ignition wiring, stuffing it deep, into the pocket of its white overalls. Next it smashed the valves of each of the radios and dragged the warm bodies of the prey to the edge of the tree line.

It tore a branch and returning covered all traces of its presence, carefully working back to the seclusion of the

318

trees. It removed the ground sheet and sleeping bag from the backpack. Carefully choosing a site, close to the two bodies. Pulling the white sheet over its long body it merged into the snow covered forest floor. The bait and the snake waited for more prey.

* * *

Bushel was beginning to enjoy himself, like a composer at the first night of his concert; months of creativity were blossoming into a symphony of noise and light. His only worry was the Norwegians on his flank. Kristiansand and his father were no soldiers and could not be relied on to defend a position for long, not in the face of these seasoned mountain troops. He would be happier if Olaf was here, closer to the tunnel and their escape route. He reached a decision and taking the flare pistol crawled out of the HQ and along the shallow drainage ditch, twenty yards; there was no point in drawing Jerry's attention to the log HQ, flare signals fired from there would do just that, Jerry would soon realise it was not just another gun position. He fired the two flares in quick succession. Immediately a German voice called from the trees, bursts of heavy machine gun fire kicked earth and snow in around him as he crawled, head low and body flat back to shelter.

* * *

Suddenly two flares lit the night sky to Sieg's front. He turned on his side and yelled, "Dautel! Bring your fire to bear on that flare position!" The MG42 gunner commenced fire, tracer tracked through the trees sending splinters of wood flying.

Sieg rolled over on his back as Hoffman slid in beside him. "That could be their HQ," he yelled, jerking one thumb over his shoulder, "That's the second signal from there. Any word from HQ?"

"Not yet, Herr Leutnant."

Sieg frowned, "They're taking too long, send someone to the rear, check they're in contact."

* * *

The HQ runner backed away from the position and turning in the snow, crawled on his elbows for another fifty yards, stood up and crouching double ran back towards the vehicle park.

He saw the two radio operators sitting, their backs against the trees. He ran straight up to them. "By the Gods, you two would have been for it if I'd been the Ober…"

A hand appeared from behind his head, he had time to see a tattooed snake on an exposed wrist, before his throat contracted beneath a sinewy arm. He heard the crack of his own spine and then a painless void enveloped him.

* * *

The snake surveyed its handiwork from the comfort of its hideaway. The trap was a thing of beauty, a diorama worthy of any exhibition. The three corpses were propped against the trees. It took time to enjoy the way the fat man's hand rested gracefully on the shoulder of his neighbour. It raised a hip flask in the direction of the trio and took a swig of the fat man's Schnapps. Fat soldiers always carried little extras, little tit bits to enjoy.

It could be the last kill here… it might be necessary to move again. The dirt track to the rear? The tongue flicked across the wet lips in anticipation. It took a last look at the art of the Mentor before smiling slyly and sliding back deeper into the folds of the ground sheet.

* * *

It was as he had sensed, the others had come in

strength, too strong a force, come to see his handiwork. No chance of a quiet kill. They would send a messenger now. The Mentor had made sure of that, they had no radio. Another move in the game, how it enjoyed anticipating the 'others' move. How it would enjoy countering it. The long body slid smoothly, slowly from cover and then swiftly through the trees. As it went it laughed quietly, a hissing sound, humour absent in the sick eyes.

The snake had already chosen the position, a sharp turn in the path. The prey would be cautious here. It would check the road ahead making sure it was clear; its whole attention would be on that. Strike time! It laughed again. It was laughing a lot lately, a sign the Mentor was enjoying the work, was pleased with him. Knew the snake did not want to return to England with the others. It smiled, nodding in understanding. Here it was no crime, here it could kill at will. Here there were hundreds, thousands of prey... enough for even the snake's insatiable needs. He must remain here with the Mentor, they must never be parted.

* * *

The Norwegian Sea, 0550 hrs, Monday, 28th May, 1940.

'Eddy'

Grant cursed; the moon had appeared from behind thick cloud. In the ghost-white light he could see every detail of Crosswall-Brown's boat as if it was day. The M.T.B. leapt over the waves like a racehorse taking fences, eager to be taking the next.

Abruptly the coast of Norway appeared from the sea, peaks of snow capped mountains shrouded in mist tipped with silver from the setting moon.

Too much light, by entering the Inlet now he was risking the secret base, the Network", just about everything they had worked for. In any other circumstances he would have veered off, abandoned the mission, and returned home. This time was different, he had no choice, his orders were to get their people out.

As dawn's first light painted the sky, quenching the darkness behind the rugged silhouette, the line of the coast began to grow in stature. Ten miles to go, at thirty knots, twenty minutes. They would make it now, but only just.

"Ship! Green two five!" the lookout's cry shattered that brief moment of triumph and relief. As he whipped his binoculars up, struggling to focus both the glasses and his tired brain, a star-shaped light, winked its challenge. Beyond the loom of the light he instantly recognised the sleek head-on silhouette of an enemy destroyer.

* * *

Inlet

It had grown cold as the dawn approached; already the sky had started to lighten in the east. Sieg surveyed the enemy's position through the powerful Zeiss binoculars. He had hoped that the reinforcements, he had sent for, would arrive before dawn, unlikely now. He had set sentries in the rear to counter any more of the dissident behaviour that had cost him valuable men. He lowered the glasses and turned round to continue his briefing of Hoffman.

"I will attack at zero six-thirty hours even if the extra men have not arrived. I am certain there are no more than eight or ten men against our thirty. It is enough…the fewer of us the greater the glory, No?"

Hoffman's eyes flashed momentarily to his leader's face. He was serious. The blue eyes flashed back to the tree above Sieg's shaven head. "Yes. Herr Jager Leutnant!"

"I want you to take half the men around to the right flank, go well to the rear before moving across, I don't want the enemy to know of your movements. At zero six-thirty, precisely, we attack together. That will give you plenty of time to move into position, no skis until you are well out of ear-shot."

The Oberjager, bobbed his head, clicked his heels and turning smartly away checked for the reassuring presence of the hip flask.

* * *

The Mentor was all knowing...all seeing. Hadn't he prophesied exactly what the prey would do. The other had arrived exactly as he had foretold. He travelled on foot, the Mentor had made sure of that when he had the vehicles destroyed. He slowed at the bend, as it had been decreed he would, the snake must now ensure that the man died in the way ordained by his Mentor.

It smelt the man's fear as he died, as he wriggled pathetically in the last long embrace. The fear was strong, rank, acrid; he sucked it deep into his lungs. It gave him strength... it made him one with his Mentor. There would be no reinforcements for the others now, but the snake had one more kill, at a hut in the forest....

* * *

'Eddy'

Grant had a moment of doubt, by now the German destroyer, for that matter the whole occupied coastline, must know of the captured E-boats. Try to bluff it out or not?...It might buy Crosswall-Brown some time, some breathing space: it might not. Without taking the binoculars from his eyes he shouted, "Middy! the youngster appeared alongside him, oilskin shining like black oil. "Make to Jerry, We have a captured enemy Schnellboote. Others are in the area. Last known position Latitude 64 degrees north Longitude nine degrees east'... Get that off quickly, and then..." he paused, the moment he had dreaded, since that last leave, had now arrived, "Signal the 'Dirty Four'... 'Act independently... Engage the enemy...'" Something caught in his throat. He swallowed quickly. "Add, 'God's speed'. " Fighting to keep his voice steady he bent to the wheelhouse voice pipe. "Come to port, steer west twenty north. Full ahead all engines."

* * *

The snake could see the hut now as he slid steadily nearer through the misty half-light before dawn. When the light came he would take another. It would be his last task, the last of the commands, for a moment he felt confusion, were they the commands of the Mentor or of the other called Bushel. It mattered not for it knew it was what the Mentor wanted.

It heard the sound of men in whispered conversation. The snake stretched its long body forward, turned towards the sound, a half smile on its face as it tasted the air with a wet tongue. Here he would take only one, the head one. It would remove the head like a chicken and leave the body to die in its own juices. Something laughed quietly.

The snake had known the head-prey would be here even if the other called Bushel hadn't; a testimony to the superiority of the snake over the other. It had to stop himself from chuckling, the Mentor did not like noise...noise was the enemy of the hunter. It grinned, half sneer, half revulsion at man's inadequacy, its head extended, tongue licking at its stained teeth. A devil's face, sick with sin. It would wait...wait until the prey was ready, ripe...it would be soon. The striped-blackened face with the mad yellow eyes merged silently back into the dense foliage.

* * *

It had fallen quiet as Bushel had expected. Jerry would

be re-positioning, waiting for first light, readying for the off, what he would have done in the same circumstances.

There wouldn't have been more than fifty Germans in those three half-tracks. No one would have survived the mining of that first vehicle that would leave thirty... maybe more....but then they had accounted for a few since...less than thirty then. If 'Snake' had survived to do his bit there would be no reinforcements. Thirty...It was still enough to take this place if they knew their stuff ... if their officers were still alive.

* * *

Marine Blake, unseen, watched Oberjager Hofmann and his men removing their skis. Another five or ten yards and they would have been in the perfect position, in amongst the first of the explosives. As it was they had stopped too far back. He would have to be patient. They would have to come nearer, plenty of time. They looked like experienced soldiers, judging by their kit, possibly Alpine Troops. He had trained with their sort in Norway before the war. He knew how good they had to be... they wouldn't be squadies on skis. About fifteen as far as he could see, though it was difficult to tell exactly. He eased the safety on the Bren and checked the sights for snow.

By the time he looked back they were spreading out and had begun to move forward. He gave one quick burst on the Bren... Brrrr! They were good, inside one second there was nobody there. He'd got one for definite, maybe another wounded, he could hear groaning.

He reached out to his right and pushed down on the first plunger. The explosion was muffled by the snow...disappointing, anticlimactic even, but the effects weren't. Men flew out from behind trees. He guessed five...six, somersaulting through the air like rag dolls, dead before they hit the snow.

Angry orange tongues flickered back from the trees as

the troops returned fire. As he'd hoped his earlier short burst had gone undetected, the fire was erratic, random, a gut-scared reaction. They had no idea where he was... and he had no plans to enlighten them...yet.

* * *

M.T.B.34

Crosswall-Brown's signalman struggled to read the message from Grant's boat; it was directed towards the enemy destroyer, not towards them, a mere loom of light.

"Enemy destroyer has challenged the 'Eddy', sir. She replied, I think she asked if the destroyer had sighted something or the other, but I couldn't be sure... 'Eddy' signalling us now sir...reads...'Act independently... Engage the enemy...God's Speed'."

Crosswall-Brown yelled above the roar of the engines. "Hoist Battle Ensigns... Stand by torpedo tubes...Stand by depth charges. Guns hold your fire until my order. "Helmsman! Starboard wheel..." he leant quickly over the compass, "Steer east twenty south!"

Crosswall-Brown looked down at his hands, they had been shaking badly, now they had stopped, it was always like that. He'd be all right now. He had always known he was more afraid of being afraid then of anything else.

"Middy we'll go in... close range... torpedoes first then depth charges," he yelled, "Signalman make to enemy destroyer, "Enemy astern of you... am attacking."

They bounced in, the roar of the aero engines mounting to a screaming crescendo; twenty knots... twenty-five knots. She began to punch into each wave like a prize-fighter at a punch bag. Thirty knots. She wouldn't take much more... not in this sea. The range was closing at a colossal sixty knots. They were hurtling towards each other at a mile a minute. His beloved 'Dirty Four' was banging across the sea's surface like a skipping stone, great spurts of water jetting from her wooden sides each time she hit solid water. He loved this boat! He wished he'd had time to circle round, come in from windward. Then she would have flown across the surface like an albatross. Suddenly he remembered one of Barr's saying 'War affords very few luxuries, time isn't one of them.'

He wiped his binoculars dry on the towel hanging damp around his neck and, choosing his moment carefully, peered at the enemy warship. Time for one quick look and then the spray drenched them again. Time enough to see the barrels were training in his direction. He looked astern, they were hard to miss, the spray they displaced as their full weight smacked into each wave, shone with a luminance better than any flare.

"Enemy vessel signalling, 'Veer away... or I will... fire."

He wiped quickly at the glasses, snatched another look. He was looking straight down the barrels of the destroyer. He felt like a man about to commit suicide. He been in action before, many times, but not like this. This was different. This was no dead-end decision, devoid of choice. He had time to turn and run, time to think of the consequences if he didn't. The crew had no choice, another 'luxury' not afforded. So this was bravery; this selfish unthinking madness. He shut out the thought. He'd become good at that at least. Another quick look, she'd turned broadside on, he could see her entire length. Suddenly the destroyer disappeared, obliterated by smoke and stabbing flame. A full broadside was on its way.

He bawled, "Come to port two points!" and then above the roar of salvo crashing by, "Torpedomen... Ready torpedoes... Standby... Standby...The bow steadied like a training gun. "Launch!...Launch!...Launch!" Immediately there was a flash of liquid silver light and two ghostly shapes shot forward into the soaring bow wave.

"We're going round her stern...Stand by depth charges. Set shallow."

The swerving, leaping, vulnerable M.T.B. shot down the destroyer's port side. Close in, too fast for the main armament to follow. The cannon on the destroyer's bridge opened up, rounds of deadly 20 mil bullets, kicking water, chased the sprinting grey form. The destroyer was swinging now, under full helm, towards the torpedo's glittering moonlit tracks; swinging to present the smallest target possible to the thousand pounds of high explosive hurtling towards her.

Abruptly the bridge began to shake to a well remembered, inescapable beat. The destroyer's cannon had found the range, punching quick holes through the wooden structure, they drilled their way forward, scattering splinters and men as they went. They penetrated the flimsy bridge screen as if it were paper, lifting Crosswall-Brown off his feet with consummate ease. The impact threw him the width of his bridge. His hurtling body crashed through the thick glass, smacked into the starboard machine gun's smoking barrel and dropped at the feet of the young and horrified gunner.

On what was left of the bridge, an appalled midshipman, now in sole command of thirty knots of careering metal stood in catatonic shock. The enemy's stern reared to port and he screamed, "Hard aport… launch depth charge!"

The careering battered M.T.B. took the corner like a greyhound on a racetrack bend. A wall of foaming water enveloped her as she bounced across the destroyer's foaming wake.

The depth charge was sucked into the foam-mountain, as if it had never been. The men on the destroyer's bridge knew nothing of the deadly drum as it disappeared quickly into their wake. A second later the sea astern inflated, ballooned into a green hill by the high explosive, it burst, detonated, lifting the destroyer's stern, high, into the evening sky.

Trembling from the huge blast, she lost way,

staggering to a halt like a wounded deer, instantly she began to settle by the stern; her head rising slowly in the air, rearing in one last graceful, dying gesture. Frantic men were jumping into the sea, spewing from her bowels in an endless stream, her warm lifeblood chilled in the icy cold of the sea.

The M.T.B. sped on into the dawn, steady on a course to intercept her consort, the blood of her young commanding officer washing crimson from her scuppers.

* * *

Dawn 27th May 1940

Bushel heard the German's dawn attack going in on the left flank and waited to receive his own. He had called the Norwegians in from the right and sent them below; at least they would be safe... Here they come ... white figures, moving from tree to tree, criss-crossing his front. Well trained all right... but his training was better...white overalls too clean against the pine needle covered snow, for instance; big mistake.

He was sure they knew roughly where he was, no point in trying to conceal that now. He fired a long sweeping burst and saw at least four fall backwards... not forwards. The rest had gone, disappeared. He ducked away from the firing slit, just in time, the return fire chipped viciously at the thick logs, sending splinters of pine flying about him. He waited patiently while they crawled for the tree cover... about now... he gripped the handle... pushed down hard, the explosion echoed back from the mountain, it acted like a switch, the firing stopped and he snatched a quick look. A haze of smoke obscuring the site wafted gently away... two men hung from the lower branches of one pine, swinging like string puppets. He thought he saw three others in piles of dirty snow. He gave a quick burst at a running figure and saw him topple, bow- backed and screaming.

A lull then he heard shouted commands...they would be orders to go back rather than forward, in either case...time to duck. The expected covering fire was heavy... that MG42 again.

* * *

Oberjager Hofmann had no idea where this third firing position was, they had moved to out-flank the first two only to be attacked from a third that had remained quiet. The English only played by the rules when it suited them.

Sieg had his hands full judging by the explosions on the left flank. Where were the reinforcements? He raised his head quickly above the cover and took a quick look round. A ditch to his right seemed to run forward, if he sent a section down there they would at least get a different angle on things and maybe spot this arschloch wherever he was. They might even outflank him.

* * *

They had found the ditch; Blake had seen the heads bobbing, like targets at a fairground stall. They were still way out, along the far sector, still in the tree line. Bushel knew his stuff all right...he'd predicted their every move so far. Blake waited for a count of twenty, took another quick look and pushed down hard on the hand generator, a ripple of explosions shot along the ditch. He bobbed up ...huge amounts of soil was erupting from the drainage ditch, spraying into the air... earth fountains... and three bodies... two landed clear of the ditch the other toppled on its edge, gave up the ghost and slowly slid back in. Nine-ish down seven-ish to go.

* * *

Jager Leutnant Sieg knew the whole thing was falling

apart, no reinforcements, massive explosions to his front and on his right flank. He reached behind for his binoculars, his elbow touched something soft...It moved, he swung round expecting to see one of his men. Nothing, his eyes dropped to the level of his waist Crouched on the floor at his side was a figure, green face hideously striped in black, yellow teeth, mad eyes. He recoiled in horror, uttering a strangled cry. The figure uncoiled in a sinewy leap, reaching up, grabbing for his throat. In a reflex, born of repulsion, he hit out with the binoculars and made contact. The figure fell back; Sieg threw a kick, a swinging pile driver, with all of his fourteen stone behind it. Abruptly a knife flickered up in front of the swinging leg stabbing deep between his legs. Sieg's kick never made contact; his leg snapped back in another reflex jerk, he lost balance falling back. He looked down, from between his legs blood was gushing from the severed artery. He felt cold...everything was cold, only the blood was warm. The figure had gone... slipped away into the darker recesses of the room. He could hear quiet laughter coming in short bursts, like the hissing of a snake. He was floating, drifting in a sea of numbing pain; he rose...floated, drifted and rose into the blackness and that one distant light beckoning...

Chapter 19

A Seed of Doubt

Morning Watch, 27th May, 1940.

Every rivet on the 'Nishga' seemed to be vibrating with the strain as she fought to keep up with her swifter consorts.

Barr had retired to his sea cabin; he laid fully clothed, except for his salt stained duffel coat and dog-eared sea boots. He had dozed off for a few minutes when he heard the lid lifting on the bridge voice pipe; after eight months of war that was all it took.

"Yes?" he asked quickly before the bridge could say a word or worse, sound the hated bell.

"Captain, sir?" It was Grey, his voice echoing eerily in the confines of the metal pipe, "Signal from Flag, I'm afraid."

Barr breathed in resignedly, "Read it, please."

"Time 0435. 'Nishga' repeated Admiral Ramsey. Message reads 'Enemy cruiser sighted. Position four degrees two minutes east, fifty two degrees ten minutes north ... course south twenty east... speed twenty-five knots. Intercept and delay until re-enforced'...Message ends.

In the dark of his cabin Barr pulled a face, "I'll be right up."

He thundered up the bridge ladder, his heavy boots rattling the metal treads. The fresh damp air blew the cobwebs of sleep away.

The destroyer was lifting to the long swell rolling rhythmically in from astern. He made for the chart table and the muffled figure of Grey bent over the wind-rippled chart.

"Morning, sir...She's here, west of Amsterdam, steaming south, out to interfere with the evacuation?"

"I should say almost certainly, and we're here?" Barr pointed.

"Yes, sir and that's an interception course," he pointed to pencilled calculations on the chart margin.

"Very good, Number One... Acknowledge the signal and come round onto the new course." He tapped a gloved finger on the chart margin, his mind racing. "We'll go to Action Stations in one hour, inform Hogg and Kendel." He looked back down at the chart while Grey moved to the array of voice pipes on the bridge screen "Bridge, Wheelhouse."

"Wheelhouse." replied the helmsman.

"Port twenty... steer south thirty east". He lifted another lid while he listened to the wheel order being repeated. He pressed the bell, a signalman below answered. "This is the bridge, "Make to Flag, Proceeding in accordance with your 0435 stroke 28 stroke 5."

* * *

The Action Station Alarm brought the watch below stumbling bleary-eyed to join their mates already closed up. Grey stood by the voice pipes acknowledging each of the closing up reports as they came in. A quarter sea corkscrewed the racing warship.

"Coxswain on the wheel!"... "Depth Charge Crews closed up"..."Short range weapons closed up"...he checked them off one by one until satisfied he turned to Barr and saluted, "Ship at Action Stations, sir."

"Very good, Number One," Barr handed him a sheet of paper, "These are my intentions when we flush out the enemy cruiser... have it sent to the 'Ethel' and the 'Dirty Five' by lamp. Keep the copy for yourself, in case. You'll see Hogg's E-boat is to go ahead of us, so as to be in a position to attack the cruiser from landward. With luck, the enemy's attention will be on us and the M.T.B. and Hogg's 'Ethel' will go undetected, especially against the mass of the land. I intend to hold that attention long enough for him to get into a good firing position. We will be attacking from seaward. Should Jerry sight Hogg there's a good chance he'll be fooled into believing her to be on his side and coming to his aid. It may give us an edge...it may not."

* * *

The faint pall of smoke smudging the horizon to the south-east was reported at 0732 by the crow's nest lookout from his position high above the bridge on the tripod mast. It was duly noted in the ship's log.

At 0735 the massive cruiser turned towards and opened fire at extreme range. The lookout reported the smoke and flash long before they heard the distant rumble of the guns; time 0738.

Barr fancied he could see the shells as they flew through the air towards his 'Nishga'. He tensed as the scream of shot filled the air, but the giant shells passed over. The cruiser was closing rapidly, an awesome sight, towering above the horizon, terrace upon terrace of grey metal and dazzle paint, brisling with guns.

The Yeoman of Signals looked up from his copy of Jane's Fighting Ships. "She's the 'Nienburg', sir... heavy cruiser, six eight inch guns... twelve four inch, double mounted torpedo tubes and the usual Ack-Ack stuff." He ducked involuntarily as the 'Nisgha's' bridge was suddenly drenched by the second salvo.

"Nice to know exactly what is trying to kill you." remarked a voice from the back of the bridge.

Barr was watching the enemy through his binoculars. Why wasn't she keeping her distance those big guns had a range of over twenty miles, why risk closing. She was now heading due south, hull up on the horizon. Through the powerful glasses he could make out the 'bone in her teeth', the white bow wave thrown up in front of her as she surged forward. Every few seconds she became shrouded in the smoke from her own massive guns, emerging from it like a grey ghost through cemetery mist. She must be averaging four salvoes a minute, two hundred and sixty pound shells and four of the buggers in each salvo. Travelling at close to two thousand miles an hour, sending the sea around them into dancing spouts of water higher than the 'Nishga's' mainmast.

The next salvo landed to their front; she'd managed to straddle them, time for a course alteration, if ever there was one.

* * *

Sub Lieutenant Hogg watched, gripping the windscreen, as the third salvo roared in towards the 'Nishga'. She was now way over to port, her low silhouette almost hull down and turning away from the anticipated fall of shot. As yet he had no sighting of the enemy and was reacting purely to the 'Nishga's' 'Enemy in sight to the south east'. He had immediately turned to starboard. Altering towards where there was a chance that they might go undetected against the rocky coastline, but at their top speed they would need fifteen perhaps twenty minutes to circle round onto the enemy's flank; would the 'Nishga' survive that long?

* * *

The 'Nishga's' two Battle Ensigns, cracked like whips in her own thirty knot slipstream as she raced in towards the 'Nienburg'. Barr anxious to close the range so his own four-point sevens, hopelessly out-gunned, as they were, could at least return fire.

Way out to starboard, Kendel's M.T.B. flew her own tiny ensigns, like her bigger consort she flew two, in case one was shot away. Barr saw the irony of it, if her flimsy wooden hull took just one 'brick' there would be no need to worry about ensigns still flying. She was steering south east, her high-octane aero-engines opening the gap between them at a terrific rate.

The fourth salvo screamed overhead as Barr scribbled in the chart table note book. He turned to a white-faced young signalman. "Get this off to the 'Ethel'… Pilot! Tell 'Torps' Ready both tubes. I will be attacking at very close range. The cruiser will turn towards the torpedoes, she'll be expecting them, I will keep pace with her turn, and make smoke. Then, I will attack with…" Another salvo straddled the speeding 'Nishga' as their own four point sevens came into range…but the Pilot had heard alright, he nodded and turned away.

The range was closing at sixty knots. This German captain was playing it safe; bow on he was showing only fifty feet of target to his enemy he could have sacrificed that in order to use his after turrets; he had chosen otherwise.

Hogg's E-boat, must be somewhere out there, broad on 'Nishga's' starboard bow, and hopefully already turning to run parallel to the coastline.

* * *

"What's she saying signalman?" Hogg's eyes were

riveted on the cruiser, she was on their port bow hidden in smoke from her last broadside, but they could still see the giant searchlight they were using as a signal lamp " 'Heave to.'" reported the signalman, "And now…she wants us to clear our decks of all crew."

The captured E Boats had never operated this far south, but this chap wasn't relying on history, wasn't taking any risks, doubtless he'd heard of the rogue E-Boats' exploits further north. It was a clever move, if the E-Boat was a rogue, with no men on deck, she'd be incapable of aggressive action, and if they disobeyed the order her skipper would know they were the enemy.

"Make, 'Repeat your last.' and send it slowly." He had to play for time, anything to gain precious minutes. That's all it would take for him to get in position for an attack, an attack that, at the very least, should draw some attention away from the embattled 'Nishga'.

As Barr was fond of saying, 'Doubt was a powerful weapon, everyone had it, make sure that the enemy has more than you' He was right, if he could make this German Captain hesitate for just thirty seconds, they would be five hundred yards closer to target. His life, the lives of his crew and probably the lives of the entire flotilla depended on sowing that seed of doubt.

* * *

Through his glasses, Barr saw the cruiser's close range guns open up on Kendel's M.T.B., a withering fire, throwing the sea around the tiny craft into turmoil of leaping spray. Kendel had turned onto his attack course only seconds before. He was racing in, with a bow wave that reached twice the height of his main deck. A magnificent sight, David and Goliath, armour against wood, raw courage against impossible odds. Suddenly a huge flash lit the sea, Barr gasped. The M.T.B. had gone, vanished in a ball of fire that spewed burning fuel along her boiling wake. The flaming ball tore on towards the enemy cruiser as if the ghosts of her incinerated crew were set on a fiery revenge, but she dropped lower and lower, slowed and finally stopped. It burned on, Kendel his boat and his crew wrapped in a flaming shroud of their own fuel.

Barr tore his gaze from the flames, forced himself to concentrate on the enemy cruiser. Her for'ard turrets erupted fire, the after turrets were silent, then he realised why, they were training round onto the remaining patrol boat; Hogg's 'Ethel'. The eight inch guns spit fire and venom. The German Captain had not been fooled for long, was it long enough? Beyond the enemy's bow Barr could see the 'Ethel' dancing in towards her towering target, the first fall of shot from the cruiser's guns were over ranged...the second under. Bracketed; the third could well destroy the speeding E-boat...Hogg's boat began a broad weave, presenting each of her sides to the smoking barrels of the enemy cruiser in turn. The third salvo was way to one side, Hogg was handling his tiny boat beautifully managing to upset the enemy's gun aimers... but for how long ... he would need to get in close, close enough for the small boat to even the odds in her favour.

On her next weave she kept going to starboard... kept going while the cruiser's guns wrongly, anticipated a turn back to port. The tactic worked, Barr saw the terrible eight-inch shells bouncing across the sea, way out to port of the leaping, swerving E-boat.

* * *

'Ethel'

The German gunnery control team had realised their mistake the huge after turrets of the enemy cruiser were already swinging laboriously back towards them. They shuddered to a halt, pointing directly at him, smoke drifted lazily from the blackened end of the barrels. It was as if five hundred tons of turret was trying to anticipate his next move.

He kept the starboard helm on. Kept it on until he saw the guns traversed left to follow him and then he turned the 'Ethel' rapidly in a tight turn the other way, until the broad, fat, port side of the cruiser filled the horizon like a giant block of flats.

"Midships, steady!"

Soaked to the skin, water streaming from his oilskin he yelled, "Stand by both tubes!" Then, "Launch...Launch...Launch!"

The two torpedoes leapt from their tubes, momentarily skimming the wave crests and them plunging deeper, chasing the speeding cruiser as she turned away, all her close range weaponry were blazing away at the tiny 'Ethel'. Then 'X' and 'Y' turrets caught up and opened fire. As first, through the great spouts of water the massive shells threw up, the torpedoes leapt and cavorted, twisted and weaved, but gradually they matched the enemy's speed, knot for knot until slowly they began to better it, overhauling her, closer and closer.

* * *

The cruiser's captain faced with the unenviable choice of torpedoes astern of him and the destroyer abeam, chose to keep to his course. Hoping to outpace the torpedoes and let his big guns take care of the destroyer.

The cruiser's turn away from Hogg's torpedoes had presented Barr with just what he'd hoped and planned for. The enemy cruiser was now directly down wind and broadside on to the 'Nishga' as the destroyer raced in.

"Both mountings stand by for a torpedo attack, starboard side, all tubes." Barr turned to the engine room voice pipe "Make smoke".

He was looking aft towards the funnels anticipating the clouds of concealing smoke when the eight-inch shell struck.

The blast threw him back against the for'ard screen with incredible force, pain shot through his whole body, the impact drove the air from his lungs, he managed to rise shakily to one knee. Gasping for air, his head spinning with pain, he looked about him. The smoke screen was billowing from the funnel, stinging his eyes, but, by the grace of God, sweeping downwind towards the enemy. His mouth opened in surprise the main mast had gone. He staggered to the rear of the bridge and looked down; the 'Nishga's' tripod mast hung over the port side, a mass of wires and crippled steel girders. The crews of the depth charge throwers were already running forward to clear the wreckage. "Petty Officer," he yelled, "Leave that to your leading hand, take two men aft, stand by to jettison the E boat's fuel drums on my order likewise the charges in their racks, set shallow."

"Aye, Aye, sir," the burly P.O. grabbed two men by the scruff of their necks and propelled them aft, Barr smiled, action speaking louder than words, or at least more quickly.

He reached the for'ard screen and caught a fleeting glimpse of the enemy. At last 'Nishga's' four point sevens were doing damage, the forward turret of the cruiser had taken a hit at its base, toppling it from its turntable, its barrels pointing harmlessly at the sky. Then she was gone enveloped once again in choking smoke. The 'Nishga's' four sevens fell silent. The smoke screen had rendered both ships' gunnery control useless, blind, wrapped in an acrid, oily blackness.

He yelled to the torpedo communications rating, "Torpedo action starboard! Open sights...Launch when ready...Pilot! Port fifteen take her across the enemy's bow!"

Barr watched from the starboard wing of the bridge as the tubes fired, the deadly fish slipping gracefully into the swell, disappearing rapidly from sight.

The cruiser's captain had been waiting, had glimpsed the torpedoes launching, despite the choking smoke. He executed an emergency turn to port, but the sleek destroyer was turning faster, tucking herself in across the cruiser's projected path, she was still in danger of taking that pointed bow full square in her vitals.

Barr whirled the handle of the quarterdeck phone. "Jettison the aviation fuel drums."

Aft, the drums rolled eagerly from their stern ramps. Four depth charges sank in to the foaming wake at the same time.

At thirty knots the six-thousand tons of cruiser charged headlong into the drums; the explosion spewed blazing fuel oil high over the cruiser's fo'c's'le.

The E-boat's torpedoes sped by missing their burning target, passing only feet from the 'Nishga's' stern.

The 'Ethel' was now coming in from astern of the cruiser. The cruiser's after eight-inch fell silent unable to bear on so close a target. Abruptly Hogg turned the 'Ethel' across her stern. Two depth charges dropped into the sea as the cruiser continued her turn, Hogg tried to follow her round, to keep close in, fearful of the cruiser's burning bow section, he had left the turn a matter of seconds too late. The remaining forward eight inch was ready on the bearing as the E-boat emerged from the cruiser's shadow. The huge shell hit the speeding boat amidships, her aluminium hull disintegrated completely and immediately. For several seconds, propelled by her own momentum, 'Ethel's' blazing remains sped on at top speed, skipping across the waves, then slowed, her bow dropping back into the water. As the 'Ethel' died so her depth charges exploded in the wake of the already blazing 'Nienburg', lifting the vast bulk from the water, blowing off her rudder and screws. The mighty cruiser instantly lost way, smoke and flames pouring from her gaping wounds, she settled slowly back into the waves, like some huge factory she spewed clouds of black smoke. Then abruptly the after magazine exploded with unbelievable force, wrapping her in orange flame. She dropped back onto her shattered stern, her blazing bow swung skywards, men cascading from her like ants.

Chapter 20

The Miracle

HMS Nishga, off Dunkirk, France. Monday, 27th May 1940.

Dunkirk lay along a grey horizon, stretching away to pencil thickness wreathed in black smoke from the town's burning storage tanks. To the east a cold red sun rose, flooding its rouged reflection into a pewter-coloured sea.

Between the battered 'Nishga' and the shore, a myriad of crowded small boats bobbed and tossed their way west. All were laden to the gunwales with the dispirited remnants of the expeditionary force which had landed on the shores of France, so gloriously, a few short months before.

The crew of the destroyer were stood to at their action stations as she nosed her way carefully in towards the shore. It was thus, carefully, watchfully, excited and afraid that they entered, not only the harbour, but history, the way fighting men had entered it since time immemorial.

This was the second day of Dunkirk, but for the crew of the 'Nishga' it was the first. No one had experience anything like it before, a panorama filled with ships and boats of all shapes and sizes, horizon to horizon, and beyond. Thousands of men adrift, upon hundreds of boats; ferries, freighters, fishing boats, every conceivable craft had been enlisted for the vital job of saving the Army. Small overcrowded boats, mere dots on a vast canvas, passed alarmingly close to the destroyer, slipping by in her frothing wake. Their gunwales hung with doll-like khaki-clad and sea sick soldiers, French, British, the wounded and the exhausted.

Ashore long lines of men, like human breakwaters, stretched seaward from the long beaches. In the harbour itself, a huge queue, snaked its way, three-deep for almost a mile around the rocky mole that protected it from the sea.

In the smoke flecked and shell torn sky a confusing array of aircraft, climbed and dived, twisted and turned in noiseless dog-fights.

The 'Nishga' entered through the breakwater astern of a rust streaked pleasure steamer, the two ships weaving in and out of the treacherous sandy shoals that littered the harbour approaches. Every shoal carried its wrecked ship, some still in flames, some still with men on board. From deeper water, funnels and the tops of shattered masts rose from the oil- slicks; broken tombstones in a bleak and desolate graveyard.

Suddenly every anti-aircraft gun, ashore and afloat, opened up as tiny bent-winged specks dived out of the sky. A terrible wailing-scream filled the air as the Stuka dive-bombers swooped onto the sitting ducks. Hemmed in by the mole and the treacherous sand banks, they could take no avoiding action, there wasn't enough sea room to swing a cat. The steamer ahead took two direct hits and staggered out of line like a wounded swan, smoke billowing from her gaping fo'c's'le. Immediately she began to sink. With her fore-ends already under water her crew were desperately rigging pumps and hoses, frantic to keep her afloat long enough to ground her on the sandbanks. They made it; as she settled by the bow a shroud of bubbling water and steam rose from her flooded boilers.

All the while the sea around churned and leapt under the relentless onslaught from the Stuka's five hundred pound bombs. As the pleasure steamer moved aside to her last resting place they saw the next in line, an old paddle steamer burning like a torch, full to capacity with soldiers. A mass of flames, her captain had already run her aground.

The last of the bombers, dropped like a stone, straight towards a now, barely moving 'Nishga'. The after pom-pom caught it, blowing off one wing; it spiralled on, spinning madly, like a badly made child's paper plane. While fragments of its port wing showered across the open bridge, the main body of the crippled Stuka, wailing like a banshee, hit the fo'c's'le and disintegrated among the anchor cables, the wreckage burst into an orange-bright ball of flames. The bomb itself had exploded in the water alongside, drenching the men from 'A' turret as they ran forward to tackle the blaze.

The flight of Stukas took off to the west, chased by the black flowers of exploding Ack Ack.

Mercifully a respite was in the offering for the wind veered and the whole sky became black with the smoke from Dunkirk's blazing oil tanks. Unable to see the beleaguered harbour, scores of enemy aircraft turned away, searching out other more visible targets.

"Sir, they're making our call sign from the beach. Message reads berth at the eastern breakwater. It's from a Captain Tennant, sir, SNOD."

"Snod?" queried Barr, watching his men stowing away the hoses on the blackened fo'c's'le.

"Yes, sir, Senior Naval Officer Dunkirk."

"Tennant! said Barr, turning to Lieutenant Usbourne in sudden realisation, "That'll be Bill Tennant, well at least we're in the best possible hands. I served under him in my first ship... Acknowledge please, Yeo and add, 'Congratulations on your new appointment, but the initials would have been more appropriate if you'd left the naval part out.' "

Even before they had the first line across, the harbour came alive with small craft ferrying soldiers to the 'Nishga's' waiting scrambling nets. Barr leant on the bridge screen watching the tired soldiers being dragged inboard by his sailors. He could only image the comments. He walked across the width of the open bridge. Low tide had the mole towering a good five feet above the 'Nishga's' iron deck, but it was no impediment to the impatient soldiery who, even before the gangway, was out were crossing the yawning gap under their own steam.

Within the hour and fully loaded, they were nosing their way back out through the treacherous shoals and the burning wrecks.

They took Route Y that first time... the longest of the three routes. It took them a torturous three and a half hours, first north east along the French coast as far as Bray-Dunes, then west to the North Goodwin Light and finally south for Dover and home. They were not destined to help Lieutenant Grant, far to the north; indeed he had finished his assignment long before the 'Nishga' had finished hers.

The next day, Tuesday, saw the 'Nishga' entering harbour to the news that General Brook's II Corp were trying hastily to plug the hole in the line left by the surrendering Belgian Army.

The congestion ashore and in the harbour had, if anything, become worse. As they entered harbour the old ferry, 'Queen of the Channel' came out through the mole, black smoke from her funnel swirling about her in a fitful breeze from the west, her decks alive with nearly a thousand men.

Suddenly the sky seemed filled with German aircraft, the 'Nishga's' guns opened up with a tremendous roar. Every gun on the shore, as well as on the gathered ships, joined in a furious barrage, sowing the sky around the aircraft with deadly white tracer and the blossoming black and brown flowers of exploding A.A.

The old ferry took the brunt of the attack as, laden to the gunwales, she chugged lady-like towards the harbour mouth. Time and time, again she disappeared behind the spray from the exploding bombs only to reappear on the other side, unharmed and seemingly unconcerned. Then she started to list over, a near miss must have damaged her below the waterline, she was taking on water through her sprung plates.

The yeoman of signals called from the bridge wing, "She's flying, 'Need assistance', sir.

"Very good, make to her, repeated SNOD, 'Going to assistance of foundering ship.' "

"Hard astarboard...Half astern starboard, half ahead port. Barely underway the 'Nishga' began to turn in her own length as her engines spun her round like a top, at the same time all her guns continued to blaze away.

Grey climbed the bridge ladder, shouting "We going alongside, sir?"

"Affirmative, Number One... Port side to."

"Aye, Aye, sir, shall I rig hoses?"

"Yes..." said Barr, and then turned away yelling, "Bridge messenger! Inform the sickbay that they may be having some customers shortly... Bosun's Mate! Ring down to the Engine Room tell them we will be stopping engines. Make sure they understand they are not to turn the screws without permission. There will be men in the water."

Grey called down to the sea boat between the crack and boom of the four-point -sevens, the rattle tat of the machine guns. "Bosun! Prepare to go alongside... port side to... rig fenders...scrambling nets over the starboard side... run hoses out ready in case of fire."

The Bosun's gravel voice could be heard seemingly louder that four-point- sevens; but then their whole attention was focused on the ferry, as she swung into view on the starboard bow.

"Midships! Stop engines...Slow ahead both engines.

Port ten...Steady!" For'ard the 'Nishga's' lowered jack staff centred on the ferry's stern, like an unerring gun sight, as, in the wheelhouse, the coxswain countered the destroyer's rapid swing.

His steady matter-of-fact voice repeating the orders, somehow extinguished all excitement like a damp blanket.

"Course south, sir, both engines repeated slow ahead."

The willowy destroyer passed slowly down the starboard side of the plump little ferry, all gun's still firing madly at the swooping aircraft. There was a rising spiral of foam from her stern; a plate-rattling shudder ran through her as her twin turbines went astern. Abruptly the way came off her and she settled within feet of the listing ferry, rolling lazily.

Lines were passed, they were brought to the capstan forward and the winch aft and the two vessels were dragged together like reluctant lovers.

A well ordered evacuation of the doomed ferry began under the cover of the rapidly firing guns. Soldiers were soon leaping across the treacherous gaps, created by the difference in the shape of the hull.

* * *

That day the only workable jetty, the harbour breakwater, was judged too dangerous for merchant shipping. From then on it was used only by the warships.

The merchantmen waited off shore, out of range of German shore guns, their human cargo ferried to them by the hundreds of small craft, requisitioned by the Ministry of Shipping.

On the morning of Thursday the 30th they heard news of the casualties The 'Wakeful' had been torpedoed the day before by an E-boat and had sank in fifteen seconds, only a handful of the six-hundred crew had survived. The 'Grafton' had also gone, torpedoed by a U Boat. The 'Grenade' had burned, like a torch, after she had been attacked and there had been few survivors. In the close family that was the regular Navy, most of 'Nishga's' crew knew someone who had been lost. Many had served on those very ships; all mourned the loss of not only the men, but their fine ships.

There was some good news; a thick fog had crept in, keeping the enemy aircraft away for most of the day.

The men fighting in Norway, were fairing no better than the men in France, the evacuations of the Bodo and Mo were both under way, Norway was being abandoned, along with France.

That day, also, the old paddle minesweeper 'Waverley' and the Anti aircraft ship 'Crested Eagle' were both sunk in the harbour.

On Friday the wind increased to force three from the south-west; nothing to the 'Nishga', but the small boats found it hard going, several were swamped, troops were seen frantically bailing water out of the frail craft, using their battered helmets as balers.

A rising wind cleared the fog, and in came the Heinkels, the Junkers and the dreaded Stukas.

The surf, whipped up by the wind ran up the exposed beach making it impossible to land boats. Evacuation was now only possible from the sheltered harbour. Inevitably the orderly queues of men waiting to board lengthened, winding their way back through the smoking ruins of the dockyard.

The Germans continued around the clock to shell and to bomb. Ghastly gaping holes were blown in the queues and in the breakwater they trod. The bodies of the wounded and the dead were removed and makeshift bridges constructed to get the men across to the waiting destroyers.

By Saturday, 1st of June, the bone-weary crew of the 'Nishga' were near to collapse; they had been closed up at their action stations, almost continuously, for five days and nights, managing only to catch a few hours sleep on the longer routes across the channel. There was no rest, even when the ship was away from poor decrepit Dunkirk. For then they moved under perpetual threat of attack from the fighters and bombers that were constantly overhead and, of course, there were always the U Boats and E-boats known to be in the Channel.

At one point Barr was an interested listener to a conversation between his Gunnery Officer, and the Cockney gun layer of 'A' gun. It concerned their last target. 'Guns' was apparently concerned over the exact identity of the target.

"Director to 'A' Gun."

" 'A' Gun"

"You were blazing away there, Petty Officer…Are you absolutely certain that was a Jerry?"

"Yes, sir," came the confident reply.

"What makes you so sure?"

"I used colour recognition to identify her, sir." replied the gun layer technically.

"Well, Erh…Well spotted…The colours aren't that different, though, are they?"

"Oh it's Dolly Dimple when you get the 'ang of it, sir," replied the seaman gunner, condescendingly.

"Well, perhaps you could let us all in on your secret. All stations listen in a minute, will you?"

Gun layer: "It's pretty straight forward, sir…If it's grey… it one of theirs. If it's black… it's one of theirs at night."

* * *

Saturday, 1st June; 1940

Adding to the tension, the Germans were now known to be laying mines, not only in the Dunkirk area, but also around the south coast ports that were being used to land the evacuees. By the end of that most terrible of days thirty-one ships had been sunk or disabled. Six destroyers were included in the toll, the brave 'Keith' amongst them; they were losing old friends at an alarming rate.

* * *

On Sunday the 'Nishga', returning empty from Dover via 'X' Route, received a distress call from two hospital ships, the 'Paris' and the 'Worthing', they were under attack in the channel. By the time they reached the 'Paris's position, three quarters of a mile east of W buoy she had already sunk.

The 'Worthing' badly damaged, following the attack by twelve German aircraft, had turned back for England.

They joined the other Navy ships in the search for survivors. Both vessels had been clearly marked as hospital ships and the Germans had been given notice that they would be carrying wounded from Dunkirk. Outraged by the brutality of the enemy the 'Nishgas' worked through their exhaustion in an angry silence, removing body after body from the water.

When they eventually reached Dunkirk they had to wait outside the breakwater. All the berths alongside were occupied; but the ships were empty. The seemingly endless stream of men had suddenly dried up. There were still thousands inland, but there had been a communication failure between Tennant's staff and Army Headquarters. Before long the news that there were empty ships in the harbour had spread verbally and the flood-gates reopened, but by that time, the 'Nishgas' had other things on their minds. They had orders to join the screen of destroyers, submarines and A.S.W. Trawlers protecting the evacuation from the packs of U Boats prowling the Channel. They sailed immediately: That day Dunkirk fell.

Epilogue

Barr settled back in his chair, drained the last of his pink gin and lit his battered pipe. He had dined alone, with only his steward to disturb his thoughts. It was his custom on these increasingly rare moments, to let his mind wander over the events of the day. Mentally he ticked off the day's tasks, occasionally leaning across and making notes in his salt stained diary.

That morning he had finished the last of the letters to the relatives of the dead, killed in the Dunkirk operation.

Dunkirk...Distracted by the memory, his pipe hung unnoticed from his mouth, the smoke twisting its way upwards. Scene after scene flashed before his eyes, memory after memory, shouted order after shouted order, bloody incident after worse.

Dunkirk had changed everything. Several brutal lifetimes had been condensed into those few days. A sort of shorthand in intense living, a brief alarming seminar that would remain with them for the rest of their days.

Before Dunkirk he had been a bit player, totally absorbed in his own part, with little thought for the greater plot. It was all those men, all those ships that had finally brought home to him the sheer immensity of the all. It was a tragedy performed on a world stage with a cast of thousands that was set to run and run. It had it all, death, calamity, horror even comedy; a play with surreal, gruesomely indelible scenes. Unrehearsed scenes of death and destruction, performances of heroism and self sacrifice on a scale he had never envisaged.

Out of defeat had come triumph. A triumph of organisation helped by heroism and not a small amount of prayer. Out of it too had come a dogged determination to prevail in the final act, whenever that might be.

He rose, a little unsteadily, from his chair, banged his pipe out in the desk ashtray and turning out the light, staggered to his bunk.

* * *

Lieutenant Crosswall-Brown's grave lay two miles north-east of Olaf's Inlet in eighty fathoms of cold water. The graves of Sub Lieutenants Hogg and Kendel and their men lie one hundred and ten miles north of Dunkirk, just part of the terrible human loss that was the beginnings of the Second World War. They were mourned by few of the many they had fought and died for... Some never forgot, told the tale to their grandchildren who although they understood the story could not begin to comprehend the sacrifice. Theirs was to be a very different world.

* * *

"So you see gentlemen," said Churchill, addressing the senior officers of Special Operations, "You are part of the greater plan..." He paused to puff an expensive cloud of blue Havana smoke at the Georgian cornice. "It will be your job to carry the war to the enemy, to pick us up off the canvas. The nastiest of bullies hesitates when he's being punched in his fat soft belly, and that is what you and your men will be doing. I call it 'Butcher and Bolt'. You are my strong left jab and the coast of Europe is the Hun's soft underbelly. I'll lead with you while I build up my strength for the right's knockout blow. When we left France, we left, by far, the greater part of our equipment behind. We need time...time, gentlemen...time to consolidate...time to build anew. You will buy me that time with the lives of your warriors... The cost will be high, but we so desperately need that time, for we stand on the edge of darkness."

* * *

The power of the unseen was infinite, the 'others' knew nothing of his presence, knew less of his power. He saw all, yet remained himself unseen. They were the unaware, they were the watched, they were the powerless, they were the prey, his amusement ... his game. Now he was alone...free...free to continue the lethal game he loved.

* * *

The King, in the uniform of Admiral of the Fleet stood on the rostrum, his gold braid startlingly bright against the red carpet and the blue velvet curtains. An aide gave him the first medal. There was just the one Victoria Cross to be presented today. It was posthumous...they nearly always were... They were always the first in the long line. He looked in the direction of the queue of recipients... the George Crosses were next, the... The quiet beauty of the first woman in the queue took his breath away. She wore black. He had never seen a woman look more beautiful in black, dignified and solemn yet somehow... radiant. At her side one of his uniformed aides leant forward and spoke to her. He could not hear what was said, but she walked towards him... head held high, the sparkling chandeliers reflected in the tears that filled her eyes.

* * *

Grant and Charlotte joined the throng leaving

Buckingham Palace Charlotte looked down at the Victoria Cross in its small box. Suddenly she gave a short laugh…

"What's wrong? asked Grant surprised.

"I was just thinking of Ben's last signal, wasn't it 'Enemy astern of you…am attacking'… that's the old 'look behind you trick' isn't it. He used it when we were kids…Old as the hills… but it worked… He would have liked that… He would have found that funny… oh so very, very very funny."

He looked down at her…She had begun to sob softly.

THE END

Author's Notes

When I began to write this series of books, I started to think that, perhaps, I had gone a bit too far with the exploits of the entirely fictitious 'Orca'. Making them perhaps a little too daring, a little too farfetched.

Then one day, I read an account of the war time experiences of the men who served on M.T.B.s and M.G.B.s and I began to wonder if I had done them justice

These men took on enormous odds in their frail craft. For the most part these boats ran on aviation fuel, their crews literally went to war sitting on a bomb.

Men like the blockade-runners who, aboard converted M.T.B.s, ran the gauntlet of Skagerrak, a hundred mile wide channel with German occupied Norway on one side and German occupied Denmark on the other; they brought vital supplies of ball bearings from Sweden, the only supplier.

Men like the crew of M.T.B. 345, who were trapped by the Germans when they were spotted in a Norwegian Fjord. They managed to hide their boat for four days under camouflage netting. They were eventually caught and shot. Their bodies were tied to depth charges that were then fired into the cold waters of a fjord.

Men still carried on this work knowing full well that if they were caught, they could suffer a similar fate.

Men like Lieutenant Commander Tommy Fuller, R.C.N. who won the Distinguished Service Cross for taking on twenty- two German E-boats single-handed.

The eight hundred craft involved in the huge operation that was Dunkirk were finally stood down on June 4th. The exploits of the 'Keith', 'Vimey', 'Whitshed' and the 'Venamous' in the port of Boulogne are based on eye witness accounts.

Three hundred and thirty eight thousand two hundred and twenty six allied troops had been ferried to safety from Dunkirk; forty thousand had been left behind in France. Ten thousand French soldiers died in defence of the embarkation. Britain had her army back, but now she and her Empire stood alone.

It wasn't until I'd finished the sixth book in the series that I discovered that there was actually a Norwegian M.T.B. flotilla, the 30th Flotilla, based at Lerwick in the Shetlands and their task was to be as big a thorn in the side of the enemy as they could along the entire coast of Norway. By the exploits of these brave men, the Germans were obliged to reinforce their coastal defences and use men and equipment, badly needed elsewhere, to counter their offensive.

In 1940 The New York Times said of Great Britain

'There, beaten, but unconquered, in shining splendour, she faced the enemy.'

Tony Molloy, Spain, 1st July, 2003

I hope you have enjoyed reading Book 1 of what is now part of the longest book ever written in the English language. I know, from my reviews on Kindle, that a lot of you do enjoy the series. I mean to cover the whole of WW2 with my good friends from Special Force Orca and hope you will join me on my journey.

June 2014

Below is a list of the books so far. You can find them all at

amazon.com: anthony molloy: Books, or on my website at anthonymolloy.weebly.com.
Both of which you can access through twitter.com/MolloyAnthony.

1 ON THE EDGE OF DARKNESS
2 DEAD RECKONING
3 STANDING INTO DANGER
4 ON FORTUNE'S SIDE
5 LONG DAYS NIGHT
6 TO CATCH A RAT
7 MOST IMMEDIATE
8 BY NIGHT'S DARK SHADOW
9 NOTICE FOR STEAM
10 BY THOUGHT AND BY DEED
11 CONQUEROR OF THE OCEANS
12 RING ON MAIN ENGINES
13 REJOIN WITH ALL SPEED

To wet your whistle, try this for starters, a mouth-waterer from the next book in the series.

CHAPTER 1

CONTACT!

Anti-submarine screen protecting the evacuation of Dunkirk, Western Approaches, 1900 hrs, Wednesday, 5th June: 1940.

The two destroyers headed west, in line abreast, their raked bows biting deep into a choppy sea, thrusting great cascades of foam up over their bridges, for all the world like two dogs at play.

The monotonous drawn out ping of the Asdic, played through HMS Nishga's bridge speakers, grating across tired nerve ends, like chalk across a blackboard. The starboard watch had been listening to it for over an hour. It had not yet reached the point where it blended into the background, along with the vibrating rigging, the hiss of the sea and the throb of the engines.

They had joined the 'Bantu', another Tribal Class destroyer, a little after sixteen hundred hours that afternoon. They were now into the Last Dog watch and already, they were losing the light.

Commander Alexander Barr, DSO, RN, the commanding officer of the 'Nishga' was in his thirties, tall and thin, almost gaunt, the third ring on his sleeve bright, untarnished and new. He sat huddled in his bridge chair, glumly staring out at the grey sea. He was attired, as befitted his nickname, acquired at Dartmouth, of 'the clothes horse'. Normally that would indicate a man with an enviable taste in clothes. Not so with our recently promoted commander. He had acquired his nickname with more than the usual sarcasm customary in such establishments. His frame was adorned with a jumble of outer garments placed with no reference to style or taste and as and when it arrived to hand. Even in full dress uniform he cut a less than satisfactory naval figure.

'The clothes horse' suddenly sat bolt upright. Over the last nine months his brain had taught itself to filter out the routine noises of one of His Majesty's Ships at sea. Something had passed through that filter, something was different. Then he heard the second echo returning from the contact.

"Asdic…Bridge! In contact! Green four oh, range two thousand yards, Doppler… slight high."

Barr reached the voice pipe. "Bridge…Asdic; we have nothing on the surface, on that bearing."

A pause: then, "Classified possible submarine…Bearing moving left, Green four three, range one thousand nine hundred yards. Strong echo."

Barr nodded to Grey, the officer of the watch, his hand moved to the red button and the hated alarm rang through the ship.

"Hands to Action Stations! Hands to Action Stations!"

The ship sprung from routine inertia into rattling, stamping life. Bridge messengers clattered up ladders, lookouts checked their guns, men crossed and criss-crossed the bridge making for their stations, guns trained round on greased turntables. Within minutes the reports started arriving from all over the ship, adding to the organised chaos on the open bridge.

"Torpedo tubes closed up." "Coxswain on the wheel". "Engine room at action stations."

Barr shouted above the clamour, "Yeoman!"

A grey haired petty officer appeared at his shoulder, "Sir?"

"Hoist the 'In Contact' pennant and then make to Admiralty repeated 'Bantu' and F.O.C.F.; 'Submarine submerged, position fifty degrees thirty minutes north; one degree twenty minutes east, estimate course north thirty east, speed five knots. Am engaging'." He leaned over the wheelhouse voice pipe, "Starboard ten… steer two one five. Revolutions for twenty knots."

Barr looked across at the 'Bantu', No in contact flag flying... Yes! There it was! He crossed to the Asdic voice pipe. "Bridge...Asdic!"

"Asdic."

"That you Hastings?"

"Yes, sir."

Hastings the senior operator, good man, 'Ping Bosun', the lads called him, slept beside the Asdic set. "Echo still good?"

"Affirmative, sir, we have engine noise on the bearing, she's doing about...five knots... Definite submarine."

Barr bent down into the lee of the fore screen ear near to the bridge speaker, to blot out the other noises around him. The echo sounded solid, a metallic jump at the end of a breathless drawn out transmission. Ping... shh... bip...ping...shh...bip. Was it slight high, difficult to tell. Leave that to Hastings, he knew what he was doing.

"Yeoman! Hoist, 'Am attacking my contact'."

The ship's tannoy crackled into life. "Do you hear there! Darken Ship, Darken Ship." It clicked off... The routine of the ship went on regardless.

Hastings's voice cracked through his thoughts, "Contact right ahead...range five-hundred...Doppler changing, mod high. Submarine turning towards."

The echo was noticeably nearer, the interval between transmissions shortening, the two vessels closing at a relative speed of twenty-five knots.

"Stand by depth-charge!" Barr heard his order repeated and successfully resisted looking aft, no need to double check. Instead he tuned back in to Hastings's continuous report, "….ahead…range two hundred yards, Doppler high, submarine on reciprocal course to ours."

"Permission to fire, sir?"

"Granted."

"Doppler changing, mod high, submarine turning away…Instant echoes!"

A bell clanged down aft, the new depth charge throwers coughed and three hundred pounds of high explosive shot out to starboard and port, splashing into the sea, others rolled sluggishly, down the ramps, over the stern and disappeared from sight.

Hastings was still reporting, "Lost contact, carrying out stern sweep"…The submarine was directly underneath them now as they rushed onwards at twenty knots. Hastings would be rapidly training the oscillator through one hundred and eighty degrees to try and pick her up as she came out of the wake.

He had to reduce the noise from the screws, give Hastings a better chance to pick it out amongst the background noise. "Half ahead both". He heard the roar from the speakers lessen. He looked astern 'Bantu's' 'In contact' flag was down, she too had lost contact. Abruptly there came a deep-throated boom and, aft, the sea convulsed in shock. Hundreds of pounds of H.E.

exploding a hundred feet below, great spouts of dirty water shot into the air, spraying back over the pristine-white wave tops. From the speakers he heard Hastings' nautical curse. He hadn't got his earphones off quick enough…too keen to regain contact.

Hundreds of tiny echoes were being returned to the receiver, like a shower of static on a badly tuned radio. Difficult to find her in all that, Hastings will have to be as good as they say he is.

"Starboard twenty," the steady gravel voice of the coxswain, repeating the order. Barr knew he had to get the Nishga' around that turbulence astern. It was casting a 'shadow' that was hiding the enemy boat.

The ship's head began to swing right, slowly at first, then faster and faster. The sea, now beam on, rolled the narrow-shanked destroyer like a child's toy, the waves lifting and passing under her from the port side.

'Bantu' in contact, sir," The yeoman's sharp eyes honed on a thousand distant horizons missed nothing.

"Very good…Hoist, 'Attack your contact',"

As the 'Bantu's' answering flag broke at her masthead, she seemed to shoot forward, her Parson's geared turbines kicking her up to twenty knots. At her stern and masthead, her two ensigns flashed white in the fading light. Barr snatched a quick look at the 'Nishga's' own Battle Ensign snapping at the top of their one remaining mast.

The other was somewhere in Boulogne harbour.

The 'Bantu' was tearing in on her contact, brave as a lion, magnificent in her anger. She was heading for a spot slightly to the east of where 'Nishga' had lost contact. Black dots sailed into the air as she passed over the target. Again the sea convulsed as if caught unawares as more explosions rumbled into the twilight.

"In contact. Red five, woolly echo."

"Bridge, Asdic…Extent of target?"

"Wait one…Extent of target…fifteen degrees, sir, too large for the submarine, at that range."

Barr checked the bearing, "Hastings, it's right where the Bantu's depth charges exploded. The submarine could still be in amongst the turbulence… Carry out a sweep…" He checked the compass… "From red twenty to green ten. Transmission range one thousand yards."

'Bantu's' flag was down, both destroyers were now carrying out their lost contact procedure.

Lieutenant Grey stepped onto the bridge, "Everything all right below Number One?" asked Barr. Lately he'd had to check Grey's every move.

"Fine, sir…Just wondered how things were going up here."

"I think our friend's gone deep. It's what I would do… If she has, it'll be guess work and luck from now on. She could be anywhere."

"It will be a crime if she gets away, it would be sweet to bag the blighter after what Jerry did to those hospital ships in the Channel…"

365

"In contact! Green two five, range one thousand two hundred, Doppler slight low…Classified submarine… target moving left."

Barr was at the compass, "This chap's nothing if not persistent, he's back on his old course…north east. He must want to get in amongst the cross channel stuff pretty badly!…Yeoman! Hoist 'In contact'…Starboard ten, steer one four five. Revolutions for twenty knots…Bridge... Asdic."

"Asdic."

"Let me know if you get too much interference at this speed."

Hastings's voice, hoarse with excitement, "Aye, Aye, sir. Contact's fine on the starboard bow, range nine hundred yards, Doppler low. The echo's woolly, we're pinging right up her…right through her wake, sir."

Barr smiled, "Could be worse Hastings, we could be pinging right up her arse."

Printed in Great Britain
by Amazon.co.uk, Ltd.,
Marston Gate.